THE GREAT GATSBY

F. Scott Fitzgerald

edited by Michael Nowlin

broadview editions

Library and Archives Canada Cataloguing in Publication

Fitzgerald, F. Scott (Francis Scott), 1896-1940.
    The great Gatsby / F. Scott Fitzgerald ; edited by Michael Nowlin.

Includes bibliographical references.
ISBN-13: 978-1-55111-787-4
ISBN-10: 1-55111-787-8

    I. Nowlin, Michael Everett, 1962-   II. Title.

PS3511.I9G7 2007   813'.52   C2006-907022-9

Broadview Editions
The Broadview Editions series represents the ever-changing canon of literature in English by
bringing together texts long regarded as classics with valuable lesser-known works.

Advisory editor for this volume: Jennie Rubio

Broadview Press is an independent, international publishing house, incorporated in 1985.
Broadview believes in shared ownership, both with its employees and with the general public;
since the year 2000 Broadview shares have traded publicly on the Toronto Venture Exchange
under the symbol BDP.

We welcome comments and suggestions regarding any aspect of our publications—please feel
free to contact us at the addresses below or at broadview@broadviewpress.com.

North America
Post Office Box 1243, Peterborough, Ontario, Canada K9J 7H5
3576 California Road, Post Office Box 1015, Orchard Park, NY, USA 14127
Tel: (705) 743-8990; Fax: (705) 743-8353;
email: customerservice@broadviewpress.com

UK, Ireland, and continental Europe
NBN International, Estover Road, Plymouth PL6 7PY UK
Tel: 44 (0) 1752 202300   Fax: 44 (0) 1752 202330
email: enquiries@nbninternational.com

Australia and New Zealand
UNIREPS, University of New South Wales
Sydney, NSW, 2052 Australia
Tel: 61 2 9664 0999; Fax: 61 2 9664 5420
email: info.press@unsw.edu.au

www.broadviewpress.com

This book is printed on paper containing 100% post-consumer
fibre.

Broadview Press acknowledges the financial support of the Government of Canada through
the Book Publishing Industry Development Program (BPIDP) for our publishing activities.

Typesetting and assembly: True to Type Inc., Mississauga, Canada.

PRINTED IN CANADA

THE GREAT GATSBY

broadview editions
series editor: L.W. Conolly

Contents

Acknowledgements

I am very grateful to the Social Sciences and Humanities Research Council of Canada and the University of Victoria for helping fund research expenses connected to this project. Several people have helped me see this project through. I would like first of all to thank Jennifer Douglas, who gathered and photographed most of the advertisements in Appendix C as well as doing some preliminary work on the notes. My thanks are due as well to Madeline Walker, who also did some research for the notes; and to Kerry Mogg, who scanned the first edition for me and prepared it for my word-processing program. The staff at Zap Copy Services helped format the illustrations. The anonymous readers who commented on my initial proposal for this volume gave me useful advice that guided me throughout the project. And Professor Leonard Conolly of Trent University has been a valuable advisor on behalf of Broadview Press, and Jennie Rubio an excellent copy-editor.

The staffs at Princeton University's Firestone Library, the New York Public Library, and, most importantly, the University of Victoria's McPherson Library have been invariably helpful and friendly. The Interlibrary Loans office has proven indispensable, and I am grateful in particular for the interest taken in the project by Chris Petter, coordinator of Special Collections. I have relied on the first-rate secretarial staff of the English department for various jobs connected to the project: my thanks go to Puri Pazo-Torres, Diana Rutherford, Darlene Hollingsworth, and Jenny Jessa. And colleagues, friends, family, and students have helped me either by reading and commenting on material, or supplying me with useful information: I am thinking in particular of Caroline Baldwin, Luke Carson, Anthony Edwards, Christopher Nowlin, Kathleen Baldwin, John Tucker, and Gordon Alexander.

Finally, I would like to thank the following individuals and organizations for permission to reprint the material described below.

F. Scott Fitzgerald's revisions to his personal copy of the 1925 first edition of *The Great Gatsby* are published with permission of the Princeton University Library.

The excerpt from Carl Van Vechten's review, "Fitzgerald on the March" (Appendix B4), is reprinted by permission of the Carl Van Vechten Trust. My thanks go in particular to Bruce Kellner.

Introduction

While planning and writing the novel he finally called *The Great Gatsby*, F. Scott Fitzgerald revealed enough about the scope of his ambition to make a fool of himself if the novel proved, like its title character, an ultimate failure. He had recently suffered the embarrassment of seeing his 1923 play *The Vegetable*, which he trusted to make him a fortune on Broadway, flop during try-outs in Atlantic City. But by the late summer of 1924, he was feeling supremely confident again, or so his boast to his editor Maxwell Perkins suggests: "I think my novel is about the best American novel ever written."[1] The draft he was working on at that point would only get better: first as a result of his usual intensive work revising and finishing up a book before submitting it for publication, and secondly, as a result of extensive revisions he made to the galleys, largely in response to Perkins' gentle but pointed criticism of the submitted typescript. By the time the finished novel appeared in the spring of 1925, Fitzgerald's boast seemed all the more warranted, his faith in the work steeling him against the vulgar criticism of contemporary reviewers: "Some day they'll eat grass, by God! This thing, both the effort and the result have hardened me and I think now that I'm much better than any of the young Americans *without exception*."[2]

Literary history has obviously borne Fitzgerald out. The reviewers who thought *The Great Gatsby* inconsequential or downright bad (actually a minority) now suffer the punishment of all reviewers who misjudge a future classic, which is to exemplify critical obtuseness to a more knowing posterity. *The Great Gatsby* is now widely considered one of the greatest American novels, if not *the* greatest, and a recent survey of the board members of Random House's Modern Library ranks *The Great Gatsby* second only to James Joyce's *Ulysses* (1922) on a list of the one hundred greatest twentieth-century novels. But there are two aspects to this fortunate issue more interesting than Fitzgerald's bold prescience, and more pertinent to our appreciation of his novel. The first is the barely sublimated competitive spirit animating his project, his desire to beat his peers at the writing game

---

1   John Kuehl and Jackson R. Bryer, eds., *Dear Scott/Dear Max: The Fitzgerald-Perkins Correspondence* (New York: Charles Scribner's Sons, 1971), 76.
2   Ibid., 106.

and have his work live on long after theirs is forgotten. This is hardly irrelevant to a novel that has both masculine competition and the transience of human experience and achievement at its thematic core. The second is the purity of purpose or intense aesthetic commitment he brought to his work-in-progress from the moment of conception and sustained until its realization in book form. It was one thing to brag about writing the greatest American novel of his generation, another to write it.

Fitzgerald followed developments in the literary field of his day astutely enough that we can fairly ask what kind of American novel was most likely to outshine the competition in 1925, and survive as a classic for generations to come. Between the spring of 1922, when he published his second novel, *The Beautiful and Damned*, and the summer of 1924, when he was writing *The Great Gatsby*, Fitzgerald had come to appreciate the significance for all would-be literary artists of two landmark works of modernism published in 1922: Joyce's *Ulysses* and T.S. Eliot's *The Waste Land*.[1] Despite private misgivings, he put himself on record in a 1923 *Richmond Times-Dispatch* interview as a champion of *Ulysses*, proclaiming it "the great novel of the future."[2] And he sent Eliot a copy of *The Great Gatsby* bearing the inscription, "Greatest of Living Poets from his enthusiastic [sic] worshipper."[3] Though Joyce's novel had acquired extra notoriety for its obscenity (it could not be legally sold in the United States until 1934), it shared with Eliot's poem a controversial reputation for difficulty, and both epitomized for Fitzgerald the kind of writing that risked being commercially unviable (in the short run) while commanding the adulation of cosmopolitan literary elites. Following in their footsteps, Fitzgerald considered changing the title of his third novel from *The Great Gatsby* (with its show-biz evocations) to *Trimalchio*, an allusion to the vulgar banquet host of Petronius's *Satyricon* that would have puzzled readers not familiar with the Roman classic. (Fitzgerald was perhaps inspired to read a 1922 unexpurgated English translation of the *Satyricon*

---

1   Chapters of *Ulysses* had, of course, been appearing in the *Little Review* since 1918, early enough to have had a minor influence on sections of Fitzgerald's 1920 story "May Day" and *The Beautiful and Damned*.

2   Matthew J. Bruccoli with Judith S. Baughman, eds., *F. Scott Fitzgerald on Authorship* (Columbia: U of South Carolina P, 1996), 86.

3   F. Scott Fitzgerald, *A Life in Letters*, ed. Matthew J. Bruccoli (New York: Simon & Schuster, 1994), 128. Fitzgerald's spelling errors have been retained.

after Eliot used a passage from the original—in Latin and Greek—as the epigraph of his great poem.) Having elevated his literary aims, Fitzgerald sailed to France in the spring of 1924 for a long stay in Europe and soon associated himself with a relatively sophisticated circle of American expatriates. He was especially well positioned while writing *The Great Gatsby*, in effect, to measure his new work against both the kind of American writing that was still being encouraged back home and his own earlier novels, the novels that had made him a celebrity and promising literary star at a remarkably young age.

Fitzgerald knew he needed to move beyond the dominant mode of realism favored by such prominent critics as his friend H.L. Mencken, and which clearly left its imprint on *The Beautiful and Damned*. "Modern" American realism had reached a kind of apex in Sinclair Lewis's hugely successful novels about middle-America, *Main Street* (1920) and *Babbitt* (1922), and was generally the kind of writing practiced by most of the leading American novelists of the day: Edith Wharton, Willa Cather, Joseph Hergesheimer, Theodore Dreiser, and, in a more complicated vein, John Dos Passos. This was a critical realism, heavily dependent on extensive social and psychological observation, but ideological to the extent that it worked to expose untenable values or moral positions, explore social problems, or oppose America's perennially facile optimism and complacency with a pessimistic counter-vision. As early as March 1923 Fitzgerald was informing fellow writer Thomas Boyd, "I shall never write another document-novel. I have decided to be a pure artist + experiment in form and emotion."[1] "Pure" artistry, this statement implies, entailed freeing oneself from the realist's subservience to the sprawling world of external facts inimical to the very idea of artistic form. Defending *The Great Gatsby* against Mencken's criticism soon after it was published, Fitzgerald insisted: "It is in protest against my own formless two novels, and Lewis' and Dos Passos' that this was written."[2] In a novel as meticulously written as *The Great Gatsby*, it seems deliberate that George Wilson's garage sits "on the edge of the waste land, a sort of compact Main Street ministering to it, and contiguous to absolutely nothing." George and Myrtle Wilson—a plodding, inarticulate husband barely able to make a living, a vivacious wife dying from cultural

---

1 Matthew J. Bruccoli and Margaret M. Duggan, eds., *The Correspondence of F. Scott Fitzgerald* (New York: Random House, 1980), 126.
2 Fitzgerald, *A Life in Letters*, 110.

and sexual starvation—seem transplanted from Lewis's middle-American villages to a symbolic desert populated by ashen men and overseen by an ominous billboard optometrist named Dr. Eckleburg.

Fitzgerald's symbolic use of the landscape betrays his repudiation as well of the regionalist strain of modern American realism. A Minnesotan himself, by 1925 Fitzgerald had lowered his estimation of fellow mid-Western writers like Sherwood Anderson, Thomas Boyd, and Glenway Wescott, and wrote contemptuously of attempts to find authentic subject-matter in the lives of rural Americans. His hero Jay Gatsby's parents, notably, are "shiftless and unsuccessful farm people," and Gatsby's roots are as provincial as any main character of the above writers. But that part of his life is of little intrinsic interest and thus recalled in the most cursory manner. Jay Gatsby is of interest—and his story of a potentially mythical cast—because of his in some ways typically modern, in some ways typically American transformation from provincial "rough-neck" to glamorous and fabulously wealthy host of parties on Long Island, the ostentatious suburban enclave of the nation's cosmopolitan center, New York City. Fitzgerald was adept enough at depicting place, as he demonstrated in writing about Princeton in his first novel, *This Side of Paradise* (1920), and about New York City in "May Day" and *The Beautiful and Damned*. But more so than in his second novel, the carefully registered locale of *The Great Gatsby* is an explicitly modernist terrain, a site of regionally dislocated people, distorted perceptions, and experimental mores. Gatsby unabashedly claims to be from the mid-Western city of San Francisco; Nick Carraway feels his mid-Western roots most profoundly while traveling across the country on a train. The particularities of place matter less than what might be rendered through what Fitzgerald called "the sustained imagination of a sincere and radiant world."[1] Thus Fitzgerald poetically transforms the two actual (and physically dissimilar) peninsulas of Great Neck and Manhasset Neck into "a pair of enormous eggs, identical in contour," West Egg and East Egg respectively, so as to underscore the incongruity between the very real social distinctions they represent and the inability to see these from the transcendental perspective of the seagulls overhead. The artist who can hold such incongruities in his own mind recognizes the need for, and, to a limited but important extent, the authority of, personal vision—

1 Kuehl and Bryer, 70.

vision that finds the terrain from Long Island to New York composed of a false pastoral suburb linked by ash-heaps to a corrupting "city" that nonetheless appears before initiates "in white heaps and sugar lumps all built with a wish out of non-olfactory money."

Fitzgerald's newfound appreciation for the centrality of form to art brought him not only beyond the putative formlessness, the verbal crudity, and the situational clichés of American realism (his own instances included), but promised him some much needed distance from the autobiographical material he had exploited for his first two novels. As he wrote Perkins in 1924, "I don't know anyone who has used up so much personal experience as I have at 27."[1] Not that *The Great Gatsby* left autobiographical content behind. On the contrary, it drew more honestly than Fitzgerald had before on his most intimate, emotionally charged experience: his rejection at the hands of Ginevra King years earlier (see below, 15-16), his wife Zelda's infidelity in the summer of 1924, his anxiety about his own celebrity and the expensive and often wasteful life he was indulging in, his deep-rooted ambivalence (not untainted by resentment) towards wealth and privilege. His aim of achieving formal perfection—structural concision, stylistic precision, deft character and scene development, careful use of leitmotifs, rigorous modulation of tone throughout—gave him emotional control over his material without sacrificing the passionate insight garnered from experience. Fitzgerald undoubtedly identified with his romantic, upstart hero; indeed, he might have echoed the French father of the artistically rigorous modern novel and proclaimed of Jay Gatsby what Flaubert supposedly said of Emma Bovary: "c'est moi!" But he cast his novel so that Gatsby might be seen as he really is, conveyed by a lucid, objectifying imagination at once aware of his crass ambition and attuned to his uncanny purity of purpose. Gatsby needed to be seen by a controlling intelligence that could grasp his emblematic significance for an aimless generation; for the over-confident, materialistic democracy that many identified with the twentieth century; and for the whole modern (i.e., Western) world irrevocably unmoored from compelling traditions or religious beliefs.

Fitzgerald surely felt delight when reviewer William Curtis wrote of *The Great Gatsby* that, precisely because of its technical accomplishment, "it can be put on the same book shelf with the best of

---

1   Ibid., 76.

London, Vienna, Paris, or Rome."[1] Fitzgerald had reached before his thirtieth birthday what in hindsight he recognized as the high point of his artistic career. Near the end of his relatively short life he wrote to his daughter Scottie, "I wish now I'd *never* relaxed or looked back—but said at the end of *The Great Gatsby*: 'I've found my line—from now on this comes first. This is my immediate duty—without this I am nothing.'"[2] What followed *The Great Gatsby* can hardly be called an unproductive career, but in obvious respects it fell short of the promise opened up by his triumph in 1925. His subsequent artistic struggles were exacerbated by nearly insurmountable personal woes, so that from the vantage point of his death in 1940 his claim to have written "about the best American novel ever" seems an act of hubris that set the stage for the romantic tragedy Fitzgerald's life became.

F. Scott Fitzgerald: Life, Works, and Critical Reputation

Late in his life Fitzgerald described himself as a perennial outsider, marked by the experience of having been "a poor boy in a rich town; a poor boy in a rich boy's school; a poor boy in a rich man's club at Princeton."[3] As the antithetical phrasing betrays, his poverty was relative. Born in St. Paul, Minnesota on 24 September 1896, he enjoyed an only moderately unstable middle-class upbringing and, christened Francis Scott Key after the remote cousin who wrote the American national anthem, was encouraged to cultivate upper middle-class social aspirations.

His namesake belonged to the paternal branch of the family, which traced its roots back to colonial Maryland and fought on the Confederate side during the Civil War. His father Edward Fitzgerald showed some of the traces of his Southern pedigree in his fine manners and taste for romantic legend, particularly tales of Confederate war heroes and the novels of Sir Walter Scott. Fortunately, the family was not wholly dependent on him as breadwinner. His furniture manufacturing business failed soon after Scott was born. He then took a job as a wholesale grocery salesman with Proctor & Gamble, which took the family to Buffalo and Syracuse. He was fired in 1908, when Scott was twelve, and as his son later recollected, he never quite recovered

---

1 See Appendix B3.
2 Fitzgerald, *A Life in Letters*, 451.
3 Fitzgerald, *A Life in Letters*, 352.

from that blow. The real money propping up the Fitzgerald household came from his mother Mollie McQuillan's side of the family. Her father was an Irish immigrant who had come to America in the 1850s and built up a successful wholesale grocery business. When the Fitzgeralds returned to St. Paul in 1908, Scott's father worked for the McQuillans; and it was McQuillan money that paid for Scott's elite education at Newman preparatory school and Princeton University.

The Fitzgeralds never owned their own home, but after returning to St. Paul rented decent housing in the respectable Summit Avenue neighborhood. The teenage Fitzgerald grew up with his younger sister Annabel among wealthy and socially prominent families, and not far from the imposing mansion of financier and railroad tycoon James J. Hill (who died there in 1916). His parents enrolled him in the private St. Paul Academy, his mother sent him to a dance school to mingle with the right social set, and he tried unsuccessfully to shine as an athlete. By most accounts something of a show-off, Fitzgerald discovered early a talent for writing amusing stories and plays that he could star in for the city's amateur Elizabethan Dramatic Club. He carried this talent first to Newman School and then Princeton, where among other things he discovered models of intellectual seriousness—first in Father Sigourney Fay, the eventual headmaster who served as a crucial mentor until his untimely death in 1919, then in contemporaries like the future men of letters Edmund Wilson and John Peale Bishop and the politically rebellious Henry Stater (who led a failed revolt against the exclusive eating clubs at Princeton). These would leave their mark on his emerging literary aspirations, which were more fundamentally rooted in a desire for popular recognition.

Probably the most formative experience of his youth was his romance with Ginevra King, the daughter of a Chicago stockbroker with a home in the affluent suburb of Lake Forest. The eighteen-year-old Fitzgerald met her in St. Paul in January 1915 while home for Christmas during his sophomore year at Princeton. She was sixteen and home from Westover, an exclusive finishing school in Connecticut. Ginevra King was beautiful, popular, and immensely rich, and Fitzgerald fell in love with her—or, so it might seem in hindsight, with the idea of her—almost immediately. His talent for writing held him in good stead as he carried on an intense epistolary relationship with her, punctuated by visits to Westover and Lake Forest, prom and football dates, and the odd trip to New York. Though Scott undoubtedly charmed her for a while, Ginevra King could have her pick of wealthy suitors and inevitably recognized the social obstacles that stood in the way of any serious future with him. Fitzgerald was made to recognize them too. After an unsatisfying visit to Lake Forest in August 1916, he entered into his ledger the quoted statement, "Poor boys shouldn't think of marrying rich girls."[1]

Ginevra King's rejection of Fitzgerald—or Fitzgerald's pursuit of a woman who for social reasons was bound to reject him—ended up facilitating his writing career, and indirectly affected his relationship with his future wife, Zelda Sayre. Before Ginevra formally broke with him in January 1917, Fitzgerald had written a piece about her for Princeton's *Nassau Literary Magazine* called "The Débutante," which would eventually find its way into his first novel. And she provided the model for several of his heroines thereafter, including Daisy Buchanan in *The Great Gatsby*.

America's entry into the First World War in April 1917 gave him an escape route from his sorrows and from his academic difficulties at Princeton (he never graduated). He received a commission as second lieutenant in the infantry, and while stationed at Fort Leavenworth in the fall began the novel that would soon make him famous. He finished what he first fittingly called "The Romantic Egotist" in March of 1918, while at Princeton on a furlough. He had the author Shane Leslie recommend it to his publisher, the respectable and conservative firm of Charles Scribner's Sons, which rejected it twice in that year. In the meantime he met Zelda while stationed from June to November at Camp Sheridan outside Montgomery, Alabama. She was the daughter of a justice of the Alabama Supreme Court, and a flamboyant, mischievous Southern belle who, like Ginevra, thrived on the attention of many men. Fitzgerald fell in love with her in September (notably, the month Ginevra married William Mitchell). He acquired pride of place in Zelda's affections, but again held it precariously. Though the Sayres were not rich, they had social standing, and Zelda would have looked to make an economically sensible match. After being discharged from the army (the war ended just before Fitzgerald was sent overseas), Fitzgerald continued courting Zelda from New York both by letter and by trips South that he could ill afford. The relationship reached a crisis by July 1919, when she broke off their unofficial engagement. Fitzgerald's efforts to make it as a writer in New York were going nowhere,

---

1 Cited in James L.W. West III, *The Perfect Hour: The Romance of F. Scott Fitzgerald and Ginevra King* (New York: Random House, 2005), 62.

and despite Zelda's romantic temperament, she realistically balked at the idea of marrying a struggling writer.

But Fitzgerald's life took the kind of dramatic turn for the better that would contribute to his most memorable characters' sense that, as he wrote in a late retrospective essay, "life is a romantic matter."[1] Zelda's rejection spurred him back home to St. Paul to revise his novel and send it to Scribner's one more time. Now called *This Side of Paradise*, it drew the favorable attention of the firm's most forward looking editor, Maxwell Perkins, and was finally accepted. Fitzgerald also had the good luck to place his stories in the high-paying and widely circulating *Saturday Evening Post* as well as low-paying but more prestigious venues like Mencken and George Jean Nathan's *The Smart Set*. Fitzgerald had become "a professional," as he wrote in "Early Success."[2] He convinced Zelda to marry him at the outset of 1920, when a promising career seemed to be unfolding before him. She left Montgomery for New York in April 1920; they married on 3 April, a week after *This Side of Paradise* was published.

Based on his life at Princeton, *This Side of Paradise* struck a chord with a generation of readers, and gave Fitzgerald a notoriety to capitalize upon as a spokesperson for rebellious and disenchanted youth. Very tame by today's standards, it was mildly shocking for its revelations about the sexual escapades and drinking sprees of the young and privileged. And it sold well for a first novel, abetted by the generally comic stories about leisure-class youth Fitzgerald was writing for magazines. Both Fitzgeralds were quick to encourage publicity depicting them as a glamorously wild, sexy, and carefree couple, epitomizing the spirit of the new post-war era Fitzgerald would dub "the jazz age." But privately the marriage soon manifested destructive tendencies. Zelda could behave impetuously to get the attention Scott could not always give her while meeting his commitments as a writer. Scott was well on his way to becoming a chronic alcoholic. And they enjoyed living beyond their means, an effect of the bad habit Fitzgerald established early in his career of writing from debt. He drew advances from his publisher and his agent on the strength of future book sales and his ability to churn out high quality magazine fiction with apparent ease. This habit led him frequently to

---

1   F. Scott Fitzgerald, "Early Success," in *The Crack-Up*, ed. Edmund Wilson (New York: New Directions, 1945), 89.
2   Ibid.

disparage his short stories—a few of which are among the best in American literature—because he wrote them primarily to raise quick money either to pay his bills or leave him free to write his novels.

Fitzgerald used the first year of their marriage—spent in New York and a rented house in Westport, Connecticut—as material for his second novel, *The Beautiful and Damned*, published in book form in the spring of 1922. The novel precociously followed its young couple to a sordid end, in keeping with the naturalistic emphasis on "character in decay" championed by the influential critic H.L. Mencken.[1] To Fitzgerald's discerning friend Edmund Wilson in an ambivalent profile published in time for its release, *The Beautiful and Damned* was too self-consciously made to the order of "the ironical-pessimistic" school of fiction its opportunistic author thought fashionable.[2] Though generally regarded as Fitzgerald's least appealing novel today, it sold better than any of his other novels during his lifetime.

The Fitzgeralds returned from their first trip to Europe in 1921 to St. Paul, where their daughter "Scottie" was born and Scott saw his second novel published. He began projecting his third novel as early as the summer of 1922, but he was also working on the play he hoped would make it to Broadway. In the fall of that year the Fitzgeralds moved to Great Neck on Long Island, a community boasting a good share of show-business people and journalists, and well-supplied with liquor. Fitzgerald lived there for a year and a half, writing and partying, and would immortalize the experience in his next novel. There he made good friends with journalist and humorist Ring Lardner, who had covered the 1919 World Series and the ensuing "Black Sox" scandal; followed the trials of Edward Fuller and William McGee, a pair of stockbrokers charged (and ultimately convicted) for misusing clients' funds; and met models for his most memorable hero Jay Gatsby—including Max Gerlach, an alleged bootlegger, and Robert C. Kerr, Jr.[3] He also saw his satiric comedy *The Vegetable* fail so conclusively that he never took up

---

1   See H.L. Mencken, "The National Letters," in *Prejudices: Second Series* (New York: Knopf, 1920), 41.

2   [Edmund Wilson], "F. Scott Fitzgerald," *The Bookman* 55 (March 1922), 23.

3   See the indispensable "Backgrounds" chapter in Matthew J. Bruccoli, ed., *F. Scott Fitzgerald's "The Great Gatsby": A Literary Reference* (New York: Carroll & Graf, 2000), especially 12-45.

playwriting again. As surely as the Great Neck period provided Fitzgerald with crucial material for The Great Gatsby, so did his move to France in April 1924 provide him with the atmosphere and leisure needed to turn that material to literary account.

Fitzgerald's second trip to Europe lasted nearly three years, and helped transform a still somewhat provincial writer into the world-class author he became. He first settled in St. Raphael on the Riviera, where he became good friends with the charming expatriate couple Gerald and Sara Murphy, who drew on family wealth to establish a villa in Cap d'Antibes (as well as a residence in Paris) dedicated to enjoying the best life has to offer. They were especially hospitable to artists and attuned to the latest continental developments in painting and music; they counted among their friends and guests American writers John Dos Passos and Archibald MacLeish, the popular composer Cole Porter, European painters Fernand Léger and Pablo Picasso, and soon after Fitzgerald befriended him in Paris in May 1925, Ernest Hemingway. When Fitzgerald later settled in Paris, he became acquainted with such key figures in the development of international literary modernism as Gertrude Stein, Sylvia Beach, Robert McAlmon, and even James Joyce. (This despite his telling decision to live on Paris's more conservative and commercially oriented Right Bank.) Fitzgerald wrote the bulk of The Great Gatsby on the Riviera in the summer of 1924. His work on the novel may have been critically disrupted by Zelda's brief affair that summer with a handsome French aviator named Edouard Jozan; but her affair would also have deepened the integrity of the theme of disillusionment so fundamental to his novel. He revised it for publication while traveling in Italy in the winter of 1925, and The Great Gatsby appeared to generally favorable reviews in April 1925.

After the publication of The Great Gatsby, the story of Fitzgerald's embattled and dissipated life tends to overshadow his work. He lived nearly sixteen more years, but finished just one more novel, left substantial fragments and notes toward another, and published numerous short stories and essays. Buoyed especially by the kind of response he was getting from his peers about Gatsby, he proclaimed to Perkins in May 1925 that his new novel was "something really NEW in form, idea, structure—the model for the age that Joyce and Stien [sic] are searching for, that Conrad didn't find."[1] The novel that finally appeared in 1934 as Tender is

---

1   Fitzgerald, A Life in Letters, 108.

the Night is by most estimates an important one; but it can hardly be characterized as the epoch-defining aesthetic wonder-work Fitzgerald enthusiastically projected while feeling at the peak of his powers.

A number of factors contributed to Fitzgerald's slide, though his much chronicled alcoholism surely ranks among the foremost. He had also grown used to lavish living, so that he had continually to set aside the novel-in-progress to write short stories and potentially lucrative scenarios for the movies. By 1929 he was one of the highest paid contributors of magazine fiction in the United States (the *Saturday Evening Post* was paying him $4000 per story), but financial exigencies continued to press upon him. Drinking and spending habits as well as sexual jealousy were a constant source of friction in the Fitzgeralds' marriage, which was exacerbated further when Zelda took up ballet dancing with a passion under the tutelage of the Russian emigré Lubov Egorova. Finally, it seems in hindsight as though Fitzgerald had chosen intractable material for his fourth novel. His projected plot about a young Hollywood technician who murders his mother on the Riviera generated some fine writing that he would later transpose to good effect, but he kept coming to a dead end with it. Meanwhile he watched Hemingway, the writer whose career he had helped launch with Scribner's, surpass him as the decade's most acclaimed American novelist and become at best a condescending friend.

Taking a rather austere view of things, one could say that public and personal catastrophe rescued Fitzgerald. The stock market crash of October 1929 and Zelda's coincidental mental breakdown six months later came brimming with dramatic meaning for an author in search of material, as his superb story "Babylon Revisited" (published December 1930) attested. As he finished his years in Europe overseeing Zelda's treatment in a high-priced Swiss psychiatric clinic and witnessing the onset of what would prove one of the worst economic depressions in modern history, Fitzgerald was bringing a complex historical perspective and a hard-earned moral vision to the American experience of the 1920s. Upon returning to the United States in the fall of 1931, he conveyed these in the now classic essay "Echoes of the Jazz Age." By the end of 1932, living outside Baltimore, and after a bitter struggle with Zelda over her own novel about their experience, *Save Me the Waltz* (1932), he found the plot of his fourth novel in a promising psychiatrist's demise after marrying a wealthy patient and cultivating the kind of high-order life of leisure modeled in real life by Gerald and Sara Murphy. Fitzgerald's long-awaited novel *Tender is the Night* appeared in 1934. Though it sold reasonably well under depression conditions and, contrary to common assumption, received more favorable than unfavorable reviews, Fitzgerald's financial and critical hopes for the novel were disappointed.

Fitzgerald reached the sorriest stage of his life in the three years following the publication of *Tender is the Night*. His heart was no longer into writing the kind of magazine fiction desired by the *Saturday Evening Post*, and prices were in any case dropping. An ill-conceived project about a medieval French count was soon aborted. Relations with Zelda, who would remain in and out of costly mental institutions for the rest of her life, were as fraught as ever. Living in North Carolina for health reasons, he carried on at least one extra-marital affair and continued to drink heavily. At the outset of 1936 he published in *Esquire* a series of confessional essays known as "The Crack-Up," which were regarded by peers as maudlin and self-indulgent. (The essays have been more kindly judged by posterity, and show symptoms of a lingering literary vitality.) A suicide attempt followed an unflattering *New York Post* profile written on the occasion of his fortieth birthday. Fitzgerald found his reprieve from this hellish existence when he was offered a generous six-month contract as a screen-writer with Metro-Goldwyn-Mayer. Overwhelmingly in debt, he could hardly refuse.

When Fitzgerald moved to Los Angeles in the summer of 1937, he was making his third attempt as a Hollywood screenwriter (he had gone there in 1927 and 1931 for specific assignments that were not adopted). This time, as things turned out, he was going for good, and he went open to the possibility of establishing a second career in the movie industry (though his disdain for it never ceased to surface). His life was enriched there by the relationship he soon began with gossip-columnist Sheilah Graham. He gained screen credit for his work on the film *Three Comrades*, had his contract renewed for a year, and managed (temporarily) to pay off his debts. His contract was not renewed at the outset of 1939, however, and he would struggle as a freelancer from this point forward. Certain that in the long run he would not be forgotten as an important American novelist, Fitzgerald worked during his final years both to consolidate and renew his reputation, even as he courageously came to grips with what he took to be a very different set of historical circumstances from the ones that had allowed for his quick rise to literary stardom at the outset of the 1920s. He became more politically astute, supporting Roosevelt's New Deal policies at home while following the developments that were leading the world to what might prove an apocalyptic war abroad. He tried with some success to quit drinking. He admonished his daughter to take full advantage of the education at Vassar College he was paying for and created a liberal-arts curriculum for his companion Graham. And perhaps most importantly, he outlined and began writing a new novel about Hollywood (now known as *The Love of the Last Tycoon*), basing his hero on the late Irving Thalberg, M-G-M's visionary production chief. That last novel was still in progress when Fitzgerald died of a heart attack in Graham's apartment on 21 December 1940.

By the measure of his early success, Fitzgerald died a failure: his books were hard to come by, he tried to no avail to get Scribner's to issue an omnibus edition of his novels, and he could not get a magazine interested in serializing his new novel. Editorials following on the heels of his obituaries pegged him as a passé product of the twenties. But Fitzgerald's resurrection was not slow in coming. In 1941, the *New Republic* magazine published a series of appreciations by noteworthy writers and critics. This preceded by six months the publication of *The Last Tycoon*, the unfinished novel introduced and edited by Edmund Wilson, in a volume also containing *The Great Gatsby* and some of his best stories. Wilson did more for his friend's reputation when in 1945 he published *The Crack-Up* (New Directions), a collection of Fitzgerald's essays and notebook entries, along with the *New Republic* tributes and other testimonials to his importance. In the same year, Viking published the two major novels and other writings in *The Portable F. Scott Fitzgerald*, and a Fitzgerald revival was well under way. It was bolstered by Arthur Mizener's popular and scholarly biography *The Far Side of Paradise* (1951) and Alfred Kazin's collection of the better essays on Fitzgerald to date, *F. Scott Fitzgerald: The Man and His Work* (1951).

By the 1960s, largely on the strength of *The Great Gatsby* and *Tender is the Night*, F. Scott Fitzgerald held the secure place he enjoys today among critics and common readers as one of the major twentieth-century American novelists. Editions of his novels and stories became widely available, as they are to this day, and academic criticism on every facet of his work began appearing with the steadiness American literary scholars have become accustomed to. Fitzgerald facilitated his posthumous canonization by leaving so much organized information about himself—

his ledger, manuscripts, notebooks, correspondence. No one has worked so tirelessly with this material as Matthew J. Bruccoli to establish the soundest possible foundation for studying Fitzgerald's writing, though this same foundation may account for the relatively conservative and repetitive character of much Fitzgerald scholarship. To the extent that there are any divisive controversies they have been over textual matters and, since Nancy Milford's 1970 biography *Zelda*, the place of Zelda in Scott's life and art. Bruccoli's textual scholarship and emphatically fact-laden biographical work have proven especially influential in displacing the problematic editions of *The Last Tycoon* and *Tender is the Night* put forth, respectively, by Wilson in 1941 and Malcolm Cowley in 1951, and challenging superficial and overly romantic assumptions about Fitzgerald. But such assumptions have inevitably and perhaps intractably gathered around a figure who, with Zelda, circulates among the iconography of American popular culture as the handsome, muse-bidden, fast living, tragic representative of the jazz age.

The Great Gatsby: Composition and Critical Reception

Though Fitzgerald was envisioning his third novel as early as mid-1922, he did not really devote himself to writing it until he went to France in April 1924.

Fitzgerald's tendency to disparage his short stories as "trash" obscures the extent to which they often served as more than an economic foundation for his "art." Short fiction served as the medium through which he tried out thematic material and verbal passages for his novels. Thus he could later describe the story "Winter Dreams," published in *Metropolitan Magazine* in December 1922, as "A sort of 1st draft of the Gatsby idea."[1] "Winter Dreams" dealt with a young mid-Westerner rejected by the wealthier girl of his dreams only to hear later in life, after he has made his success, that time and experience have not been kind to Judy Jones. The story is less about the lost dream girl than the loss of the dream she embodies, a theme that clearly anticipates the romantic disillusionment of Jay Gatsby. His second most important proto-Gatsby story was "Absolution," written in the summer of 1923 and published a year later in Mencken's *American Mercury*. Sometimes referred to as the "Ur-Gatsby," it may be closer to what Fitzgerald had in mind when he wrote Perkins in

---

1   Ibid., 121.

1922 that his next novel would be set in "the middle west and New York" and "have a catholic element."[1] Young Rudolph Miller, in conflict with his religious, immigrant father and baffled by a priest unhinged by his attraction to the world, can be recognized as an early avatar of Gatsby; Fitzgerald later said his story was "intended to be a picture of [Gatsby's] early life, but that [he] cut it [...] to preserve the sense of mystery."[2] Finally, in late 1923 he wrote "The Sensible Thing" (published in *Liberty*, July 1924), a story that recalled his painful experience of being rejected by Zelda because of insufficient prospects. Like Fitzgerald, its protagonist opportunely makes his fortune and returns to re-win his beloved's hand, but without seeking, as Gatsby will, to restore the former magic of their relationship.

With such stories and his Great Neck experience behind him, Fitzgerald wrote *The Great Gatsby* within about eight months, finishing his working draft by September 1924 and revising in the early fall. Perkins received his finished typescript in November 1924, and while acknowledging its brilliance offered what turned out to be very valuable criticism. Perkins got Fitzgerald to see two fundamental flaws in the book. The first was that the title character was inadequately developed. Granting that Gatsby was supposed to be shrouded in mystery, Perkins thought the reader still needed to have a better physical picture of him, recognize him through a few more telling characteristics, and gain a surer sense of how he made his money. Secondly, he thought that by having Gatsby tell the bulk of his story in the first-person late in the novel, Fitzgerald violated his own narrative method of sticking to Nick Carraway's impressionistic recollection of events.[3] The unusual upshot of this was that, while traveling in Italy, Fitzgerald substantially revised his novel after it had already been set in galleys to meet the scheduled April publication date. Alongside some extensive re-writing of passages and scenes (especially in Chapters III, VI, and VII) that alters our impressions of characters and their motives, Fitzgerald broke up the account of Gatsby's real history in Chapter VIII and transposed part of it to the beginning of Chapter VI, even as he had done more to hint at the nature of Gatsby's character throughout the course of the novel. He also made Nick's splendid lyrical description of Gatsby

---

1   See Appendix A, p. 177.

2   Andrew Turnbull, ed. *The Letters of F. Scott Fitzgerald* (New York: Charles Scribner's Sons, 1963), 509.

3   For Perkins' important letters, see Appendix A, pp. 181-83, 184-85.

and Daisy's first kiss the climax of Chapter VI, rather than burying it early in Chapter VII. And he took most of Gatsby's story out of Gatsby's own mouth, for the sake of the more aesthetically effective order Nick could recount it in. Most readers agree with Fitzgerald that Perkins' criticism helped him bring the novel closer to perfection.

Fitzgerald was destined to have his high commercial expectations for the novel disappointed: the novel sold reasonably well (over 20,000 copies in the first four months), but was no bestseller, and he made more money selling the dramatization rights than he did from sales.[1] He characteristically gnawed over the matter, blaming low sales on the fact that it did not appeal enough to women readers. On the other hand, he should have been more pleased than he was with the critical response. There were some daft, dismissive reviews, as the early one appearing in the *New York World* with the title "F. Scott Fitzgerald's Latest a Dud"; and even an admiring critic like Isabel Paterson in the *New York Herald Tribune* deemed it "a book of the season only [...]."[2] But most reviewers, whether they read the novel as satiric or as tragic, acknowledged it to be the best work yet of a noteworthy young writer. Critics were compelled to recognize the force of Fitzgerald's style and the novel's formal ingenuity. They may have been divided as to whether *The Great Gatsby* fulfilled the promise suggested by Fitzgerald's earlier novels, or was itself the surer promise of greater work to come. But a characteristic refrain in the early criticism was that *The Great Gatsby* signaled a new maturity in Fitzgerald, not merely on account of its craftsmanship but because it showed him taking a more objective look at the rebellious cultural milieu with which he had become identified. Most flattering of all for Fitzgerald—on top of Perkins' praise and the laudatory reviews in high places (see Appendix B)—must have been the private congratulations of his peers, most notably those of John Peale Bishop, Edith Wharton, Gertrude Stein, and T.S. Eliot, who deemed it "the first step that American fiction has taken since Henry James."[3]

In hindsight, it is hard to appreciate the extent to which *The Great Gatsby*, despite a 1934 Modern Library edition, was nearly

---

1 Owen Davis's dramatic treatment was produced on Broadway in 1926, and the novel was made into a silent film in 1926.
2 Jackson R. Bryer, ed. *F. Scott Fitzgerald: The Critical Reception* (New York: Burt Franklin & Co., 1978), 195, 202.
3 See Fitzgerald, *The Crack Up*, 310.

forgotten by the time of Fitzgerald's death in 1940. Fitzgerald would have been as vindicated by the fact that the judgment of its earliest "highbrow" admirers has been generally endorsed as he would have been delighted by the fact that it became one of the twentieth century's more popular classics. Its central love story and evocation of an historical moment both glamorous and decadent have made ideal fodder for movies (1949 and 1975), mass market paperback editions, a ballet (1996), and an opera (1999). Most recently, it has even inspired a "black" movie variation called *G* (2005). At the same time its less alienable literary virtues have long made it a staple of undergraduate and even high school English curricula throughout North America and abroad.

Reading *The Great Gatsby*

The Great Gatsby's earliest admirers recognized that Fitzgerald's new level of technical accomplishment and ability to penetrate beneath the surface details of his material stemmed from his narrative method. "You adopted exactly the right method of telling it," Perkins told him, "that of employing a narrator who is more of a spectator than an actor: this puts the reader upon a point of observation on a higher level than that on which the characters stand and at a distance that gives perspective. In no other way could your irony have been so immensely effective [...]."[1] One could go so far as to claim that Nick Carraway makes the novel the "beautiful and simple + intricately patterned" work Fitzgerald projected in the summer of 1922.[2] And yet by the same token, one need look no farther than Nick to find a flaw in the design. His status poses interpretive problems that may not be resolvable; at the very least it demands of us a certain suspension of disbelief. For as narrator Nick is at once *a relatively objective witness* of events, *an interested participant* who helps determine the events, and, as the last section of Chapter III suggests, *the author-surrogate*, that is, the writer of the very text we are reading, with a capacity for brilliant flights of lyricism, deadpan satire, symbolic organization, and tragic insight one would hardly expect from a bond salesman, even one who "was rather literary in college." As arguably the novel's most complex character, Nick has a specific social background and hinted-at psychological conflicts that presumably compromise the accuracy and determine the economy

---

1   Kuehl and Bryer, 82.
2   See Appendix A, p. 178.

of his point-of-view. But if we are tempted to read Nick as an unreliable narrator, as some critics have, we must face the problem of how to interpret his self-exposure as an unreliable narrator in the novel he appears to have written.

Most critics have followed Perkins in granting Nick Carraway a special authority to tell Gatsby's story because of qualities of perception and judgment that set him apart from the other characters in the novel. Such qualities would have to be grounded in the succinct but revealing information about himself Nick gives us in the novel's opening pages and at key junctures throughout the novel (most notably in Chapters III and IX). Nick begins by recalling the advice of an apparently honored father, and his sense of himself is inseparable from his sense of the respectable, solidly bourgeois, mid-Western, three-generation American "clan" to which he belongs. Nick refers ironically enough to his family's aristocratic pretensions, but this kind of self-deprecation in no way undermines his social and economic security. Despite the imagery of pioneering he attaches to his journey eastward at the outset of the novel, he is in fact an Ivy League graduate backed by his family for a career on Wall Street. And though he rents a modest home at West Egg, his kinship with Daisy Buchanan aligns him to some degree with the "old money" class across the bay from him at East Egg, which Daisy's husband Tom also thinks of as the pinnacle of the white race. Nick is self-evidently included in Tom's assertion, "we're Nordics."

But what has happened to draw Nick to a man like Jay Gatsby—someone, he tells us at the outset, "who represented everything for which I have an unaffected scorn"? And why has Gatsby's story left him so profoundly disillusioned? These are the enigmas Nick's narrative purports to answer. Crucial to our understanding of this narrative is its retrospective and melancholic quality. The man who set out to make his fortune in New York in the summer of 1922 has returned west to his family home to tell the story of Gatsby, which becomes the story of an ever-elusive, because forever lost, American dream of regeneration.

As several of its initial reviewers noted, *The Great Gatsby* departs from Fitzgerald's earlier novels in no longer concerning itself with young people. Nick turns thirty midway through the novel; Gatsby is described as looking just over thirty; Daisy is in her early twenties, but married and a mother; Tom is Nick's contemporary. These are grown ups, in Fitzgerald's terms, who have lived past the moment of youth when the horizon lay open for glorious deeds and erotic bliss, the moment the incorrigibly romantic Fitzgerald took to be the high point of life. Gatsby from the outset epitomizes the spirit of youth, with his "extraordinary gift for hope" and "romantic readiness" that Nick feels sure he will never meet with again. It might seem odd that Nick, a veteran of some nasty campaigns during the First World War, had any illusions intact, or was receptive to the illusions of others, when he ventured east in 1922. But we must accept what Fitzgerald, who did not see combat, shows us: the experiences of that summer doing for Nick what the war somehow did not manage to do.

The war that left Nick as "restless" as so many others of his generation presumably made him more receptive to the modern, sensually alluring, morally emancipated, mildly anarchic terrain of jazz-age America he encounters on Long Island and in New York. But he inhabits this world still psychologically bound to the moral sureties of his father's house, so to speak, "within and without" the scenes he describes, "simultaneously enchanted and repelled by the inexhaustible variety of life." It is precisely his deep-seated ambivalence toward the cultural shift epitomized by Gatsby's spectacular parties that makes him a witness capable of bringing perspective to Gatsby's project of winning back his lost love Daisy. Before he learns of Gatsby's plan, he becomes privy to Tom's adultery with Myrtle Wilson, indulges in some aimless partying, has one brief affair before taking up with the incorrigibly dishonest Jordan Baker, lunches with a shady Jewish gangster responsible for fixing the 1919 World's Series, and experiences what we might call the restorative power of alcoholic vision: "I had taken two finger-bowls of champagne, and the scene had changed before my eyes into something significant, elemental, and profound." Soon after he learns of Gatsby's plan, he helps him realize it by arranging the tryst with Daisy that re-kindles their romance. By this time, even as we see Nick incrementally compromising his provincial, bourgeois code of conduct, we acquire a fuller picture of who the mysterious Gatsby is and what he is all about—though we will not get a complete picture until the end. Nick artfully reveals Gatsby to us as Gatsby was revealed to him (he does not appear until a quarter's way into the book), withholding crucial information about him that he gathered later and adumbrating his deeper significance as it occurred to him.

Nick's artfulness is essential to the novel's power, and we diminish that power if we reduce artfulness here to a strategy for exonerating himself for his role in the catastrophe that unfolds. In a novel as time-haunted as *The Great Gatsby*, which above all things is about a man striving to re-capture an ideal moment in his past, a poetic reconstruction of the potentially forgettable summer of 1922 seems all the more imperative. Nick does not simply narrate events but, to the extent that we are invited to regard him as the author of what we are reading, imposes an "intricate pattern" on them, to recall Fitzgerald's terms for what he was aspiring to do. *The Great Gatsby* shares with other noteworthy modernist prose works the quality Joseph Frank some time ago described as "spatial form," the quality by which, as he says with reference to Djuna Barnes's *Nightwood* (1936), a novel is held together "by the continual reference and cross reference of images and symbols that must be referred to each other spatially throughout the time-act of reading."[1]

There are plenty of these images, symbols, and even leitmotifs (to draw on a term from the temporal art of music) we can attend to in *The Great Gatsby*, beginning with Nick's acknowledgment of his father's saying—in a novel about a man who disowns his father—and culminating in Nick's vision of the original Dutch sailors spellbound before the "fresh, green breast of the new world." That return to the origins of America, and to the possibilities inherent in "the new world" figured as a natural, erotic object, becomes the prototype, once we get to the end of the novel, of Gatsby's desire to return to the moment in time before he "took" Daisy. That "green breast" invites comparison at once with "the green light at the end of Daisy's dock" and the green card Daisy gives out at Gatsby's party. It also recalls the more prosaic breast of Myrtle Wilson, the other female character named after something natural rather than, like Jordan, something mechanical, despite ironically being married to a garage keeper and living in an anti-pastoral wasteland. The Dutch sailors traveling westward remind us of the westward and eastward movement and the East/West binary pervading the novel, both laden with meanings accrued from American history and mythography. And the Dutch sailors' vision brings to a climax the recurring trope of blindness and vision introduced in Chapter II through the reference to T.J. Eckleburg's billboard. One could go on citing such details as evidence for how composed a work we have here.

Such artful patterning tends, as modernist art generally does, toward abstraction, and reflects in Nick's case the rage for moral

---

1   Joseph Frank, *The Widening Gyre: Crisis and Mastery in Modern Literature* (New Brunswick: Rutgers UP, 1963), 32.

order he expresses after the unsettling journey east. But it is kept from becoming overly abstract by the messy historical particulars through which Gatsby's peculiar vitality makes itself felt. The dominant trope for the novel's concrete, historical circumstances seems to be, paradoxically, music—specifically, the musical sound of Daisy Buchanan's seductive voice, the sound of the world's (feminine) body alluring masculine fortune seekers with what Nick hears as "an arrangement of notes that will never be played again." There is something inherently deadly in this appeal. To Gatsby's crassly materialistic ears, as we discover, Daisy's voice "is full of money"; and those with lots of money, so Nick judges, are part of the "foul dust" floating in the wake of Gatsby's dreams. But Gatsby intuitively knows that whatever ideal Self he envisions must be embodied according to the possibilities offered by modern America's "vast, vulgar, and meretricious beauty." Ambivalent toward it though he is, Nick deftly captures the numerous forms this beauty takes, beginning with the vernacular someone like Myrtle Wilson retains even after her transformation from garage keeper's wife to high-born lady ("The only *crazy* I was was when I married him"). Myrtle's transformation is buttressed, of course, by consumer products: cosmetics, a puppy, a new dress, an apartment with furniture upholstered in images of Versailles. The small party she hosts anticipates Gatsby's parties, which manifest conspicuous consumption and oddly assorted company on a far grander scale. The sensually entrancing and thoroughly alcoholic character of Gatsby's parties barely veil the social leveling they facilitate, paid for as they are by money furnished by Prohibition and a bullish stock market, and gravitating as they do around a new celebrity class created by Broadway and the movie industry. In the "amusement park" atmosphere of Gatsby's newly acquired mansion, characters dance promiscuously to the music that gave the era its name; and as Fitzgerald well knew, "jazz"—like so much of the nation's modern popular culture—was largely created by Jewish immigrants and African-Americans. Gatsby gets associated throughout the novel with these "alien" or abject Americans,[1] newcomers or perennial outsiders laying their claim to America's

---

1 Gatsby's association with Jews is more detailed in the manuscript, where the "Jazz History of the World" composer is Les Epstien, not Vladimir Tostoff; where Gatsby sings a Tin Pan Alley-style song of his own composition; and where Tom bristles at finding himself among a crowd of Jews at Gatsby's party: see F. Scott Fitzgerald, *The Great Gatsby: A Facsimile of the Manuscript*, ed. Matthew J. Bruccoli (Washington, DC: Bruccoli Clark/NCR Microcard Books, 1973), 54, 162-63, 170.

promise in fancy suits and shiny automobiles. Though Nick underscores the association in places, his narrative on the whole works to redeem Gatsby from its more sordid implications, to purify his ambition so that we recognize in Gatsby something more than a tasteless, social-climbing, racially suspect, criminally opportunistic poor boy trying to win the hand of a rich, white Southern belle. In purifying Gatsby's designs, Nick sacrifices his cousin Daisy, her Siren-like voice included, as (like Jordan presumably, and perhaps even Myrtle) too shallow and unworthy a vessel.

The surer vessel for embodying Gatsby's extraordinary romantic idealism—his belief in the green light, his project of self-regeneration—is the book we are reading. For against the story's thematic admonitions about the folly of trying to repeat the past, its intricate formal pattern compels us instead to re-read. In Gatsby's desire to recapture everything signified by Daisy, Nick recognizes a "purposeless splendor" such as we attribute to the boldest artistic endeavors, and which, in writing the otherwise forgettable Gatsby's story, he appropriates as his own. Re-reading Nick's artful rendering of that story brings us again and again to that "transitory enchanted moment" when universal "man" is imagined to be staring breathless before an unsullied America, "compelled into an aesthetic contemplation he neither understood nor desired, face to face for the last time in history with something commensurate to his capacity for wonder." This great passage figures forth the ideal reader response to the wonder work of American literature it concludes. *The Great Gatsby* stands in as best it can for a transcendental aesthetic experience forever irrecoverable, and yet forever bound to the irreversible, materialistic course of American history its most representative men fall prey to.

The Great Gatsby in Cultural Context: A Note on the Appendices

Though *The Great Gatsby* should be enjoyed as the art object Fitzgerald conceived it to be, like all great works of art literature it was a product of its time and place and spoke to that time and place before managing to speak beyond them. If this introduction has suggested ways in which the novel resonates with Fitzgerald's biography, the five appendices that follow the text should encourage readers to think about ways in which it resonates with the cultural context Fitzgerald observed acutely without being able to dissociate himself from it.

Appendices A and B—selections from Fitzgerald's correspondence and contemporary reviews—reveal something to readers of the literary field Fitzgerald was working in. As the correspondence shows, his aesthetic goals were bound up with more ordinary commercial interests and domestic concerns; and his artistic success depended on professional savvy, a sympathetic and intelligent editor, and, when it was demanded, self-discipline and understanding of his craft. The reviews by some of the leading critics of the day give us a good sense of what we might call contemporary scales of literary expectation by which the measure of an original work like *The Great Gatsby* could be taken. The first reviewers inevitably read the novel against the backdrop of Fitzgerald's reputation, and inevitably judged it not merely for its intrinsic qualities or deficiencies, but for how it could be related positively or negatively to his other works and to a familiar range of other authors, novels, and literary trends.

Appendix C, "Consumption, Class, and Selfhood," reproduces eight advertisements from 1922 to reflect Fitzgerald's grasp of the kind of imagery and language shaping his contemporaries' sense of "class" in a world where money could be imagined to buy anything. The novel's numerous references to commodities, to sporadic buying, to large scale waste, and especially to the extravagant tokens of Gatsby's pseudo-aristocratic status (a "real" library, multi-colored shirts from London, an aquaplane) suggest that Fitzgerald was attending to the deep cultural transformation being wrought by an economy increasingly oriented toward mass consumption. The most disturbing symptom of this in the novel is not so much the demise of America's much touted Protestant work ethic as it is the epistemological and aesthetic difficulty of distinguishing the real from the fake.

Appendix D, "The Irreverent Spirit of the Jazz Age," offers a selection of writings that either illustrate the exuberant, youth-oriented rebelliousness for which the period became famous or seek to describe and diagnose it. In looking back to 1922, as I suggested above, *The Great Gatsby* already anticipates the kind of objectifying, retrospective assessment of the jazz age spirit that one finds in Fitzgerald's marvelous 1931 essay "Echoes of the Jazz Age" (reprinted in part here). "Jazz" in this section refers less to the specific music of the period than to the mocking, anti-authoritarian, experimental ethos that the music supposedly expressed. That ethos is put on trial by the guardians of public morality in a *Vanity Fair* satire, which appears here with a representative H.L. Mencken editorial on the stupidity of Prohibition (which went into effect in January 1920) and a wistful piece by Zelda Fitzgerald on one of the dominant icons of the period, the flapper.[1] The section concludes with public intellectual Walter Lippmann's somber assessment at decade's end of the nihilism afflicting the post-war generation—a nihilism Fitzgerald's novel also exposes in suggestive ways.

Appendix E, "Race and the National Culture, 1920-25," recalls the racially charged discourse about "American" national and cultural identity that culminated in the passage of restrictive immigration laws in 1921 and 1924 while federal anti-lynching legislation was blocked.[2] Though we are surely meant to read Tom Buchanan's white supremacist paranoia ironically, the novel nonetheless tends to go on figuring distinctions of class—and distinctions based on family origins in America—in racial terms. According to this tendency, the novel is not merely about a poor boy making himself a fortune so as to win the heart of a rich girl, but about an outsider with suspicious origins trying to claim America's legacy as his own and conquer a paragon of white Southern womanhood. Readers will find here selections from well-known racist literature by Lothrop Stoddard and Henry Ford that made itself felt between the period in which *The Great Gatsby* is set and the time in which it was written. Whether or not Fitzgerald read their writings, he was familiar with the racist ideas, narratives, and tropes they typify, and must have been familiar with the kind of counter-racist argument represented here by Frederick C. Howe. It is hard not to conclude that *The Great Gatsby* engages the question throughout of how race, culture, and American identity interpenetrate, given its early reference to a book called "The Rise of the Colored Empires," its several notations of an immigrant presence, its iconic "modish Negroes," its unforgettable Jewish gangster, its offhand allu-

---

1 "Flapper" was the contemporary slang term for the rebellious, carefree, supposedly sexually licentious young women notable for their bobbed hair styles, slim physiques, clothing styles that downplayed maternal-feminine attributes such as large breasts and broad hips, and open indulgence of traditionally masculine vices like smoking and drinking. The term probably derived from the fashion of wearing unbuttoned, flapping galoshes as well as hats with flapping ear muffs, though it was also associated with the term "fledgling," as in a young bird learning to flap its wings.

2 See Geoffrey Perrett, *America in the Twenties: A History* (New York: Simon & Schuster, 1982), 82-83, 183-84, 245.

sions to a vibrant American popular culture being created from the bottom up, and perhaps most troublingly its melancholic white narrator. How it engages the question—or what exactly it seems to say to the question: this should remain a vexing issue so long as we appreciate the sustained self-reflexivity of Fitzgerald's masterpiece.

F. Scott Fitzgerald: A Brief Chronology

1896   24 September: Francis Scott Key Fitzgerald born, at 481
Laurel Avenue in St. Paul, Minnesota.

1898-1908

The Fitzgerald family moves to upstate New York following the failure of Edward Fitzgerald's wicker furniture business. Fitzgerald's father works as a salesman for Proctor & Gamble, first in Buffalo, then in Syracuse (1901-03), then in Buffalo again, until he loses his job in 1908.

1908-11

The Fitzgeralds return to St. Paul, living in rented quarters on or near Summit Avenue. Fitzgerald enters St. Paul Academy in the fall of 1908. Begins publishing stories in the St. Paul Academy newspaper as early as 1909, and writing (and acting in) plays for the Elizabethan Dramatic Club by 1911.

1911-13

Sent to Newman School, a preparatory boarding school in Hackensack, New Jersey, September 1911. In 1912 comes under the influence there of Father Sigourney Fay, who introduces him to Anglo-Irish writer Shane Leslie and American historian Henry Adams.

1913-17

Fitzgerald enters Princeton University in the fall of 1913. By 1914, meets two of his most influential classmates, Edmund Wilson and John Peale Bishop. Writes for the *Princeton Tiger*, publishes stories, poems, and reviews in the *Nassau Literary Magazine*, and writes lyrics (as well as one book) for three annual Triangle Club musical-theatre productions. Poor grades keep him from acting in Triangle Club shows, and force him to withdraw for nearly a year in the fall of 1915, and return home. During the Christmas holiday of 1914-15, he meets and falls in love with Ginevra King, daughter of a wealthy stockbroker from Lake Forest, Illinois. Though the relationship is precarious by the summer of 1916, when Ginevra formally breaks with Fitzgerald in January 1917, he is devastated.

1917   Enlists following America's entry into the First World
        War. Receives his infantry commission as Second Lieu-
        tenant in the fall while at Princeton, and reports for duty
        at Fort Leavenworth, Kansas. There he begins writing
        his first novel.

1918   Finishes "The Romantic Egotist" in March, and sends it
        to Shane Leslie, who forwards it to his own publisher,
        Charles Scribner's Sons, in May. After brief stays at
        Camp Zachary Taylor outside Louisville and Camp
        Gordon in Georgia, Fitzgerald ends up at Camp Sheri-
        dan outside Montgomery, Alabama in June. Meets Zelda
        Sayre at a country-club dance in July and becomes
        romantically involved. Scribner's rejects "The Romantic
        Egotist" in August, and again in October after Fitzgerald
        revises and re-submits it. Sent to Camp Mills, New York
        for deployment overseas just before the war ends.

1919   Moves to New York City after being discharged from the
        army; works for the Barron Collier advertising company
        and tries with little success to make it as a writer. Takes
        several trips to Montgomery to woo Zelda, but she
        breaks off their unofficial engagement in July. Devastated
        again, he returns to St. Paul to revise his novel again.
        Scribner's accepts *This Side of Paradise* in September.
        Fitzgerald begins placing several stories in noteworthy
        periodicals like *The Smart Set*, *Scribner's Magazine*, and
        the *Saturday Evening Post*. Hires Harold Ober as his
        agent.

1920   Fitzgerald's success wins over Zelda and their engage-
        ment is renewed. Stories begin appearing with some reg-
        ularity in the *Saturday Evening Post*, and will continue to
        throughout the 1920s for increasingly higher prices; *Met-
        ropolitan Magazine* also shows a lucrative interest in his
        stories. Publication of *This Side of Paradise* in March
        makes Fitzgerald a celebrity. Marries Zelda in April.
        They rent a house in Westport, Connecticut for the
        summer, and a Manhattan apartment in the fall.
        Becomes friends with the popular, iconoclastic intellec-
        tual H.L. Mencken. *Flappers and Philosophers*, his first
        collection of stories, published in September.

1921   With Zelda pregnant, the Fitzgeralds visit England,
        France, and Italy from May through July. They return to
        St. Paul, where Scott finishes his second novel and
        begins a play. *The Beautiful and Damned* runs serially in

Metropolitan September to December. Daughter Frances Scott (Scottie) Fitzgerald born in October.

1922 *The Beautiful and Damned* published in March; *Tales of the Jazz Age*, his second collection of stories, published in September; "Winter Dreams" appears in *Metropolitan* in December. After summering at White Bear Lake, near St. Paul, moves to the wealthy Long Island community of Great Neck in October. Befriends writers Ring Lardner and John Dos Passos.

1923 Fitzgerald's play, *The Vegetable*, published in April, bombs in production at Atlantic City in November.

1924 Sails for France in April, begins a nearly three-year sojourn abroad. "Absolution" appears in *American Mercury* in June. Settles for the summer at St. Raphael on the Riviera; works on *The Great Gatsby* and befriends Gerald and Sara Murphy. Zelda has marriage-threatening affair with French aviator Edouard Jozan in July. Travels with Zelda to Rome and Capri for the winter, where he revises galleys of his novel.

1925 Divides time between the Riviera in the summer and Paris in spring and fall. *The Great Gatsby* published in April. Begins close friendship with Ernest Hemingway in May, and helps launch his career at Scribner's. Also meets key figures of the expatriate avant-garde: Gertrude Stein, Sylvia Beach, and Robert McAlmon.

1926 *All the Sad Young Men*, his third collection of stories, published in February; includes "The Rich Boy," published in January and February issues of *Redbook*. Helps Hemingway improve *The Sun Also Rises* before publication. Returns with family to the US in December.

1927 First trip to Hollywood in January and February to work (unsuccessfully) on "Lipstick," a flapper vehicle for Constance Talmadge. Meets producer Irving Thalberg, and has romantic liaison with actress Lois Moran. In March rents Ellerslie, a mansion outside Wilmington, Delaware.

1928 Returns to Paris in the spring. Meets James Joyce at dinner hosted by Sylvia Beach. Writes Basil Duke Lee stories for the *Saturday Evening Post*. Zelda studies ballet under the Russian emigré Lubov Egorova. Returns to Ellerslie in the fall.

1929 Returns to Paris in April, divides the year between Cannes in the summer and Paris in spring and fall.

1930 Zelda's first serious mental breakdown: she enters Malmaison clinic outside Paris in April, and spends summer in Dr. Oscar Forel's Les Rives de Prangins clinic on Lake Geneva. In Lausanne, Fitzgerald has brief affair with Bijou O'Conor. Writes several high priced stories for the *Post*, including "Babylon Revisited" (published December) and the Josephine Perry stories.

1931 Fitzgerald's father dies in January, and he returns to the US alone for funeral. Zelda discharged from Prangins in June. Fitzgeralds return to the U.S. for good in September, stopping at Montgomery. "Echoes of the Jazz Age" published in *Scribner's Magazine* in November. Brief trip to Hollywood in November to work on Jean Harlow vehicle.

1932 Zelda enters Phipps Clinic in Baltimore in February, and works on novel she began in late 1931. In May, Fitzgerald rents La Paix, a house on the Turnbull estate outside Baltimore. Zelda's novel, *Save Me the Waltz*, published by Scribner's in October.

1933 Works intensely on re-conceived fourth novel. Moves from La Paix to Baltimore town house in December.

1934 *Tender is the Night* serialized in *Scribner's Magazine* January through April; book published in April. Zelda returns to Phipps Clinic in February, ends up in Sheppard and Enoch Pratt Hospital in May. Fitzgerald begins "Philippe, Count of Darkness" series, soon aborted.

1935 *Taps at Reveille*, his fourth collection of stories, published in March. Travels to Tryon, North Carolina for health reasons in the winter; stays the summer in Asheville, where he has brief affair with Beatrice Dance. Rents an apartment in Baltimore in the fall, and goes back to North Carolina (Hendersonville) in the winter.

1936 The three autobiographical "Crack-Up" essays appear in *Esquire* from February through April. Zelda transferred to Highlands Hospital in Asheville in April. Fitzgerald's mother dies in August. In September, Fitzgerald interviewed while drunk by Michel Mok of the *New York Post*, and made the subject of a humiliating profile, which leads to a suicide attempt.

1937 In Tryon, Fitzgerald's debts accumulate to $40,000. Goes to Hollywood in July on a six-month contract with Metro-Goldwyn-Mayer. Meets gossip columnist Sheilah Graham in July, and begins affair that will last until his death. Works on and gets only screen credit for adaptation of Erich Maria Remarque's *Three Comrades*, starring Robert Taylor and Margaret Sullavan.

1938   M-G-M renews Fitzgerald's contract for the year. Works on "Infidelity," a Joan Crawford vehicle; an adaptation of Claire Booth Luce's "The Women"; and "Madame Curie," a Greta Garbo vehicle. Moves to Malibu Beach and later Encino. Daughter Scottie enters Vassar College in Poughkeepsie, New York. Begins his "College of One" course in Western civilization with Graham.

1939   M-G-M does not renew contract; Fitzgerald goes freelance. Works briefly on "Gone With the Wind" script. With Budd Schulberg, takes trip to Dartmouth College to work on the movie "Winter Carnival"; ends up fired and hospitalized for alcoholism. In October, begins novel about Hollywood. Breaks with Harold Ober over the latter's refusal to lend him any more money.

1940   Pat Hobby stories appear regularly in *Esquire*. Tries to sell screenplay "Cosmopolitan," based on "Babylon Revisited," as Shirley Temple vehicle. Moves to Laurel Avenue apartment to be closer to Graham. Dies of a heart attack in Graham's apartment, 21 December. As a lapsed Catholic, he was refused burial in St. Mary's Church cemetery in Rockville, Maryland; he was buried in Rockville Union Cemetery (St. Mary's Church relented in 1975, and he was re-buried alongside Zelda; see below).

1941   *The Last Tycoon* appears in its unfinished form with *The Great Gatsby*, edited by Edmund Wilson.

1975   Re-buried in St. Mary's alongside Zelda, who died in a fire at Highlands Hospital in 1948.

A Note on the Text

The copy-text for this edition of *The Great Gatsby* is the 1925 first edition, published by Charles Scribner's Sons in April 1925. Amendments to the copy-text are as follows.

Six changes (revisions or corrections) were introduced into subsequent imprints of the text in accordance with Fitzgerald's directions, and are included here:

1) Chapter 3, page 84, line 2: "echolalia" replaced "chatter";

2) Chapter 6, page 119, line 18: "northern" was corrected to "southern";

3) Chapter 7, page 145, line 31: "it's" was corrected to "its";

4) Chapter 7, page 145, line 42: period was put in after "away";

5) Chapter 9, page 168, line 29: "sickantired" replaced "sick and tired";

6) Chapter 9, page 172, line 30: "Union Street station" was corrected to "Union Station."[1]

This edition restores three words from the existent holograph manuscript that underwent corruption in the course of being typed and set in galleys:

1) Chapter 1, page 60, line 15: "startlingly" replaces "startingly";

2) Chapter 2, page 73, line 41: "was" replaces "saw" (a change further authorized by F. Scott Fitzgerald's marked personal copy);

3) Chapter 3, page 84, line 26: "with" replaces "for."

Despite the dubious authority of the holograph manuscript in the case of *The Great Gatsby* (since the intervening and undoubtedly revised typescript from which the galleys were set has been lost), the restored words here either accord with usage or make better sense.

This edition also restores two space-breaks indicated by Fitzgerald in his revisions to the galleys, the space-breaks marking either a change of scene or the passage of time:

1) Chapter 6, page 122, after line 38;

2) Chapter 6, page 126, after line 19.

---

1 See Matthew J. Bruccoli, *F. Scott Fitzgerald: A Descriptive Bibliography*, rev. ed. (Pittsburgh: U of Pittsburgh P, 1987), 67.

It retains two double space-breaks Fitzgerald insisted on—in Chapter 3 and in Chapter 4—that appear in the 1925 edition but which subsequent editions (including the Cambridge University Press edition) have changed to a single space-break. In both cases, the double-spacing seems to mark a significant narrative shift: the first, from Nick's narration of the story about Gatsby to a key passage of self-reflection; the second, from Nick's version of events to Jordan's account of Gatsby and Daisy's initial affair.

This Broadview Edition furthermore incorporates most of the roughly forty holograph revisions Fitzgerald made in his personal copy of the first edition now housed at the Firestone Library at Princeton University (Rare Books and Manuscripts, C0187, Box 5b). These have been documented by Jennifer E. Atkinson, in "Fitzgerald's Marked Copy of *The Great Gatsby*," *Fitzgerald/Hemingway Annual* 2 (1970), 28-33; and by Matthew J. Bruccoli, in *Apparatus for F. Scott Fitzgerald's "The Great Gatsby"* (Columbia: U of South Carolina P, 1974), 61-64. In practically every instance these changes improve upon the printed version, either by excising redundant words or phrases, making descriptions more precise, or correcting details. My own examination of Fitzgerald's marked copy leads me to depart from Professor Atkinson's and Professor Bruccoli's description in only one instance:

1) Chapter 4, page 101, line 6: "on" should replace "with." I have not incorporated any of the changes beside which Fitzgerald put a question mark, for the obvious reason that he himself was not sure whether he should or would make it. In the one instance where Fitzgerald suggested alternative changes—inserting "sub-or suppressed" before the word "journalism" in Chapter 6, page 119, line 33—I have chosen the former as better conveying what I take to be his intended meaning. Finally, I have adopted the change from "children" to "little girls" in Chapter 4, page 104, lines 21-22, on the assumption that it is authorized in Fitzgerald's handwriting.

Fitzgerald was a notoriously bad speller and I have corrected four obvious errors that withstood his (and Scribner's copy-editors') scrutiny. I have corrected "Vladmir" to Vladimir" (twice in Chapter 3); "Jaqueline" to "Jacqueline" (in Chapter 4); "self-absorbtion" to "self-absorption" (in Chapter 6); and "rythmic" to "rhythmic" (in Chapter 8). In Chapter 9, I have corrected one instance of "Wolfsheim" to Fitzgerald's usual spelling of "Wolfshiem," resisting the temptation to follow Edmund Wilson and make "Wolfsheim" the proper spelling throughout. (Fitzgerald almost invariably mis-spelled "ei" as "ie," and "Wolfs-heim" would carry the presumably intended suggestive meaning "wolf's home."[1])

I have made two substantive corrections to diction or phrasing errors that have withstood editorial scrutiny:

1) "urbane" for "urban" (Chapter 3, page 83, line 35), which more precisely conveys Fitzgerald's meaning;

2) "in" for "on" (Chapter 5, page 116, line 36), which conforms with usage and Fitzgerald's use of the phrase "in the air" elsewhere in the novel.

I have also silently corrected a few accidental errors: commas instead of periods, a period missing after "Mr," three ellipses points where there should be four. I have changed "33d" to "33rd," and capitalized "village" after "West Egg" in Chapter 9.

Finally, I have allowed errors of fact (eg. chronological, geographical, physical) to stand, noting some of these if they might prove disconcerting. I have also allowed Scribner's house-style to stand (notably in the matters of punctuation and the use of quotation marks around titles) on the ground that there is little to no evidence that Fitzgerald was ever troubled by it. He did, however, pointedly request that "some one" be printed as one word. I have accordingly made this change, and by analogy made single words of "any one" and "every one."

1   See Robert M. Crunden, *Body and Soul: The Making of American Modernism* (New York: Basic Books, 2000), 437, n48.

The Great Gatsby

Then wear the gold hat, if that will move her;
If you can bounce high, bounce for her too,
Till she cry "Lover, gold-hatted, high-bouncing lover,
I must have you!"
—THOMAS PARKE D'INVILLIERS.[1]

---

1 D'Invilliers is a fictional character from Fitzgerald's first novel, *This Side of Paradise*, modeled on Princeton classmate and fellow writer John Peale Bishop (1892-1944).

ONCE AGAIN
TO
ZELDA

Chapter I

IN my younger and more vulnerable years my father gave me some advice that I've been turning over in my mind ever since.

"Whenever you feel like criticising anyone," he told me, "just remember that all the people in this world haven't had the advantages that you've had."

He didn't say any more, but we've always been unusually communicative in a reserved way, and I understood that he meant a great deal more than that. In consequence, I'm inclined to reserve all judgments, a habit that has opened up many curious natures to me and also made me the victim of not a few veteran bores. The abnormal mind is quick to detect and attach itself to this quality when it appears in a normal person, and so it came about that in college I was unjustly accused of being a politician, because I was privy to the secret griefs of wild, unknown men. Most of the confidences were unsought—frequently I have feigned sleep, preoccupation, or a hostile levity when I realized by some unmistakable sign that an intimate revelation was quivering on the horizon; for the intimate revelations of young men, or at least the terms in which they express them, are usually plagiaristic and marred by obvious suppressions. Reserving judgments is a matter of infinite hope. I am still a little afraid of missing something if I forget that, as my father snobbishly suggested, and I snobbishly repeat, a sense of the fundamental decencies is parcelled out unequally at birth.

And, after boasting this way of my tolerance, I come to the admission that it has a limit. Conduct may be founded on the hard rock or the wet marshes, but after a certain point I don't care what it's founded on. When I came back from the East last autumn I felt that I wanted the world to be in uniform and at a sort of moral attention forever; I wanted no more riotous excursions with privileged glimpses into the human heart. Only Gatsby, the man who gives his name to this book, was exempt from my reaction—Gatsby, who represented everything for which I have an unaffected scorn. If personality is an unbroken series of successful gestures, then there was something gorgeous about him, some heightened sensitivity to the promises of life, as if he were related to one of those intricate machines that register earthquakes ten thousand miles away. This responsiveness had nothing to do with that flabby impressionability which is dignified under the name of the "creative temperament"—it was an extraordinary gift for hope, a romantic readiness such as I have never found in any other person and which it is not likely I shall ever find again. No—Gatsby turned out all right at the end; it is what preyed on Gatsby, what foul dust floated in the wake of his dreams that temporarily closed out my interest in the abortive sorrows and short-winded elations of men.

My family have been prominent, well-to-do people in this Middle Western city for three generations. The Carraways are something of a clan, and we have a tradition that we're descended from the Dukes of Buccleuch, but the actual founder of my line was my grandfather's brother, who came here in fifty-one, sent a substitute to the Civil War, and started the wholesale hardware business that my father carries on to-day.[1]

I never saw this great-uncle, but I'm supposed to look like him—with special reference to the rather hard-boiled painting that hangs in father's office. I graduated from New Haven in 1915, just a quarter of a century after my father, and a little later I participated in that delayed Teutonic migration known as the Great War.[2] I enjoyed the counter-raid so thoroughly that I came back restless. Instead of being the warm centre of the world, the Middle West now seemed like the ragged edge of the universe—so I decided to go East and learn the bond business. Everybody I knew was in the bond business, so I supposed it could support one more single man. All my aunts and uncles talked it over as if they were choosing a prep school[3] for me, and finally said, "Why—ye-es," with very grave, hesitant faces. Father agreed to finance me for a year, and after various delays I came East, permanently, I thought, in the spring of twenty-two.

---

1   "The Dukes of Buccleuch" refers to a Scottish ducal house going back to the fifteenth century, commemorated among other places in Sir Walter Scott's romantic poem *The Lay of the Last Minstrel* (1805). The Carraways' claim to descend from the aristocratic Scotts of Buccleuch makes all the more ironic Nick's detail about his great-uncle sending "a substitute to the Civil War": that is, paying the $300 required by the Conscription Act of March 1863 to have someone less fortunate take his place on the battlefield.

2   New Haven is a city in southern Connecticut, home of Yale University, Nick's alma mater. "Teutonic migration" is an ironic reference to the First World War, specifically Germany's invasion of Belgium and France.

3   Short for "preparatory school," usually a private school preparing in-residence students for elite colleges and universities.

The practical thing was to find rooms in the city, but it was a warm season, and I had just left a country of wide lawns and friendly trees, so when a young man at the office suggested that we take a house together in a commuting town, it sounded like a great idea. He found the house, a weather-beaten cardboard bungalow at eighty a month, but at the last minute the firm ordered him to Washington, and I went out to the country alone. I had a dog—at least I had him for a few days until he ran away—and an old Dodge and a Finnish woman, who made my bed and cooked breakfast and muttered Finnish wisdom to herself over the electric stove.

It was lonely for a day or so until one morning some man, more recently arrived than I, stopped me on the road.

"How do you get to West Egg village?" he asked helplessly.

I told him. And as I walked on I was lonely no longer. I was a guide, a pathfinder, an original settler. He had casually conferred on me the freedom of the neighborhood.

And so with the sunshine and the great bursts of leaves growing on the trees, just as things grow in fast movies, I had that familiar conviction that life was beginning over again with the summer.

There was so much to read, for one thing, and so much fine health to be pulled down out of the young breath-giving air. I bought a dozen volumes on banking and credit and investment securities, and they stood on my shelf in red and gold like new money from the mint, promising to unfold the shining secrets that only Midas and Morgan and Maecenas knew.[1] And I had the high intention of reading many other books besides. I was rather literary in college—one year I wrote a series of very solemn and obvious editorials for the Yale News—and now I was going to bring back all such things into my life and become again that most limited of all specialists, the "well-rounded man." This isn't just an epigram—life is much more successfully looked at from a single window, after all.

It was a matter of chance that I should have rented a house in

---

1 "Midas," a king in classical mythology with the power to turn anything he touched into gold; John Pierpont Morgan (1837-1913), American financier, founder of the powerful banking firm J.P. Morgan and Company in 1895; one of the wealthiest and (reputedly) most powerful men in the world when he died; "Maecenas" (70-78 BCE), close adviser to Caesar Augustus and patron of the Roman poets Virgil and Horace; the name now connotes a wealthy patron of the arts.

one of the strangest communities in North America. It was on that slender riotous island which extends itself due east of New York—and where there are, among other natural curiosities, two unusual formations of land. Twenty miles from the city a pair of enormous eggs, identical in contour and separated only by a courtesy bay, jut out into the most domesticated body of salt water in the Western hemisphere, the great wet barnyard of Long Island Sound. They are not perfect ovals—like the egg in the Columbus story, they are both crushed flat at the contact end—but their physical resemblance must be a source of perpetual confusion to the gulls that fly overhead. To the wingless a more arresting phenomenon is their dissimilarity in every particular except shape and size.[1]

I lived at West Egg, the—well, the less fashionable of the two, though this is a most superficial tag to express the bizarre and not a little sinister contrast between them. My house was at the very tip of the egg, only fifty yards from the Sound, and squeezed between two huge places that rented for twelve or fifteen thousand a season. The one on my right was a colossal affair by any standard—it was a factual imitation of some Hôtel de Ville in Normandy,[2] with a tower on one side, spanking new under a thin beard of raw ivy, and a marble swimming pool, and more than forty acres of lawn and garden. It was Gatsby's mansion. Or, rather, as I didn't know Mr. Gatsby, it was a mansion inhabited by a gentleman of that name. My own house was an eyesore, but it was a small eyesore, and it had been overlooked, so I had a view of the water, a partial view of my neighbor's lawn, and the consoling proximity of millionaires—all for eighty dollars a month.

Across the courtesy bay the white palaces of fashionable East Egg glittered along the water, and the history of the summer really begins on the evening I drove over there to have dinner with the Tom Buchanans. Daisy was my second cousin once

---

1 Fitzgerald's Long Island setting is imaginatively based on the peninsulas known as Great Neck and Manhasset Neck (West and East Egg, respectively). They are not in fact as geographically identical as Nick's metaphorical description suggests. "The egg in the Columbus story" recalls how Columbus reputedly bet members of the Spanish nobility that he could make an egg stand on end, which he won by crushing the end of the egg; the legend originates in Girolamo Benzini's *Historia del Mondo Nuovo* (1565).

2 A city hall in Normandy, a Northwest coastal region of France.

removed, and I'd known Tom in college. And just after the war I spent two days with them in Chicago.

Her husband, among various physical accomplishments, had been one of the most powerful ends that ever played football at New Haven—a national figure in a way, one of those men who reach such an acute limited excellence at twenty-one that everything afterward savors of anti-climax. His family were enormously wealthy—even in college his freedom with money was a matter for reproach—but now he'd left Chicago and come East in a fashion that rather took your breath away: for instance, he'd brought down a string of polo ponies from Lake Forest.[1] It was hard to realize that a man in my own generation was wealthy enough to do that.

Why they came East I don't know. They had spent a year in France for no particular reason, and then drifted here and there unrestfully wherever people played polo and were rich together. This was a permanent move, said Daisy over the telephone, but I didn't believe it—I had no sight into Daisy's heart, but I felt that Tom would drift on forever seeking, a little wistfully, for the dramatic turbulence of some irrecoverable football game.

And so it happened that on a warm windy evening I drove over to East Egg to see two old friends whom I scarcely knew at all. Their house was even more elaborate than I expected, a cheerful red-and-white Georgian Colonial mansion,[2] overlooking the bay. The lawn started at the beach and ran toward the front door for a quarter of a mile, jumping over sun-dials and brick walks and burning gardens—finally when it reached the house drifting up the side in bright vines as though from the momentum of its run. The front was broken by a line of French windows, glowing now with reflected gold and wide open to the warm windy afternoon, and Tom Buchanan in riding clothes was standing with his legs apart on the front porch.

He had changed since his New Haven years. Now he was a sturdy straw-haired man of thirty with a rather hard mouth and a supercilious manner. Two shining arrogant eyes had established

---

1 Affluent suburb of Chicago on the southwest shore of Lake Michigan, the home of Fitzgerald's first serious love, Ginevra King.

2 Style of architecture most prevalent in the eighteenth century (during the reigns of Kings George I, II, and III). Homes in this style were symmetrical and elegant, featuring flattened columns on either side of the front door, windows across the facade, and twinned chimneys. They were especially prominent in New England and the American South.

dominance over his face and gave him the appearance of always leaning aggressively forward. Not even the effeminate swank of his riding clothes could hide the enormous power of that body—he seemed to fill those glistening boots until he strained the top lacing, and you could see a great pack of muscle shifting when his shoulder moved under his thin coat. It was a body capable of enormous leverage—a cruel body.

His speaking voice, a gruff husky tenor, added to the impression of fractiousness he conveyed. There was a touch of paternal contempt in it, even toward people he liked—and there were men at New Haven who had hated his guts.

"Now, don't think my opinion on these matters is final," he seemed to say, "just because I'm stronger and more of a man than you are." We were in the same senior society, and while we were never intimate I always had the impression that he approved of me and wanted me to like him with some harsh, defiant wistfulness of his own.

We talked for a few minutes on the sunny porch.

"I've got a nice place here," he said, his eyes flashing about restlessly.

Turning me around by one arm, he moved a broad flat hand along the front vista, including in its sweep a sunken Italian garden, a half acre of deep, pungent roses, and a snub-nosed motor-boat that bumped the tide offshore.

"It belonged to Demaine, the oil man." He turned me around again, politely and abruptly. "We'll go inside."

We walked through a high hallway into a bright rosy-colored space, fragilely bound into the house by French windows at either end. The windows were ajar and gleaming white against the fresh grass outside that seemed to grow a little way into the house. A breeze blew through the room, blew curtains in at one end and out the other like pale flags, twisting them up toward the frosted wedding-cake of the ceiling, and then rippled over the wine-colored rug, making a shadow on it as wind does on the sea.

The only completely stationary object in the room was an enormous couch on which two young women were buoyed up as though upon an anchored balloon. They were both in white, and their dresses were rippling and fluttering as if they had just been blown back in after a short flight around the house. I must have stood for a few moments listening to the whip and snap of the curtains and the groan of a picture on the wall. Then there was a boom as Tom Buchanan shut the rear windows and the caught wind died out about the room, and the curtains and the rugs and the two young women ballooned slowly to the floor.

The younger of the two was a stranger to me. She was extended full length at her end of the divan, completely motionless, and with her chin raised a little, as if she were balancing something on it which was quite likely to fall. If she saw me out of the corner of her eyes she gave no hint of it—indeed, I was almost surprised into murmuring an apology for having disturbed her by coming in.

The other girl, Daisy, made an attempt to rise—she leaned slightly forward with a conscientious expression—then she laughed, an absurd, charming little laugh, and I laughed too and came forward into the room.

"I'm p-paralyzed with happiness."

She laughed again, as if she said something very witty, and held my hand for a moment, looking up into my face, promising that there was no one in the world she so much wanted to see. That was a way she had. She hinted in a murmur that the surname of the balancing girl was Baker. (I've heard it said that Daisy's murmur was only to make people lean toward her; an irrelevant criticism that made it no less charming.)

At any rate, Miss Baker's lips fluttered, she nodded at me almost imperceptibly, and then quickly tipped her head back again—the object she was balancing had obviously tottered a little and given her something of a fright. Again a sort of apology arose to my lips. Almost any exhibition of complete self-sufficiency draws a stunned tribute from me.

I looked back at my cousin, who began to ask me questions in her low, thrilling voice. It was the kind of voice that the ear follows up and down, as if each speech is an arrangement of notes that will never be played again. Her face was sad and lovely with bright things in it, bright eyes and a bright passionate mouth, but there was an excitement in her voice that men who had cared for her found difficult to forget: a singing compulsion, a whispered "Listen," a promise that she had done gay, exciting things just a while since and that there were gay, exciting things hovering in the next hour.

I told her how I had stopped off in Chicago for a day on my way East, and how a dozen people had sent their love through me.

"Do they miss me?" she cried ecstatically.

"The whole town is desolate. All the cars have the left rear wheel painted black as a mourning wreath, and there's a persistent wail all night along the north shore."

"How gorgeous! Let's go back, Tom. To-morrow!" Then she added irrelevantly: "You ought to see the baby."

"I'd like to."

"She's asleep. She's three years old.[1] Haven't you ever seen her?"

"Never."

"Well, you ought to see her. She's——"

Tom Buchanan, who had been hovering restlessly about the room, stopped and rested his hand on my shoulder.

"What you doing, Nick?"

"I'm a bond man."

"Who with?"

I told him.

"Never heard of them," he remarked decisively.

This annoyed me.

"You will," I answered shortly. "You will if you stay in the East."

"Oh, I'll stay in the East, don't you worry," he said, glancing at Daisy and then back at me, as if he were alert for something more. "I'd be a God damned fool to live anywhere else."

At this point Miss Baker said: "Absolutely!" with such suddenness that I started—it was the first word she had uttered since I came into the room. Evidently it surprised her as much as it did me, for she yawned and with a series of rapid, deft movements stood up into the room.

"I'm stiff," she complained, "I've been lying on that sofa for as long as I can remember."

"Don't look at me," Daisy retorted, "I've been trying to get you to New York all afternoon."

"No, thanks," said Miss Baker to the four cocktails just in from the pantry, "I'm absolutely in training."

Her host looked at her incredulously.

"You are!" He took down his drink as if it were a drop in the bottom of a glass. "How you ever get anything done is beyond me."

I looked at Miss Baker, wondering what it was she "got done." I enjoyed looking at her. She was a slender, small-breasted girl, with an erect carriage, which she accentuated by throwing her body backward at the shoulders like a young cadet. Her gray sun-

---

1 This is an error on Fitzgerald's part: Daisy and Tom's daughter would have to be two years old according to the account of their engagement and marriage in Chapter IV.

strained eyes looked back at me with polite reciprocal curiosity out of a wan, charming, discontented face. It occurred to me now that I had seen her, or a picture of her, somewhere before.

"You live in West Egg," she remarked contemptuously. "I know somebody there."

"I don't know a single——"

"You must know Gatsby."

"Gatsby?" demanded Daisy. "What Gatsby?"

Before I could reply that he was my neighbor dinner was announced; wedging his tense arm imperatively under mine, Tom Buchanan compelled me from the room as though he were moving a checker to another square.

Slenderly, languidly, their hands set lightly on their hips, the two young women preceded us out onto a rosy-colored porch, open toward the sunset, where four candles flickered on the table in the diminished wind.

"Why *candles*?" objected Daisy, frowning. She snapped them out with her fingers. "In two weeks it'll be the longest day in the year." She looked at us all radiantly. "Do you always watch for the longest day of the year and then miss it? I always watch for the longest day in the year and then miss it."

"We ought to plan something," yawned Miss Baker, sitting down at the table as if she were getting into bed.

"All right," said Daisy. "What'll we plan?" She turned to me helplessly. "What do people plan?"

Before I could answer her eyes fastened with an awed expression on her little finger.

"Look!" she complained; "I hurt it."

We all looked—the knuckle was black and blue.

"You did it, Tom," she said accusingly. "I know you didn't mean to, but you *did* do it. That's what I get for marrying a brute of a man, a great, big, hulking physical specimen of a——"

"I hate that word hulking," objected Tom crossly, "even in kidding."

"Hulking," insisted Daisy.

Sometimes she and Miss Baker talked at once, unobtrusively and with a bantering inconsequence that was never quite chatter, that was as cool as their white dresses and their impersonal eyes in the absence of all desire. They were here, and they accepted Tom and me, making only a polite pleasant effort to entertain or to be entertained. They knew that presently dinner would be over and a little later the evening too would be over and casually put away. It was sharply different from the West, where an evening was hurried from phase to phase toward its close, in a continually disappointed anticipation or else in sheer nervous dread of the moment itself.

"You make me feel uncivilized, Daisy," I confessed on my second glass of corky but rather impressive claret. "Can't you talk about crops or something?"

I meant nothing in particular by this remark, but it was taken up in an unexpected way.

"Civilization's going to pieces," broke out Tom violently. "I've gotten to be a terrible pessimist about things. Have you read 'The Rise of the Colored Empires' by this man Goddard?"[1]

"Why, no," I answered, rather surprised by his tone.

"Well, it's a fine book, and everybody ought to read it. The idea is if we don't look out the white race will be—will be utterly submerged. It's all scientific stuff; it's been proved."

"Tom's getting very profound," said Daisy, with an expression of unthoughtful sadness. "He reads deep books with long words in them. What was that word we——"

"Well, these books are all scientific," insisted Tom, glancing at her impatiently. "This fellow has worked out the whole thing. It's up to us, who are the dominant race, to watch out or these other races will have control of things."

"We've got to beat them down," whispered Daisy, winking ferociously toward the fervent sun.

"You ought to live in California—" began Miss Baker, but Tom interrupted her by shifting heavily in his chair.

"This idea is that we're Nordics. I am, and you are, and you are, and—" After an infinitesimal hesitation he included Daisy with a slight nod, and she winked at me again. "—And we've produced all the things that go to make civilization—oh, science and art, and all that. Do you see?"

There was something pathetic in his concentration, as if his complacency, more acute than of old, was not enough to him any more. When, almost immediately, the telephone rang inside and the butler left the porch Daisy seized upon the momentary interruption and leaned toward me.

"I'll tell you a family secret," she whispered enthusiastically. "It's about the butler's nose. Do you want to hear about the butler's nose?"

---

1 Fitzgerald likely has in mind here *The Rising Tide of Color Against White World-Supremacy* by Lothrop Stoddard, published by Charles Scribner's Sons in 1920 (see Appendix E1).

"That's why I came over to-night."

"Well, he wasn't always a butler; he used to be the silver polisher for some people in New York that had a silver service for two hundred people. He had to polish it from morning till night, until finally it began to affect his nose——"

"Things went from bad to worse," suggested Miss Baker.

"Yes. Things went from bad to worse, until finally he had to give up his position."

For a moment the last sunshine fell with romantic affection upon her glowing face; her voice compelled me forward breathlessly as I listened—then the glow faded, each light deserting her with lingering regret, like children leaving a pleasant street at dusk.

The butler came back and murmured something close to Tom's ear, whereupon Tom frowned, pushed back his chair, and without a word went inside. As if his absence quickened something within her, Daisy leaned forward again, her voice glowing and singing.

"I love to see you at my table, Nick. You remind me of a—of a rose, an absolute rose. Doesn't he?" She turned to Miss Baker for confirmation: "An absolute rose?"

This was untrue. I am not even faintly like a rose. She was only extemporizing, but a stirring warmth flowed from her, as if her heart was trying to come out to you concealed in one of those breathless, thrilling words. Then suddenly she threw her napkin on the table and excused herself and went into the house.

Miss Baker and I exchanged a short glance consciously devoid of meaning. I was about to speak when she sat up alertly and said "Sh!" in a warning voice. A subdued impassioned murmur was audible in the room beyond, and Miss Baker leaned forward unashamed, trying to hear. The murmur trembled on the verge of coherence, sank down, mounted excitedly, and then ceased altogether.

"This Mr. Gatsby you spoke of is my neighbor—" I said.

"Don't talk. I want to hear what happens."

"Is something happening?" I inquired innocently.

"You mean to say you don't know?" said Miss Baker, honestly surprised. "I thought everybody knew."

"I don't."

"Why—" she said hesitantly, "Tom's got some woman in New York."

"Got some woman?" I repeated blankly.

Miss Baker nodded.

"She might have the decency not to telephone him at dinner time. Don't you think?"

Almost before I had grasped her meaning there was the flutter of a dress and the crunch of leather boots, and Tom and Daisy were back at the table.

"It couldn't be helped!" cried Daisy with tense gayety.

She sat down, glanced searchingly at Miss Baker and then at me, and continued: "I looked outdoors for a minute, and it's very romantic outdoors. There's a bird on the lawn that I think must be a nightingale come over on the Cunard or White Star Line.[1] He's singing away—" Her voice sang: "It's romantic, isn't it, Tom?"

"Very romantic," he said, and then miserably to me: "If it's light enough after dinner, I want to take you down to the stables."

The telephone rang inside, startlingly, and as Daisy shook her head decisively at Tom the subject of the stables, in fact all subjects, vanished into air. Among the broken fragments of the last five minutes at table I remember the candles being lit again, pointlessly, and I was conscious of wanting to look squarely at everyone, and yet to avoid all eyes. I couldn't guess what Daisy and Tom were thinking, but I doubt if even Miss Baker, who seemed to have mastered a certain hardy scepticism, was able utterly to put this fifth guest's shrill metallic urgency out of mind. To a certain temperament the situation might have seemed intriguing—my own instinct was to telephone immediately for the police.

The horses, needless to say, were not mentioned again. Tom and Miss Baker, with several feet of twilight between them, strolled back into the library, as if to a vigil beside a perfectly tangible body, while, trying to look pleasantly interested and a little deaf, I followed Daisy around a chain of connecting verandas to the porch in front. In its deep gloom we sat down side by side on a wicker settee.

Daisy took her face in her hands as if feeling its lovely shape, and her eyes moved gradually out into the velvet dusk. I saw that turbulent emotions possessed her, so I asked what I thought would be some sedative questions about her little girl.

"We don't know each other very well, Nick," she said suddenly. "Even if we are cousins. You didn't come to my wedding."

"I wasn't back from the war."

---

1 The two largest transatlantic steamship companies. They merged in 1934 to become Cunard-White Star Limited.

"That's true." She hesitated. "Well, I've had a very bad time, Nick, and I'm pretty cynical about everything."

Evidently she had reason to be. I waited but she didn't say any more, and after a moment I returned rather feebly to the subject of her daughter.

"I suppose she talks, and—eats, and everything."

"Oh, yes." She looked at me absently. "Listen, Nick; let me tell you what I said when she was born. Would you like to hear?"

"Very much."

"It'll show you how I've gotten to feel about—things. Well, she was less than an hour old and Tom was God knows where. I woke up out of the ether with an utterly abandoned feeling, and asked the nurse right away if it was a boy or a girl. She told me it was a girl, and so I turned my head away and wept. 'All right,' I said, 'I'm glad it's a girl. And I hope she'll be a fool—that's the best thing a girl can be in this world, a beautiful little fool.'

"You see I think everything's terrible anyhow," she went on in a convinced way. "Everybody thinks so—the most advanced people. And I *know*. I've been everywhere and seen everything and done everything." Her eyes flashed around her in a defiant way, rather like Tom's, and she laughed with thrilling scorn. "Sophisticated—God, I'm sophisticated!"

The instant her voice broke off, ceasing to compel my attention, my belief, I felt the basic insincerity of what she had said. It made me uneasy, as though the whole evening had been a trick of some sort to exact a contributary emotion from me. I waited, and sure enough, in a moment she looked at me with an absolute smirk on her lovely face, as if she had asserted her membership in a rather distinguished secret society to which she and Tom belonged.

Inside, the crimson room bloomed with light. Tom and Miss Baker sat at either end of the long couch and she read aloud to him from the Saturday Evening Post[1]—the words, murmurous and uninflected, running together in a soothing tune. The lamplight, bright on his boots and dull on the autumn-leaf yellow of her hair, glinted along the paper as she turned a page with a flutter of slender muscles in her arms.

---

1 At the time, America's most popular and commercially successful weekly periodical. Fitzgerald earned a good part of his money writing stories for it from 1920 until 1937.

When we came in she held us silent for a moment with a lifted hand.

"To be continued," she said, tossing the magazine on the table, "in our very next issue."

Her body asserted itself with a restless movement of her knee, and she stood up.

"Ten o'clock," she remarked, apparently finding the time on the ceiling. "Time for this good girl to go to bed."

"Jordan's going to play in the tournament to-morrow," explained Daisy, "over at Westchester."[1]

"Oh—you're *Jor*dan Baker."

I knew now why her face was familiar—its pleasing contemptuous expression had looked out at me from many rotogravure pictures of the sporting life at Asheville and Hot Springs and Palm Beach.[2] I had heard some story of her too, a critical, unpleasant story, but what it was I had forgotten long ago.

"Good night," she said softly. "Wake me at eight, won't you."

"If you'll get up."

"I will. Good night, Mr. Carraway. See you anon."

"Of course you will," confirmed Daisy. "In fact I think I'll arrange a marriage. Come over often, Nick, and I'll sort of—oh—fling you together. You know—lock you up accidentally in linen closets and push you out to sea in a boat, and all that sort of thing——"

"Good night," called Miss Baker from the stairs. "I haven't heard a word."

"She's a nice girl," said Tom after a moment. "They oughtn't to let her run around the country this way."

"Who oughtn't to?" inquired Daisy coldly.

"Her family."

"Her family is one aunt about a thousand years old. Besides, Nick's going to look after her, aren't you, Nick? She's going to spend lots of week-ends out here this summer. I think the home influence will be very good for her."

Daisy and Tom looked at each other for a moment in silence.

"Is she from New York?" I asked quickly.

---

1 Westchester County is the New York suburb on the other side of Long Island Sound from Great Neck and Manhasset Neck.

2 "Rotogravure" refers to magazine or newspaper photographs, a feature of weekend supplements. Asheville, Hot Springs, Palm Beach are all affluent Southern resort towns popular with the northeastern sporting set, located in North Carolina, Arkansas, and Florida respectively.

"From Louisville. Our white girlhood was passed together there. Our beautiful white——"

"Did you give Nick a little heart to heart talk on the veranda?" demanded Tom suddenly.

"Did I?" She looked at me. "I can't seem to remember, but I think we talked about the Nordic race. Yes, I'm sure we did. It sort of crept up on us and first thing you know——"

"Don't believe everything you hear, Nick," he advised me.

I said lightly that I had heard nothing at all, and a few minutes later I got up to go home. They came to the door with me and stood side by side in a cheerful square of light. As I started my motor Daisy peremptorily called: "Wait!

"I forgot to ask you something, and it's important. We heard you were engaged to a girl out West."

"That's right," corroborated Tom kindly. "We heard that you were engaged."

"It's a libel. I'm too poor."

"But we heard it," insisted Daisy, surprising me by opening up again in a flower-like way. "We heard it from three people, so it must be true."

Of course I knew what they were referring to, but I wasn't even vaguely engaged. The fact that gossip had published the banns was one of the reasons I had come East. You can't stop going with an old friend on account of rumors, and on the other hand I had no intention of being rumored into marriage.

Their interest rather touched me and made them less remotely rich—nevertheless, I was confused and a little disgusted as I drove away. It seemed to me that the thing for Daisy to do was to rush out of the house, child in arms—but apparently there were no such intentions in her head. As for Tom, the fact that he "had some woman in New York" was really less surprising than that he had been depressed by a book. Something was making him nibble at the edge of stale ideas as if his sturdy physical egotism no longer nourished his peremptory heart.

Already it was deep summer on roadhouse roofs and in front of wayside garages, where new red gas-pumps sat out in pools of light, and when I reached my estate at West Egg I ran the car under its shed and sat for a while on an abandoned grass roller in the yard. The wind had blown off, leaving a loud, bright night, with wings beating in the trees and a persistent organ sound as the full bellows of the earth blew the frogs full of life. The silhouette of a moving cat wavered across the moonlight, and turning my head to watch it, I saw that I was not alone—fifty feet away a figure had emerged from the shadow of my neighbor's mansion and was standing with his hands in his pockets regarding the silver pepper of the stars. Something in his leisurely movements and the secure position of his feet upon the lawn suggested that it was Mr. Gatsby himself, come out to determine what share was his of our local heavens.

I decided to call to him. Miss Baker had mentioned him at dinner, and that would do for an introduction. But I didn't call to him, for he gave a sudden intimation that he was content to be alone—he stretched out his arms toward the dark water in a curious way, and, far as I was from him, I could have sworn he was trembling. Involuntarily I glanced seaward—and distinguished nothing except a single green light, minute and far away, that might have been the end of a dock. When I looked once more for Gatsby he had vanished, and I was alone again in the unquiet darkness.

Chapter II

ABOUT half way between West Egg and New York the motor road hastily joins the railroad and runs beside it for a quarter of a mile, so as to shrink away from a certain desolate area of land. This is a valley of ashes—a fantastic farm where ashes grow like wheat into ridges and hills and grotesque gardens; where ashes take the forms of houses and chimneys and rising smoke and, finally, with a transcendent effort, of men, who move dimly and already crumbling through the powdery air.[1] Occasionally a line of gray cars crawls along an invisible track, gives out a ghastly creak, and comes to rest, and immediately the ash-gray men swarm up with leaden spades and stir up an impenetrable cloud, which screens their obscure operations from your sight.

But above the gray land and the spasms of bleak dust which drift endlessly over it, you perceive, after a moment, the eyes of Doctor T.J. Eckleburg. The eyes of Doctor T.J. Eckleburg are blue and gigantic—their retinas[2] are one yard high. They look out of

---

1 The basis for the valley of ashes is probably the Corona dumps (now Flushing Meadows-Corona Park) on the border of Flushing in the borough of Queens.

2 Matthew J. Bruccoli reminds us that the retina is invisible, and that Fitzgerald probably means irises or pupils here. See *Apparatus for F. Scott Fitzgerald's "The Great Gatsby"* (Columbia: U of South Carolina P, 1974), 33.

no face, but, instead, from a pair of enormous yellow spectacles which pass over a non-existent nose. Evidently some wild wag of an oculist set them there to fatten his practice in the borough of Queens, and then sank down himself into eternal blindness, or forgot them and moved away. But his eyes, dimmed a little by many paintless days under sun and rain, brood on over the solemn dumping ground.

The valley of ashes is bounded on one side by a small foul river, and, when the drawbridge is up to let barges through, the passengers on waiting trains can stare at the dismal scene for as long as half an hour. There is always a halt there of at least a minute, and it was because of this that I first met Tom Buchanan's mistress.

The fact that he had one was insisted upon wherever he was known. His acquaintances resented the fact that he turned up in popular restaurants with her and, leaving her at a table, sauntered about, chatting with whomsoever he knew. Though I was curious to see her, I had no desire to meet her—but I did. I went up to New York with Tom on the train one afternoon, and when we stopped by the ashheaps he jumped to his feet and, taking hold of my elbow, literally forced me from the car.

"We're getting off," he insisted. "I want you to meet my girl."

I think he'd tanked up a good deal at luncheon, and his determination to have my company bordered on violence. The supercilious assumption was that on Sunday afternoon I had nothing better to do.

I followed him over a low whitewashed railroad fence, and we walked back a hundred yards along the road under Doctor Eckleburg's persistent stare. The only building in sight was a small block of yellow brick sitting on the edge of the waste land, a sort of compact Main Street ministering to it, and contiguous to absolutely nothing. One of the three shops it contained was for rent and another was an all-night restaurant, approached by a trail of ashes; the third was a garage—*Repairs*. GEORGE B. WILSON. *Cars bought and sold.*—and I followed Tom inside.

The interior was unprosperous and bare; the only car visible was the dust-covered wreck of a Ford which crouched in a dim corner. It had occurred to me that this shadow of a garage must be a blind, and that sumptuous and romantic apartments were concealed overhead, when the proprietor himself appeared in the door of an office, wiping his hands on a piece of waste. He was a blond, spiritless man, anæmic, and faintly handsome. When he saw us a damp gleam of hope sprang into his light blue eyes.

"Hello, Wilson, old man," said Tom, slapping him jovially on the shoulder. "How's business?"

"I can't complain," answered Wilson unconvincingly. "When are you going to sell me that car?"

"Next week; I've got my man working on it now."

"Works pretty slow, don't he?"

"No, he doesn't," said Tom coldly. "And if you feel that way about it, maybe I'd better sell it somewhere else after all."

"I don't mean that," explained Wilson quickly. "I just meant——"

His voice faded off and Tom glanced impatiently around the garage. Then I heard footsteps on a stairs, and in a moment the thickish figure of a woman blocked out the light from the office door. She was in the middle thirties, and faintly stout, but she carried her surplus flesh sensuously as some women can. Her face, above a spotted dress of dark blue crêpe-de-chine, contained no facet or gleam of beauty, but there was an immediately perceptible vitality about her as if the nerves of her body were continually smouldering. She smiled slowly and, walking through her husband as if he were a ghost, shook hands with Tom, looking him flush in the eye. Then she wet her lips, and without turning around spoke to her husband in a soft, coarse voice:

"Get some chairs, why don't you, so somebody can sit down."

"Oh, sure," agreed Wilson hurriedly, and went toward the little office, mingling immediately with the cement color of the walls. A white ashen dust veiled his dark suit and his pale hair as it veiled everything in the vicinity—except his wife, who moved close to Tom.

"I want to see you," said Tom intently. "Get on the next train."

"All right."

"I'll meet you by the news-stand on the lower level."

She nodded and moved away from him just as George Wilson emerged with two chairs from his office door.

We waited for her down the road and out of sight. It was a few days before the Fourth of July, and a gray, scrawny Italian child was setting torpedoes in a row along the railroad track.

"Terrible place, isn't it," said Tom, exchanging a frown with Doctor Eckleburg.

"Awful."

"It does her good to get away."

"Doesn't her husband object?"

"Wilson? He thinks she goes to see her sister in New York. He's so dumb he doesn't know he's alive."

So Tom Buchanan and his girl and I went up together to New York—or not quite together, for Mrs. Wilson sat discreetly in another car. Tom deferred that much to the sensibilities of those East Eggers who might be on the train.

She had changed her dress to a brown figured muslin, which stretched tight over her rather wide hips as Tom helped her to the platform in New York. At the news-stand she bought a copy of Town Tattle and a moving-picture magazine,[1] and in the station drug-store some cold cream and a small flask of perfume. Upstairs, in the solemn echoing drive she let four taxicabs drive away before she selected a new one, lavender-colored with gray upholstery, and in this we slid out from the mass of the station into the glowing sunshine. But immediately she turned sharply from the window and, leaning forward, tapped on the front glass.

"I want to get one of those dogs," she said earnestly. "I want to get one for the apartment. They're nice to have—a dog."

We backed up to a gray old man who bore an absurd resemblance to John D. Rockefeller.[2] In a basket swung from his neck cowered a dozen very recent puppies of an indeterminate breed.

"What kind are they?" asked Mrs. Wilson eagerly, as he came to the taxi-window.

"All kinds. What kind do you want, lady?"

"I'd like to get one of those police dogs; I don't suppose you got that kind?"

The man peered doubtfully into the basket, plunged in his hand and drew one up, wriggling, by the back of the neck.

"That's no police dog," said Tom.

"No, it's not exactly a po*lice* dog," said the man with disappointment in his voice. "It's more of an Airedale." He passed his hand over the brown wash-rag of a back. "Look at that coat. Some coat. That's a dog that'll never bother you with catching cold."

"I think it's cute," said Mrs. Wilson enthusiastically. "How much is it?"

"That dog?" He looked at it admiringly. "That dog will cost you ten dollars."

The Airedale—undoubtedly there was an Airedale concerned

---

1 Fictional periodical probably based on the gossip magazine *Town Topics*, which, like moving-picture magazines, provided titillating glimpses into the lives of the wealthy and famous.
2 John D. Rockefeller (1839-1937), wealthy oil-industry leader and philanthropist, founder of Standard Oil.

in it somewhere, though its feet were startlingly white—changed hands and settled down into Mrs. Wilson's lap, where she fondled the weatherproof coat with rapture.

"Is it a boy or a girl?" she asked delicately.

"That dog? That dog's a boy."

"It's a bitch," said Tom decisively. "Here's your money. Go and buy ten more dogs with it."

We drove over to Fifth Avenue, so warm and soft, almost pastoral, on the summer Sunday afternoon that I wouldn't have been surprised to see a great flock of white sheep turn the corner.

"Hold on," I said, "I have to leave you here."

"No, you don't," interposed Tom quickly. "Myrtle'll be hurt if you don't come up to the apartment. Won't you, Myrtle?"

"Come on," she urged. "I'll telephone my sister Catherine. She's said to be very beautiful by people who ought to know."

"Well, I'd like to, but——"

We went on, cutting back again over the Park toward the West Hundreds. At 158th Street the cab stopped at one slice in a long white cake of apartment-houses. Throwing a regal homecoming glance around the neighborhood, Mrs. Wilson gathered up her dog and her other purchases, and went haughtily in.

"I'm going to have the McKees come up," she announced as we rose in the elevator. "And, of course, I got to call up my sister, too."

The apartment was on the top floor—a small living-room, a small dining-room, a small bedroom, and a bath. The living-room was crowded to the doors with a set of tapestried furniture entirely too large for it, so that to move about was to stumble continually over scenes of ladies swinging in the gardens of Versailles.[1] The only picture was an over-enlarged photograph, apparently a hen sitting on a blurred rock. Looked at from a distance, however, the hen resolved itself into a bonnet, and the countenance of a stout old lady beamed down into the room. Several old copies of Town Tattle lay on the table together with a copy of "Simon Called Peter,"[2] and some of the small scandal

---

1 Wealthy suburb outside of Paris, the unofficial seat of the French court and government through most of the eighteenth century, and site of the post-war peace negotiations in 1919.

2 Popular 1921 British novel by Robert Keable (1887-1927) about a high-minded minister morally transformed by his war-time experience. Its overall realism and generally frank depiction of sexuality made it somewhat risqué at the time.

magazines of Broadway. Mrs. Wilson was first concerned with the dog. A reluctant elevator-boy went for a box full of straw and some milk, to which he added on his own initiative a tin of large, hard dog-biscuits—one of which decomposed apathetically in the saucer of milk all afternoon. Meanwhile Tom brought out a bottle of whiskey from a locked bureau door.

I have been drunk just twice in my life, and the second time was that afternoon; so everything that happened has a dim, hazy cast over it, although until after eight o'clock the apartment was full of cheerful sun. Sitting on Tom's lap Mrs. Wilson called up several people on the telephone; then there were no cigarettes, and I went out to buy some at the drug-store on the corner. When I came back they had disappeared, so I sat down discreetly in the living-room and read a chapter of "Simon Called Peter"—either it was terrible stuff or the whiskey distorted things, because it didn't make any sense to me.

Just as Tom and Myrtle (after the first drink Mrs. Wilson and I called each other by our first names) reappeared, company commenced to arrive at the apartment-door.

The sister, Catherine, was a slender, worldly girl of about thirty, with a solid, sticky bob of red hair, and a complexion powdered milky white. Her eyebrows had been plucked and then drawn on again at a more rakish angle, but the efforts of nature toward the restoration of the old alignment gave a blurred air to her face. When she moved about there was an incessant clicking as innumerable pottery bracelets jingled up and down upon her arms. She came in with such a proprietary haste, and looked around so possessively at the furniture that I wondered if she lived here. But when I asked her she laughed immoderately, repeated my question aloud, and told me she lived with a girl friend at a hotel.

Mr. McKee was a pale, feminine man from the flat below. He had just shaved, for there was a white spot of lather on his cheekbone, and he was most respectful in his greeting to everyone in the room. He informed me that he was in the "artistic game," and I gathered later that he was a photographer and had made the dim enlargement of Mrs. Wilson's mother which hovered like an ectoplasm[1] on the wall. His wife was shrill, languid, handsome, and horrible. She told me with pride that her husband had photographed her a hundred and twenty-seven times since they had been married.

---

1 A term drawn from spiritualism that refers to the materialized form taken by ghosts or mediums.

Mrs. Wilson had changed her costume some time before, and was now attired in an elaborate afternoon dress of cream-colored chiffon, which gave out a continual rustle as she swept about the room. With the influence of the dress her personality had also undergone a change. The intense vitality that had been so remarkable in the garage was converted into impressive hauteur. Her laughter, her gestures, her assertions became more violently affected moment by moment, and as she expanded the room grew smaller around her, until she seemed to be revolving on a noisy, creaking pivot through the smoky air.

"My dear," she told her sister in a high, mincing shout, "most of these fellas will cheat you every time. All they think of is money. I had a woman up here last week to look at my feet, and when she gave me the bill you'd of thought she had my appendicitus out."

"What was the name of the woman?" asked Mrs. McKee.

"Mrs. Eberhardt. She goes around looking at people's feet in their own homes."

"I like your dress," remarked Mrs. McKee, "I think it's adorable."

Mrs. Wilson rejected the compliment by raising her eyebrow in disdain.

"It's just a crazy old thing," she said. "I just slip it on sometimes when I don't care what I look like."

"But it looks wonderful on you, if you know what I mean," pursued Mrs. McKee. "If Chester could only get you in that pose I think he could make something of it."

We all looked in silence at Mrs. Wilson, who removed a strand of hair from over her eyes and looked back at us with a brilliant smile. Mr. McKee regarded her intently with his head on one side, and then moved his hand back and forth slowly in front of his face.

"I should change the light," he said after a moment. "I'd like to bring out the modelling of the features. And I'd try to get hold of all the back hair."

"I wouldn't think of changing the light," cried Mrs. McKee. "I think it's——"

Her husband said "*Sh!*" and we all looked at the subject again, whereupon Tom Buchanan yawned audibly and got to his feet.

"You McKees have something to drink," he said. "Get some more ice and mineral water, Myrtle, before everybody goes to sleep."

"I told that boy about the ice." Myrtle raised her eyebrows in despair at the shiftlessness of the lower orders. "These people! You have to keep after them all the time."

She looked at me and laughed pointlessly. Then she flounced over to the dog, kissed it with ecstasy, and swept into the kitchen, implying that a dozen chefs awaited her orders there.

"I've done some nice things out on Long Island," asserted Mr. McKee.

Tom looked at him blankly.

"Two of them we have framed down-stairs."

"Two what?" demanded Tom.

"Two studies. One of them I call 'Montauk Point—The Gulls,' and the other I call 'Montauk Point—The Sea.'"

The sister Catherine sat down beside me on the couch.

"Do you live down on Long Island, too?" she inquired.

"I live at West Egg."

"Really? I was down there at a party about a month ago. At a man named Gatsby's. Do you know him?"

"I live next door to him."

"Well, they say he's a nephew or a cousin of Kaiser Wilhelm's.[1] That's where all his money comes from."

"Really?"

She nodded.

"I'm scared of him. I'd hate to have him get anything on me."

This absorbing information about my neighbor was interrupted by Mrs. McKee's pointing suddenly at Catherine:

"Chester, I think you could do something with *her*," she broke out, but Mr. McKee only nodded in a bored way, and turned his attention to Tom.

"I'd like to do more work on Long Island, if I could get the entry. All I ask is that they should give me a start."

"Ask Myrtle," said Tom, breaking into a short shout of laughter as Mrs. Wilson entered with a tray. "She'll give you a letter of introduction, won't you, Myrtle?"

"Do what?" she asked, startled.

"You'll give McKee a letter of introduction to your husband, so he can do some studies of him." His lips moved silently for a

---

1 Kaiser Wilhelm II (1859-1941), German king since 1888 and leader of the Central Powers in the First World War; he was forced to abdicate after the armistice and died in exile.

moment as he invented. "'George B. Wilson at the Gasoline Pump,' or something like that."

Catherine leaned close to me and whispered in my ear:

"Neither of them can stand the person they're married to."

"Can't they?"

"Can't *stand* them." She looked at Myrtle and then at Tom. "What I say is, why go on living with them if they can't stand them? If I was them I'd get a divorce and get married to each other right away."

"Doesn't she like Wilson either?"

The answer to this was unexpected. It came from Myrtle, who had overheard the question, and it was violent and obscene.

"You see," cried Catherine triumphantly. She lowered her voice again. "It's really his wife that's keeping them apart. She's a Catholic, and they don't believe in divorce."

Daisy was not a Catholic, and I was a little shocked at the elaborateness of the lie.

"When they do get married," continued Catherine, "they're going West to live for a while until it blows over."

"It'd be more discreet to go to Europe."

"Oh, do you like Europe?" she exclaimed surprisingly. "I just got back from Monte Carlo."

"Really."

"Just last year. I went over there with another girl."

"Stay long?"

"No, we just went to Monte Carlo and back. We went by way of Marseilles.[1] We had over twelve hundred dollars when we started, but we got gyped[2] out of it all in two days in the private rooms. We had an awful time getting back, I can tell you. God, how I hated that town!"

The late afternoon sky bloomed in the window for a moment like the blue honey of the Mediterranean—then the shrill voice of Mrs. McKee called me back into the room.

"I almost made a mistake, too," she declared vigorously. "I almost married a little kyke[3] who'd been after me for years. I knew he was below me. Everybody kept saying to me: Lucille,

---

1 Monte Carlo is a gambling resort in the principality of Monaco, in south-eastern France. Marseilles is the major seaport in southeastern France.

2 Gyped (Fitzgerald's spelling: more commonly spelled "gypped"): American slang for being cheated, probably derived from racist conceptions of gypsies.

3 Derogatory term for a Jew, usually spelt "kike."

that man's 'way below you!' But if I hadn't met Chester, he'd of got me sure."

"Yes, but listen," said Myrtle Wilson, nodding her head up and down, "at least you didn't marry him."

"I know I didn't."

"Well, I married him," said Myrtle, ambiguously. "And that's the difference between your case and mine."

"Why did you, Myrtle?" demanded Catherine. "Nobody forced you to."

Myrtle considered.

"I married him because I thought he was a gentleman," she said finally. "I thought he knew something about breeding, but he wasn't fit to lick my shoe."

"You were crazy about him for a while," said Catherine.

"Crazy about him!" cried Myrtle incredulously. "Who said I was crazy about him? I never was any more crazy about him than I was about that man there."

She pointed suddenly at me, and everyone looked at me accusingly. I tried to show by my expression that I had played no part in her past.

"The only *crazy* I was was when I married him. I knew right away I made a mistake. He borrowed somebody's best suit to get married in, and never even told me about it, and the man came after it one day when he was out." She looked around to see who was listening: "'Oh, is that your suit?' I said. 'This is the first I ever heard about it.' But I gave it to him and then I lay down and cried to beat the band all afternoon."

"She really ought to get away from him," resumed Catherine to me. "They've been living over that garage for eleven years. And Tom's the first sweetie she ever had."

The bottle of whiskey—a second one—was now in constant demand by all present, excepting Catherine, who "felt just as good on nothing at all." Tom rang for the janitor and sent him for some celebrated sandwiches, which were a complete supper in themselves. I wanted to get out and walk eastward toward the park through the soft twilight, but each time I tried to go I became entangled in some wild, strident argument which pulled me back, as if with ropes, into my chair. Yet high over the city our line of yellow windows must have contributed their share of human secrecy to the casual watcher in the darkening streets, and I was him too, looking up and wondering. I was within and without, simultaneously enchanted and repelled by the inexhaustible variety of life.

Myrtle pulled her chair close to mine, and suddenly her warm breath poured over me the story of her first meeting with Tom.

"It was on the two little seats facing each other that are always the last ones left on the train. I was going up to New York to see my sister and spend the night. He had on a dress suit and patent leather shoes, and I couldn't keep my eyes off him, but every time he looked at me I had to pretend to be looking at the advertisement over his head. When we came into the station he was next to me, and his white shirt-front pressed against my arm, and so I told him I'd have to call a policeman, but he knew I lied. I was so excited that when I got into a taxi with him I didn't hardly know I wasn't getting into a subway train. All I kept thinking about, over and over, was 'You can't live forever; you can't live forever.'"

She turned to Mrs. McKee and the room rang full of her artificial laughter.

"My dear," she cried, "I'm going to give you this dress as soon as I'm through with it. I've got to get another one to-morrow. I'm going to make a list of all the things I've got to get. A massage and a wave, and a collar for the dog, and one of those cute little ash-trays where you touch a spring, and a wreath with a black silk bow for mother's grave that'll last all summer. I got to write down a list so I won't forget all the things I got to do."

It was nine o'clock—almost immediately afterward I looked at my watch and found it was ten. Mr. McKee was asleep on a chair with his fists clenched in his lap, like a photograph of a man of action. Taking out my handkerchief I wiped from his cheek the spot of dried lather that had worried me all the afternoon.

The little dog was sitting on the table looking with blind eyes through the smoke, and from time to time groaning faintly. People disappeared, reappeared, made plans to go somewhere, and then lost each other, searched for each other, found each other a few feet away. Some time toward midnight Tom Buchanan and Mrs. Wilson stood face to face discussing, in impassioned voices, whether Mrs. Wilson had any right to mention Daisy's name.

"Daisy! Daisy! Daisy!" shouted Mrs. Wilson. "I'll say it whenever I want to! Daisy! Dai——"

Making a short deft movement, Tom Buchanan broke her nose with his open hand.

Then there were bloody towels upon the bathroom floor, and women's voices scolding, and high over the confusion a long broken wail of pain. Mr. McKee awoke from his doze and started in a daze toward the door. When he had gone half way he turned around and stared at the scene—his wife and Catherine scolding and consoling as they stumbled here and there among the crowded furniture with articles of aid, and the despairing figure on the couch, bleeding fluently, and trying to spread a copy of Town Tattle over the tapestry scenes of Versailles. Then Mr. McKee turned and continued on out the door. Taking my hat from the chandelier, I followed.

"Come to lunch some day," he suggested, as we groaned down in the elevator.

"Where?"

"Anywhere."

"Keep your hands off the lever," snapped the elevator boy.

"I beg your pardon," said Mr. McKee with dignity, "I didn't know I was touching it."

"All right," I agreed, "I'll be glad to."

... I was standing beside his bed and he was sitting up between the sheets, clad in his underwear, with a great portfolio in his hands.

"Beauty and the Beast ... Loneliness ... Old Grocery Horse ... Brook'n Bridge ..."

Then I was lying half asleep in the cold lower level of the Pennsylvania Station, staring at the morning Tribune, and waiting for the four o'clock train.[1]

Chapter III

THERE was music from my neighbor's house through the summer nights. In his blue gardens men and girls came and went like moths among the whisperings and the champagne and the stars. At high tide in the afternoon I watched his guests diving from the tower of his raft, or taking the sun on the hot sand of his

---

1 Pennsylvania Station is New York City's second major railroad station spanning from 33rd to 31st streets between 7th and 8th avenues, completed in 1911, terminal of the commuter-carrying Long Island Railroad; it was re-built in the 1960s. The *Tribune* is a New York daily newspaper of a conservative turn; merged with the *Herald* to become the *New York Herald Tribune* in 1924.

beach while his two motor-boats slit the waters of the Sound, drawing aquaplanes over cataracts of foam. On week-ends his Rolls-Royce[1] became an omnibus, bearing parties to and from the city between nine in the morning and long past midnight, while his station wagon scampered like a brisk yellow bug to meet all trains. And on Mondays eight servants, including an extra gardener, toiled all day with mops and scrubbing-brushes and hammers and garden-shears, repairing the ravages of the night before.

Every Friday five crates of oranges and lemons arrived from a fruiterer in New York—every Monday these same oranges and lemons left his back door in a pyramid of pulpless halves. There was a machine in the kitchen which could extract the juice of two hundred oranges in half an hour if a little button was pressed two hundred times by a butler's thumb.

At least once a fortnight a corps of caterers came down with several hundred feet of canvas and enough colored lights to make a Christmas tree of Gatsby's enormous garden. On buffet tables, garnished with glistening hors-d'oeuvre, spiced baked hams crowded against salads of harlequin designs and pastry pigs and turkeys bewitched to a dark gold. In the main hall a bar with a real brass rail was set up, and stocked with gins and liquors and with cordials so long forgotten that most of his female guests were too young to know one from another.

By seven o'clock the orchestra has arrived, no thin five-piece affair, but a whole pitful of oboes and trombones and saxophones and viols and cornets and piccolos, and low and high drums. The last swimmers have come in from the beach now and are dressing up-stairs; the cars from New York are parked five deep in the drive, and already the halls and salons and verandas are gaudy with primary colors, and hair shorn in strange new ways, and shawls beyond the dreams of Castile.[2] The bar is in full swing, and floating rounds of cocktails permeate the garden outside, until the air is alive with chatter and laughter, and casual innuendo and introductions forgotten on the spot, and enthusiastic meetings between women who never knew each other's names.

The lights grow brighter as the earth lurches away from the sun, and now the orchestra is playing yellow cocktail music, and

---

1   Top-quality British car, more readily available in the United States after the American Rolls-Royce Co. opened its plant in November 1919.
2   Region in northern Spain, known for the ornate and colorfully embroidered traditional women's shawls.

the opera of voices pitches a key higher. Laughter is easier minute by minute, spilled with prodigality, tipped out at a cheerful word. The groups change more swiftly, swell with new arrivals, dissolve and form in the same breath; already there are wanderers, confident girls who weave here and there among the stouter and more stable, become for a sharp, joyous moment the centre of a group, and then, excited with triumph, glide on through the sea-change of faces and voices and color under the constantly changing light.

Suddenly one of these gypsies, in trembling opal, seizes a cocktail out of the air, dumps it down for courage and, moving her hands like Frisco, dances out alone on the canvas platform. A momentary hush; the orchestra leader varies his rhythm obligingly for her, and there is a burst of chatter as the erroneous news goes around that she is Gilda Gray's understudy from the Follies.[1] The party has begun.

I believe that on the first night I went to Gatsby's house I was one of the few guests who had actually been invited. People were not invited—they went there. They got into automobiles which bore them out to Long Island, and somehow they ended up at Gatsby's door. Once there they were introduced by somebody who knew Gatsby, and after that they conducted themselves according to the rules of behavior associated with amusement parks. Sometimes they came and went without having met Gatsby at all, came for the party with a simplicity of heart that was its own ticket of admission.

I had been actually invited. A chauffeur in a uniform of robin's-egg blue crossed my lawn early that Saturday morning with a surprisingly formal note from his employer: the honor would be entirely Gatsby's, it said, if I would attend his "little party" that night. He had seen me several times, and had intended to call on me long before, but a peculiar combination of circumstances had prevented it—signed Jay Gatsby, in a majestic hand.

---

1 Joe Frisco (1889-1958), stage name of Louis Wilson Joseph, famous jazz dancer from the period known for his rendition of the "Black Bottom." Gilda Gray (1901-59), stage name of Polish-born dancer and actress Marianna Michalski, famous for her rendition of the provocative dance called the "shimmy." Both Frisco and Gray were members of the Zeigfield Follies, the singing and dance revue highlighting the attributes of "the American girl," which ran from 1907 to 1925, and in 1927 and 1931.

Dressed up in white flannels I went over to his lawn a little after seven, and wandered around rather ill at ease among swirls and eddies of people I didn't know—though here and there was a face I had noticed on the commuting train. I was immediately struck by the number of young Englishmen dotted about; all well dressed, all looking a little hungry, and all talking in low, earnest voices to solid and prosperous Americans. I was sure that they were selling something: bonds or insurance or automobiles. They were at least agonizingly aware of the easy money in the vicinity and convinced that it was theirs for a few words in the right key.

As soon as I arrived I made an attempt to find my host, but the two or three people of whom I asked his whereabouts stared at me in such an amazed way, and denied so vehemently any knowledge of his movements, that I slunk off in the direction of the cocktail table—the only place in the garden where a single man could linger without looking purposeless and alone.

I was on my way to get roaring drunk from sheer embarrassment when Jordan Baker came out of the house and stood at the head of the marble steps, leaning a little backward and looking with contemptuous interest down into the garden.

Welcome or not, I found it necessary to attach myself to someone before I should begin to address cordial remarks to the passers-by.

"Hello!" I roared, advancing toward her. My voice seemed unnaturally loud across the garden.

"I thought you might be here," she responded absently as I came up. "I remembered you lived next door to——"

She held my hand impersonally, as a promise that she'd take care of me in a minute, and gave ear to two girls in twin yellow dresses, who stopped at the foot of the steps.

"Hello!" they cried together. "Sorry you didn't win."

That was for the golf tournament. She had lost in the finals the week before.

"You don't know who we are," said one of the girls in yellow, "but we met you here about a month ago."

"You've dyed your hair since then," remarked Jordan, and I started, but the girls had moved casually on and her remark was addressed to the premature moon, produced like the supper, no doubt, out of a caterer's basket. With Jordan's slender golden arm resting in mine, we descended the steps and sauntered about the garden. A tray of cocktails floated at us through the twilight, and we sat down at a table with the two girls in yellow and three men, each one introduced to us as Mr. Mumble.

"Do you come to these parties often?" inquired Jordan of the girl beside her.

"The last one was the one I met you at," answered the girl, in an alert confident voice. She turned to her companion: "Wasn't it for you, Lucille?"

It was for Lucille, too.

"I like to come," Lucille said. "I never care what I do, so I always have a good time. When I was here last I tore my gown on a chair, and he asked me my name and address—inside of a week I got a package from Croirier's[1] with a new evening gown in it."

"Did you keep it?" asked Jordan.

"Sure I did. I was going to wear it to-night, but it was too big in the bust and had to be altered. It was gas blue with lavender beads. Two hundred and sixty-five dollars."

"There's something funny about a fellow that'll do a thing like that," said the other girl eagerly. "He doesn't want any trouble with *any*body."

"Who doesn't?" I inquired.

"Gatsby. Somebody told me——"

The two girls and Jordan leaned together confidentially.

"Somebody told me they thought he killed a man once."

A thrill passed over all of us. The three Mr. Mumbles bent forward and listened eagerly.

"I don't think it's so much *that*," argued Lucille sceptically; "it's more that he was a German spy during the war."

One of the men nodded in confirmation.

"I heard that from a man who knew all about him, grew up with him in Germany," he assured us positively.

"Oh, no," said the first girl, "it couldn't be that, because he was in the American army during the war." As our credulity switched back to her she leaned forward with enthusiasm. "You look at him sometimes when he thinks nobody's looking at him. I'll bet he killed a man."

She narrowed her eyes and shivered. Lucille shivered. We all turned and looked around for Gatsby. It was testimony to the romantic speculation he inspired that there were whispers about him from those who had found little that it was necessary to whisper about in this world.

The first supper—there would be another one after mid-

---

1 Fictional store, the name of which plays on the French verb "croire," to believe.

night—was now being served, and Jordan invited me to join her own party, who were spread around a table on the other side of the garden. There were three married couples and Jordan's escort, a persistent undergraduate given to violent innuendo, and obviously under the impression that sooner or later Jordan was going to yield him up her person to a greater or lesser degree. Instead of rambling this party had preserved a dignified homogeneity, and assumed to itself the function of representing the staid nobility of the country-side—East Egg condescending to West Egg, and carefully on guard against its spectroscopic gayety.

"Let's get out," whispered Jordan, after a somehow wasteful and inappropriate half-hour; "this is much too polite for me."

We got up, and she explained that we were going to find the host: I had never met him, she said, and it was making me uneasy. The undergraduate nodded in a cynical, melancholy way.

The bar, where we glanced first, was crowded, but Gatsby was not there. She couldn't find him from the top of the steps, and he wasn't on the veranda. On a chance we tried an important-looking door, and walked into a high Gothic library, panelled with carved English oak, and probably transported complete from some ruin overseas.[1]

A stout, middle-aged man, with enormous owl-eyed spectacles, was sitting somewhat drunk on the edge of a great table, staring with unsteady concentration at the shelves of books. As we entered he wheeled excitedly around and examined Jordan from head to foot.

"What do you think?" he demanded impetuously.

"About what?"

He waved his hand toward the book-shelves.

"About that. As a matter of fact you needn't bother to ascertain. I ascertained. They're real."

"The books?"

He nodded.

"Absolutely real—have pages and everything. I thought they'd be a nice durable cardboard. Matter of fact, they're absolutely real. Pages and—Here! Lemme show you."

---

1   "Gothic library" suggests the style of medieval architecture prominent in France and England from the twelfth through sixteenth centuries; Nick later refers to Gatsby's library as the "Merton College Library," Oxford University's most famous library, founded in 1373. See Chapter V, p. 113, n. 1.

Taking our scepticism for granted, he rushed to the bookcases and returned with Volume One of the "Stoddard Lectures."[1]

"See!" he cried triumphantly. "It's a bona-fide piece of printed matter. It fooled me. This fella's a regular Belasco.[2] It's a triumph. What thoroughness! What realism! Knew when to stop, too—didn't cut the pages. But what do you want? What do you expect?"

He snatched the book from me and replaced it hastily on its shelf, muttering that if one brick was removed the whole library was liable to collapse.

"Who brought you?" he demanded. "Or did you just come? I was brought. Most people were brought."

Jordan looked at him alertly, cheerfully, without answering.

"I was brought by a woman named Roosevelt," he continued. "Mrs. Claud Roosevelt. Do you know her? I met her somewhere last night. I've been drunk for about a week now, and I thought it might sober me up to sit in a library."

"Has it?"

"A little bit, I think. I can't tell yet. I've only been here an hour. Did I tell you about the books? They're real. They're——"

"You told us."

We shook hands with him gravely and went back outdoors.

There was dancing now on the canvas in the garden; old men pushing young girls backward in eternal graceless circles, superior couples holding each other tortuously, fashionably, and keeping in the corners—and a great number of single girls dancing individualistically or relieving the orchestra for a moment of the burden of the banjo or the traps. By midnight the hilarity had increased. A celebrated tenor had sung in Italian, and a notorious contralto had sung in jazz, and between the numbers people were doing "stunts" all over the garden, while happy, vacuous bursts of laughter rose toward the summer sky. A pair of stage twins, who turned out to be the girls in yellow, did a baby act in costume, and champagne was served in glasses bigger than finger-bowls. The moon had risen higher, and floating in the Sound was a triangle of silver scales, trembling a little to the stiff, tinny drip of the banjoes on the lawn.

---

1 A popular ten-volume set of illustrated travel books by the globetrotter John Stoddard (1850-1931), first issued in 1897-98. Well into the 1920s, leather bound sets with supplementary volumes were a staple of home libraries.

2 David Belasco (1853-1931), prolific playwright and legendary New York theater producer known for his theatrical realism.

I was still with Jordan Baker. We were sitting at a table with a man of about my age and a rowdy little girl, who gave way upon the slightest provocation to uncontrollable laughter. I was enjoying myself now. I had taken two finger-bowls of champagne, and the scene had changed before my eyes into something significant, elemental, and profound.

At a lull in the entertainment the man looked at me and smiled.

"Your face is familiar," he said, politely. "Weren't you in the Third Division during the war?"

"Why, yes. I was in the Ninth Machine-Gun Battalion."

"I was in the Seventh Infantry until June nineteen-eighteen. I knew I'd seen you somewhere before."

We talked for a moment about some wet, gray little villages in France. Evidently he lived in this vicinity, for he told me that he had just bought a hydroplane,[1] and was going to try it out in the morning.

"Want to go with me, old sport? Just near the shore along the Sound."

"What time?"

"Any time that suits you best."

It was on the tip of my tongue to ask his name when Jordan looked around and smiled.

"Having a gay time now?" she inquired.

"Much better." I turned again to my new acquaintance. "This is an unusual party for me. I haven't even seen the host. I live over there—" I waved my hand at the invisible hedge in the distance, "and this man Gatsby sent over his chauffeur with an invitation."

For a moment he looked at me as if he failed to understand.

"I'm Gatsby," he said suddenly.

"What!" I exclaimed. "Oh, I beg your pardon."

"I thought you knew, old sport. I'm afraid I'm not a very good host."

He smiled understandingly—much more than understandingly. It was one of those rare smiles with a quality of eternal reassurance in it, that you may come across four or five times in life. It faced—or seemed to face—the whole external world for an instant, and then concentrated on *you* with an irresistible prejudice in your favor. It understood you just so far as you wanted to be understood, believed in you as you would like to believe in

---

1 Seaplane or speedboat; in this case it would have to be the latter, as Gatsby later speaks of going "up" in it.

yourself, and assured you that it had precisely the impression of you that, at your best, you hoped to convey. Precisely at that point it vanished—and I was looking at an elegant young rough-neck, a year or two over thirty, whose elaborate formality of speech just missed being absurd. Some time before he introduced himself I'd got a strong impression that he was picking his words with care.

Almost at the moment when Mr. Gatsby identified himself a butler hurried toward him with the information that Chicago was calling him on the wire. He excused himself with a small bow that included each of us in turn.

"If you want anything just ask for it, old sport," he urged me. "Excuse me. I will rejoin you later."

When he was gone I turned immediately to Jordan—constrained to assure her of my surprise. I had expected that Mr. Gatsby would be a florid and corpulent person in his middle years.

"Who is he?" I demanded. "Do you know?"

"He's just a man named Gatsby."

"Where is he from, I mean? And what does he do?"

"Now *you*'re started on the subject," she answered with a wan smile. "Well, he told me once he was an Oxford man."

A dim background started to take shape behind him, but at her next remark it faded away. "However, I don't believe it."

"Why not?"

"I don't know," she insisted, "I just don't think he went there."

Something in her tone reminded me of the other girl's "I think he killed a man," and had the effect of stimulating my curiosity. I would have accepted without question the information that Gatsby sprang from the swamps of Louisiana or from the lower East Side of New York.[1] That was comprehensible. But young men didn't—at least in my provincial inexperience I believed they didn't—drift coolly out of nowhere and buy a palace on Long Island Sound.

"Anyhow, he gives large parties," said Jordan, changing the subject with an urbane distaste for the concrete. "And I like large parties. They're so intimate. At small parties there isn't any privacy."

---

1   The implication here seems to be that Gatsby most plausibly fits the type of a self-made migrant from the South (with presumably "white trash" origins or even black blood in him), or the self-made man from New York's densely populated immigrant enclave. By 1920, the lower East Side was well known for its large Jewish population in particular, numbering 400,000.

There was the boom of a bass drum, and the voice of the orchestra leader rang out suddenly above the echolalia[1] of the garden.

"Ladies and gentlemen," he cried. "At the request of Mr. Gatsby we are going to play for you Mr. Vladimir Tostoff's latest work, which attracted so much attention at Carnegie Hall last May.[2] If you read the papers you know there was a big sensation." He smiled with jovial condescension, and added: "Some sensation!" Whereupon everybody laughed.

"The piece is known," he concluded lustily, "as 'Vladimir Tostoff's Jazz History of the World.'"[3]

The nature of Mr. Tostoff's composition eluded me, because just as it began my eyes fell on Gatsby, standing alone on the marble steps and looking from one group to another with approving eyes. His tanned skin was drawn attractively tight on his face and his short hair looked as though it were trimmed every day. I could see nothing sinister about him. I wondered if the fact that he was not drinking helped to set him off from his guests, for it seemed to me that he grew more correct as the fraternal hilarity increased. When the "Jazz History of the World" was over, girls were putting their heads on men's shoulders in a puppyish, convivial way, girls were swooning backward playfully into men's arms, even into groups, knowing that someone would arrest their falls—but no one swooned backward on Gatsby, and no French bob touched Gatsby's shoulder, and no singing quartets were formed with Gatsby's head for one link.

"I beg your pardon."

Gatsby's butler was suddenly standing beside us.

---

1 Pathological condition wherein one compulsively repeats others' words or phrases, or, more generally, the subordination of sense to sound. Fitzgerald chose this word at the last minute to replace "chatter" (too late for the first imprint of the first edition).

2 Elegant Manhattan concert hall on 7th Avenue and 57th St.

3 This fictional piece was probably inspired by popular bandleader Paul Whiteman's 1924 Aeolian Hall concert, "An Experiment in Modern Music," which culminated in the premier of George Gershwin's "Rhapsody in Blue." Fitzgerald may have also had in mind French composer Darius Milhaud's "La création du monde," which premiered in Paris in 1923. The description of the piece is far more extensive in the manuscript and unrevised galleys of the novel; Fitzgerald changed the composer's name from "Les Epstein" to "Vladimir Tostoff" while revising the galleys. For illuminating commentary, see Breitwieser's essays listed in the Select Bibliography.

"Miss Baker?" he inquired. "I beg your pardon, but Mr. Gatsby would like to speak to you alone."

"With me?" she exclaimed in surprise.

"Yes, madame."

She got up slowly, raising her eyebrows at me in astonishment, and followed the butler toward the house. I noticed that she wore her evening-dress, all her dresses, like sports clothes—there was a jauntiness about her movements as if she had first learned to walk upon golf courses on clean, crisp mornings.

I was alone and it was almost two. For some time confused and intriguing sounds had issued from a long, many-windowed room which overhung the terrace. Eluding Jordan's undergraduate, who was now engaged in an obstetrical conversation with two chorus girls, and who implored me to join him, I went inside.

The large room was full of people. One of the girls in yellow was playing the piano, and beside her stood a tall, red-haired young lady from a famous chorus, engaged in song. She had drunk a quantity of champagne, and during the course of her song she had decided, ineptly, that everything was very, very sad—she was not only singing, she was weeping too. Whenever there was a pause in the song she filled it with gasping, broken sobs, and then took up the lyric again in a quavering soprano. The tears coursed down her cheeks—not freely, however, for when they came into contact with her heavily beaded eyelashes they assumed an inky color, and pursued the rest of their way in slow black rivulets. A humorous suggestion was made that she sing the notes on her face, whereupon she threw up her hands, sank into a chair, and went off into a deep vinous sleep.

"She had a fight with a man who says he's her husband," explained a girl at my elbow.

I looked around. Most of the remaining women were now having fights with men said to be their husbands. Even Jordan's party, the quartet from East Egg, were rent asunder by dissension. One of the men was talking with curious intensity to a young actress, and his wife, after attempting to laugh at the situation in a dignified and indifferent way, broke down entirely and resorted to flank attacks—at intervals she appeared suddenly at his side like an angry diamond, and hissed: "You promised!" into his ear.[1]

---

1 Perhaps Fitzgerald meant "diamondback" here, in which case his simile would make better sense. See A.S.G. Edwards, "F. Scott Fitzgerald, *The Great Gatsby*, 'Like an Angry Diamond,'" *ANQ* 19.2 (2006): 51–52.

The reluctance to go home was not confined to wayward men. The hall was at present occupied by two deplorably sober men and their highly indignant wives. The wives were sympathizing with each other in slightly raised voices.

"Whenever he sees I'm having a good time he wants to go home."

"Never heard anything so selfish in my life."

"We're always the first ones to leave."

"So are we."

"Well, we're almost the last to-night," said one of the men sheepishly. "The orchestra left half an hour ago."

In spite of the wives' agreement that such malevolence was beyond credibility, the dispute ended in a short struggle, and both wives were lifted, kicking, into the night.

As I waited for my hat in the hall the door of the library opened and Jordan Baker and Gatsby came out together. He was saying some last word to her, but the eagerness in his manner tightened abruptly into formality as several people approached him to say good-by.

Jordan's party were calling impatiently to her from the porch, but she lingered for a moment to shake hands.

"I've just heard the most amazing thing," she whispered. "How long were we in there?"

"Why, about an hour."

"It was ... simply amazing," she repeated abstractedly. "But I swore I wouldn't tell it and here I am tantalizing you." She yawned gracefully in my face. "Please come and see me.... Phone book.... Under the name of Mrs. Sigourney Howard.... My aunt...." She was hurrying off as she talked—her brown hand waved a jaunty salute as she melted into her party at the door.

Rather ashamed that on my first appearance I had stayed so late, I joined the last of Gatsby's guests, who were clustered around him. I wanted to explain that I'd hunted for him early in the evening and to apologize for not having known him in the garden.

"Don't mention it," he enjoined me eagerly. "Don't give it another thought, old sport." The familiar expression held no more familiarity than the hand which reassuringly brushed my shoulder. "And don't forget we're going up in the hydroplane to-morrow morning, at nine o'clock."

Then the butler, behind his shoulder:

"Philadelphia wants you on the 'phone, sir."

"All right, in a minute. Tell them I'll be right there.... Good night."

"Good night."

"Good night." He smiled—and suddenly there seemed to be a pleasant significance in having been among the last to go, as if he had desired it all the time. "Good night, old sport.... Good night."

But as I walked down the steps I saw that the evening was not quite over. Fifty feet from the door a dozen headlights illuminated a bizarre and tumultuous scene. In the ditch beside the road, right side up, but violently shorn of one wheel, rested a new coupé[1] which had left Gatsby's drive not two minutes before. The sharp jut of a wall accounted for the detachment of the wheel, which was now getting considerable attention from half a dozen curious chauffeurs. However, as they had left their cars blocking the road, a harsh, discordant din from those in the rear had been audible for some time, and added to the already violent confusion of the scene.

A man in a long duster[2] had dismounted from the wreck and now stood in the middle of the road, looking from the car to the tire and from the tire to the observers in a pleasant, puzzled way.

"See!" he explained. "It went in the ditch."

The fact was infinitely astonishing to him, and I recognized first the unusual quality of wonder, and then the man—it was the late patron of Gatsby's library.

"How'd it happen?"

He shrugged his shoulders.

"I know nothing whatever about mechanics," he said decisively.

"But how did it happen? Did you run into the wall?"

"Don't ask me," said Owl Eyes, washing his hands of the whole matter. "I know very little about driving—next to nothing. It happened, and that's all I know."

"Well, if you're a poor driver you oughtn't to try driving at night."

"But I wasn't even trying," he explained indignantly, "I wasn't even trying."

An awed hush fell upon the bystanders.

"Do you want to commit suicide?"

"You're lucky it was just a wheel! A bad driver and not even *try*ing!"

---

1 Closed, two-door car.
2 A long light overcoat worn in the early days of the automobile to protect oneself from dust.

"You don't understand," explained the criminal. "I wasn't driving. There's another man in the car."

The shock that followed this declaration found voice in a sustained "Ah-h-h!" as the door of the coupé swung slowly open. The crowd—it was now a crowd—stepped back involuntarily, and when the door had opened wide there was a ghostly pause. Then, very gradually, part by part, a pale, dangling individual stepped out of the wreck, pawing tentatively at the ground with a large uncertain dancing shoe.

Blinded by the glare of the headlights and confused by the incessant groaning of the horns, the apparition stood swaying for a moment before he perceived the man in the duster.

"Wha's matter?" he inquired calmly. "Did we run outa gas?"

"Look!"

Half a dozen fingers pointed at the amputated wheel—he stared at it for a moment, and then looked upward as though he suspected that it had dropped from the sky.

"It came off," someone explained.

He nodded.

"At first I din' notice we'd stopped."

A pause. Then, taking a long breath and straightening his shoulders, he remarked in a determined voice:

"Wonder'ff tell me where there's a gas'line station?"

At least a dozen men, some of them a little better off than he was, explained to him that wheel and car were no longer joined by any physical bond.

"Back out," he suggested after a moment. "Put her in reverse."

"But the *wheel's* off!"

He hesitated.

"No harm in trying," he said.

The caterwauling horns had reached a crescendo and I turned away and cut across the lawn toward home. I glanced back once. A wafer of a moon was shining over Gatsby's house, making the night fine as before, and surviving the laughter and the sound of his still glowing garden. A sudden emptiness seemed to flow now from the windows and the great doors, endowing with complete isolation the figure of the host, who stood on the porch, his hand up in a formal gesture of farewell.

Reading over what I have written so far, I see I have given the impression that the events of three nights several weeks apart were all that absorbed me. On the contrary, they were merely casual events in a crowded summer, and, until much later, they absorbed me infinitely less than my personal affairs.

Most of the time I worked. In the early morning the sun threw my shadow westward as I hurried down the white chasms of lower New York to the Probity Trust. I knew the other clerks and young bond-salesmen by their first names, and lunched with them in dark, crowded restaurants on little pig sausages and mashed potatoes and coffee. I even had a short affair with a girl who lived in Jersey City[1] and worked in the accounting department, but her brother began throwing mean looks in my direction, so when she went on her vacation in July I let it blow quietly away.

I took dinner usually at the Yale Club[2]—for some reason it was the gloomiest event of my day—and then I went up-stairs to the library and studied investments and securities for a conscientious hour. There were generally a few rioters around, but they never came into the library, so it was a good place to work. After that, if the night was mellow, I strolled down Madison Avenue past the old Murray Hill Hotel, and over 33rd Street to the Pennsylvania Station.

I began to like New York, the racy, adventurous feel of it at night, and the satisfaction that the constant flicker of men and women and machines gives to the restless eye. I liked to walk up Fifth Avenue and pick out romantic women from the crowd and imagine that in a few minutes I was going to enter into their lives, and no one would ever know or disapprove. Sometimes, in my mind, I followed them to their apartments on the corners of hidden streets, and they turned and smiled back at me before they faded through a door into warm darkness. At the enchanted metropolitan twilight I felt a haunting loneliness sometimes, and felt it in others—poor young clerks who loitered in front of windows waiting until it was time for a solitary restaurant dinner—young clerks in the dusk, wasting the most poignant moments of night and life.

Again at eight o'clock, when the dark lanes of the Forties[3] were five deep with throbbing taxi-cabs, bound for the theatre district, I felt a sinking in my heart. Forms leaned together in the taxis as they waited, and voices sang, and there was laughter from

---

1 New Jersey port city across the Hudson River from Manhattan.
2 Exclusive club at Vanderbilt Avenue and 44th St., founded by Yale University's alumni association in 1897.
3 Mid-town area of Manhattan, famous as the theatre district.

unheard jokes, and lighted cigarettes outlined unintelligible gestures inside. Imagining that I, too, was hurrying toward gayety and sharing their intimate excitement, I wished them well.

For a while I lost sight of Jordan Baker, and then in midsummer I found her again. At first I was flattered to go places with her, because she was a golf champion, and everyone knew her name. Then it was something more. I wasn't actually in love, but I felt a sort of tender curiosity. The bored haughty face that she turned to the world concealed something—most affectations conceal something eventually, even though they don't in the beginning—and one day I found what it was. When we were on a house-party together up in Warwick,[1] she left a borrowed car out in the rain with the top down, and then lied about it—and suddenly I remembered the story about her that had eluded me that night at Daisy's. At her first big golf tournament there was a row that nearly reached the newspapers—a suggestion that she had moved her ball from a bad lie in the semi-final round. The thing approached the proportions of a scandal—then died away. A caddy retracted his statement, and the only other witness admitted that he might have been mistaken. The incident and the name had remained together in my mind.

Jordan Baker instinctively avoided clever, shrewd men, and now I saw that this was because she felt safer on a plane where any divergence from a code would be thought impossible. She was incurably dishonest. She wasn't able to endure being at a disadvantage and, given this unwillingness, I suppose she had begun dealing in subterfuges when she was very young in order to keep that cool, insolent smile turned to the world and yet satisfy the demands of her hard, jaunty body.

It made no difference to me. Dishonesty in a woman is a thing you never blame deeply—I was casually sorry, and then I forgot. It was on that same house party that we had a curious conversation about driving a car. It started because she passed so close to some workmen that our fender flicked a button on one man's coat.

"You're a rotten driver," I protested. "Either you ought to be more careful, or you oughtn't to drive at all."

"I am careful."

"No, you're not."

"Well, other people are," she said lightly.

"What's that got to do with it?"

---

1 Rural getaway fifty miles north of New York City.

"They'll keep out of my way," she insisted. "It takes two to make an accident."

"Suppose you met somebody just as careless as yourself."

"I hope I never will," she answered. "I hate careless people. That's why I like you."

Her gray, sun-strained eyes stared straight ahead, but she had deliberately shifted our relations, and for a moment I thought I loved her. But I am slow-thinking and full of interior rules that act as brakes on my desires, and I knew that first I had to get myself definitely out of that tangle back home. I'd been writing letters once a week and signing them: "Love, Nick," and all I could think of was how, when that certain girl played tennis, a faint mustache of perspiration appeared on her upper lip. Nevertheless there was a vague understanding that had to be tactfully broken off before I was free.

Everyone suspects himself of at least one of the cardinal virtues, and this is mine: I am one of the few honest people that I have ever known.

Chapter IV

ON Sunday morning while church bells rang in the villages alongshore, the world and its mistress returned to Gatsby's house and twinkled hilariously on his lawn.

"He's a bootlegger," said the young ladies, moving somewhere between his cocktails and his flowers. "One time he killed a man who had found out that he was nephew to Von Hindenburg[1] and second cousin to the devil. Reach me a rose, honey, and pour me a last drop into that there crystal glass."

Once I wrote down on the empty spaces of a time-table the names of those who came to Gatsby's house that summer. It is an old time-table now, disintegrating at its folds, and headed "This schedule in effect July 5th, 1922." But I can still read the gray names, and they will give you a better impression than my generalities of those who accepted Gatsby's hospitality and paid him the subtle tribute of knowing nothing whatever about him.

From East Egg, then, came the Chester Beckers and the

---

1 Paul Von Hindenburg (1847-1934), commander-in-chief of the German army during the last half of the First World War, and German president from 1925 to 1934.

Leeches, and a man named Bunsen, whom I knew at Yale, and Doctor Webster Civet, who was drowned last summer up in Maine. And the Hornbeams and the Willie Voltaires, and a whole clan named Blackbuck, who always gathered in a corner and flipped up their noses like goats at whosoever came near. And the Ismays and the Chrysties (or rather Hubert Auerbach and Mr. Chrystie's wife), and Edgar Beaver, whose hair, they say, turned cotton-white one winter afternoon for no good reason at all.

Clarence Endive was from East Egg, as I remember. He came only once, in white knickerbockers, and had a fight with a bum named Etty in the garden. From farther out on the Island came the Cheadles and the O.R.P. Schraeders, and the Stonewall Jackson Abrams of Georgia, and the Fishguards and the Ripley Snells. Snell was there three days before he went to the penitentiary, so drunk out on the gravel drive that Mrs. Ulysses Swett's automobile ran over his right hand. The Dancies came, too, and S.B. Whitebait, who was well over sixty, and Maurice A. Flink, and the Hammerheads, and Beluga the tobacco importer, and Beluga's girls.

From West Egg came the Poles and the Mulreadys and Cecil Roebuck and Cecil Schoen and Gulick the State senator and Newton Orchid, who controlled Films Par Excellence, and Eckhaust and Clyde Cohen and Don S. Schwartze (the son) and Arthur McCarty, all connected with the movies in one way or another. And the Catlips and the Bembergs and G. Earl Muldoon, brother to that Muldoon who afterward strangled his wife. Da Fontano the promoter came there, and Ed Legros and James B. ("Rot-Gut") Ferret and the De Jongs and Ernest Lilly—they came to gamble, and when Ferret wandered into the garden it meant he was cleaned out and Associated Traction would have to fluctuate profitably next day.

A man named Klipspringer was there so often and so long that he became known as "the boarder"—I doubt if he had any other home. Of theatrical people there were Gus Waize and Horace O'Donavan and Lester Myer and George Duckweed and Francis Bull. Also from New York were the Chromes and the Backhyssons and the Dennickers and Russel Betty and the Corrigans and the Kellehers and the Dewars and the Scullys and S.W. Belcher and the Smirkes and the young Quinns, divorced now, and Henry L. Palmetto, who killed himself by jumping in front of a subway train in Times Square.

Benny McClenahan arrived always with four girls. They were never quite the same ones in physical person, but they were so identical one with another that it inevitably seemed they had been there before. I have forgotten their names—Jacqueline, I think, or else Consuela, or Gloria or Judy or June, and their last names were either the melodious names of flowers and months or the sterner ones of the great American capitalists whose cousins, if pressed, they would confess themselves to be.

In addition to all these I can remember that Faustina O'Brien came there at least once and the Baedeker girls and young Brewer, who had his nose shot off in the war, and Mr. Albrucksburger and Miss Haag, his fiancée, and Ardita Fitz-Peters and Mr. P. Jewett, once head of the American Legion,[1] and Miss Claudia Hip, with a man reputed to be her chauffeur, and a prince of something, whom we called Duke, and whose name, if I ever knew it, I have forgotten.

All these people came to Gatsby's house in the summer.

At nine o'clock, one morning late in July, Gatsby's gorgeous car lurched up the rocky drive to my door and gave out a burst of melody from its three-noted horn. It was the first time he had called on me, though I had gone to two of his parties, mounted in his hydroplane, and, at his urgent invitation, made frequent use of his beach.

"Good morning, old sport. You're having lunch with me today and I thought we'd ride up together."

He was balancing himself on the dashboard of his car with that resourcefulness of movement that is so peculiarly American—that comes, I suppose, with the absence of lifting work or rigid sitting in youth and, even more, with the formless grace of our nervous, sporadic games. This quality was continually breaking through his punctilious manner in the shape of restlessness. He was never quite still; there was always a tapping foot somewhere or the impatient opening and closing of a hand.

He saw me looking with admiration at his car.

"It's pretty, isn't it, old sport?" He jumped off to give me a better view. "Haven't you ever seen it before?"

I'd seen it. Everybody had seen it. It was a rich cream color, bright with nickel, swollen here and there in its monstrous length with triumphant hat-boxes and supper-boxes and tool-boxes, and

---

1 Patriotic veterans' organization formed in 1919 and committed to, among other things, indoctrinating immigrants in the ways of "Americanism."

terraced with a labyrinth of wind-shields that mirrored a dozen suns. Sitting down behind many layers of glass in a sort of green leather conservatory, we started to town.

I had talked with him perhaps half a dozen times in the past month and found, to my disappointment, that he had little to say. So my first impression, that he was a person of some undefined consequence, had gradually faded and he had become simply the proprietor of an elaborate road-house next door.

And then came that disconcerting ride. We hadn't reached West Egg Village before Gatsby began leaving his elegant sentences unfinished and slapping himself indecisively on the knee of his caramel-colored suit.

"Look here, old sport," he broke out surprisingly, "what's your opinion of me, anyhow?"

A little overwhelmed, I began the generalized evasions which that question deserves.

"Well, I'm going to tell you something about my life," he interrupted. "I don't want you to get a wrong idea of me from all these stories you hear."

So he was aware of the bizarre accusations that flavored conversation in his halls.

"I'll tell you God's truth." His right hand suddenly ordered divine retribution to stand by. "I am the son of some wealthy people in the Middle West—all dead now. I was brought up in America but educated at Oxford, because all my ancestors have been educated there for many years. It is a family tradition."

He looked at me sideways—and I knew why Jordan Baker had believed he was lying. He hurried the phrase "educated at Oxford," or swallowed it, or choked on it, as though it had bothered him before. And with this doubt, his whole statement fell to pieces, and I wondered if there wasn't something a little sinister about him, after all.

"What part of the Middle West?" I inquired casually.

"San Francisco."

"I see."

"My family all died and I came into a good deal of money."

His voice was solemn, as if the memory of that sudden extinction of a clan still haunted him. For a moment I suspected that he was pulling my leg, but a glance at him convinced me otherwise.

"After that I lived like a young rajah in all the capitals of Europe—Paris, Venice, Rome—collecting jewels, chiefly rubies, hunting big game, painting a little, things for myself only, and trying to forget something very sad that had happened to me long ago."

With an effort I managed to restrain my incredulous laughter. The very phrases were worn so threadbare that they evoked no image except that of a turbaned "character" leaking sawdust at every pore as he pursued a tiger through the Bois de Boulogne.[1]

"Then came the war, old sport. It was a great relief, and I tried very hard to die, but I seemed to bear an enchanted life. I accepted a commission as first lieutenant when it began. In the Argonne Forest I took two machine-gun detachments so far forward that there was a half mile gap on either side of us where the infantry couldn't advance. We stayed there two days and two nights, a hundred and thirty men with sixteen Lewis guns, and when the infantry came up at last they found the insignia of three German divisions among the piles of dead. I was promoted to be a major, and every Allied government gave me a decoration— even Montenegro, little Montenegro down on the Adriatic Sea!"[2]

Little Montenegro! He lifted up the words and nodded at them—with his smile. The smile comprehended Montenegro's troubled history and sympathized with the brave struggles of the Montenegrin people. It appreciated fully the chain of national circumstances which had elicited this tribute from Montenegro's warm little heart. My incredulity was submerged in fascination now; it was like skimming hastily through a dozen magazines.

He reached in his pocket, and a piece of metal, slung on a ribbon, fell into my palm.

"That's the one from Montenegro."

To my astonishment, the thing had an authentic look. "Orderi di Danilo," ran the circular legend, "Montenegro, Nicolas Rex."

"Turn it."

"Major Jay Gatsby," I read, "For Valour Extraordinary."

---

1 Vast park on the western edge of Paris, created in the nineteenth century under Napoleon III.

2 The reference to "Argonne Forest" suggests that Gatsby has participated in American-led offensive battles that began on 26 September 1918. Lewis guns are machine-guns invented by American Colonel Isaac Newton Lewis in 1911; they were used by the Belgians and British before being belatedly adopted by the American forces in 1917. Montenegro was an independent kingdom on the Adriatic coastline in the southern part of the Balkan peninsula. It fought on the side of the allies during the First World War; despite popular resistance and the principles laid out at the Treaty of Versailles by American president Woodrow Wilson, it was annexed by Serbia and eventually became part of Yugoslavia after the war.

"Here's another thing I always carry. A souvenir of Oxford days. It was taken in Trinity Quad—the man on my left is now the Earl of Doncaster."

It was a photograph of half a dozen young men in blazers loafing in an archway through which were visible a host of spires. There was Gatsby, looking a little, not much, younger—with a cricket bat in his hand.

Then it was all true. I saw the skins of tigers flaming in his palace on the Grand Canal;[1] I saw him opening a chest of rubies to ease, with their crimson-lighted depths, the gnawings of his broken heart.

"I'm going to make a big request of you to-day," he said, pocketing his souvenirs with satisfaction, "so I thought you ought to know something about me. I didn't want you to think I was just some nobody. You see, I usually find myself among strangers because I drift here and there trying to forget the sad thing that happened to me." He hesitated. "You'll hear about it this afternoon."

"At lunch?"

"No, this afternoon. I happened to find out that you're taking Miss Baker to tea."

"Do you mean you're in love with Miss Baker?"

"No, old sport, I'm not. But Miss Baker has kindly consented to speak to you about this matter."

I hadn't the faintest idea what "this matter" was, but I was more annoyed than interested. I hadn't asked Jordan to tea in order to discuss Mr. Jay Gatsby. I was sure the request would be something utterly fantastic, and for a moment I was sorry I'd ever set foot upon his overpopulated lawn.

He wouldn't say another word. His correctness grew on him as we neared the city. We passed Port Roosevelt,[2] where there was a glimpse of red-belted ocean-going ships, and sped along a cobbled slum lined with the dark, undeserted saloons of the faded-gilt nineteen-hundreds. Then the valley of ashes opened out on both sides of us, and I had a glimpse of Mrs. Wilson straining at the garage pump with panting vitality as we went by.

With fenders spread like wings we scattered light through half Astoria[3]—only half, for as we twisted among the pillars of the ele-

---

1 Largest waterway in Venice, Italy.
2 Fitzgerald's invention.
3 The reference to "Astoria" is an error on Fitzgerald's part, pointed out to him by friend Ring Lardner. He had in mind Long Island City, which has an elevated train and is connected to Manhattan by the Queensboro Bridge.

vated I heard the familiar "jug-jug-*spat!*" of a motorcycle, and a frantic policeman rode alongside.

"All right, old sport," called Gatsby. We slowed down. Taking a white card from his wallet, he waved it before the man's eyes.

"Right you are," agreed the policeman, tipping his cap. "Know you next time, Mr. Gatsby. Excuse *me!*"

"What was that?" I inquired. "The picture of Oxford?"

"I was able to do the commissioner a favor once, and he sends me a Christmas card every year."

Over the great bridge, with the sunlight through the girders making a constant flicker upon the moving cars, with the city rising up across the river in white heaps and sugar lumps all built with a wish out of non-olfactory money. The city seen from the Queensboro Bridge is always the city seen for the first time, in its first wild promise of all the mystery and the beauty in the world.

A dead man passed us in a hearse heaped with blooms, followed by two carriages with drawn blinds, and by more cheerful carriages for friends. The friends looked out at us with the tragic eyes and short upper lips of southeastern Europe, and I was glad that the sight of Gatsby's splendid car was included in their sombre holiday. As we crossed Blackwell's Island[1] a limousine passed us, driven by a white chauffeur, in which sat three modish negroes, two bucks and a girl. I laughed aloud as the yolks of their eyeballs rolled toward us in haughty rivalry.

"Anything can happen now that we've slid over this bridge," I thought; "anything at all...."

Even Gatsby could happen, without any particular wonder.

Roaring noon. In a well-fanned Forty-second Street cellar I met Gatsby for lunch. Blinking away the brightness of the street outside, my eyes picked him out obscurely in the anteroom, talking to another man.

"Mr. Carraway, this is my friend Mr. Wolfshiem."

A small, flat-nosed Jew raised his large head and regarded me with two fine growths of hair which luxuriated in either nostril. After a moment I discovered his tiny eyes in the half-darkness.

"—So I took one look at him," said Mr. Wolfshiem, shaking my hand earnestly, "and what do you think I did?"

---

1 Island in the East River between Manhattan and Queens, notorious for its prison, almshouse, workhouse, and insane asylum. Re-named Welfare Island in 1921.

"What?" I inquired politely.

But evidently he was not addressing me, for he dropped my hand and covered Gatsby with his expressive nose.

"I handed the money to Katspaugh and I sid: 'All right, Katspaugh, don't pay him a penny till he shuts his mouth.' He shut it then and there."

Gatsby took an arm of each of us and moved forward into the restaurant, whereupon Mr. Wolfshiem swallowed a new sentence he was starting and lapsed into a somnambulatory abstraction.

"Highballs?" asked the head waiter.

"This is a nice restaurant here," said Mr. Wolfshiem, looking at the Presbyterian nymphs on the ceiling. "But I like across the street better!"

"Yes, highballs," agreed Gatsby, and then to Mr. Wolfshiem: "It's too hot over there."

"Hot and small—yes," said Mr. Wolfshiem, "but full of memories."

"What place is that?" I asked.

"The old Metropole."[1]

"The old Metropole," brooded Mr. Wolfshiem gloomily. "Filled with faces dead and gone. Filled with friends gone now forever. I can't forget so long as I live the night they shot Rosy Rosenthal there. It was six of us at the table, and Rosy had eat and drunk a lot all evening. When it was almost morning the waiter came up to him with a funny look and says somebody wants to speak to him outside. 'All right,' says Rosy, and begins to get up, and I pulled him down in his chair.

"'Let the bastards come in here if they want you, Rosy, but don't you, so help me, move outside this room.'

"It was four o'clock in the morning then, and if we'd of raised the blinds we'd of seen daylight."

"Did he go?" I asked innocently.

"Sure he went." Mr. Wolfshiem's nose flashed at me indignantly. "He turned around in the door and says: 'Don't let that waiter take away my coffee!' Then he went out on the sidewalk, and they shot him three times in his full belly and drove away."

"Four of them were electrocuted," I said, remembering.

---

1 Popular hotel restaurant and bar at Broadway and 42nd Street, patronized by show-business celebrities and underworld figures, it was the site of the notorious mob murder described below.

"Five, with Becker."[1] His nostrils turned to me in an interested way. "I understand you're looking for a business gonnegtion."

The juxtaposition of these two remarks was startling. Gatsby answered for me:

"Oh, no," he exclaimed, "this isn't the man."

"No?" Mr. Wolfshiem seemed disappointed.

"This is just a friend. I told you we'd talk about that some other time."

"I beg your pardon," said Mr. Wolfshiem, "I had a wrong man."

A succulent hash arrived, and Mr. Wolfshiem, forgetting the more sentimental atmosphere of the old Metropole, began to eat with ferocious delicacy. His eyes, meanwhile, roved very slowly all around the room—he completed the arc by turning to inspect the people directly behind. I think that, except for my presence, he would have taken one short glance beneath our own table.

"Look here, old sport," said Gatsby, leaning toward me, "I'm afraid I made you a little angry this morning in the car."

There was the smile again, but this time I held out against it.

"I don't like mysteries," I answered, "and I don't understand why you won't come out frankly and tell me what you want. Why has it all got to come through Miss Baker?"

"Oh, it's nothing underhand," he assured me. "Miss Baker's a great sportswoman, you know, and she'd never do anything that wasn't all right."

Suddenly he looked at his watch, jumped up, and hurried from the room, leaving me with Mr. Wolfshiem at the table.

"He has to telephone," said Mr. Wolfshiem, following him with his eyes. "Fine fellow, isn't he? Handsome to look at and a perfect gentleman."

"Yes."

"He's an Oggsford man."

"Oh!"

"He went to Oggsford College in England. You know Oggsford College?"

"I've heard of it."

"It's one of the most famous colleges in the world."

---

1   Herman "Beansy" Rosenthal was a gambler gunned down on 16 July 1912 by mobsters following the orders of New York City police lieutenant Charles Becker (1869-1915), whom Rosenthal was in the process of exposing for corruption. Becker was soon implicated in the murder, tried, and executed in 1915.

"Have you known Gatsby for a long time?" I inquired.

"Several years," he answered in a gratified way. "I made the pleasure of his acquaintance just after the war. But I knew I had discovered a man of fine breeding after I talked with him an hour. I said to myself: 'There's the kind of man you'd like to take home and introduce to your mother and sister.'" He paused. "I see you're looking at my cuff buttons."

I hadn't been looking at them, but I did now. They were composed of oddly familiar pieces of ivory.

"Finest specimens of human molars," he informed me.

"Well!" I inspected them. "That's a very interesting idea."

"Yeah." He flipped his sleeves up under his coat. "Yeah, Gatsby's very careful about women. He would never so much as look at a friend's wife."

When the subject of this instinctive trust returned to the table and sat down Mr. Wolfshiem drank his coffee with a jerk and got to his feet.

"I have enjoyed my lunch," he said, "and I'm going to run off from you two young men before I outstay my welcome."

"Don't hurry, Meyer," said Gatsby, without enthusiasm. Mr. Wolfshiem raised his hand in a sort of benediction.

"You're very polite, but I belong to another generation," he announced solemnly. "You sit here and discuss your sports and your young ladies and your—" He supplied an imaginary noun with another wave of his hand. "As for me, I am fifty years old, and I won't impose myself on you any longer."

As he shook hands and turned away his tragic nose was trembling. I wondered if I had said anything to offend him.

"He becomes very sentimental sometimes," explained Gatsby. "This is one of his sentimental days. He's quite a character around New York—a denizen of Broadway."

"Who is he, anyhow, an actor?"

"No."

"A dentist?"

"Meyer Wolfshiem? No, he's a gambler." Gatsby hesitated, then added coolly: "He's the man who fixed the World's Series back in 1919."[1]

---

1 Eight members of the heavily favored Chicago White Sox were paid by gamblers to lose the series to the Cincinnati Reds. Arnold Rothstein (1882-1928), a businessman and gambler tied to organized crime, was reputed to be the mastermind behind the scheme but was never indicted. See Appendix E2. Wolfshiem was loosely modeled on Rothstein.

"Fixed the World's Series?" I repeated.

The idea staggered me. I remembered, of course, that the World's Series had been fixed in 1919, but if I had thought of it at all I would have thought of it as a thing that merely *happened*, the end of some inevitable chain. It never occurred to me that one man could start to play on the faith of fifty million people— with the single-mindedness of a burglar blowing a safe.

"How did he happen to do that?" I asked after a minute.

"He just saw the opportunity."

"Why isn't he in jail?"

"They can't get him, old sport. He's a smart man."

I insisted on paying the check. As the waiter brought my change I caught sight of Tom Buchanan across the crowded room.

"Come along with me for a minute," I said; "I've got to say hello to someone."

When he saw us Tom jumped up and took half a dozen steps in our direction.

"Where've you been?" he demanded eagerly. "Daisy's furious because you haven't called up."

"This is Mr. Gatsby, Mr. Buchanan."

They shook hands briefly, and a strained, unfamiliar look of embarrassment came over Gatsby's face.

"How've you been, anyhow?" demanded Tom of me. "How'd you happen to come up this far to eat?"

"I've been having lunch with Mr. Gatsby."

I turned toward Mr. Gatsby, but he was no longer there.

One October day in nineteen-seventeen——

(said Jordan Baker that afternoon, sitting up very straight on a straight chair in the tea-garden at the Plaza Hotel)[1]

—I was walking along from one place to another, half on the sidewalks and half on the lawns. I was happier on the lawns because I had on shoes from England with rubber nobs on the soles that bit into the soft ground. I had on a new plaid skirt also that blew a little in the wind, and whenever this happened the red, white, and blue banners in front of all the houses stretched out stiff and said *tut-tut-tut-tut*, in a disapproving way.

---

1 Luxurious, Edwardian-style hotel overlooking Central Park on 59th Street, built in its present form in 1907.

The largest of the banners and the largest of the lawns belonged to Daisy Fay's house. She was just eighteen, two years older than me, and by far the most popular of all the young girls in Louisville. She dressed in white, and had a little white road-ster,[1] and all day long the telephone rang in her house and excited young officers from Camp Taylor demanded the privilege of monopolizing her that night. "Anyways, for an hour!"

When I came opposite her house that morning her white road-ster was beside the curb, and she was sitting in it with a lieutenant I had never seen before. They were so engrossed in each other that she didn't see me until I was five feet away.

"Hello, Jordan," she called unexpectedly. "Please come here."

I was flattered that she wanted to speak to me, because of all the older girls I admired her most. She asked me if I was going to the Red Cross and make bandages. I was. Well, then, would I tell them that she couldn't come that day? The officer looked at Daisy while she was speaking, in a way that every young girl wants to be looked at sometime, and because it seemed romantic to me I have remembered the incident ever since. His name was Jay Gatsby, and I didn't lay eyes on him again for over four years—even after I'd met him on Long Island I didn't realize it was the same man.

That was nineteen-seventeen. By the next year I had a few beaux myself, and I began to play in tournaments, so I didn't see Daisy very often. She went with a slightly older crowd—when she went with anyone at all. Wild rumors were circulating about her—how her mother had found her packing her bag one winter night to go to New York and say good-by to a soldier who was going overseas. She was effectually prevented, but she wasn't on speaking terms with her family for several weeks. After that she didn't play around with the soldiers any more, but only with a few flat-footed, short-sighted young men in town, who couldn't get into the army at all.

By the next autumn she was gay again, gay as ever. She had a début after the armistice, and in February she was presumably engaged to a man from New Orleans. In June she married Tom Buchanan of Chicago, with more pomp and circumstance than Louisville ever knew before. He came down with a hundred people in four private cars, and hired a whole floor of the Seal-bach Hotel, and the day before the wedding he gave her a string of pearls valued at three hundred and fifty thousand dollars.

I was a bridesmaid. I came into her room half an hour before the bridal dinner, and found her lying on her bed as lovely as the

---

1 Sporty-styled convertible, seating two.

June night in her flowered dress—and as drunk as a monkey. She had a bottle of Sauterne in one hand and a letter in the other.

"'Gratulate me," she muttered. "Never had a drink before, but oh how I do enjoy it."

"What's the matter, Daisy?"

I was scared, I can tell you; I'd never seen a girl like that before.

"Here, deares'." She groped around in a waste-basket she had with her on the bed and pulled out the string of pearls. "Take 'em down-stairs and give 'em back to whoever they belong to. Tell 'em all Daisy's change' her mine. Say: 'Daisy's change' her mine!'"

She began to cry—she cried and cried. I rushed out and found her mother's maid, and we locked the door and got her into a cold bath. She wouldn't let go of the letter. She took it into the tub with her and squeezed it up into a wet ball, and only let me leave it in the soap-dish when she saw that it was coming to pieces like snow.

But she didn't say another word. We gave her spirits of ammonia and put ice on her forehead and hooked her back into her dress, and half an hour later, when we walked out of the room, the pearls were around her neck and the incident was over. Next day at five o'clock she married Tom Buchanan without so much as a shiver, and started off on a three months' trip to the South Seas.

I saw them in Santa Barbara when they came back, and I thought I'd never seen a girl so mad about her husband. If he left the room for a minute she'd look around uneasily, and say: "Where's Tom gone?" and wear the most abstracted expression until she saw him coming in the door. She used to sit on the sand with his head in her lap by the hour, rubbing her fingers over his eyes and looking at him with unfathomable delight. It was touching to see them together—it made you laugh in a hushed, fascinated way. That was in August. A week after I left Santa Barbara Tom ran into a wagon on the Ventura road[1] one night, and ripped a front wheel off his car. The girl who was with him got into the papers, too, because her arm was broken she was one of the chambermaids in the Santa Barbara Hotel.

The next April Daisy had her little girl, and they went to France for a year. I saw them one spring in Cannes, and later in Deauville, and then they came back to Chicago to settle down.

---

1 California highway connecting the coastal city of Santa Barbara to Los Angeles to the south.

Daisy was popular in Chicago, as you know. They moved with a fast crowd, all of them young and rich and wild, but she came out with an absolutely perfect reputation. Perhaps because she doesn't drink. It's a great advantage not to drink among hard-drinking people. You can hold your tongue, and, moreover, you can time any little irregularity of your own so that everybody else is so blind that they don't see or care. Perhaps Daisy never went in for amour at all—and yet there's something in that voice of hers....

Well, about six weeks ago, she heard the name Gatsby for the first time in years. It was when I asked you—do you remember?—if you knew Gatsby in West Egg. After you had gone home she came into my room and woke me up, and said: "What Gatsby?" and when I described him—I was half asleep—she said in the strangest voice that it must be the man she used to know. It wasn't until then that I connected this Gatsby with the officer in her white car.

When Jordan Baker had finished telling all this we had left the Plaza for half an hour and were driving in a victoria[1] through Central Park. The sun had gone down behind the tall apartments of the movie stars in the West Fifties, and the clear voices of little girls, already gathered like crickets on the grass, rose through the hot twilight:

> "I'm the Sheik of Araby.
> Your love belongs to me.
> At night when you're asleep
> Into your tent I'll creep——"[2]

"It was a strange coincidence," I said.

"But it wasn't a coincidence at all."

"Why not?"

"Gatsby bought that house so that Daisy would be just across the bay."

Then it had not been merely the stars to which he had aspired

---

1 Horse-drawn four-wheel carriage for two with raised seat for the driver; still a feature of Central Park today.

2 From the popular 1921 song "The Sheik of Araby," music by Ted Snyder, lyrics by Harry B. Smith and Francis Wheeler, inspired by the hit 1921 movie "The Sheik" starring Rudolph Valentino and Agnes Ayres.

on that June night. He came alive to me, delivered suddenly from the womb of his purposeless splendor.

"He wants to know," continued Jordan, "if you'll invite Daisy to your house some afternoon and then let him come over."

The modesty of the demand shook me. He had waited five years and bought a mansion where he dispensed starlight to casual moths—so that he could "come over" some afternoon to a stranger's garden.

"Did I have to know all this before he could ask such a little thing?"

"He's afraid, he's waited so long. He thought you might be offended. You see, he's a regular tough underneath it all."

Something worried me.

"Why didn't he ask you to arrange a meeting?"

"He wants her to see his house," she explained. "And your house is right next door."

"Oh!"

"I think he half expected her to wander into one of his parties, some night," went on Jordan, "but she never did. Then he began asking people casually if they knew her, and I was the first one he found. It was that night he sent for me at his dance, and you should have heard the elaborate way he worked up to it. Of course, I immediately suggested a luncheon in New York—and I thought he'd go mad:

"'I don't want to do anything out of the way!' he kept saying. 'I want to see her right next door.'

"When I said you were a particular friend of Tom's, he started to abandon the whole idea. He doesn't know very much about Tom, though he says he's read a Chicago paper for years just on the chance of catching a glimpse of Daisy's name."

It was dark now, and as we dipped under a little bridge I put my arm around Jordan's golden shoulder and drew her toward me and asked her to dinner. Suddenly I wasn't thinking of Daisy and Gatsby any more, but of this clean, hard, limited person, who dealt in universal scepticism, and who leaned back jauntily just within the circle of my arm. A phrase began to beat in my ears with a sort of heady excitement: "There are only the pursued, the pursuing, the busy and the tired."

"And Daisy ought to have something in her life," murmured Jordan to me.

"Does she want to see Gatsby?"

"She's not to know about it. Gatsby doesn't want her to know. You're just supposed to invite her to tea."

We passed a barrier of dark trees, and then the façade of Fifty-ninth Street, a block of delicate pale light, beamed down into the park. Unlike Gatsby and Tom Buchanan, I had no girl whose disembodied face floated along the dark cornices and blinding signs, and so I drew up the girl beside me, tightening my arms. Her wan, scornful mouth smiled, and so I drew her up again closer, this time to my face.

Chapter V

WHEN I came home to West Egg that night I was afraid for a moment that my house was on fire. Two o'clock and the whole corner of the peninsula was blazing with light, which fell unreal on the shrubbery and made thin elongating glints upon the roadside wires. Turning a corner, I saw that it was Gatsby's house, lit from tower to cellar.

At first I thought it was another party, a wild rout that had resolved itself into "hide-and-go-seek" or "sardines-in-the-box" with all the house thrown open to the game. But there wasn't a sound. Only wind in the trees, which blew the wires and made the lights go off and on again as if the house had winked into the darkness. As my taxi groaned away I saw Gatsby walking toward me across his lawn.

"Your place looks like the World's Fair," I said.

"Does it?" He turned his eyes toward it absently. "I have been glancing into some of the rooms. Let's go to Coney Island,[1] old sport. In my car."

"It's too late."

"Well, suppose we take a plunge in the swimming-pool? I haven't made use of it all summer."

"I've got to go to bed."

"All right."

He waited, looking at me with suppressed eagerness.

"I talked with Miss Baker," I said after a moment. "I'm going to call up Daisy to-morrow and invite her over here to tea."

"Oh, that's all right," he said carelessly. "I don't want to put you to any trouble."

"What day would suit you?"

---

1 Neighborhood of Brooklyn famous by the 1920s for its gaudy, state-of-the-art amusement parks.

"What day would suit *you?*" he corrected me quickly. "I don't want to put you to any trouble, you see."

"How about the day after to-morrow?"

He considered for a moment. Then, with reluctance:

"I want to get the grass cut," he said.

We both looked at the grass—there was a sharp line where my ragged lawn ended and the darker, well-kept expanse of his began. I suspected that he meant my grass.

"There's another little thing," he said uncertainly, and hesitated.

"Would you rather put it off for a few days?" I asked.

"Oh, it isn't about that. At least—" He fumbled with a series of beginnings. "Why, I thought—why, look here, old sport, you don't make much money, do you?"

"Not very much."

This seemed to reassure him and he continued more confidently.

"I thought you didn't, if you'll pardon my—you see, I carry on a little business on the side, a sort of side line, you understand. And I thought that if you don't make very much—You're selling bonds, aren't you, old sport?"

"Trying to."

"Well, this would interest you. It wouldn't take up much of your time and you might pick up a nice bit of money. It happens to be a rather confidential sort of thing."

I realize now that under different circumstances that conversation might have been one of the crises of my life. But, because the offer was obviously and tactlessly for a service to be rendered, I had no choice except to cut him off there.

"I've got my hands full," I said. "I'm much obliged but I couldn't take on any more work."

"You wouldn't have to do any business with Wolfshiem." Evidently he thought that I was shying away from the "gonnegtion" mentioned at lunch, but I assured him he was wrong. He waited a moment longer, hoping I'd begin a conversation, but I was too absorbed to be responsive, so he went unwillingly home.

The evening had made me light-headed and happy; I think I walked into a deep sleep as I entered my front door. So I don't know whether or not Gatsby went to Coney Island, or for how many hours he "glanced into rooms" while his house blazed gaudily on. I called up Daisy from the office next morning, and invited her to come to tea.

"Don't bring Tom," I warned her.

"What?"

"Don't bring Tom."

"Who is 'Tom'?" she asked innocently.

The day agreed upon was pouring rain. At eleven o'clock a man in a raincoat, dragging a lawn-mower, tapped at my front door and said that Mr. Gatsby had sent him over to cut my grass. This reminded me that I had forgotten to tell my Finn to come back, so I drove into West Egg Village to search for her among soggy whitewashed alleys and to buy some cups and lemons and flowers.

The flowers were unnecessary, for at two o'clock a greenhouse arrived from Gatsby's, with innumerable receptacles to contain it. An hour later the front door opened nervously, and Gatsby, in a white flannel suit, silver shirt, and gold-colored tie, hurried in. He was pale, and there were dark signs of sleeplessness beneath his eyes.

"Is everything all right?" he asked immediately.

"The grass looks fine, if that's what you mean."

"What grass?" he inquired blankly. "Oh, the grass in the yard." He looked out the window at it, but, judging from his expression, I don't believe he saw a thing.

"Looks very good," he remarked vaguely. "One of the papers said they thought the rain would stop about four. I think it was The Journal. Have you got everything you need in the shape of— of tea?"

I took him into the pantry, where he looked a little reproachfully at the Finn. Together we scrutinized the twelve lemon cakes from the delicatessen shop.

"Will they do?" I asked.

"Of course, of course! They're fine!" and he added hollowly, " ... old sport."

The rain cooled about half-past three to a damp mist, through which occasional thin drops swam like dew. Gatsby looked with vacant eyes through a copy of Clay's "Economics,"[1] starting at the Finnish tread that shook the kitchen floor, and peering toward the bleared windows from time to time as if a series of invisible but alarming happenings were taking place outside. Finally he got up and informed me, in an uncertain voice, that he was going home.

"Why's that?"

---

1 British economist Henry Clay's *Economics: An Introduction for the General Reader*, first published in England in 1916, in the United States in 1918.

"Nobody's coming to tea. It's too late!" He looked at his watch as if there was some pressing demand on his time elsewhere. "I can't wait all day."

"Don't be silly; it's just two minutes to four."

He sat down miserably, as if I had pushed him, and simultaneously there was the sound of a motor turning into my lane. We both jumped up, and, a little harrowed myself, I went out into the yard.

Under the dripping bare lilac-trees a large open car was coming up the drive. It stopped. Daisy's face, tipped sideways beneath a three-cornered lavender hat, looked out at me with a bright ecstatic smile.

"Is this absolutely where you live, my dearest one?"

The exhilarating ripple of her voice was a wild tonic in the rain. I had to follow the sound of it for a moment, up and down, with my ear alone, before any words came through. A damp streak of hair lay like a dash of blue paint across her cheek, and her hand was wet with glistening drops as I took it to help her from the car.

"Are you in love with me," she said low in my ear, "or why did I have to come alone?"

"That's the secret of Castle Rackrent.[1] Tell your chauffeur to go far away and spend an hour."

"Come back in an hour, Ferdie." Then in a grave murmur: "His name is Ferdie."

"Does the gasoline affect his nose?"

"I don't think so," she said innocently. "Why?"

We went in. To my overwhelming surprise the living-room was deserted.

"Well, that's funny," I exclaimed.

"What's funny?"

She turned her head as there was a light dignified knocking at the front door. I went out and opened it. Gatsby, pale as death, with his hands plunged like weights in his coat pockets, was standing in a puddle of water glaring tragically into my eyes.

With his hands still in his coat pockets he stalked by me into the hall, turned sharply as if he were on a wire, and disappeared into the living-room. It wasn't a bit funny. Aware of the loud beating of my own heart I pulled the door to against the increasing rain.

---

1   Title of 1800 gothic-historical novel by Irish novelist Maria Edgeworth (1767-1849).

For half a minute there wasn't a sound. Then from the living-room I heard a sort of choking murmur and part of a laugh, followed by Daisy's voice on a clear artificial note:

"I certainly am awfully glad to see you again."

A pause; it endured horribly. I had nothing to do in the hall, so I went into the room.

Gatsby, his hands still in his pockets, was reclining against the mantelpiece in a strained counterfeit of perfect ease, even of boredom. His head leaned back so far that it rested against the face of a defunct mantelpiece clock, and from this position his distraught eyes stared down at Daisy, who was sitting, frightened but graceful, on the edge of a stiff chair.

"We've met before," muttered Gatsby. His eyes glanced momentarily at me, and his lips parted with an abortive attempt at a laugh. Luckily the clock took this moment to tilt dangerously at the pressure of his head, whereupon he turned and caught it with trembling fingers, and set it back in place. Then he sat down, rigidly, his elbow on the arm of the sofa and his chin in his hand.

"I'm sorry about the clock," he said.

My own face had now assumed a deep tropical burn. I couldn't muster up a single commonplace out of the thousand in my head.

"It's an old clock," I told them idiotically.

I think we all believed for a moment that it had smashed in pieces on the floor.

"We haven't met for many years," said Daisy, her voice as matter-of-fact as it could ever be.

"Five years next November."

The automatic quality of Gatsby's answer set us all back at least another minute. I had them both on their feet with the desperate suggestion that they help me make tea in the kitchen when the demoniac Finn brought it in on a tray.

Amid the welcome confusion of cups and cakes a certain physical decency established itself. Gatsby got himself into a shadow and, while Daisy and I talked, looked conscientiously from one to the other of us with tense, unhappy eyes. However, as calmness wasn't an end in itself, I made an excuse at the first possible moment, and got to my feet.

"Where are you going?" demanded Gatsby in immediate alarm.

"I'll be back."

"I've got to speak to you about something before you go."

He followed me wildly into the kitchen, closed the door, and whispered: "Oh, God!" in a miserable way.

"What's the matter?"

"This is a terrible mistake," he said, shaking his head from side to side, "a terrible, terrible mistake."

"You're just embarrassed, that's all," and luckily I added: "Daisy's embarrassed too."

"She's embarrassed?" he repeated incredulously.

"Just as much as you are."

"Don't talk so loud."

"You're acting like a little boy," I broke out impatiently. "Not only that, but you're rude. Daisy's sitting in there all alone."

He raised his hand to stop my words, looked at me with unforgettable reproach, and, opening the door cautiously, went back into the other room.

I walked out the back way—just as Gatsby had when he had made his nervous circuit of the house half an hour before—and ran for a huge black knotted tree, whose massed leaves made a fabric against the rain. Once more it was pouring, and my irregular lawn, well-shaved by Gatsby's gardener, abounded in small muddy swamps and prehistoric marshes. There was nothing to look at from under the tree except Gatsby's enormous house, so I stared at it, like Kant at his church steeple,[1] for half an hour. A brewer had built it early in the "period" craze, a decade before, and there was a story that he'd agreed to pay five years' taxes on all the neighboring cottages if the owners would have their roofs thatched with straw. Perhaps their refusal took the heart out of his plan to Found a Family—he went into an immediate decline. His children sold his house with the black wreath still on the door. Americans, while occasionally willing to be serfs, have always been obstinate about being peasantry.

After half an hour, the sun shone again, and the grocer's automobile rounded Gatsby's drive with the raw material for his servants' dinner—I felt sure he wouldn't eat a spoonful. A maid began opening the upper windows of his house, appeared momentarily in each, and, leaning from a large central bay, spat meditatively into the garden. It was time I went back. While the rain continued it had seemed like the murmur of their voices, rising and swelling a little now and then with gusts of emotion. But in the new silence I felt that silence had fallen within the house too.

---

1 German Romantic philosopher Immanuel Kant (1724-84) of Königsberg reputedly had the habit of staring while deep in thought at the church steeple in view of his study window.

I went in—after making every possible noise in the kitchen, short of pushing over the stove—but I don't believe they heard a sound. They were sitting at either end of the couch, looking at each other as if some question had been asked, or was in the air, and every vestige of embarrassment was gone. Daisy's face was smeared with tears, and when I came in she jumped up and began wiping at it with her handkerchief before a mirror. But there was a change in Gatsby that was simply confounding. He literally glowed; without a word or a gesture of exultation a new well-being radiated from him and filled the little room.

"Oh, hello, old sport," he said, as if he hadn't seen me for years. I thought for a moment he was going to shake hands.

"It's stopped raining."

"Has it?" When he realized what I was talking about, that there were twinkle-bells of sunshine in the room, he smiled like a weather man, like an ecstatic patron of recurrent light, and repeated the news to Daisy. "What do you think of that? It's stopped raining."

"I'm glad, Jay." Her throat, full of aching, grieving beauty, told only of her unexpected joy.

"I want you and Daisy to come over to my house," he said, "I'd like to show her around."

"You're sure you want me to come?"

"Absolutely, old sport."

Daisy went up-stairs to wash her face—too late I thought with humiliation of my towels—while Gatsby and I waited on the lawn.

"My house looks well, doesn't it?" he demanded. "See how the whole front of it catches the light."

I agreed that it was splendid.

"Yes." His eyes went over it, every arched door and square tower. "It took me just three years to earn the money that bought it."

"I thought you inherited your money."

"I did, old sport," he said automatically, "but I lost most of it in the big panic—the panic of the war."

I think he hardly knew what he was saying, for when I asked him what business he was in he answered: "That's my affair," before he realized that it wasn't an appropriate reply.

"Oh, I've been in several things," he corrected himself. "I was in the drug business and then I was in the oil business. But I'm not in either one now." He looked at me with more attention. "Do you mean you've been thinking over what I proposed the other night?"

Before I could answer, Daisy came out of the house and two rows of brass buttons on her dress gleamed in the sunlight.

"That huge place *there?*" she cried pointing.

"Do you like it?"

"I love it, but I don't see how you live there all alone."

"I keep it always full of interesting people, night and day. People who do interesting things. Celebrated people."

Instead of taking the short cut along the Sound we went down to the road and entered by the big postern. With enchanting murmurs Daisy admired this aspect or that of the feudal silhouette against the sky, admired the gardens, the sparkling odor of jonquils and the frothy odor of hawthorn and plum blossoms and the pale gold odor of kiss-me-at-the-gate. It was strange to reach the marble steps and find no stir of bright dresses in and out the door, and hear no sound but bird voices in the trees.

And inside, as we wandered through Marie Antoinette music-rooms and Restoration Salons, I felt that there were guests concealed behind every couch and table, under orders to be breathlessly silent until we had passed through. As Gatsby closed the door of "the Merton College Library" I could have sworn I heard the owl-eyed man break into ghostly laughter.[1]

We went up-stairs, through period bedrooms swathed in rose and lavender silk and vivid with new flowers, through dressing-rooms and poolrooms, and bathrooms with sunken baths— intruding into one chamber where a dishevelled man in pajamas was doing liver exercises on the floor. It was Mr. Klipspringer, the "boarder." I had seen him wandering hungrily about the beach that morning. Finally we came to Gatsby's own apartment, a bedroom and a bath, and an Adam's study,[2] where we sat down and drank a glass of some Chartreuse he took from a cupboard in the wall.

---

1   Marie Antoinette music rooms: after Marie Antoinette (1755-93), extravagant wife of Louis XVI, executed during the "Reign of Terror" phase of the French Revolution; Restoration Salons: probably after the Restoration of the Bourbon monarchy in France, 1814-30; Merton College Library: at Oxford University, one of the oldest academic libraries in the world, founded in 1373.

2   After the predominantly neo-classical style of Scottish architect, interior decorator, and furniture designer Robert Adams (1728-92) and his brother James (1730-94). As with the details above, Nick is underscoring the bizarre mélange of Old World styles making up Gatsby's house, collectively signifying a cultivated appropriation of the past.

He hadn't once ceased looking at Daisy, and I think he revalued everything in his house according to the measure of response it drew from her well-loved eyes. Sometimes, too, he stared around at his possessions in a dazed way, as though in her actual and astounding presence none of it was any longer real. Once he nearly toppled down a flight of stairs.

His bedroom was the simplest room of all—except where the dresser was garnished with a toilet set of pure dull gold. Daisy took the brush with delight, and smoothed her hair, whereupon Gatsby sat down and shaded his eyes and began to laugh.

"It's the funniest thing, old sport," he said hilariously. "I can't—When I try to——"

He had passed visibly through two states and was entering upon a third. After his embarrassment and his unreasoning joy he was consumed with wonder at her presence. He had been full of the idea so long, dreamed it right through to the end, waited with his teeth set, so to speak, at an inconceivable pitch of intensity. Now, in the reaction, he was running down like an overwound clock.

Recovering himself in a minute he opened for us two hulking patent cabinets which held his massed suits and dressing-gowns and ties, and his shirts, piled like bricks in stacks a dozen high.

"I've got a man in England who buys me clothes. He sends over a selection of things at the beginning of each season, spring and fall."

He took out a pile of shirts and began throwing them, one by one, before us, shirts of sheer linen and thick silk and fine flannel, which lost their folds as they fell and covered the table in many colored disarray. While we admired he brought more and the soft rich heap mounted higher—shirts with stripes and scrolls and plaids in coral and apple-green and lavender and faint orange, with monograms of Indian blue. Suddenly, with a strained sound, Daisy bent her head into the shirts and began to cry stormily.

"They're such beautiful shirts," she sobbed, her voice muffled in the thick folds. "It makes me sad because I've never seen such—such beautiful shirts before."

After the house, we were to see the grounds and the swimming-pool, and the hydroplane and the midsummer flowers—but outside Gatsby's window it began to rain again, so we stood in a row looking at the corrugated surface of the Sound.

"If it wasn't for the mist we could see your home across the bay," said Gatsby. "You always have a green light that burns all night at the end of your dock."

Daisy put her arm through his abruptly, but he seemed absorbed in what he had just said. Possibly it had occurred to him that the colossal significance of that light had now vanished forever. Compared to the great distance that had separated him from Daisy it had seemed very near to her, almost touching her. It had seemed as close as a star to the moon. Now it was again a green light on a dock. His count of enchanted objects had diminished by one.

I began to walk about the room, examining various indefinite objects in the half darkness. A large photograph of an elderly man in yachting costume attracted me, hung on the wall over his desk.

"Who's this?"

"That? That's Mr. Dan Cody, old sport."

The name sounded faintly familiar.

"He's dead now. He used to be my best friend years ago."

There was a small picture of Gatsby, also in yachting costume, on the bureau—Gatsby with his head thrown back defiantly—taken apparently when he was about eighteen.

"I adore it," exclaimed Daisy. "The pompadour![1] You never told me you had a pompadour—or a yacht."

"Look at this," said Gatsby quickly. "Here's a lot of clippings—about you."

They stood side by side examining it. I was going to ask to see the rubies when the phone rang, and Gatsby took up the receiver.

"Yes.... Well, I can't talk now.... I can't talk now, old sport.... I said a *small* town.... He must know what a small town is.... Well, he's no use to us if Detroit is his idea of a small town...."

He rang off.

"Come here *quick!*" cried Daisy at the window.

The rain was still falling, but the darkness had parted in the west, and there was a pink and golden billow of foamy clouds above the sea.

"Look at that," she whispered, and then after a moment: "I'd like to just get one of those pink clouds and put you in it and push you around."

I tried to go then, but they wouldn't hear of it; perhaps my presence made them feel more satisfactorily alone.

---

1 Hairdo in which hair is combed high in the front.

"I know what we'll do," said Gatsby, "we'll have Klipspringer play the piano."

He went out of the room calling "Ewing!" and returned in a few minutes accompanied by an embarrassed, slightly worn young man, with shell-rimmed glasses and scanty blond hair. He was now decently clothed in a "sport shirt," open at the neck, sneakers, and duck trousers[1] of a nebulous hue.

"Did we interrupt your exercises?" inquired Daisy politely.

"I was asleep," cried Mr. Klipspringer, in a spasm of embarrassment. "That is, I'd *been* asleep. Then I got up..."

"Klipspringer plays the piano," said Gatsby, cutting him off. "Don't you, Ewing, old sport?"

"I don't play well. I don't—I hardly play at all. I'm all out of prac——"

"We'll go down-stairs," interrupted Gatsby. He flipped a switch. The gray windows disappeared as the house glowed full of light.

In the music-room Gatsby turned on a solitary lamp beside the piano. He lit Daisy's cigarette from a trembling match, and sat down with her on a couch far across the room, where there was no light save what the gleaming floor bounced in from the hall.

When Klipspringer had played "The Love Nest"[2] he turned around on the bench and searched unhappily for Gatsby in the gloom.

"I'm all out of practice, you see. I told you I couldn't play. I'm all out of prac——"

"Don't talk so much, old sport," commanded Gatsby. "Play!"

> "In the morning,
>   In the evening,
>   Ain't we got fun——"

Outside the wind was loud and there was a faint flow of thunder along the Sound. All the lights were going on in West Egg now; the electric trains, men-carrying, were plunging home through the rain from New York. It was the hour of a profound human change, and excitement was generating in the air.

---

1   Pants of a light, though durable cotton.
2   Popular 1920 song, music by Louis A. Hirsch, lyrics by Otto Harbach, from the musical comedy *Mary*.

"One thing's sure and nothing's surer
The rich get richer and the poor get—children.
In the meantime,
In between time——"[1]

As I went over to say good-by I saw that the expression of bewilderment had come back into Gatsby's face, as though a faint doubt had occurred to him as to the quality of his present happiness. Almost five years! There must have been moments even that afternoon when Daisy tumbled short of his dreams—not through her own fault, but because of the colossal vitality of his illusion. It had gone beyond her, beyond everything. He had thrown himself into it with a creative passion, adding to it all the time, decking it out with every bright feather that drifted his way. No amount of fire or freshness can challenge what a man will store up in his ghostly heart.

As I watched him he adjusted himself a little, visibly. His hand took hold of hers, and as she said something low in his ear he turned toward her with a rush of emotion. I think that voice held him most, with its fluctuating, feverish warmth, because it couldn't be over-dreamed—that voice was a deathless song.

They had forgotten me, but Daisy glanced up and held out her hand; Gatsby didn't know me now at all. I looked once more at them and they looked back at me, remotely, possessed by intense life. Then I went out of the room and down the marble steps into the rain, leaving them there together.

Chapter VI

ABOUT this time an ambitious young reporter from New York arrived one morning at Gatsby's door and asked him if he had anything to say.

"Anything to say about what?" inquired Gatsby politely.

"Why—any statement to give out."

It transpired after a confused five minutes that the man had heard Gatsby's name around his office in a connection which he either wouldn't reveal or didn't fully understand. This was his day off and with laudable initiative he had hurried out "to see."

---

1 From the popular 1921 song "Ain't We Got Fun," music and lyrics by Richard A. Whiting.

It was a random shot, and yet the reporter's instinct was right. Gatsby's notoriety, spread about by the hundreds who had accepted his hospitality and so become authorities upon his past, had increased all summer until he fell just short of being news. Contemporary legends such as the "underground pipe-line to Canada"[1] attached themselves to him, and there was one persistent story that he didn't live in a house at all, but in a boat that looked like a house and was moved secretly up and down the Long Island shore. Just why these inventions were a source of satisfaction to James Gatz of North Dakota, isn't easy to say.

James Gatz—that was really, or at least legally, his name. He had changed it at the age of seventeen and at the specific moment that witnessed the beginning of his career—when he saw Dan Cody's yacht drop anchor over the most insidious flat on Lake Superior. It was James Gatz who had been loafing along the beach that afternoon in a torn green jersey and a pair of canvas pants, but it was already Jay Gatsby who borrowed a rowboat, pulled out to the *Tuolomee*,[2] and informed Cody that a wind might catch him and break him up in half an hour.

I suppose he'd had the name ready for a long time, even then. His parents were shiftless and unsuccessful farm people—his imagination had never really accepted them as his parents at all. The truth was that Jay Gatsby of West Egg, Long Island, sprang from his Platonic[3] conception of himself. He was a son of God— a phrase which, if it means anything, means just that—and he must be about His Father's business, the service of a vast, vulgar, and meretricious beauty.[4] So he invented just the sort of Jay Gatsby that a seventeen year-old boy would be likely to invent, and to this conception he was faithful to the end.

For over a year he had been beating his way along the south shore of Lake Superior as a clam-digger and a salmon-fisher or in any other capacity that brought him food and bed. His brown,

---

1 This legend originated from the fact that Canada was a primary source of bootleg liquor, both by land and sea.

2 Probably named after Tuolumne County in California, gold mining site during the 1850s and 1860s, given some notoriety by Mark Twain's description of it in *Roughing It* (1872).

3 I.e., ideal.

4 See *St. Luke* 2.v.41-49. Searching anxiously for their missing son, Joseph and Mary find the twelve-year old Jesus discoursing with his teachers in the temple and admonish him. "And he said to them: How is it that you sought me? did you not know, that I must be about my Father's business?" (Rheims-Douay Bible).

hardening body lived naturally through the half-fierce, half-lazy work of the bracing days. He knew women early, and since they spoiled him he became contemptuous of them, of young virgins because they were ignorant, of the others because they were hysterical about things which in his overwhelming self-absorption he took for granted.

But his heart was in a constant, turbulent riot. The most grotesque and fantastic conceits haunted him in his bed at night. A universe of ineffable gaudiness spun itself out in his brain while the clock ticked on the wash-stand and the moon soaked with wet light his tangled clothes upon the floor. Each night he added to the pattern of his fancies until drowsiness closed down upon some vivid scene with an oblivious embrace. For a while these reveries provided an outlet for his imagination; they were a satisfactory hint of the unreality of reality, a promise that the rock of the world was founded securely on a fairy's wing.

An instinct toward his future glory had led him, some months before, to the small Lutheran College of St. Olaf's in southern Minnesota.[1] He stayed there two weeks, dismayed at its ferocious indifference to the drums of his destiny, to destiny itself, and despising the janitor's work with which he was to pay his way through. Then he drifted back to Lake Superior, and he was still searching for something to do on the day that Dan Cody's yacht dropped anchor in the shallows alongshore.

Cody was fifty years old then, a product of the Nevada silver fields, of the Yukon, of every rush for metal since seventy-five. The transactions in Montana copper that made him many times a millionaire found him physically robust but on the verge of soft-mindedness, and, suspecting this, an infinite number of women tried to separate him from his money. The none too savory ramifications by which Ella Kaye, the newspaper woman, played Madame de Maintenon[2] to his weakness and sent him to sea in a yacht, were common knowledge to the turgid sub-journalism of 1902. He had been coasting along all too hospitable shores for five years when he turned up as James Gatz's destiny in Little Girl Bay.

To young Gatz, resting on his oars and looking up at the railed deck, that yacht represented all the beauty and glamour in the

---

1   Located in Northfield, south of Minneapolis-St. Paul.
2   Title bestowed by France's King Louis XIV upon Françoise d'Aubigné (1636-1719), educator who acted as governess to his illegitimate children, and eventually became his second wife.

world. I suppose he smiled at Cody—he had probably discovered that people liked him when he smiled. At any rate Cody asked him a few questions (one of them elicited the brand new name) and found that he was quick and extravagantly ambitious. A few days later he took him to Duluth[1] and bought him a blue coat, six pair of white duck trousers, and a yachting cap. And when the *Tuolomee* left for the West Indies and the Barbary Coast[2] Gatsby left too.

He was employed in a vague personal capacity—while he remained with Cody he was in turn steward, mate, skipper, secretary, and even jailor, for Dan Cody sober knew what lavish doings Dan Cody drunk might soon be about, and he provided for such contingencies by reposing more and more trust in Gatsby. The arrangement lasted five years, during which the boat went three times around the Continent. It might have lasted indefinitely except for the fact that Ella Kaye came on board one night in Boston and a week later Dan Cody inhospitably died.

I remember the portrait of him up in Gatsby's bedroom, a gray, florid man with a hard, empty face—the pioneer debauchee, who during one phase of American life brought back to the Eastern seaboard the savage violence of the frontier brothel and saloon. It was indirectly due to Cody that Gatsby drank so little. Sometimes in the course of gay parties women used to rub champagne into his hair; for himself he formed the habit of letting liquor alone.

And it was from Cody that he inherited money—a legacy of twenty-five thousand dollars. He didn't get it. He never understood the legal device that was used against him, but what remained of the millions went intact to Ella Kaye. He was left with his singularly appropriate education; the vague contour of Jay Gatsby had filled out to the substantiality of a man.

He told me all this very much later, but I've put it down here with the idea of exploding those first wild rumors about his antecedents, which weren't even faintly true. Moreover he told it to me at a time of confusion, when I had reached the point of believing everything and nothing about him. So I take advantage of this short halt, while Gatsby, so to speak, caught his breath, to clear this set of misconceptions away.

---

1 Port city on Lake Superior in north-east Minnesota.
2 Probably the saloon and brothel district in old San Francisco, as the yacht travels "around the continent."

It was a halt, too, in my association with his affairs. For several weeks I didn't see him or hear his voice on the phone—mostly I was in New York, trotting around with Jordan and trying to ingratiate myself with her senile aunt—but finally I went over to his house one Sunday afternoon. I hadn't been there two minutes when somebody brought Tom Buchanan in for a drink. I was startled, naturally, but the really surprising thing was that it hadn't happened before.

They were a party of three on horseback—Tom and a man named Sloane and a pretty woman in a brown riding-habit, who had been there previously.

"I'm delighted to see you," said Gatsby, standing on his porch. "I'm delighted that you dropped in."

As though they cared!

"Sit right down. Have a cigarette or a cigar." He walked around the room quickly, ringing bells. "I'll have something to drink for you in just a minute."

He was profoundly affected by the fact that Tom was there. But he would be uneasy anyhow until he had given them something, realizing in a vague way that that was all they came for. Mr. Sloane wanted nothing. A lemonade? No, thanks. A little champagne? Nothing at all, thanks.... I'm sorry——

"Did you have a nice ride?"

"Very good roads around here."

"I suppose the automobiles——"

"Yeah."

Moved by an irresistible impulse, Gatsby turned to Tom, who had accepted the introduction as a stranger.

"I believe we've met somewhere before, Mr. Buchanan."

"Oh, yes," said Tom, gruffly polite, but obviously not remembering. "So we did. I remember very well."

"About two weeks ago."

"That's right. You were with Nick here."

"I know your wife," continued Gatsby, almost aggressively.

"That so?"

Tom turned to me.

"You live near here, Nick?"

"Next door."

"That so?"

Mr. Sloane didn't enter into the conversation, but lounged back haughtily in his chair; the woman said nothing either—until unexpectedly, after two highballs, she became cordial.

"We'll all come over to your next party, Mr. Gatsby," she suggested. "What do you say?"

"Certainly; I'd be delighted to have you."

"Be ver' nice," said Mr. Sloane, without gratitude. "Well— think ought to be starting home."

"Please don't hurry," Gatsby urged them. He had control of himself now, and he wanted to see more of Tom. "Why don't you—why don't you stay for supper? I wouldn't be surprised if some other people dropped in from New York."

"You come to supper with *me*," said the lady enthusiastically. "Both of you."

This included me. Mr. Sloane got to his feet.

"Come along," he said—but to her only.

"I mean it," she insisted. "I'd love to have you. Lots of room."

Gatsby looked at me questioningly. He wanted to go, and he didn't see that Mr. Sloane had determined he shouldn't.

"I'm afraid I won't be able to," I said.

"Well, you come," she urged, concentrating on Gatsby.

Mr. Sloane murmured something close to her ear.

"We won't be late if we start now," she insisted aloud.

"I haven't got a horse," said Gatsby. "I used to ride in the army, but I've never bought a horse. I'll have to follow you in my car. Excuse me for just a minute."

The rest of us walked out on the porch, where Sloane and the lady began an impassioned conversation aside.

"My God, I believe the man's coming," said Tom. "Doesn't he know she doesn't want him?"

"She says she does want him."

"She has a big dinner party and he won't know a soul there." He frowned. "I wonder where in the devil he met Daisy. By God, I may be old-fashioned in my ideas, but women run around too much these days to suit me. They meet all kinds of crazy fish."

Suddenly Mr. Sloane and the lady walked down the steps and mounted their horses.

"Come on," said Mr. Sloane to Tom, "we're late. We've got to go." And then to me: "Tell him we couldn't wait, will you?"

Tom and I shook hands, the rest of us exchanged a cool nod, and they trotted quickly down the drive, disappearing under the August foliage just as Gatsby, with hat and light overcoat in hand, came out the front door.

Tom was evidently perturbed at Daisy's running around alone, for on the following Saturday night he came with her to Gatsby's party. Perhaps his presence gave the evening its peculiar quality of oppressiveness—it stands out in my memory from Gatsby's other parties that summer. There were the same people, or at least the same sort of people, the same profusion of champagne, the same many-colored, many-keyed commotion, but I felt an unpleasantness in the air, a pervading harshness that hadn't been there before. Or perhaps I had merely grown used to it, grown to accept West Egg as a world complete in itself, with its own standards and its own great figures, second to nothing because it had no consciousness of being so, and now I was looking at it again, through Daisy's eyes. It is invariably saddening to look through new eyes at things upon which you have expended your own powers of adjustment.

They arrived at twilight, and, as we strolled out among the sparkling hundreds, Daisy's voice was playing murmurous tricks in her throat.

"These things excite me *so*," she whispered. "If you want to kiss me any time during the evening, Nick, just let me know and I'll be glad to arrange it for you. Just mention my name. Or present a green card. I'm giving out green——"

"Look around," suggested Gatsby.

"I'm looking around. I'm having a marvellous——"

"You must see the faces of many people you've heard about." Tom's arrogant eyes roamed the crowd.

"We don't go around very much," he said; "in fact, I was just thinking I don't know a soul here."

"Perhaps you know that lady." Gatsby indicated a gorgeous, scarcely human orchid of a woman who sat in state under a white-plum tree. Tom and Daisy stared, with that peculiarly unreal feeling that accompanies the recognition of a hitherto ghostly celebrity of the movies.

"She's lovely," said Daisy.

"The man bending over her is her director."

He took them ceremoniously from group to group:

"Mrs. Buchanan ... and Mr. Buchanan—" After an instant's hesitation he added: "the polo player."

"Oh no," objected Tom quickly, "not me."

But evidently the sound of it pleased Gatsby for Tom remained "the polo player" for the rest of the evening.

"I've never met so many celebrities," Daisy exclaimed, "I liked that man—what was his name?—with the sort of blue nose."

Gatsby identified him, adding that he was a small producer.

"Well, I liked him anyhow."

"I'd a little rather not be the polo player," said Tom pleasantly, "I'd rather look at all these famous people in—in oblivion."

Daisy and Gatsby danced. I remember being surprised by his graceful, conservative fox-trot—I had never seen him dance before. Then they sauntered over to my house and sat on the steps for half an hour, while at her request I remained watchfully in the garden. "In case there's a fire or a flood," she explained, "or any act of God."

Tom appeared from his oblivion as we were sitting down to supper together. "Do you mind if I eat with some people over here?" he said. "A fellow's getting off some funny stuff."

"Go ahead," answered Daisy genially, "and if you want to take down any addresses here's my little gold pencil...." She looked around after a moment and told me the girl was "common but pretty," and I knew that except for the half-hour she'd been alone with Gatsby she wasn't having a good time.

We were at a particularly tipsy table. That was my fault—Gatsby had been called to the phone, and I'd enjoyed these same people only two weeks before. But what had amused me then turned septic on the air now.

"How do you feel, Miss Baedeker?"

The girl addressed was trying, unsuccessfully, to slump against my shoulder. At this inquiry she sat up and opened her eyes.

"Wha'?"

A massive and lethargic woman, who had been urging Daisy to play golf with her at the local club to-morrow, spoke in Miss Baedeker's defence:

"Oh, she's all right now. When she's had five or six cocktails she always starts screaming like that. I tell her she ought to leave it alone."

"I do leave it alone," affirmed the accused hollowly.

"We heard you yelling, so I said to Doc Civet here: 'There's somebody that needs your help, Doc.'"

"She's much obliged, I'm sure," said another friend, without gratitude, "but you got her dress all wet when you stuck her head in the pool."

"Anything I hate is to get my head stuck in a pool," mumbled Miss Baedeker. "They almost drowned me once over in New Jersey."

"Then you ought to leave it alone," countered Doctor Civet.

"Speak for yourself!" cried Miss Baedeker violently. "Your hand shakes. I wouldn't let you operate on me!"

It was like that. Almost the last thing I remember was standing with Daisy and watching the moving-picture director and his Star. They were still under the white-plum tree and their faces were touching except for a pale, thin ray of moonlight between. It occurred to me that he had been very slowly bending toward her all evening to attain this proximity, and even while I watched I saw him stoop one ultimate degree and kiss at her cheek.

"I like her," said Daisy, "I think she's lovely."

But the rest offended her—and inarguably, because it wasn't a gesture but an emotion. She was appalled by West Egg, this unprecedented "place" that Broadway had begotten upon a Long Island fishing village—appalled by its raw vigor that chafed under the old euphemisms and by the too obtrusive fate that herded its inhabitants along a short-cut from nothing to nothing. She saw something awful in the very simplicity she failed to understand.

I sat on the front steps with them while they waited for their car. It was dark here in front; only the bright door sent ten square feet of light volleying out into the soft black morning. Sometimes a shadow moved against a dressing-room blind above, gave way to another shadow, an indefinite procession of shadows, who rouged and powdered in an invisible glass.

"Who is this Gatsby anyhow?" demanded Tom suddenly. "Some big bootlegger?"

"Where'd you hear that?" I inquired.

"I didn't hear it. I imagined it. A lot of these newly rich people are just big bootleggers, you know."

"Not Gatsby," I said shortly.

He was silent for a moment. The pebbles of the drive crunched under his feet.

"Well, he certainly must have strained himself to get this menagerie together."

A breeze stirred the gray haze of Daisy's fur collar.

"At least they're more interesting than the people we know," she said with an effort.

"You didn't look so interested."

"Well, I was."

Tom laughed and turned to me.

"Did you notice Daisy's face when that girl asked her to put her under a cold shower?"

Daisy began to sing with the music in a husky, rhythmic whisper, bringing out a meaning in each word that it had never had before and would never have again. When the melody rose her voice broke up sweetly, following it, in a way contralto voices have, and each change tipped out a little of her warm human magic upon the air.

"Lots of people come who haven't been invited," she said suddenly. "That girl hadn't been invited. They simply force their way in and he's too polite to object."

"I'd like to know who he is and what he does," insisted Tom. "And I think I'll make a point of finding out."

"I can tell you right now," she answered. "He owned some drug-stores, a lot of drug-stores. He built them up himself."

The dilatory limousine came rolling up the drive.

"Good night, Nick," said Daisy.

Her glance left me and sought the lighted top of the steps, where "Three o'Clock in the Morning," a neat, sad little waltz of that year,[1] was drifting out the open door. After all, in the very casualness of Gatsby's party there were romantic possibilities totally absent from her world. What was it up there in the song that seemed to be calling her back inside? What would happen now in the dim, incalculable hours? Perhaps some unbelievable guest would arrive, a person infinitely rare and to be marvelled at, some authentically radiant young girl who with one fresh glance at Gatsby, one moment of magical encounter, would blot out those five years of unwavering devotion.

I stayed late that night, Gatsby asked me to wait until he was free, and I lingered in the garden until the inevitable swimming party had run up, chilled and exalted, from the black beach, until the lights were extinguished in the guest-rooms overhead. When he came down the steps at last the tanned skin was drawn unusually tight on his face, and his eyes were bright and tired.

"She didn't like it," he said immediately.

"Of course she did."

"She didn't like it," he insisted. "She didn't have a good time."

He was silent, and I guessed at his unutterable depression.

"I feel far away from her," he said. "It's hard to make her understand."

"You mean about the dance?"

"The dance?" He dismissed all the dances he had given with a snap of his fingers. "Old sport, the dance is unimportant."

He wanted nothing less of Daisy than that she should go to Tom and say: "I never loved you." After she had obliterated four years with that sentence they could decide upon the more practical measures to be taken. One of them was that, after she was

---

1 Actually published in 1919, the song was popular in 1921; music by Julian Robledo, lyrics by Dorothy Terriss.

free, they were to go back to Louisville and be married from her house—just as if it were five years ago.

"And she doesn't understand," he said. "She used to be able to understand. We'd sit for hours——"

He broke off and began to walk up and down a desolate path of fruit rinds and discarded favors and crushed flowers.

"I wouldn't ask too much of her," I ventured. "You can't repeat the past."

"Can't repeat the past?" he cried incredulously. "Why of course you can!"

He looked around him wildly, as if the past were lurking here in the shadow of his house, just out of reach of his hand.

"I'm going to fix everything just the way it was before," he said, nodding determinedly. "She'll see."

He talked a lot about the past, and I gathered that he wanted to recover something, some idea of himself perhaps, that had gone into loving Daisy. His life had been confused and disordered since then, but if he could once return to a certain starting place and go over it all slowly, he could find out what that thing was....

... One autumn night, five years before, they had been walking down the street when the leaves were falling, and they came to a place where there were no trees and the sidewalk was white with moonlight. They stopped here and turned toward each other. Now it was a cool night with that mysterious excitement in it which comes at the two changes of the year. The quiet lights in the houses were humming out into the darkness and there was a stir and bustle among the stars. Out of the corner of his eye Gatsby saw that the blocks of the sidewalks really formed a ladder and mounted to a secret place above the trees—he could climb to it, if he climbed alone, and once there he could suck on the pap of life, gulp down the incomparable milk of wonder.

His heart beat faster and faster as Daisy's white face came up to his own. He knew that when he kissed this girl, and forever wed his unutterable visions to her perishable breath, his mind would never romp again like the mind of God. So he waited, listening for a moment longer to the tuning-fork that had been struck upon a star. Then he kissed her. At his lips' touch she blossomed for him like a flower and the incarnation was complete.

Through all he said, even through his appalling sentimentality, I was reminded of something—an elusive rhythm, a fragment of lost words, that I had heard somewhere a long time ago. For a moment a phrase tried to take shape in my mouth and my lips parted like a dumb man's, as though there was more struggling upon them than a wisp of startled air. But they made no sound, and what I had almost remembered was uncommunicable forever.

Chapter VII

IT was when curiosity about Gatsby was at its highest that the lights in his house failed to go on one Saturday night—and, as obscurely as it had begun, his career as Trimalchio[1] was over. Only gradually did I become aware that the automobiles which turned expectantly into his drive stayed for just a minute and then drove sulkily away. Wondering if he were sick I went over to find out—an unfamiliar butler with a villainous face squinted at me suspiciously from the door.

"Is Mr. Gatsby sick?"

"Nope." After a pause he added "sir" in a dilatory, grudging way.

"I hadn't seen him around, and I was rather worried. Tell him Mr. Carraway came over."

"Who?" he demanded rudely.

"Carraway."

"Carraway. All right, I'll tell him."

Abruptly he slammed the door.

My Finn informed me that Gatsby had dismissed every servant in his house a week ago and replaced them with half a dozen others, who never went into West Egg Village to be bribed by the tradesmen, but ordered moderate supplies over the telephone. The grocery boy reported that the kitchen looked like a pigsty, and the general opinion in the village was that the new people weren't servants at all.

Next day Gatsby called me on the phone.

"Going away?" I inquired.

"No, old sport."

"I hear you fired all your servants."

"I wanted somebody who wouldn't gossip. Daisy comes over quite often—in the afternoons."

---

1 Fitzgerald seriously considered naming his novel after the wealthy ex-slave who gives a lavish, alcoholic banquet in the *Satyricon*, a satiric treatment of a decadent Roman empire by Petronius (27-66 AD). Fitzgerald likely read an unexpurgated translation issued in 1922 by the small publishing firm Boni and Liveright.

So the whole caravansary[1] had fallen in like a card house at the disapproval in her eyes.

"They're some people Wolfshiem wanted to do something for. They're all brothers and sisters. They used to run a small hotel."

"I see."

He was calling up at Daisy's request—would I come to lunch at her house to-morrow? Miss Baker would be there. Half an hour later Daisy herself telephoned and seemed relieved to find that I was coming. Something was up. And yet I couldn't believe that they would choose this occasion for a scene—especially for the rather harrowing scene that Gatsby had outlined in the garden.

The next day was broiling, almost the last, certainly the warmest, of the summer. As my train emerged from the tunnel into sunlight, only the hot whistles of the National Biscuit Company broke the simmering hush at noon. The straw seats of the car hovered on the edge of combustion; the woman next to me perspired delicately for a while into her white shirtwaist,[2] and then, as her newspaper dampened under her fingers, lapsed despairingly into deep heat with a desolate cry. Her pocket-book slapped to the floor.

"Oh, my!" she gasped.

I picked it up with a weary bend and handed it back to her, holding it at arm's length and by the extreme tip of the corners to indicate that I had no designs upon it—but every one near by, including the woman, suspected me just the same.

"Hot!" said the conductor to familiar faces. "Some weather!... Hot!... Hot!... Hot!... Is it hot enough for you? Is it hot? Is it ... ?"

My commutation ticket came back to me with a dark stain from his hand. That any one should care in this heat whose flushed lips he kissed, whose head made damp the pajama pocket over his heart!

... Through the hall of the Buchanans' house blew a faint wind, carrying the sound of the telephone bell out to Gatsby and me as we waited at the door.

"The master's body!" roared the butler into the mouthpiece. "I'm sorry, madame, but we can't furnish it—it's far too hot to touch this noon!"

What he really said was: "Yes ... Yes ... I'll see."

---

1 An inn with a courtyard for caravans, once common to western and central Asia.

2 A woman's tailored shirt or blouse.

He set down the receiver and came toward us, glistening slightly, to take our stiff straw hats. "Madame expects you in the salon!" he cried, needlessly indicating the direction. In this heat every extra gesture was an affront to the common store of life.

The room, shadowed well with awnings, was dark and cool. Daisy and Jordan lay upon an enormous couch, like silver idols weighing down their own white dresses against the singing breeze of the fans.

"We can't move," they said together.

Jordan's fingers, powdered white over their tan, rested for a moment in mine.

"And Mr. Thomas Buchanan, the athlete?" I inquired.

Simultaneously I heard his voice, gruff, muffled, husky, at the hall telephone.

Gatsby stood in the centre of the crimson carpet and gazed around with fascinated eyes. Daisy watched him and laughed, her sweet, exciting laugh; a tiny gust of powder rose from her bosom into the air.

"The rumor is," whispered Jordan, "that that's Tom's girl on the telephone."

We were silent. The voice in the hall rose high with annoyance: "Very well, then, I won't sell you the car at all.... I'm under no obligations to you at all.... And as for your bothering me about it at lunch time, I won't stand that at all!"

"Holding down the receiver," said Daisy cynically.

"No, he's not," I assured her. "It's a bona-fide deal. I happen to know about it."

Tom flung open the door, blocked out its space for a moment with his thick body, and hurried into the room.

"Mr. Gatsby!" He put out his broad, flat hand with well-concealed dislike. "I'm glad to see you, sir.... Nick...."

"Make us a cold drink," cried Daisy.

As he left the room again she got up and went over to Gatsby and pulled his face down, kissing him on the mouth.

"You know I love you," she murmured.

"You forget there's a lady present," said Jordan. Daisy looked around doubtfully.

"You kiss Nick too."

"What a low, vulgar girl!"

"I don't care!" cried Daisy, and began to clog[1] on the brick fireplace. Then she remembered the heat and sat down guiltily on

---

1 Do a clog dance, beat out a clattering rhythm with clog heeled shoes.

the couch just as a freshly laundered nurse leading a little girl came into the room.

"Bles-sed pre-cious," she crooned, holding out her arms. "Come to your own mother that loves you."

The child, relinquished by the nurse, rushed across the room and rooted shyly into her mother's dress.

"The bles-sed pre-cious! Did mother get powder on your old yellowy hair? Stand up now, and say—How-de-do."

Gatsby and I in turn leaned down and took the small reluctant hand. Afterward he kept looking at the child with surprise. I don't think he had ever really believed in its existence before.

"I got dressed before luncheon," said the child, turning eagerly to Daisy.

"That's because your mother wanted to show you off." Her face bent into the single wrinkle of the small white neck. "You dream, you. You absolute little dream."

"Yes," admitted the child calmly. "Aunt Jordan's got on a white dress too."

"How do you like mother's friends?" Daisy turned her around so that she faced Gatsby. "Do you think they're pretty?"

"Where's Daddy?"

"She doesn't look like her father," explained Daisy. "She looks like me. She's got my hair and shape of the face."

Daisy sat back upon the couch. The nurse took a step forward and held out her hand.

"Come, Pammy."

"Good-by, sweetheart!"

With a reluctant backward glance the well-disciplined child held to her nurse's hand and was pulled out the door, just as Tom came back, preceding four gin rickeys that clicked full of ice.

Gatsby took up his drink.

"They certainly look cool," he said, with visible tension.

We drank in long, greedy swallows.

"I read somewhere that the sun's getting hotter every year," said Tom genially. "It seems that pretty soon the earth's going to fall into the sun—or wait a minute—it's just the opposite—the sun's getting colder every year.

"Come outside," he suggested to Gatsby, "I'd like you to have a look at the place."

I went with them out to the veranda. On the green Sound, stagnant in the heat, one small sail crawled slowly toward the fresher sea. Gatsby's eyes followed it momentarily; he raised his hand and pointed across the bay.

"I'm right across from you."

"So you are."

Our eyes lifted over the rose-beds and the hot lawn and the weedy refuse of the dog-days alongshore. Slowly the white wings of the boat moved against the blue cool limit of the sky. Ahead lay the scalloped ocean and the abounding blessed isles.

"There's sport for you," said Tom, nodding. "I'd like to be out there with him for about an hour."

We had luncheon in the dining-room, darkened too against the heat, and drank down nervous gayety with the cold ale.

"What'll we do with ourselves this afternoon?" cried Daisy, "and the day after that, and the next thirty years?"

"Don't be morbid," Jordan said. "Life starts all over again when it gets crisp in the fall."

"But it's so hot," insisted Daisy, on the verge of tears, "and everything's so confused. Let's all go to town!"

Her voice struggled on through the heat, beating against it, molding its senselessness into forms.

"I've heard of making a garage out of a stable," Tom was saying to Gatsby, "but I'm the first man who ever made a stable out of a garage."

"Who wants to go to town?" demanded Daisy insistently. Gatsby's eyes floated toward her. "Ah," she cried, "you look so cool."

Their eyes met, and they stared together at each other, alone in space. With an effort she glanced down at the table.

"You always look so cool," she repeated.

She had told him that she loved him, and Tom Buchanan saw. He was astounded. His mouth opened a little, and he looked at Gatsby, and then back at Daisy as if he had just recognized her as someone he knew a long time ago.

"You resemble the advertisement of the man," she went on innocently. "You know the advertisement of the man——"

"All right," broke in Tom quickly, "I'm perfectly willing to go to town. Come on—we're all going to town."

He got up, his eyes still flashing between Gatsby and his wife. No one moved.

"Come on!" His temper cracked a little. "What's the matter, anyhow? If we're going to town, let's start."

His hand, trembling with his effort at self-control, bore to his lips the last of his glass of ale. Daisy's voice got us to our feet and out on to the blazing gravel drive.

"Are we just going to go?" she objected. "Like this? Aren't we going to let any one smoke a cigarette first?"

"Everybody smoked all through lunch."

"Oh, let's have fun," she begged him. "It's too hot to fuss."

He didn't answer.

"Have it your own way," she said. "Come on, Jordan."

They went up-stairs to get ready while we three men stood there shuffling the hot pebbles with our feet. A silver curve of the moon hovered already in the western sky. Gatsby started to speak, changed his mind, but not before Tom wheeled and faced him expectantly.

"Have you got your stables here?" asked Gatsby with an effort.

"About a quarter of a mile down the road."

"Oh."

A pause.

"I don't see the idea of going to town," broke out Tom savagely. "Women get these notions in their heads——"

"Shall we take anything to drink?" called Daisy from an upper window.

"I'll get some whiskey," answered Tom. He went inside.

Gatsby turned to me rigidly:

"I can't say anything in his house, old sport."

"She's got an indiscreet voice," I remarked. "It's full of——" I hesitated.

"Her voice is full of money," he said suddenly.

That was it. I'd never understood before. It was full of money—that was the inexhaustible charm that rose and fell in it, the jingle of it, the cymbals' song of it.... High in a white palace the king's daughter, the golden girl....

Tom came out of the house wrapping a quart bottle in a towel, followed by Daisy and Jordan wearing small tight hats of metallic cloth and carrying light capes over their arms.

"Shall we all go in my car?" suggested Gatsby. He felt the hot, green leather of the seat. "I ought to have left it in the shade."

"Is it standard shift?" demanded Tom.

"Yes."

"Well, you take my coupé and let me drive your car to town."

The suggestion was distasteful to Gatsby.

"I don't think there's much gas," he objected.

"Plenty of gas," said Tom boisterously. He looked at the gauge. "And if it runs out I can stop at a drug-store. You can buy anything at a drug-store nowadays."

A pause followed this apparently pointless remark. Daisy looked at Tom frowning, and an indefinable expression, at once definitely unfamiliar and vaguely recognizable, as if I had only heard it described in words, passed over Gatsby's face.

"Come on, Daisy," said Tom, pressing her with his hand toward Gatsby's car. "I'll take you in this circus wagon."

He opened the door, but she moved out from the circle of his arm.

"You take Nick and Jordan. We'll follow you in the coupé."

She walked close to Gatsby, touching his coat with her hand. Jordan and Tom and I got into the front seat of Gatsby's car, Tom pushed the unfamiliar gears tentatively, and we shot off into the oppressive heat, leaving them out of sight behind.

"Did you see that?" demanded Tom.

"See what?"

He looked at me keenly, realizing that Jordan and I must have known all along.

"You think I'm pretty dumb, don't you?" he suggested. "Perhaps I am, but I have a—almost a second sight, sometimes, that tells me what to do. Maybe you don't believe that, but science——"

He paused. The immediate contingency overtook him, pulled him back from the edge of the theoretical abyss.

"I've made a small investigation of this fellow," he continued. "I could have gone deeper if I'd known——"

"Do you mean you've been to a medium?" inquired Jordan humorously.

"What?" Confused, he stared at us as we laughed. "A medium?"

"About Gatsby."

"About Gatsby! No, I haven't. I said I'd been making a small investigation of his past."

"And you found he was an Oxford man," said Jordan helpfully.

"An Oxford man!" He was incredulous. "Like hell he is! He wears a pink suit."

"Nevertheless he's an Oxford man."

"Oxford, New Mexico," snorted Tom contemptuously, "or something like that."

"Listen, Tom. If you're such a snob, why did you invite him to lunch?" demanded Jordan crossly.

"Daisy invited him; she knew him before we were married— God knows where!"

We were all irritable now with the fading ale, and aware of it we drove for a while in silence. Then as Doctor T.J. Eckleburg's faded eyes came into sight down the road, I remembered Gatsby's caution about gasoline.

"We've got enough to get us to town," said Tom.

"But there's a garage right here," objected Jordan. "I don't want to get stalled in this baking heat."

Tom threw on both brakes impatiently, and we slid to an abrupt dusty spot under Wilson's sign. After a moment the proprietor emerged from the interior of his establishment and gazed hollow-eyed at the car.

"Let's have some gas!" cried Tom roughly. "What do you think we stopped for—to admire the view?"

"I'm sick," said Wilson without moving. "Been sick all day."

"What's the matter?"

"I'm all run down."

"Well, shall I help myself?" Tom demanded. "You sounded well enough on the phone."

With an effort Wilson left the shade and support of the doorway and, breathing hard, unscrewed the cap of the tank. In the sunlight his face was green.

"I didn't mean to interrupt your lunch," he said. "But I need money pretty bad, and I was wondering what you were going to do with your old car."

"How do you like this one?" inquired Tom. "I bought it last week."

"It's a nice yellow one," said Wilson, as he strained at the handle.

"Like to buy it?"

"Big chance," Wilson smiled faintly. "No, but I could make some money on the other."

"What do you want money for, all of a sudden?"

"I've been here too long. I want to get away. My wife and I want to go West."

"Your wife does," exclaimed Tom, startled.

"She's been talking about it for ten years." He rested for a moment against the pump, shading his eyes. "And now she's going whether she wants to or not. I'm going to get her away."

The coupé flashed by us with a flurry of dust and the flash of a waving hand.

"What do I owe you?" demanded Tom harshly.

"I just got wised up to something funny the last two days," remarked Wilson. "That's why I want to get away. That's why I been bothering you about the car."

"What do I owe you?"

"Dollar twenty."

The relentless beating heat was beginning to confuse me and I had a bad moment there before I realized that so far his suspicions hadn't alighted on Tom. He had discovered that Myrtle had some sort of life apart from him in another world, and the shock had made him physically sick. I stared at him and then at Tom, who had made a parallel discovery less than an hour before—and it occurred to me that there was no difference between men, in intelligence or race, so profound as the difference between the sick and the well. Wilson was so sick that he looked guilty, unforgivably guilty—as if he had just got some poor girl with child.

"I'll let you have that car," said Tom. "I'll send it over to-morrow afternoon."

That locality was always vaguely disquieting, even in the broad glare of afternoon, and now I turned my head as though I had been warned of something behind. Over the ashheaps the giant eyes of Doctor T. J. Eckleburg kept their vigil, but I perceived, after a moment, that other eyes were regarding us with peculiar intensity from less than twenty feet away.

In one of the windows over the garage the curtains had been moved aside a little, and Myrtle Wilson was peering down at the car. So engrossed was she that she had no consciousness of being observed, and one emotion after another crept into her face like objects into a slowly developing picture. Her expression was curiously familiar—it was an expression I had often seen on women's faces, but on Myrtle Wilson's face it seemed purposeless and inexplicable until I realized that her eyes, wide with jealous terror, were fixed not on Tom, but on Jordan Baker, whom she took to be his wife.

There is no confusion like the confusion of a simple mind, and as we drove away Tom was feeling the hot whips of panic. His wife and his mistress, until an hour ago secure and inviolate, were slipping precipitately from his control. Instinct made him step on the accelerator with the double purpose of overtaking Daisy and leaving Wilson behind, and we sped along toward Astoria at fifty miles an hour, until, among the spidery girders of the elevated, we came in sight of the easy-going blue coupé.

"Those big movies around Fiftieth Street are cool," suggested Jordan. "I love New York on summer afternoons when everyone's away. There's something very sensuous about it—overripe, as if all sorts of funny fruits were going to fall into your hands."

The word "sensuous" had the effect of further disquieting Tom, but before he could invent a protest the coupé came to a stop, and Daisy signalled us to draw up alongside.

"Where are we going?" she cried.

"How about the movies?"

"It's so hot," she complained. "You go. We'll ride around and meet you after." With an effort her wit rose faintly, "We'll meet you on some corner. I'll be the man smoking two cigarettes."

"We can't argue about it here," Tom said impatiently, as a truck gave out a cursing whistle behind us. "You follow me to the south side of Central Park, in front of the Plaza."

Several times he turned his head and looked back for their car, and if the traffic delayed them he slowed up until they came into sight. I think he was afraid they would dart down a side street and out of his life forever.

But they didn't. And we all took the less explicable step of engaging the parlor of a suite in the Plaza Hotel.

The prolonged and tumultuous argument that ended by herding us into that room eludes me, though I have a sharp physical memory that, in the course of it, my underwear kept climbing like a damp snake around my legs and intermittent beads of sweat raced cool across my back. The notion originated with Daisy's suggestion that we hire five bathrooms and take cold baths, and then assumed more tangible form as "a place to have a mint julep." Each of us said over and over that it was a "crazy idea"—we all talked at once to a baffled clerk and thought, or pretended to think, that we were being very funny....

The room was large and stifling, and, though it was already four o'clock, opening the windows admitted only a gust of hot shrubbery from the Park. Daisy went to the mirror and stood with her back to us, fixing her hair.

"It's a swell suite," whispered Jordan respectfully, and every one laughed.

"Open another window," commanded Daisy, without turning around.

"There aren't any more."

"Well, we'd better telephone for an axe——"

"The thing to do is to forget about the heat," said Tom impatiently. "You make it ten times worse by crabbing about it."

He unrolled the bottle of whiskey from the towel and put it on the table.

"Why not let her alone, old sport?" remarked Gatsby. "You're the one that wanted to come to town."

There was a moment of silence. The telephone book slipped from its nail and splashed to the floor, whereupon Jordan whispered, "Excuse me"—but this time no one laughed.

"I'll pick it up," I offered.

"I've got it." Gatsby examined the parted string, muttered "Hum!" in an interested way, and tossed the book on a chair.

"That's a great expression of yours, isn't it?" said Tom sharply.

"What is?"

"All this 'old sport' business. Where'd you pick that up?"

"Now see here, Tom," said Daisy, turning around from the mirror, "if you're going to make personal remarks I won't stay here a minute. Call up and order some ice for the mint julep."

As Tom took up the receiver the compressed heat exploded into sound and we were listening to the portentous chords of Mendelssohn's Wedding March from the ballroom below.[1]

"Imagine marrying anybody in this heat!" cried Jordan dismally.

"Still—I was married in the middle of June," Daisy remembered, "Louisville in June! Somebody fainted. Who was it fainted, Tom?"

"Biloxi," he answered shortly.

"A man named Biloxi. 'Blocks' Biloxi, and he made boxes—that's a fact—and he was from Biloxi, Tennessee."[2]

"They carried him into my house," appended Jordan, "because we lived just two doors from the church. And he stayed three weeks, until Daddy told him he had to get out. The day after he left Daddy died." After a moment she added, as if she might have sounded irreverent, "There wasn't any connection."

"I used to know a Bill Biloxi from Memphis," I remarked.

"That was his cousin. I knew his whole family history before he left. He gave me an aluminum putter that I use to-day."

The music had died down as the ceremony began and now a long cheer floated in at the window, followed by intermittent cries of "Yea—ea—ea!" and finally by a burst of jazz as the dancing began.

"We're getting old," said Daisy. "If we were young we'd rise and dance."

---

1 The traditional "Wedding March," originally from *A Midsummer Night's Dream* (1842) by Felix Mendelssohn (1809-47).
2 The city of Biloxi is in Mississippi, not Tennessee.

"Remember Biloxi," Jordan warned her. "Where'd you know him, Tom?"

"Biloxi?" He concentrated with an effort. "I didn't know him. He was a friend of Daisy's."

"He was not," she denied. "I'd never seen him before. He came down in the private car."

"Well, he said he knew you. He said he was raised in Louisville. Asa Bird brought him around at the last minute and asked if we had room for him."

Jordan smiled.

"He was probably bumming his way home. He told me he was president of your class at Yale."

Tom and I looked at each other blankly.

"Biloxi?"

"First place, we didn't have any president——"

Gatsby's foot beat a short, restless tattoo and Tom eyed him suddenly.

"By the way, Mr. Gatsby, I understand you're an Oxford man."

"Not exactly."

"Oh, yes, I understand you went to Oxford."

"Yes I went there."

A pause. Then Tom's voice, incredulous and insulting:

"You must have gone there about the time Biloxi went to New Haven."

Another pause. A waiter knocked and came in with crushed mint and ice but the silence was unbroken by his "thank you" and the soft closing of the door. This tremendous detail was to be cleared up at last.

"I told you I went there," said Gatsby.

"I heard you, but I'd like to know when."

"It was in nineteen-nineteen, I only stayed five months. That's why I can't really call myself an Oxford man."

Tom glanced around to see if we mirrored his unbelief. But we were all looking at Gatsby.

"It was an opportunity they gave to some of the officers after the armistice," he continued. "We could go to any of the universities in England or France."

I wanted to get up and slap him on the back. I had one of those renewals of complete faith in him that I'd experienced before.

Daisy rose, smiling faintly, and went to the table.

"Open the whiskey, Tom," she ordered, "and I'll make you a

mint julep. Then you won't seem so stupid to yourself.... Look at the mint!"

"Wait a minute," snapped Tom, "I want to ask Mr. Gatsby one more question."

"Go on," Gatsby said politely.

"What kind of a row are you trying to cause in my house anyhow?"

They were out in the open at last and Gatsby was content.

"He isn't causing a row." Daisy looked desperately from one to the other. "You're causing a row. Please have a little self-control."

"Self-control!" repeated Tom incredulously. "I suppose the latest thing is to sit back and let Mr. Nobody from Nowhere make love to your wife. Well, if that's the idea you can count me out.... Nowadays people begin by sneering at family life and family institutions, and next they'll throw everything overboard and have intermarriage between black and white."

Flushed with his impassioned gibberish, he saw himself standing alone on the last barrier of civilization.

"We're all white here," murmured Jordan.

"I know I'm not very popular. I don't give big parties. I suppose you've got to make your house into a pigsty in order to have any friends—in the modern world."

Angry as I was, as we all were, I was tempted to laugh whenever he opened his mouth. The transition from libertine to prig was so complete.

"I've got something to tell *you*, old sport—" began Gatsby. But Daisy guessed at his intention.

"Please don't!" she interrupted helplessly. "Please let's all go home. Why don't we all go home?"

"That's a good idea." I got up. "Come on, Tom. Nobody wants a drink."

"I want to know what Mr. Gatsby has to tell me."

"Your wife doesn't love you," said Gatsby. "She's never loved you. She loves me."

"You must be crazy!" exclaimed Tom automatically.

Gatsby sprang to his feet, vivid with excitement.

"She never loved you, do you hear?" he cried. "She only married you because I was poor and she was tired of waiting for me. It was a terrible mistake, but in her heart she never loved any one except me!"

At this point Jordan and I tried to go, but Tom and Gatsby

insisted with competitive firmness that we remain—as though neither of them had anything to conceal and it would be a privilege to partake vicariously of their emotions.

"Sit down, Daisy." Tom's voice groped unsuccessfully for the paternal note. "What's been going on? I want to hear all about it."

"I told you what's been going on," said Gatsby. "Going on for five years—and you didn't know."

Tom turned to Daisy sharply.

"You've been seeing this fellow for five years?"

"Not seeing," said Gatsby. "No, we couldn't meet. But both of us loved each other all that time, old sport, and you didn't know. I used to laugh sometimes"—but there was no laughter in his eyes—"to think that you didn't know."

"Oh—that's all." Tom tapped his thick fingers together like a clergyman and leaned back in his chair.

"You're crazy!" he exploded. "I can't speak about what happened five years ago, because I didn't know Daisy then—and I'll be damned if I see how you got within a mile of her unless you brought the groceries to the back door. But all the rest of that's a God damned lie. Daisy loved me when she married me and she loves me now."

"No," said Gatsby, shaking his head.

"She does, though. The trouble is that sometimes she gets foolish ideas in her head and doesn't know what she's doing." He nodded sagely. "And what's more, I love Daisy too. Once in a while I go off on a spree and make a fool of myself, but I always come back, and in my heart I love her all the time."

"You're revolting," said Daisy. She turned to me, and her voice, dropping an octave lower, filled the room with thrilling scorn: "Do you know why we left Chicago? I'm surprised that they didn't treat you to the story of that little spree."

Gatsby walked over and stood beside her.

"Daisy, that's all over now," he said earnestly. "It doesn't matter any more. Just tell him the truth—that you never loved him—and it's all wiped out forever."

She looked at him blindly. "Why—how could I love him possibly?"

"You never loved him."

She hesitated. Her eyes fell on Jordan and me with a sort of appeal, as though she realized at last what she was doing—and as though she had never, all along, intended doing anything at all. But it was done now. It was too late.

"I never loved him," she said, with perceptible reluctance.

"Not at Kapiolani?" demanded Tom suddenly.[1]

"No."

From the ballroom beneath, muffled and suffocating chords were drifting up on hot waves of air.

"Not that day I carried you down from the Punch Bowl[2] to keep your shoes dry?" There was a husky tenderness in his tone.... "Daisy?"

"Please don't." Her voice was cold, but the rancor was gone from it. She looked at Gatsby. "There, Jay," she said—but her hand as she tried to light a cigarette was trembling. Suddenly she threw the cigarette and the burning match on the carpet.

"Oh, you want too much!" she cried to Gatsby. "I love you now—isn't that enough? I can't help what's past." She began to sob helplessly. "I did love him once—but I loved you too."

Gatsby's eyes opened and closed.

"You loved me *too?*" he repeated.

"Even that's a lie," said Tom savagely. "She didn't know you were alive. Why—there're things between Daisy and me that you'll never know, things that neither of us can ever forget."

The words seemed to bite physically into Gatsby.

"I want to speak to Daisy alone," he insisted. "She's all excited now——"

"Even alone I can't say I never loved Tom," she admitted in a pitiful voice. "It wouldn't be true."

"Of course it wouldn't," agreed Tom.

She turned to her husband.

"As if it mattered to you," she said.

"Of course it matters. I'm going to take better care of you from now on."

"You don't understand," said Gatsby, with a touch of panic. "You're not going to take care of her any more."

"I'm not?" Tom opened his eyes wide and laughed. He could afford to control himself now. "Why's that?"

"Daisy's leaving you."

"Nonsense."

"I am, though," she said with a visible effort.

"She's not leaving me!" Tom's words suddenly leaned down over Gatsby. "Certainly not for a common swindler who'd have to steal the ring he put on her finger."

---

1   Large park bordering the Waikiki section of Honolulu, Hawaii.

2   Extinct volcanic crater overlooking Honolulu, a popular tourist site.

"I won't stand this!" cried Daisy. "Oh, please let's get out."

"Who are you, anyhow?" broke out Tom. "You're one of that bunch that hangs around with Meyer Wolfshiem—that much I happen to know. I've made a little investigation into your affairs —and I'll carry it further to-morrow."

"You can suit yourself about that, old sport," said Gatsby steadily.

"I found out what your 'drug-stores' were." He turned to us and spoke rapidly. "He and this Wolfshiem bought up a lot of side-street drug-stores here and in Chicago and sold grain alcohol over the counter. That's one of his little stunts. I picked him for a bootlegger the first time I saw him, and I wasn't far wrong."

"What about it?" said Gatsby politely. "I guess your friend Walter Chase wasn't too proud to come in on it."

"And you left him in the lurch, didn't you? You let him go to jail for a month over in New Jersey. God! You ought to hear Walter on the subject of *you.*"

"He came to us dead broke. He was very glad to pick up some money, old sport."

"Don't you call me 'old sport'!" cried Tom. Gatsby said nothing. "Walter could have you up on the betting laws too, but Wolfshiem scared him into shutting his mouth."

That unfamiliar yet recognizable look was back again in Gatsby's face.

"That drug-store business was just small change," continued Tom slowly, "but you've got something on now that Walter's afraid to tell me about."

I glanced at Daisy, who was staring terrified between Gatsby and her husband, and at Jordan, who had begun to balance an invisible but absorbing object on the tip of her chin. Then I turned back to Gatsby—and was startled at his expression. He looked—and this is said in all contempt for the babbled slander of his garden—as if he had "killed a man." For a moment the set of his face could be described in just that fantastic way.

It passed, and he began to talk excitedly to Daisy, denying everything, defending his name against accusations that had not been made. But with every word she was drawing further and further into herself, so he gave that up, and only the dead dream fought on as the afternoon slipped away, trying to touch what was no longer tangible, struggling unhappily, undespairingly, toward that lost voice across the room.

The voice begged again to go.

"*Please,* Tom! I can't stand this any more."

Her frightened eyes told that whatever intentions, whatever courage she had had, were definitely gone.

"You two start on home, Daisy," said Tom. "In Mr. Gatsby's car."

She looked at Tom, alarmed now, but he insisted with magnanimous scorn.

"Go on. He won't annoy you. I think he realizes that his presumptuous little flirtation is over."

They were gone, without a word, snapped out, made accidental, isolated, like ghosts, even from our pity.

After a moment Tom got up and began wrapping the unopened bottle of whiskey in the towel. "Want any of this stuff? Jordan?... Nick?"

I didn't answer.

"Nick?" He asked again.

"What?"

"Want any?"

"No ... I just remembered that to-day's my birthday."

I was thirty. Before me stretched the portentous, menacing road of a new decade.

It was seven o'clock when we got into the coupé with him and started for Long Island. Tom talked incessantly, exulting and laughing, but his voice was as remote from Jordan and me as the foreign clamor on the sidewalk or the tumult of the elevated overhead. Human sympathy has its limits, and we were content to let all their tragic arguments fade with the city lights behind. Thirty—the promise of a decade of loneliness, a thinning list of single men to know, a thinning brief-case of enthusiasm, thinning hair. But there was Jordan beside me, who, unlike Daisy, was too wise ever to carry well-forgotten dreams from age to age. As we passed over the dark bridge her wan face fell lazily against my coat's shoulder and the formidable stroke of thirty died away with the reassuring pressure of her hand.

So we drove on toward death through the cooling twilight.

The young Greek, Michaelis, who ran the coffee joint beside the ashheaps was the principal witness at the inquest. He had slept through the heat until after five, when he strolled over to the garage, and found George Wilson sick in his office—really sick, pale as his own pale hair and shaking all over. Michaelis advised him to go to bed, but Wilson refused, saying that he'd miss a lot of business if he did. While his neighbor was trying to persuade him a violent racket broke out overhead.

"I've got my wife locked in up there," explained Wilson calmly. "She's going to stay there till the day after to-morrow, and then we're going to move away."

Michaelis was astonished; they had been neighbors for four years, and Wilson had never seemed faintly capable of such a statement. Generally he was one of these worn-out men: when he wasn't working, he sat on a chair in the doorway and stared at the people and the cars that passed along the road. When anyone spoke to him he invariably laughed in an agreeable, colorless way. He was his wife's man and not his own.

So naturally Michaelis tried to find out what had happened, but Wilson wouldn't say a word—instead he began to throw curious, suspicious glances at his visitor and ask him what he'd been doing at certain times on certain days. Just as the latter was getting uneasy, some workmen came past the door bound for his restaurant, and Michaelis took the opportunity to get away, intending to come back later. But he didn't. He supposed he forgot to, that's all. When he came outside again, a little after seven, he was reminded of the conversation because he heard Mrs. Wilson's voice, loud and scolding, down-stairs in the garage.

"Beat me!" he heard her cry. "Throw me down and beat me, you dirty little coward!"

A moment later she rushed out into the dusk, waving her hands and shouting—before he could move from his door the business was over.

The "death car" as the newspapers called it, didn't stop; it came out of the gathering darkness, wavered tragically for a moment, and then disappeared around the next bend. Michaelis wasn't even sure of its color—he told the first policeman that it was light green. The other car, the one going toward New York, came to rest a hundred yards beyond, and its driver hurried back to where Myrtle Wilson, her life violently extinguished, knelt in the road and mingled her thick dark blood with the dust.

Michaelis and this man reached her first, but when they had torn open her shirtwaist, still damp with perspiration, they saw that her left breast was swinging loose like a flap, and there was no need to listen for the heart beneath. The mouth was wide open and ripped a little at the corners, as though she had choked a little in giving up the tremendous vitality she had stored so long.

We saw the three or four automobiles and the crowd when we were still some distance away.

"Wreck!" said Tom. "That's good. Wilson'll have a little business at last."

He slowed down, but still without any intention of stopping, until, as we came nearer, the hushed, intent faces of the people at the garage door made him automatically put on the brakes.

"We'll take a look," he said doubtfully, "just a look."

I became aware now of a hollow, wailing sound which issued incessantly from the garage, a sound which as we got out of the coupé and walked toward the door resolved itself into the words "Oh, my God!" uttered over and over in a gasping moan.

"There's some bad trouble here," said Tom excitedly.

He reached up on tiptoes and peered over a circle of heads into the garage, which was lit only by a yellow light in a swinging wire basket overhead. Then he made a harsh sound in his throat, and with a violent thrusting movement of his powerful arms pushed his way through.

The circle closed up again with a running murmur of expostulation; it was a minute before I could see anything at all. Then new arrivals deranged the line, and Jordan and I were pushed suddenly inside.

Myrtle Wilson's body, wrapped in a blanket, and then in another blanket, as though she suffered from a chill in the hot night, lay on a work-table by the wall, and Tom, with his back to us, was bending over it, motionless. Next to him stood a motorcycle policeman taking down names with much sweat and correction in a little book. At first I couldn't find the source of the high, groaning words that echoed clamorously through the bare garage—then I saw Wilson standing on the raised threshold of his office, swaying back and forth and holding to the doorposts with both hands. Some man was talking to him in a low voice and attempting, from time to time, to lay a hand on his shoulder, but Wilson neither heard nor saw. His eyes would drop slowly from the swinging light to the laden table by the wall, and then jerk back to the light again, and he gave out incessantly his high, horrible call:

"Oh, my Ga-od! Oh, my Ga-od! Oh, Ga-od! Oh, my Ga-od!"

Presently Tom lifted his head with a jerk and, after staring around the garage with glazed eyes, addressed a mumbled incoherent remark to the policeman.

"M-a-v——" the policeman was saying, "——o——"

"No, r——" corrected the man, "M-a-v-r-o——"[1]

---

1 The spelling here is an oversight of Fitzgerald's, who in his galley revisions changed the character's name from Mavromichaelis to Michaelis.

"Listen to me!" muttered Tom fiercely.

"r—" said the policeman, "o——"

"g——"

"g—" He looked up as Tom's broad hand fell sharply on his shoulder. "What you want, fella?"

"What happened?—that's what I want to know."

"Auto hit her. Ins'antly killed."

"Instantly killed," repeated Tom, staring.

"She ran out ina road. Son-of-a-bitch didn't even stopus car."

"There was two cars," said Michaelis, "one comin', one goin', see?"

"Going where?" asked the policeman keenly.

"One goin' each way. Well, she"—his hand rose toward the blankets but stopped half way and fell to his side—"she ran out there an' the one comin' from N'York knock right into her, goin' thirty or forty miles an hour."

"What's the name of this place here?" demanded the officer.

"Hasn't got any name."

A pale well-dressed negro stepped near.

"It was a yellow car," he said, "big yellow car. New."

"See the accident?" asked the policeman.

"No, but the car passed me down the road, going faster'n forty. Going fifty, sixty."

"Come here and let's have your name. Look out now. I want to get his name."

Some words of this conversation must have reached Wilson, swaying in the office door, for suddenly a new theme found voice among his gasping cries:

"You don't have to tell me what kind of car it was! I know what kind of car it was!"

Watching Tom, I saw the wad of muscle back of his shoulder tighten under his coat. He walked quickly over to Wilson and, standing in front of him seized him, firmly by the upper arms.

"You've got to pull yourself together," he said with soothing gruffness.

Wilson's eyes fell upon Tom; he started up on his tiptoes and then would have collapsed to his knees had not Tom held him upright.

"Listen," said Tom, shaking him a little. "I just got here a minute ago, from New York. I was bringing you that coupé we've been talking about. That yellow car I was driving this afternoon wasn't mine—do you hear? I haven't seen it all afternoon."

Only the negro and I were near enough to hear what he said,

but the policeman caught something in the tone and looked over with truculent eyes.

"What's all that?" he demanded.

"I'm a friend of his." Tom turned his head but kept his hands firm on Wilson's body. "He says he knows the car that did it.... It was a yellow car."

Some dim impulse moved the policeman to look suspiciously at Tom.

"And what color's your car?"

"It's a blue car, a coupé."

"We've come straight from New York," I said.

Some one who had been driving a little behind us confirmed this, and the policeman turned away.

"Now, if you'll let me have that name again correct——"

Picking up Wilson like a doll, Tom carried him into the office, set him down in a chair, and came back.

"If somebody'll come here and sit with him," he snapped authoritatively. He watched while the two men standing closest glanced at each other and went unwillingly into the room. Then Tom shut the door on them and came down the single step, his eyes avoiding the table. As he passed close to me he whispered: "Let's get out."

Self-consciously, with his authoritative arms breaking the way, we pushed through the still gathering crowd, passing a hurried doctor, case in hand, who had been sent for in wild hope half an hour ago.

Tom drove slowly until we were beyond the bend—then his foot came down hard, and the coupé raced along through the night. In a little while I heard a low husky sob, and saw that the tears were overflowing down his face.

"The God damned coward!" he whimpered. "He didn't even stop his car."

The Buchanans' house floated suddenly toward us through the dark rustling trees. Tom stopped beside the porch and looked up at the second floor, where two windows bloomed with light among the vines.

"Daisy's home," he said. As we got out of the car he glanced at me and frowned slightly.

"I ought to have dropped you in West Egg, Nick. There's nothing we can do to-night."

A change had come over him, and he spoke gravely, and with

decision. As we walked across the moonlight gravel to the porch he disposed of the situation in a few brisk phrases.

"I'll telephone for a taxi to take you home, and while you're waiting you and Jordan better go in the kitchen and have them get you some supper—if you want any." He opened the door. "Come in."

"No, thanks. But I'd be glad if you'd order me the taxi. I'll wait outside."

Jordan put her hand on my arm.

"Won't you come in, Nick?"

"No, thanks."

I was feeling a little sick and I wanted to be alone. But Jordan lingered for a moment more.

"It's only half-past nine," she said.

I'd be damned if I'd go in; I'd had enough of all of them for one day, and suddenly that included Jordan too. She must have seen something of this in my expression, for she turned abruptly away and ran up the porch steps into the house. I sat down for a few minutes with my head in my hands, until I heard the phone taken up inside and the butler's voice calling a taxi. Then I walked slowly down the drive away from the house, intending to wait by the gate.

I hadn't gone twenty yards when I heard my name and Gatsby stepped from between two bushes into the path. I must have felt pretty weird by that time, because I could think of nothing except the luminosity of his pink suit under the moon.

"What are you doing?" I inquired.

"Just standing here, old sport."

Somehow, that seemed a despicable occupation. For all I knew he was going to rob the house in a moment; I wouldn't have been surprised to see sinister faces, the faces of "Wolfshiem's people," behind him in the dark shrubbery.

"Did you see any trouble on the road?" he asked after a minute.

"Yes."

He hesitated.

"Was she killed?"

"Yes."

"I thought so; I told Daisy I thought so. It's better that the shock should all come at once. She stood it pretty well."

He spoke as if Daisy's reaction was the only thing that mattered.

"I got to West Egg by a side road," he went on, "and left the car in my garage. I don't think anybody saw us, but of course I can't be sure."

I disliked him so much by this time that I didn't find it necessary to tell him he was wrong.

"Who was the woman?" he inquired.

"Her name was Wilson. Her husband owns the garage. How the devil did it happen?"

"Well, I tried to swing the wheel——" He broke off, and suddenly I guessed at the truth.

"Was Daisy driving?"

"Yes," he said after a moment, "but of course I'll say I was. You see, when we left New York she was very nervous and she thought it would steady her to drive—and this woman rushed out at us just as we were passing a car coming the other way. It all happened in a minute, but it seemed to me that she wanted to speak to us, thought we were somebody she knew. Well, first Daisy turned away from the woman toward the other car, and then she lost her nerve and turned back. The second my hand reached the wheel I felt the shock—it must have killed her instantly."

"It ripped her open——"

"Don't tell me, old sport." He winced. "Anyhow—Daisy stepped on it. I tried to make her stop, but she couldn't, so I pulled on the emergency brake. Then she fell over into my lap and I drove on.

"She'll be all right to-morrow," he said presently. "I'm just going to wait here and see if he tries to bother her about that unpleasantness this afternoon. She's locked herself into her room, and if he tries any brutality she's going to turn the light out and on again."

"He won't touch her," I said. "He's not thinking about her."

"I don't trust him, old sport."

"How long are you going to wait?"

"All night, if necessary. Anyhow, till they all go to bed."

A new point of view occurred to me. Suppose Tom found out that Daisy had been driving. He might think he saw a connection in it—he might think anything. I looked at the house; there were two or three bright windows down-stairs and the pink glow from Daisy's room on the second floor.

"You wait here," I said. "I'll see if there's any sign of a commotion."

I walked back along the border of the lawn, traversed the gravel softly, and tiptoed up the veranda steps. The drawing-room curtains were open, and I saw that the room was empty. Crossing the porch where we had dined that June night three months before, I came to a small rectangle of light which I guessed was the pantry window. The blind was drawn, but I found a rift at the sill.

Daisy and Tom were sitting opposite each other at the kitchen table, with a plate of cold fried chicken between them, and two bottles of ale. He was talking intently across the table at her, and in his earnestness his hand had fallen upon and covered her own. Once in a while she looked up at him and nodded in agreement.

They weren't happy, and neither of them had touched the chicken or the ale—and yet they weren't unhappy either. There was an unmistakable air of natural intimacy about the picture, and anybody would have said that they were conspiring together.

As I tiptoed from the porch I heard my taxi feeling its way along the dark road toward the house. Gatsby was waiting where I had left him in the drive.

"Is it all quiet up there?" he asked anxiously.

"Yes, it's all quiet." I hesitated. "You'd better come home and get some sleep."

He shook his head.

"I want to wait here till Daisy goes to bed. Good night, old sport."

He put his hands in his coat pockets and turned back eagerly to his scrutiny of the house, as though my presence marred the sacredness of the vigil. So I walked away and left him standing there in the moonlight—watching over nothing.

Chapter VIII

I COULDN'T sleep all night; a fog-horn was groaning incessantly on the Sound, and I tossed half-sick between grotesque reality and savage, frightening dreams. Toward dawn I heard a taxi go up Gatsby's drive, and immediately I jumped out of bed and began to dress—I felt that I had something to tell him, something to warn him about, and morning would be too late.

Crossing his lawn, I saw that his front door was still open and he was leaning against a table in the hall, heavy with dejection or sleep.

"Nothing happened," he said wanly. "I waited, and about four o'clock she came to the window and stood there for a minute and then turned out the light."

His house had never seemed so enormous to me as it did that night when we hunted through the great rooms for cigarettes. We pushed aside curtains that were like pavilions, and felt over innumerable feet of dark wall for electric light switches—once I tumbled with a sort of splash upon the keys of a ghostly piano. There was an inexplicable amount of dust everywhere, and the rooms were musty, as though they hadn't been aired for many days. I found the humidor on an unfamiliar table, with two stale, dry cigarettes inside. Throwing open the French windows of the drawing-room, we sat smoking out into the darkness.

"You ought to go away," I said. "It's pretty certain they'll trace your car."

"Go away *now*, old sport?"

"Go to Atlantic City for a week, or up to Montreal."

He wouldn't consider it. He couldn't possibly leave Daisy until he knew what she was going to do. He was clutching at some last hope and I couldn't bear to shake him free.

It was this night that he told me the strange story of his youth with Dan Cody—told it to me because "Jay Gatsby" had broken up like glass against Tom's hard malice, and the long secret extravaganza was played out. I think that he would have acknowledged anything now, without reserve, but he wanted to talk about Daisy.

She was the first "nice" girl he had ever known. In various unrevealed capacities he had come in contact with such people, but always with indiscernible barbed wire between. He found her excitingly desirable. He went to her house, at first with other officers from Camp Taylor, then alone. It amazed him—he had never been in such a beautiful house before. But what gave it an air of breathless intensity, was that Daisy lived there—it was as casual a thing to her as his tent out at camp was to him. There was a ripe mystery about it, a hint of bedrooms up-stairs more beautiful and cool than other bedrooms, of gay and radiant activities taking place through its corridors, and of romances that were not musty and laid away already in lavender but fresh and breathing and redolent of this year's shining motor-cars and of dances whose flowers were scarcely withered. It excited him, too, that many men had already loved Daisy—it increased her value in his eyes. He felt their presence all about the house, pervading the air with the shades and echoes of still vibrant emotions.

But he knew that he was in Daisy's house by a colossal accident. However glorious might be his future as Jay Gatsby, he was at present a penniless young man without a past, and at any moment the invisible cloak of his uniform might slip from his shoulders. So he made the most of his time. He took what he could get, ravenously and unscrupulously—eventually he took Daisy one still October night, took her because he had no real right to touch her hand.

He might have despised himself, for he had certainly taken her under false pretenses. I don't mean that he had traded on his phantom millions, but he had deliberately given Daisy a sense of security; he let her believe that he was a person from much the same strata as herself—that he was fully able to take care of her. As a matter of fact, he had no such facilities—he had no comfortable family standing behind him, and he was liable at the whim of an impersonal government to be blown anywhere about the world.

But he didn't despise himself and it didn't turn out as he had imagined. He had intended, probably, to take what he could and go—but now he found that he had committed himself to the following of a grail. He knew that Daisy was extraordinary, but he didn't realize just how extraordinary a "nice" girl could be. She vanished into her rich house, into her rich, full life, leaving Gatsby—nothing. He felt married to her, that was all.

When they met again, two days later, it was Gatsby who was breathless, who was, somehow, betrayed. Her porch was bright with the bought luxury of star-shine; the wicker of the settee squeaked fashionably as she turned toward him and he kissed her curious and lovely mouth. She had caught a cold, and it made her voice huskier and more charming than ever, and Gatsby was overwhelmingly aware of the youth and mystery that wealth imprisons and preserves, of the freshness of many clothes, and of Daisy, gleaming like silver, safe and proud above the hot struggles of the poor.

"I can't describe to you how surprised I was to find out I loved her, old sport. I even hoped for a while that she'd throw me over, but she didn't, because she was in love with me too. She thought I knew a lot because I knew different things from her.... Well, there I was, 'way off my ambitions, getting deeper in love every minute, and all of a sudden I didn't care. What was the use of doing great things if I could have a better time telling her what I was going to do?"

On the last afternoon before he went abroad, he sat with Daisy in his arms for a long, silent time. It was a cold fall day, with fire in the room and her cheeks flushed. Now and then she moved and he changed his arm a little, and once he kissed her dark shining hair. The afternoon had made them tranquil for a while, as if to give them a deep memory for the long parting the next day promised. They had never been closer in their month of love, nor communicated more profoundly one with another, than when she brushed silent lips against his coat's shoulder or when he touched the end of her fingers, gently, as though she were asleep.

He did extraordinarily well in the war. He was a captain before he went to the front, and following the Argonne battles[1] he got his majority and the command of the divisional machine-guns. After the armistice he tried frantically to get home, but some complication or misunderstanding sent him to Oxford instead. He was worried now—there was a quality of nervous despair in Daisy's letters. She didn't see why he couldn't come. She was feeling the pressure of the world outside, and she wanted to see him and feel his presence beside her and be reassured that she was doing the right thing after all.

For Daisy was young and her artificial world was redolent of orchids and pleasant, cheerful snobbery and orchestras which set the rhythm of the year, summing up the sadness and suggestiveness of life in new tunes. All night the saxophones wailed the hopeless comment of the "Beale Street Blues"[2] while a hundred pairs of golden and silver slippers shuffled the shining dust. At the gray tea hour there were always rooms that throbbed incessantly with this low, sweet fever, while fresh faces drifted here and there like rose petals blown by the sad horns around the floor.

Through this twilight universe Daisy began to move again with the season; suddenly she was again keeping half a dozen dates a day with half a dozen men, and drowsing asleep at dawn with the beads and chiffon of an evening dress tangled among dying orchids on the floor beside her bed. And all the time something within her was crying for a decision. She wanted her life shaped now, immediately—and the decision must be made by some force—of love, of money, of unquestionable practicality—that was close at hand.

---

1 See Chapter IV, p. 95, n. 2.
2 Popular blues song of 1919, by W.C. Handy.

That force took shape in the middle of spring with the arrival of Tom Buchanan. There was a wholesome bulkiness about his person and his position, and Daisy was flattered. Doubtless there was a certain struggle and a certain relief. The letter reached Gatsby while he was still at Oxford.

It was dawn now on Long Island and we went about opening the rest of the windows down-stairs, filling the house with gray-turning, gold-turning light. The shadow of a tree fell abruptly across the dew and ghostly birds began to sing among the blue leaves. There was a slow, pleasant movement in the air, scarcely a wind, promising a cool, lovely day.

"I don't think she ever loved him." Gatsby turned around from a window and looked at me challengingly. "You must remember, old sport, she was very excited this afternoon. He told her those things in a way that frightened her—that made it look as if I was some kind of cheap sharper. And the result was she hardly knew what she was saying."

He sat down gloomily.

"Of course she might have loved him just for a minute, when they were first married—and loved me more even then, do you see?"

Suddenly he came out with a curious remark.

"In any case," he said, "it was just personal."

What could you make of that, except to suspect some intensity in his conception of the affair that couldn't be measured?

He came back from France when Tom and Daisy were still on their wedding trip, and made a miserable but irresistible journey to Louisville on the last of his army pay. He stayed there a week, walking the streets where their footsteps had clicked together through the November night and revisiting the out-of-the-way places to which they had driven in her white car. Just as Daisy's house had always seemed to him more mysterious and gay than other houses, so his idea of the city itself, even though she was gone from it, was pervaded with a melancholy beauty.

He left feeling that if he had searched harder, he might have found her—that he was leaving her behind. The day-coach—he was penniless now—was hot. He went out to the open vestibule and sat down on a folding-chair, and the station slid away and the backs of unfamiliar buildings moved by. Then out into the spring fields, where a yellow trolley raced them for a minute with people in it who might once have seen the pale magic of her face along the casual street.

The track curved and now it was going away from the sun, which, as it sank lower, seemed to spread itself in benediction over the vanishing city where she had drawn her breath. He stretched out his hand desperately as if to snatch only a wisp of air, to save a fragment of the spot that she had made lovely for him. But it was all going by too fast now for his blurred eyes and he knew that he had lost that part of it, the freshest and the best, forever.

It was nine o'clock when we finished breakfast and went out on the porch. The night had made a sharp difference in the weather and there was an autumn flavor in the air. The gardener, the last one of Gatsby's former servants, came to the foot of the steps.

"I'm going to drain the pool to-day, Mr. Gatsby. Leaves'll start falling pretty soon, and then there's always trouble with the pipes."

"Don't do it to-day," Gatsby answered. He turned to me apologetically. "You know, old sport, I've never used that pool all summer?"

I looked at my watch and stood up.

"Twelve minutes to my train."

I didn't want to go to the city. I wasn't worth a decent stroke of work, but it was more than that—I didn't want to leave Gatsby. I missed that train, and then another, before I could get myself away.

"I'll call you up," I said finally.

"Do, old sport."

"I'll call you about noon."

We walked slowly down the steps.

"I suppose Daisy'll call too." He looked at me anxiously, as if he hoped I'd corroborate this.

"I suppose so."

"Well, good-by."

We shook hands and I started away. Just before I reached the hedge I remembered something and turned around.

"They're a rotten crowd," I shouted across the lawn. "You're worth the whole damn bunch put together."

I've always been glad I said that. It was the only compliment I ever gave him, because I disapproved of him from beginning to end. First he nodded politely, and then his face broke into that radiant and understanding smile, as if we'd been in ecstatic cahoots on that fact all the time. His gorgeous pink rag of a suit made a bright spot of color against the white steps, and I thought of the night when I first came to his ancestral home, three months before. The lawn and drive had been crowded with the faces of those who guessed at his corruption—and he had stood on those steps, concealing his incorruptible dream, as he waved them good-by.

I thanked him for his hospitality. We were always thanking him for that—I and the others.

"Good-by," I called. "I enjoyed breakfast, Gatsby."

Up in the city, I tried for a while to list the quotations on an interminable amount of stock, then I fell asleep in my swivel-chair. Just before noon the phone woke me, and I started up with sweat breaking out on my forehead. It was Jordan Baker; she often called me up at this hour because the uncertainty of her own movements between hotels and clubs and private houses made her hard to find in any other way. Usually her voice came over the wire as something fresh and cool, as if a divot from a green golf-links had come sailing in at the office window, but this morning it seemed harsh and dry.

"I've left Daisy's house," she said. "I'm at Hempstead, and I'm going down to Southampton this afternoon."[1]

Probably it had been tactful to leave Daisy's house, but the act annoyed me, and her next remark made me rigid.

"You weren't so nice to me last night."

"How could it have mattered then?"

Silence for a moment. Then:

"However—I want to see you."

"I want to see you, too."

"Suppose I don't go to Southampton, and come into town this afternoon?"

"No—I don't think this afternoon."

"Very well."

"It's impossible this afternoon. Various——"

We talked like that for a while, and then abruptly we weren't

---

1 Hempstead is a town on Long Island, about thirty miles east of New York City. Southampton is a town on the south shore of the eastern end of Long Island, about one hundred miles from the city.

talking any longer. I don't know which of us hung up with a sharp click, but I know I didn't care. I couldn't have talked to her across a tea-table that day if I never talked to her again in this world.

I called Gatsby's house a few minutes later, but the line was busy. I tried four times; finally an exasperated central told me the wire was being kept open for long distance from Detroit. Taking out my time-table, I drew a small circle around the three-fifty train. Then I leaned back in my chair and tried to think. It was just noon.

When I passed the ashheaps on the train that morning I had crossed deliberately to the other side of the car. I supposed there'd be a curious crowd around there all day with little boys searching for dark spots in the dust, and some garrulous man telling over and over what had happened, until it became less and less real even to him and he could tell it no longer, and Myrtle Wilson's tragic achievement was forgotten. Now I want to go back a little and tell what happened at the garage after we left there the night before.

They had difficulty in locating the sister, Catherine. She must have broken her rule against drinking that night, for when she arrived she was stupid with liquor and unable to understand that the ambulance had already gone to Flushing.[1] When they convinced her of this, she immediately fainted, as if that was the intolerable part of the affair. Someone, kind or curious, took her in his car and drove her in the wake of her sister's body.

Until long after midnight a changing crowd lapped up against the front of the garage, while George Wilson rocked himself back and forth on the couch inside. For a while the door of the office was open, and everyone who came into the garage glanced irresistibly through it. Finally someone said it was a shame, and closed the door. Michaelis and several other men were with him; first, four or five men, later two or three men. Still later Michaelis had to ask the last stranger to wait there fifteen minutes longer, while he went back to his own place and made a pot of coffee. After that, he stayed there alone with Wilson until dawn.

About three o'clock the quality of Wilson's incoherent muttering changed—he grew quieter and began to talk about the yellow car. He announced that he had a way of finding out whom the

---

1 Eastern section of Queens on Long Island, between Manhattan and Great Neck (West Egg).

yellow car belonged to, and then he blurted out that a couple of months ago his wife had come from the city with her face bruised and her nose swollen.

But when he heard himself say this, he flinched and began to cry "Oh, my God!" again in his groaning voice. Michaelis made a clumsy attempt to distract him.

"How long have you been married, George? Come on there, try and sit still a minute and answer my question. How long have you been married?"

"Twelve years."

"Ever had any children? Come on, George, sit still—I asked you a question. Did you ever have any children?"

The hard brown beetles kept thudding against the dull light, and whenever Michaelis heard a car go tearing along the road outside it sounded to him like the car that hadn't stopped a few hours before. He didn't like to go into the garage, because the work bench was stained where the body had been lying, so he moved uncomfortably around the office—he knew every object in it before morning—and from time to time sat down beside Wilson trying to keep him more quiet.

"Have you got a church you go to sometimes, George? Maybe even if you haven't been there for a long time? Maybe I could call up the church and get a priest to come over and he could talk to you, see?"

"Don't belong to any."

"You ought to have a church, George, for times like this. You must have gone to church once. Didn't you get married in a church? Listen, George, listen to me. Didn't you get married in a church?"

"That was a long time ago."

The effort of answering broke the rhythm of his rocking—for a moment he was silent. Then the same half-knowing, half-bewildered look came back into his faded eyes.

"Look in the drawer there," he said, pointing at the desk.

"Which drawer?"

"That drawer—that one."

Michaelis opened the drawer nearest his hand. There was nothing in it but a small, expensive dog-leash, made of leather and braided silver. It was apparently new.

"This?" he inquired, holding it up.

Wilson stared and nodded.

"I found it yesterday afternoon. She tried to tell me about it, but I knew it was something funny."

"You mean your wife bought it?"

"She had it wrapped in tissue paper on her bureau."

Michaelis didn't see anything odd in that, and he gave Wilson a dozen reasons why his wife might have bought the dog-leash. But conceivably Wilson had heard some of these same explanations before, from Myrtle, because he began saying "Oh, my God!" again in a whisper—his comforter left several explanations in the air.

"Then he killed her," said Wilson. His mouth dropped open suddenly.

"Who did?"

"I have a way of finding out."

"You're morbid, George," said his friend. "This has been a strain to you and you don't know what you're saying. You'd better try and sit quiet till morning."

"He murdered her."

"It was an accident, George."

Wilson shook his head. His eyes narrowed and his mouth widened slightly with the ghost of a superior "Hm!"

"I know," he said definitely, "I'm one of these trusting fellas and I don't think any harm to *no*body, but when I get to know a thing I know it. It was the man in that car. She ran out to speak to him and he wouldn't stop."

Michaelis had seen this too, but it hadn't occurred to him that there was any special significance in it. He believed that Mrs. Wilson had been running away from her husband, rather than trying to stop any particular car.

"How could she of been like that?"

"She's a deep one," said Wilson, as if that answered the question. "Ah-h-h——"

He began to rock again, and Michaelis stood twisting the leash in his hand.

"Maybe you got some friend that I could telephone for, George?"

This was a forlorn hope—he was almost sure that Wilson had no friend: there was not enough of him for his wife. He was glad a little later when he noticed a change in the room, a blue quickening by the window, and realized that dawn wasn't far off. About five o'clock it was blue enough outside to snap off the light.

Wilson's glazed eyes turned out to the ashheaps, where small gray clouds took on fantastic shapes and scurried here and there in the faint dawn wind.

"I spoke to her," he muttered, after a long silence. "I told her she might fool me but she couldn't fool God. I took her to the window"—with an effort he got up and walked to the rear window and leaned with his face pressed against it—"and I said 'God knows what you've been doing, everything you've been doing. You may fool me, but you can't fool God!'"

Standing behind him, Michaelis saw with a shock that he was looking at the eyes of Doctor T.J. Eckleburg, which had just emerged, pale and enormous, from the dissolving night.

"God sees everything," repeated Wilson.

"That's an advertisement," Michaelis assured him. Something made him turn away from the window and look back into the room. But Wilson stood there a long time, his face close to the window pane, nodding into the twilight.

By six o'clock Michaelis was worn out, and grateful for the sound of a car stopping outside. It was one of the watchers of the night before who had promised to come back, so he cooked breakfast for three, which he and the other man ate together. Wilson was quieter now, and Michaelis went home to sleep; when he awoke four hours later and hurried back to the garage, Wilson was gone.

His movements—he was on foot all the time—were afterward traced to Port Roosevelt and then to Gad's Hill,[1] where he bought a sandwich that he didn't eat, and a cup of coffee. He must have been tired and walking slowly, for he didn't reach Gad's Hill until noon. Thus far there was no difficulty in accounting for his time—there were boys who had seen a man "acting sort of crazy," and motorists at whom he stared oddly from the side of the road. Then for three hours he disappeared from view. The police, on the strength of what he said to Michaelis, that he "had a way of finding out," supposed that he spent that time going from garage to garage thereabout, inquiring for a yellow car. On the other hand, no garage man who had seen him ever came forward, and perhaps he had an easier, surer way of finding out what he wanted to know. By half-past two he was in West Egg, where he asked someone the way to Gatsby's house. So by that time he knew Gatsby's name.

---

1 Like Port Roosevelt (see Chapter 4, p. 96, n. 2), Gad's Hill seems to be Fitzgerald's invention.

At two o'clock Gatsby put on his bathing-suit and left word with the butler that if anyone phoned word was to be brought to him at the pool. He stopped at the garage for a pneumatic mattress that had amused his guests during the summer, and the chauffeur helped him pump it up. Then he gave instructions that the open car wasn't to be taken out under any circumstances—and this was strange, because the front right fender needed repair.

Gatsby shouldered the mattress and started for the pool. Once he stopped and shifted it a little, and the chauffeur asked him if he needed help, but he shook his head and in a moment disappeared among the yellowing trees.

No telephone message arrived, but the butler went without his sleep and waited for it until four o'clock—until long after there was anyone to give it to if it came. I have an idea that Gatsby himself didn't believe it would come, and perhaps he no longer cared. If that was true he must have felt that he had lost the old warm world, paid a high price for living too long with a single dream. He must have looked up at an unfamiliar sky through frightening leaves and shivered as he found what a grotesque thing a rose is and how raw the sunlight was upon the scarcely created grass. A new world, material without being real, where poor ghosts, breathing dreams like air, drifted fortuitously about ... like that ashen, fantastic figure gliding toward him through the amorphous trees.

The chauffeur—he was one of Wolfshiem's protégés—heard the shots—afterward he could only say that he hadn't thought anything much about them. I drove from the station directly to Gatsby's house and my rushing anxiously up the front steps was the first thing that alarmed anyone. But they knew then, I firmly believe. With scarcely a word said, four of us, the chauffeur, butler, gardener, and I, hurried down to the pool.

There was a faint, barely perceptible movement of the water as the fresh flow from one end urged its way toward the drain at the other. With little ripples that were hardly the shadows of waves, the laden mattress moved irregularly down the pool. A small gust of wind that scarcely corrugated the surface was enough to disturb its accidental course with its accidental burden. The touch of a cluster of leaves revolved it slowly, tracing, like the leg of transit, a thin red circle in the water.

It was after we started with Gatsby toward the house that the gardener saw Wilson's body a little way off in the grass, and the holocaust was complete.

Chapter IX

AFTER two years I remember the rest of that day, and that night and the next day, only as an endless drill of police and photographers and newspaper men in and out of Gatsby's front door. A rope stretched across the main gate and a policeman by it kept out the curious, but little boys soon discovered that they could enter through my yard, and there were always a few of them clustered open-mouthed about the pool. Someone with a positive manner, perhaps a detective, used the expression "madman" as he bent over Wilson's body that afternoon, and the adventitious authority of his voice set the key for the newspaper reports next morning.

Most of those reports were a nightmare—grotesque, circumstantial, eager, and untrue. When Michaelis's testimony at the inquest brought to light Wilson's suspicions of his wife I thought the whole tale would shortly be served up in racy pasquinade[1]—but Catherine, who might have said anything, didn't say a word. She showed a surprising amount of character about it too—looked at the coroner with determined eyes under that corrected brow of hers, and swore that her sister had never seen Gatsby, that her sister was completely happy with her husband, that her sister had been into no mischief whatever. She convinced herself of it, and cried into her handkerchief, as if the very suggestion was more than she could endure. So Wilson was reduced to a man "deranged by grief" in order that the case might remain in its simplest form. And it rested there.

But all this part of it seemed remote and unessential. I found myself on Gatsby's side, and alone. From the moment I telephoned news of the catastrophe to West Egg Village, every surmise about him, and every practical question, was referred to me. At first I was surprised and confused; then, as he lay in his house and didn't move or breathe or speak, hour upon hour, it grew upon me that I was responsible, because no one else was interested—interested, I mean, with that intense personal interest to which everyone has some vague right at the end.

I called up Daisy half an hour after we found him, called her instinctively and without hesitation. But she and Tom had gone away early that afternoon, and taken baggage with them.

---

1 Lampoon or satire.

"Left no address?"

"No."

"Say when they'd be back?"

"No."

"Any idea where they are? How I could reach them?"

"I don't know. Can't say."

I wanted to get somebody for him. I wanted to go into the room where he lay and reassure him: "I'll get somebody for you, Gatsby. Don't worry. Just trust me and I'll get somebody for you——"

Meyer Wolfshiem's name wasn't in the phone book. The butler gave me his office address on Broadway, and I called Information, but by the time I had the number it was long after five, and no one answered the phone.

"Will you ring again?"

"I've rung them three times."

"It's very important."

"Sorry. I'm afraid no one's there."

I went back to the drawing-room and thought for an instant that they were chance visitors, all these official people who suddenly filled it. But, as they drew back the sheet and looked at Gatsby with unmoved eyes, his protest continued in my brain:

"Look here, old sport, you've got to get somebody for me. You've got to try hard. I can't go through this alone."

Someone started to ask me questions, but I broke away and going up-stairs looked hastily through the unlocked parts of his desk—he'd never told me definitely that his parents were dead. But there was nothing—only the picture of Dan Cody, a token of forgotten violence, staring down from the wall.

Next morning I sent the butler to New York with a letter to Wolfshiem, which asked for information and urged him to come out on the next train. That request seemed superfluous when I wrote it. I was sure he'd start when he saw the newspapers, just as I was sure there'd be a wire from Daisy before noon—but neither a wire nor Mr. Wolfshiem arrived; no one arrived except more police and photographers and newspaper men. When the butler brought back Wolfshiem's answer I began to have a feeling of defiance, of scornful solidarity between Gatsby and me against them all.

Dear Mr. Carraway. This has been one of the most terrible shocks of my life to me I hardly can believe it that it is true at all. Such a mad act as that man did should make us all think. I cannot come down now as I am tied up in some very important business and cannot get mixed up in this thing now. If there is anything I can do a little later let me know in a letter by Edgar. I hardly know where I am when I hear about a thing like this and am completely knocked down and out.

Yours truly
MEYER WOLFSHIEM

and then hasty addenda beneath:

Let me know about the funeral etc do not know his family at all.

When the phone rang that afternoon and Long Distance said Chicago was calling I thought this would be Daisy at last. But the connection came through as a man's voice, very thin and far away.

"This is Slagle speaking ..."

"Yes?" The name was unfamiliar.

"Hell of a note, isn't it? Get my wire?"

"There haven't been any wires."

"Young Parke's in trouble," he said rapidly. "They picked him up when he handed the bonds over the counter. They got a circular from New York giving 'em the numbers just five minutes before. What d'you know about that, hey? You never can tell in these hick towns——"

"Hello!" I interrupted breathlessly. "Look here—this isn't Mr. Gatsby. Mr. Gatsby's dead."

There was a long silence on the other end of the wire, followed by an exclamation ... then a quick squawk as the connection was broken.

I think it was on the third day that a telegram signed Henry C. Gatz arrived from a town in Minnesota. It said only that the sender was leaving immediately and to postpone the funeral until he came.

It was Gatsby's father, a solemn old man, very helpless and dismayed, bundled up in a long cheap ulster[1] against the warm

---

1 Long, loose-fitting overcoat made of heavy material.

September day. His eyes leaked continuously with excitement, and when I took the bag and umbrella from his hands he began to pull so incessantly at his sparse gray beard that I had difficulty in getting off his coat. He was on the point of collapse, so I took him into the music room and made him sit down while I sent for something to eat. But he wouldn't eat, and the glass of milk spilled from his trembling hand.

"I saw it in the Chicago newspaper," he said. "It was all in the Chicago newspaper. I started right away."

"I didn't know how to reach you."

His eyes, seeing nothing, moved ceaselessly about the room.

"It was a madman," he said. "He must have been mad."

"Wouldn't you like some coffee?" I urged him.

"I don't want anything. I'm all right now, Mr.——"

"Carraway."

"Well, I'm all right now. Where have they got Jimmy?"

I took him into the drawing-room, where his son lay, and left him there. Some little boys had come up on the steps and were looking into the hall; when I told them who had arrived, they went reluctantly away.

After a little while Mr. Gatz opened the door and came out, his mouth ajar, his face flushed slightly, his eyes leaking isolated and unpunctual tears. He had reached an age where death no longer has the quality of ghastly surprise, and when he looked around him now for the first time and saw the height and splendor of the hall and the great rooms opening out from it into other rooms, his grief began to be mixed with an awed pride. I helped him to a bedroom up-stairs; while he took off his coat and vest I told him that all arrangements had been deferred until he came.

"I didn't know what you'd want, Mr. Gatsby——"

"Gatz is my name."

"—Mr. Gatz. I thought you might want to take the body West."

He shook his head.

"Jimmy always liked it better down East. He rose up to his position in the East. Were you a friend of my boy's, Mr.——?"

"We were close friends."

"He had a big future before him, you know. He was only a young man, but he had a lot of brain power here."

He touched his head impressively, and I nodded.

"If he'd of lived, he'd of been a great man. A man like James J. Hill.[1] He'd of helped build up the country."

"That's true," I said, uncomfortably.

He fumbled at the embroidered coverlet, trying to take it from the bed, and lay down stiffly—was instantly asleep.

That night an obviously frightened person called up, and demanded to know who I was before he would give his name.

"This is Mr. Carraway," I said.

"Oh!" He sounded relieved. "This is Klipspringer."

I was relieved too, for that seemed to promise another friend at Gatsby's grave. I didn't want it to be in the papers and draw a sightseeing crowd, so I'd been calling up a few people myself. They were hard to find.

"The funeral's to-morrow," I said. "Three o'clock, here at the house. I wish you'd tell anybody who'd be interested."

"Oh, I will," he broke out hastily. "Of course I'm not likely to see anybody, but if I do."

His tone made me suspicious.

"Of course you'll be there yourself."

"Well, I'll certainly try. What I called up about is——"

"Wait a minute," I interrupted. "How about saying you'll come?"

"Well, the fact is—the truth of the matter is that I'm staying with some people up here in Greenwich,[2] and they rather expect me to be with them to-morrow. In fact, there's a sort of picnic or something. Of course I'll do my very best to get away."

I ejaculated an unrestrained "Huh!" and he must have heard me, for he went on nervously:

"What I called up about was a pair of shoes I left there. I wonder if it'd be too much trouble to have the butler send them on. You see, they're tennis shoes, and I'm sort of helpless without them. My address is care of B.F.——"

---

1 James J. Hill (1838-1916), self-made railroad tycoon who developed the St. Paul and Pacific Railroad into the Great Northern Railway, which was instrumental in the commercial expansion and settlement of the West. Hill's imposing mansion on Summit Avenue in St. Paul was down the street from the rented home Fitzgerald grew up in as a teenager.

2 Wealthy town in Connecticut, to the north of Westchester County on the other side of Long Island Sound from Manhasset Neck (East Egg).

I didn't hear the rest of the name, because I hung up the receiver.

After that I felt a certain shame for Gatsby—one gentleman to whom I telephoned implied that he had got what he deserved. However, that was my fault, for he was one of those who used to sneer most bitterly at Gatsby on the courage of Gatsby's liquor, and I should have known better than to call him.

The morning of the funeral I went up to New York to see Meyer Wolfshiem; I couldn't seem to reach him any other way. The door that I pushed open, on the advice of an elevator boy, was marked "The Swastika Holding Company,"[1] and at first there didn't seem to be anyone inside. But when I'd shouted "hello" several times in vain, an argument broke out behind a partition, and presently a lovely Jewess appeared at an interior door and scrutinized me with black hostile eyes.

"Nobody's in," she said. "Mr. Wolfshiem's gone to Chicago."

The first part of this was obviously untrue, for someone had begun to whistle "The Rosary,"[2] tunelessly, inside.

"Please say that Mr. Carraway wants to see him."

"I can't get him back from Chicago, can I?"

At this moment a voice, unmistakably Wolfshiem's, called "Stella!" from the other side of the door.

"Leave your name on the desk," she said quickly. "I'll give it to him when he gets back."

"But I know he's there."

She took a step toward me and began to slide her hands indignantly up and down her hips.

"You young men think you can force your way in here any time," she scolded. "We're getting sickantired of it. When I say he's in Chicago, he's in Chicago."

---

1 The name of Wolfshiem's company is plausibly read as, in hindsight, a tasteless and somewhat macabre bit of irony on Fitzgerald's part. While composing and revising the novel in Europe in 1924 and 1925, Fitzgerald must have been aware of the anti-Semitic implications of the swastika symbol adopted by Adolf Hitler's National Socialist party in Germany; like most of his contemporaries, however, he could not have foreseen Hitler's political triumph nearly a decade later or its horrific consequences. See Margolies' essay listed in the Select Bibliography.

2 1898 song still popular in the 1920s, music by Ethelbert Nevin, lyrics by Robert Cameron Rogers. Lyrics include the line, "To kiss the cross, To kiss the cross."

I mentioned Gatsby.

"Oh-h!" She looked at me over again. "Will you just— What was your name?"

She vanished. In a moment Meyer Wolfshiem stood solemnly in the doorway, holding out both hands. He drew me into his office, remarking in a reverent voice that it was a sad time for all of us, and offered me a cigar.

"My memory goes back to when first I met him," he said. "A young major just out of the army and covered over with medals he got in the war. He was so hard up he had to keep on wearing his uniform because he couldn't buy some regular clothes. First time I saw him was when he come into Winebrenner's poolroom at Forty-third Street and asked for a job. He hadn't eat anything for a couple of days. 'Come on have some lunch with me,' I sid. He ate more than four dollars' worth of food in half an hour."

"Did you start him in business?" I inquired.

"Start him! I made him."

"Oh."

"I raised him up out of nothing, right out of the gutter. I saw right away he was a fine-appearing, gentlemanly young man, and when he told me he was an Oggsford I knew I could use him good. I got him to join up in the American Legion and he used to stand high there. Right off he did some work for a client of mine up to Albany.[1] We were so thick like that in everything"— he held up two bulbous fingers—"always together."

I wondered if this partnership had included the World's Series transaction in 1919.

"Now he's dead," I said after a moment. "You were his closest friend, so I know you'll want to come to his funeral this afternoon."

"I'd like to come."

"Well, come then."

The hair in his nostrils quivered slightly, and as he shook his head his eyes filled with tears.

"I can't do it—I can't get mixed up in it," he said.

"There's nothing to get mixed up in. It's all over now."

"When a man gets killed I never like to get mixed up in it in any way. I keep out. When I was a young man it was different—if a friend of mine died, no matter how, I stuck with them to the

---

1 See Chapter IV, p. 93, n. 1. Albany is the state capital of New York.

end. You may think that's sentimental, but I mean it—to the bitter end."

I saw that for some reason of his own he was determined not to come, so I stood up.

"Are you a college man?" he inquired suddenly.

For a moment I thought he was going to suggest a "gonnegtion," but he only nodded and shook my hand.

"Let us learn to show our friendship for a man when he is alive and not after he is dead," he suggested. "After that my own rule is to let everything alone."

When I left his office the sky had turned dark and I got back to West Egg in a drizzle. After changing my clothes I went next door and found Mr. Gatz walking up and down excitedly in the hall. His pride in his son and in his son's possessions was continually increasing and now he had something to show me.

"Jimmy sent me this picture." He took out his wallet with trembling fingers. "Look there."

It was a photograph of the house, cracked in the corners and dirty with many hands. He pointed out every detail to me eagerly. "Look there!" and then sought admiration from my eyes. He had shown it so often that I think it was more real to him now than the house itself.

"Jimmy sent it to me. I think it's a very pretty picture. It shows up well."

"Very well. Had you seen him lately?"

"He come out to see me two years ago and bought me the house I live in now. Of course we was broke up when he run off from home, but I see now there was a reason for it. He knew he had a big future in front of him. And ever since he made a success he was very generous with me."

He seemed reluctant to put away the picture, held it for another minute, lingeringly, before my eyes. Then he returned the wallet and pulled from his pocket a ragged old copy of a book called "Hopalong Cassidy."[1]

"Look here, this is a book he had when he was a boy. It just shows you."

He opened it at the back cover and turned it around for me to see. On the last fly-leaf was printed the word SCHEDULE, and the date September 12, 1906. And underneath:

---

1   First in a popular series of Westerns by Clarence E. Mulford (1883-1956), first published in 1910. That Gatsby's copy is dated 1906 below is an anachronism.

```
Rise from bed . . . . . . . . . . . . . . . . . . . . . . . . .6.00      A. M.
Dumbbell exercise and wall-scaling . . . . . . . . . . .6.15-6.30   "
Study electricity, etc . . . . . . . . . . . . . . . . . . . . . .7.15-8.15   "
Work  . . . . . . . . . . . . . . . . . . . . . . . . . . . . . .8.30-4.30  P. M.
Baseball and sports  . . . . . . . . . . . . . . . . . . . . .4.30-5.00   "
Practice elocution, poise and how to attain it . . . . .5.00-6.00   "
Study needed inventions  . . . . . . . . . . . . . . . . . .7.00-9.00   "
```

GENERAL RESOLVES

No wasting time at Shafters or [a name, indecipherable]
No more smokeing or chewing.
Bath every other day
Read one improving book or magazine per week
Save $5.00 [crossed out] $3.00 per week
Be better to parents[1]

"I come across this book by accident," said the old man. "It just shows you, don't it?"

"It just shows you."

"Jimmy was bound to get ahead. He always had some resolves like this or something. Do you notice what he's got about improving his mind? He was always great for that. He told me I et like a hog once, and I beat him for it."

He was reluctant to close the book, reading each item aloud and then looking eagerly at me. I think he rather expected me to copy down the list for my own use.

A little before three the Lutheran minister arrived from Flushing, and I began to look involuntarily out the windows for other cars. So did Gatsby's father. And as the time passed and the servants came in and stood waiting in the hall, his eyes began to blink anxiously, and he spoke of the rain in a worried, uncertain way. The minister glanced several times at his watch, so I took him aside and asked him to wait for half an hour. But it wasn't any use. Nobody came.

---

1 Gatsby follows the example here of American icon Benjamin Franklin (1706-90), as established in Part Two of *The Autobiography of Benjamin Franklin* (1818; 1868).

About five o'clock our procession of three cars reached the cemetery and stopped in a thick drizzle beside the gate—first a motor hearse, horribly black and wet, then Mr. Gatz and the minister and I in the limousine, and a little later four or five servants and the postman from West Egg, in Gatsby's station wagon, all wet to the skin. As we started through the gate into the cemetery I heard a car stop and then the sound of someone splashing after us over the soggy ground. I looked around. It was the man with owl-eyed glasses whom I had found marvelling over Gatsby's books in the library one night three months before.

I'd never seen him since then. I don't know how he knew about the funeral, or even his name. The rain poured down his thick glasses, and he took them off and wiped them to see the protecting canvas unrolled from Gatsby's grave.

I tried to think about Gatsby then for a moment, but he was already too far away, and I could only remember, without resentment, that Daisy hadn't sent a message or a flower. Dimly I heard someone murmur "Blessed are the dead that the rain falls on," and then the owl-eyed man said "Amen to that," in a brave voice.

We straggled down quickly through the rain to the cars. Owl-eyes spoke to me by the gate.

"I couldn't get to the house," he remarked.

"Neither could anybody else."

"Go on!" He started. "Why, my God! they used to go there by the hundreds."

He took off his glasses and wiped them again, outside and in.

"The poor son-of-a-bitch," he said.

One of my most vivid memories is of coming back West from prep school and later from college at Christmas time. Those who went farther than Chicago would gather in the old dim Union Station at six o'clock of a December evening, with a few Chicago friends, already caught up into their own holiday gayeties, to bid them a hasty good-by. I remember the fur coats of the girls returning from Miss This-or-That's and the chatter of frozen breath and the hands waving overhead as we caught sight of old acquaintances, and the matchings of invitations: "Are you going to the Ordways'? the Herseys'? the Schultzes'?" and the long green tickets clasped tight in our gloved hands. And last the murky yellow cars of the Chicago, Milwaukee & St. Paul railroad looking cheerful as Christmas itself on the tracks beside the gate.

When we pulled out into the winter night and the real snow,

our snow, began to stretch out beside us and twinkle against the windows, and the dim lights of small Wisconsin stations moved by, a sharp wild brace came suddenly into the air. We drew in deep breaths of it as we walked back from dinner through the cold vestibules, unutterably aware of our identity with this country for one strange hour, before we melted indistinguishably into it again.

That's my Middle West—not the wheat or the prairies or the lost Swede towns, but the thrilling returning trains of my youth, and the street lamps and sleigh bells in the frosty dark and the shadows of holly wreaths thrown by lighted windows on the snow. I am part of that, a little solemn with the feel of those long winters, a little complacent from growing up in the Carraway house in a city where dwellings are still called through decades by a family's name. I see now that this has been a story of the West, after all—Tom and Gatsby, Daisy and Jordan and I, were all Westerners, and perhaps we possessed some deficiency in common which made us subtly unadaptable to Eastern life.

Even when the East excited me most, even when I was most keenly aware of its superiority to the bored, sprawling, swollen towns beyond the Ohio, with their interminable inquisitions which spared only the children and the very old—even then it had always for me a quality of distortion. West Egg, especially, still figures in my more fantastic dreams. I see it as a night scene by El Greco:[1] a hundred houses, at once conventional and grotesque, crouching under a sullen, overhanging sky and a lustreless moon. In the foreground four solemn men in dress suits are walking along the sidewalk with a stretcher on which lies a drunken woman in a white evening dress. Her hand, which dangles over the side, sparkles cold with jewels. Gravely the men turn in at a house—the wrong house. But no one knows the woman's name, and no one cares.

After Gatsby's death the East was haunted for me like that, distorted beyond my eyes' power of correction. So when the blue smoke of brittle leaves was in the air and the wind blew the wet laundry stiff on the line I decided to come back home.

There was one thing to be done before I left, an awkward, unpleasant thing that perhaps had better have been let alone. But I wanted to leave things in order and not just trust that obliging

---

1 El Greco (1541-1614), Greek artist who settled in Spain, admired by modernists for his mannered, strikingly intense style and mystical vision.

and indifferent sea to sweep my refuse away. I saw Jordan Baker and talked over and around what had happened to us together, and what had happened afterward to me, and she lay perfectly still, listening, in a big chair.

She was dressed to play golf, and I remember thinking she looked like a good illustration, her chin raised a little jauntily, her hair the color of an autumn leaf, her face the same brown tint as the fingerless glove on her knee. When I had finished she told me without comment that she was engaged to another man. I doubted that, though there were several she could have married at a nod of her head, but I pretended to be surprised. For just a minute I wondered if I wasn't making a mistake, then I thought it all over again quickly and got up to say good-by.

"Nevertheless you did throw me over," said Jordan suddenly. "You threw me over on the telephone. I don't give a damn about you now, but it was a new experience for me, and I felt a little dizzy for a while."

We shook hands.

"Oh, and do you remember"—she added—"a conversation we had once about driving a car?"

"Why—not exactly."

"You said a bad driver was only safe until she met another bad driver? Well, I met another bad driver, didn't I? I mean it was careless of me to make such a wrong guess. I thought you were rather an honest, straightforward person. I thought it was your secret pride."

"I'm thirty," I said. "I'm five years too old to lie to myself and call it honor."

She didn't answer. Angry, and half in love with her, and tremendously sorry, I turned away.

One afternoon late in October I saw Tom Buchanan. He was walking ahead of me along Fifth Avenue in his alert, aggressive way, his hands out a little from his body as if to fight off interference, his head moving sharply here and there, adapting itself to his restless eyes. Just as I slowed up to avoid overtaking him he stopped and began frowning into the windows of a jewelry store. Suddenly he saw me and walked back, holding out his hand.

"What's the matter, Nick? Do you object to shaking hands with me?"

"Yes. You know what I think of you."

"You're crazy, Nick," he said quickly. "Crazy as hell. I don't know what's the matter with you."

"Tom," I inquired, "what did you say to Wilson that afternoon?"

He stared at me without a word, and I knew I had guessed right about those missing hours. I started to turn away, but he took a step after me and grabbed my arm.

"I told him the truth," he said. "He came to the door while we were getting ready to leave, and when I sent down word that we weren't in he tried to force his way up-stairs. He was crazy enough to kill me if I hadn't told him who owned the car. His hand was on a revolver in his pocket every minute he was in the house—" He broke off defiantly. "What if I did tell him? That fellow had it coming to him. He threw dust into your eyes just like he did in Daisy's, but he was a tough one. He ran over Myrtle like you'd run over a dog and never even stopped his car."

There was nothing I could say, except the one unutterable fact that it wasn't true.

"And if you think I didn't have my share of suffering—look here, when I went to give up that flat and saw that damn box of dog biscuits sitting there on the sideboard, I sat down and cried like a baby. By God it was awful——"

I couldn't forgive him or like him, but I saw that what he had done was, to him, entirely justified. It was all very careless and confused. They were careless people, Tom and Daisy—they smashed up things and creatures and then retreated back into their money or their vast carelessness, or whatever it was that kept them together, and let other people clean up the mess they had made....

I shook hands with him; it seemed silly not to, for I felt suddenly as though I were talking to a child. Then he went into the jewelry store to buy a pearl necklace—or perhaps only a pair of cuff buttons—rid of my provincial squeamishness forever.

Gatsby's house was still empty when I left—the grass on his lawn had grown as long as mine. One of the taxi drivers in the village never took a fare past the entrance gate without stopping for a minute and pointing inside; perhaps it was he who drove Daisy and Gatsby over to East Egg the night of the accident, and perhaps he had made a story about it all his own. I didn't want to hear it and I avoided him when I got off the train.

I spent my Saturday nights in New York because those gleaming, dazzling parties of his were with me so vividly that I could still hear the music and the laughter, faint and incessant, from his garden, and the cars going up and down his drive. One night I did hear a material car there, and saw its lights stop at his front steps. But I didn't investigate. Probably it was some final guest who had been away at the ends of the earth and didn't know that the party was over.

On the last night, with my trunk packed and my car sold to the grocer, I went over and looked at that huge incoherent failure of a house once more. On the white steps an obscene word, scrawled by some boy with a piece of brick, stood out clearly in the moonlight, and I erased it, drawing my shoe raspingly along the stone. Then I wandered down to the beach and sprawled out on the sand.

Most of the big shore places were closed now and there were hardly any lights except the shadowy, moving glow of a ferryboat across the Sound. And as the moon rose higher the inessential houses began to melt away until gradually I became aware of the old island here that flowered once for Dutch sailors' eyes—a fresh, green breast of the new world. Its vanished trees, the trees that had made way for Gatsby's house, had once pandered in whispers to the last and greatest of all human dreams; for a transitory enchanted moment man must have held his breath in the presence of this continent, compelled into an æsthetic contemplation he neither understood nor desired, face to face for the last time in history with something commensurate to his capacity for wonder.

And as I sat there brooding on the old, unknown world, I thought of Gatsby's wonder when he first picked out the green light at the end of Daisy's dock. He had come a long way to this blue lawn, and his dream must have seemed so close that he could hardly fail to grasp it. He did not know that it was already behind him, somewhere back in that vast obscurity beyond the city, where the dark fields of the republic rolled on under the night.

Gatsby believed in the green light, the orgastic future that year by year recedes before us. It eluded us then, but that's no matter—to-morrow we will run faster, stretch out our arms farther.... And one fine morning——

So we beat on, boats against the current, borne back ceaselessly into the past.

Appendix A: Fitzgerald's Correspondence about The Great Gatsby *(1922-25)*

[The selections from Fitzgerald's correspondence here—including letters from his editor Maxwell Perkins—inform us about the gestation of the novel, and make up the best testimony we have to the high aesthetic achievement its author was aiming for. Most importantly, they offer Perkins's crucial response to the submitted typescript of the novel that led Fitzgerald to revise the galleys so substantially. And finally, they document Fitzgerald's worrying over the critical reception and disappointing sales. With the exception of item 3, the selections below are either excerpts from longer letters or nearly complete letters with matter not pertaining to *The Great Gatsby* edited out. The texts of the letters are derived from the three following sources: *Dear Scott/Dear Max: The Fitzgerald-Perkins Correspondence*, ed. John Kuehl and Jackson R. Bryer (New York: Charles Scribner's Sons, 1971); *The Correspondence of F. Scott Fitzgerald*, ed. Matthew J. Bruccoli and Margaret M. Duggan (New York: Random House, 1980); and F. Scott Fitzgerald, *A Life in Letters*, ed. Matthew J. Bruccoli (New York: Simon & Schuster, 1994). I have followed the policy of the editors of these volumes and left Fitzgerald's spelling and punctuation errors as written. For the sake of regularity all underlined titles and passages have been printed in italics.]

From F. Scott Fitzgerald to Maxwell Perkins, ca. 20 June 1922[1]

When I send on this last bunch of stories I may start my novel and I may not. Its locale will be the middle west and New York of 1885 I think. It will concern less superlative beauties than I run to usually & will be centered on a smaller period of time. It will have a catholic element. I'm not quite sure whether I'm ready to start it quite yet or not. I'll write next week & tell you more definate plans.

---

1 Source: *Dear Scott/Dear Max*, 61.

From F. Scott Fitzgerald to Maxwell Perkins, ca. mid-July 1922[1]

I want to write something *new*—something extraordinary and beautiful and simple + intricately patterned.

F. Scott Fitzgerald to Moran Tudury,[2] ca. 11 April 1924[3]

I am so anxious for people to see my new novel which is a new thinking out of the idea of illusion (an idea which I suppose will dominate my more serious stuff) much more mature and much more romantic than This Side of Paradise. The B & D was a better book than the first but it was a false lead ... a concession to Mencken[4] ... The business of creating illusion is much more to my taste and my talent.

From F. Scott Fitzgerald to Maxwell Perkins, ca. 10 April 1924[5]

I feel I have an enormous power in me now, more than I've ever had in a way but it works so fitfully and with so many bogeys because I've *talked so much* and not lived enough within myself to develop the nessessary self reliance. Also I don't know anyone who has used up so much personal experience as I have at 27. Copperfield & Pendennis[6] were written at past forty while This Side of Paradise was three books & the B. & D. was two. So in my new novel I'm thrown directly on purely creative work—not trashy imaginings as in my stories but the sustained imagination of a sincere and yet radiant world. So I tread slowly and carefully & at times in considerable distress. This book will be a consciously artistic achievement & must depend on that as the 1st books did not.

---

1 Source: *Correspondence of F. Scott Fitzgerald*, 112.
2 Pulp-fiction magazine writer and editor.
3 Source: *Correspondence of F. Scott Fitzgerald*, 139.
4 H.L. Mencken (1880-1956), iconoclastic intellectual and editor, and as critic a champion of literary realism and naturalism; see Appendix B1 and Appendix D3.
5 Source: *Dear Scott/Dear Max*, 70.
6 *David Copperfield* (1850), autobiographical novel by Charles Dickens (1812-70); *The History of Pendennis* (1848-50), novel by William Makepeace Thackeray (1811-63).

From F. Scott Fitzgerald to Ludlow Fowler,[1] August 1924[2]

I remember our last conversation and it makes me sad. I feel old too, this summer—I have ever since the failure of my play a year ago. Thats the whole burden of this novel—the loss of those illusions that give such color to the world so that you don't care whether things are true or false as long as they partake of the magical glory.

From F. Scott Fitzgerald to Maxwell Perkins, ca. 25 August 1924[3]

The novel will be done next week. That doesn't mean however that it'll reach America before October 1st. as Zelda and I are contemplating a careful revision after a weeks complete rest.

***

I think my novel is about the best American novel ever written. It is rough stuff in places, runs only to about 50,000 words & I hope you won't shy at it.

F. Scott Fitzgerald to Maxwell Perkins, 27 October 1924[4]

Under separate cover I'm sending you my third novel:

The Great Gatsby

(I think that at last I've done something really my own), but how good "my own" is remains to be seen.

I should suggest the following contract.

15% up to 50,000

20% after 50,000

---

1 Princeton classmate of Fitzgerald's, model for Anson Hunter in "The Rich Boy" (1926).
2 Source: *Correspondence of F. Scott Fitzgerald*, 145.
3 Source: *Dear Scott/Dear Max*, 75-76.
4 Source: *Dear Scott/Dear Max*, 80-81.

The book is only a little over fifty thousand words long but I believe, as you know, that Whitney Darrow[1] has the wrong psychology about prices (and about what class constitute the book-buying public now that the lowbrows go to the movies) and I'm anxious to charge two dollars for it and have it a *full size book*.

Of course I want the binding to be absolutely uniform with my other books—the stamping too—and the jacket we discussed before. This time I don't want any signed blurbs on the jacket—not Mencken's or Lewis' or Howard's[2] or anyone's. I'm tired of being the author of *This Side of Paradise* and I want to start over.

★★★

I have an alternative title:

Gold-hatted Gatsby

After you've read the book let me know what you think about the title. Naturally I won't get a nights sleep until I hear from you but do tell me the absolute truth, *your first impression of the book* & tell me anything that bothers you in it.

From F. Scott Fitzgerald to Maxwell Perkins, ca. 7 November 1924[3]

By now you've received the novel. There are things in it I'm not satisfied with in the middle of the book—Chapters 6 & 7. And I may write in a complete new scene in proof. I hope you got my telegram.

I have decided to stick to the title I put on the book.

Trimalchio in West Egg

The only other titles that seem to fit it are *Trimalchio* and *On the Road to West Egg*. I had two others *Gold-hatted Gatsby* and *The High-bouncing Lover* but they seemed too light.

We leave for Rome as soon as I finish the short story I'm working on.

---

1 Employee in charge of sales and promotion at Scribner's.
2 Sinclair Lewis (1885-1951), American novelist famous for *Main Street* (1920) and *Babbitt* (1922); Sidney Howard (1891-1939), playwright and screenwriter, author of the 1924 play *They Knew What They Wanted*.
3 Source: *Dear Scott/Dear Max*, 81-82.

From Maxwell Perkins to F. Scott Fitzgerald, 20 November 1924[1]

I think you have every kind of right to be proud of this book. It is an extraordinary book, suggestive of all sorts of thoughts and moods. You adopted exactly the right method of telling it, that of employing a narrator who is more of a spectator than an actor: this puts the reader upon a point of observation on a higher level than that on which the characters stand and at a distance that gives perspective. In no other way could your irony have been so immensely effective, nor the reader have been enabled so strongly to feel at times the strangeness of human circumstance in a vast heedless universe. In the eyes of Dr. Eckleberg [*sic*] various readers will see different significances; but their presence gives a superb touch to the whole thing: great unblinking eyes, expressionless, looking down upon the human scene. It's magnificent!

I could go on praising the book and speculating on its various elements and meanings, but points of criticism are more important now. I think you are right in feeling a certain slight sagging in chapters six and seven, and I don't know how to suggest a remedy. I hardly doubt that you will find one and I am only writing to say that I think it does need something to hold up here to the pace set, and ensuing. I have only two actual criticisms:—

One is that among a set of characters marvelously palpable and vital—I would know Tom Buchanan if I met him on the street and would avoid him—Gatsby is somewhat vague. The reader's eyes can never quite focus upon him, his outlines are dim. Now everything about Gatsby is more or less a mystery i.e. more or less vague, and this may be somewhat of an artistic intention, but I think it is mistaken. Couldn't *he* be physically described as distinctly as the others, and couldn't you add one or two characteristics like the use of that phrase "old sport",—not verbal, but physical ones, perhaps. I think that for some reason or other a reader—this was true of Mr. Scribner and of Louise[2]—gets an idea that Gatsby is a much older man than he is, although you have the writer say that he is little older than himself. But this would be avoided if on his first appearance he was seen as vividly as Daisy and Tom are, for instance;—and I do not think your scheme would be impaired if you made him so.

---

1   Source: *Dear Scott/Dear Max*, 82-84.
2   Charles Scribner II (1854-1930), head of the publishing firm Charles Scribner's Sons; Louise Perkins was Maxwell's wife.

The other point is also about Gatsby: his career must remain mysterious, of course. But in the end you make it pretty clear that his wealth came through his connection with Wolfsheim [*sic*]. You also suggest this much earlier. Now almost all readers numerically are going to be puzzled by his having all this wealth and are going to feel entitled to an explanation. To give a distinct and definite one would be, of course, utterly absurd. It did occur to me though, that you might here and there interpolate some phrases, and possibly incidents, little touches of various kinds, that would suggest that he was in some active way mysteriously engaged. You do have him called on the telephone, but couldn't he be seen once or twice consulting at his parties with people of some sort of mysterious significance, from the political, the gambling, the sporting world, or whatever it may be. I know I am floundering, but that fact may help you to see what I mean. The total lack of an explanation through so large a part of the story does seem to me a defect;—or not of an explanation, but of the suggestion of an explanation. I wish you were here so I could talk about it to you for then I know I could at least make you understand what I mean. What Gatsby did ought never to be definitely imparted, even if it could be. Whether he was an innocent tool in the hands of somebody else, or to what degree he was this, ought not to be explained. But if some sort of business activity of his were simply adumbrated, it would lend further probability to that part of the story.

There is one other point: in giving deliberately Gatsby's biography when he gives it to the narrator you do depart from the method of the narrative in some degree, for otherwise almost everything is told, and beautifully told, in the regular flow of it,—in the succession of events or in accompaniment with them. But you can't avoid the biography altogether. I thought you might find ways to let the truth of some of his claims like "Oxford" and his army career come out bit by bit in the course of actual narrative. I mention the point anyway for consideration in this interval before I send the proofs.

The general brilliant quality of the book makes me ashamed to make even these criticisms. The amount of meaning you get into a sentence, the dimensions and intensity of the impression you make a paragraph carry, are most extraordinary. The manuscript is full of phrases which make a scene blaze with life. If one enjoyed a rapid railroad journey I would compare the number and vividness of pictures your living words suggest, to the living scenes disclosed in that way. It seems in reading a much shorter book than it is, but it carries the mind through a series of experiences that one would think would require a book of three times its length.

The presentation of Tom, his place, Daisy and Jordan, and the unfolding of their characters is unequalled so far as I know. The description of the valley of ashes adjacent to the lovely country, the conversation and the action in Myrtle's apartment, the marvelous catalogue of those who came to Gatsby's house,—these are such things as make a man famous. And all these things, the whole pathetic episode, you have given a place in time and space, for with the help of T.J. Eckleberg and by an occasional glance at the sky, or the sea, or the city, you have imparted a sort of sense of eternity. You once told me you were not a natural writer—my God! You have plainly mastered the craft, of course; but you needed far more than craftsmanship for this.

From F. Scott Fitzgerald to Maxwell Perkins, ca. 1 December 1924[1]

Your wire & your letters made me feel like a million dollars—I'm sorry I could make no better response than a telegram whining for money. But the long siege of the novel winded me a little & I've been slow on starting the stories on which I must live.

I think all your criticisms are true

(a) About the title. I'll try my best but I don't know what I can do. Maybe simply "Trimalchio" or "Gatsby." In the former case I don't see why the note shouldn't go on the back.

(b) Chapters VI & VII I know how to fix

(c) Gatsby's business affairs I can fix. I get your point about them.

(d) His vagueness I can repair by making more pointed—this doesn't sound good but wait and see. It'll make him clear

(e) But his long narrative in Chap VIII will be difficult to split up. Zelda also thought I was a little out of key but it is good writing and I don't think I could bear to sacrifice any of it

---

1   Source: *Dear Scott/Dear Max*, 85-86.

(f) I have 1000 minor corrections which I will make on the proof & several more large ones which you didn't mention.

Your criticisms were excellent & most helpful & you picked out all my favorite spots in the book to praise as high spots. Except you didn't mention my favorite of all—the chapter where Gatsby & Daisy meet.

★★★

Another point—in Chap. II of my book when Tom & Myrt[l]e go into the bedroom while Carraway reads Simon called Peter—is that raw? Let me know. I think its pretty nessessary.

I made the royalty smaller because I wanted to make up for all money you've advanced these two years by letting it pay a sort of interest on it. But I see by calculating I made it too small—a difference of 2000 dollars. Let us call it 15% up to 40,000 and 20% after that. That's a good fair contract all around.

★★★

Anyhow thanks & thanks & thanks for your letters. I'd rather have you & Bunny[1] like it than anyone I know. And I'd rather have you like it than Bunny. If its as good as you say, when I finish with the proof it'll be perfect.

Remember, by the way, to put by some cloth for the cover uniform with my other books.

As soon as I can think about the title I'll write or wire a decision.

From Maxwell Perkins to F. Scott Fitzgerald, 16 December 1924[2]

Your cable changing the title to "The Great Gatsby" has come and has been followed [...].

★★★

---

1   Nickname of Edmund Wilson (1895-1972), prolific critic and man of letters, and good friend of Fitzgerald's since they met at Princeton.
2   Source: *Dear Scott/Dear Max*, 86-87.

I hope you are thinking over "The Great Gatsby" in this interval and will add to it freely. The most important point I think, is that of how he comes by his wealth,—some sort of suggestion about it. He was supposed to be a bootlegger, wasn't he, at least in part, and I should think a little touch here and there would give the reader the suspicion that this was so and that is all that is needed.

F. Scott Fitzgerald to Maxwell Perkins, ca. 20 December 1924[1]

With the aid you've given me I can make "Gatsby" perfect. The chapter VII (the hotel scene) will never quite be up to mark—I've worried about it too long & I can't quite place Daisy's reaction. But I can improve it a lot. It isn't imaginative energy that's lacking—its because I'm automatically prevented from thinking it out over again *because I must get all those characters to New York* in order to have the catastrophe on the road going back & I must have it pretty much that way. So there's no chance of bringing the freshness to it that a new free conception sometimes gives.

The rest is easy and I see my way so clear that I even see the mental quirks that queered it before. Strange to say my notion of Gatsby's vagueness was O.K. What you and Louise & Mr. Charles Scribner found wanting was that:

I myself didn't know what Gatsby looked like or was engaged in & you felt it. If I'd known & kept it from you you'd have been *too impressed with my knowledge to protest*. This is a complicated idea but I'm sure you'll understand. But I know now—and as a penalty for not having known first, in other words to make sure I'm going to tell more.

It seems of almost mystical significance to me that you thot he was older—the man I had in mind, half unconsciously, *was* older (a specific individual)[2] and evidently, without so much as a definate word, I conveyed the fact.—or rather, I must qualify this Shaw-Desmond-trash[3] by saying that I conveyed it without a word that I can at present and for the life of me, trace. [...]

Anyhow after careful searching of the files (of a man's mind

---

1 Source: *Dear Scott/Dear Max*, 89-90.
2 This may be a reference to Max [von] Gerlach, a known Great Neck bootlegger long presumed to be a chief model for Gatsby.
3 After Shaw Desmond (1877-1960), prolific Irish man of letters interested in psychic research.

here) for the Fuller Magee case[1] & after having had Zelda draw pictures until her fingers ache I know Gatsby better than I know my own child. My first instinct after your letter was to let him go & have Tom Buchanan dominate the book (I supposed he's the best character I've ever done [...]) but Gatsby sticks in my heart. I had him for awhile then lost him & now I know I have him again. I'm sorry Myrtle is better than Daisy. Jordan of course was a great idea (perhaps you know its Edith Cummings)[2] but she fades out. Its Chap VII that's the trouble with Daisy & it may hurt the book's popularity that its *a man's book.*

Anyhow I think (for the first time since The Vegetable failed) that I'm a wonderful writer & its your always wonderful letters that help me to go on believing in myself.

Now some practical, very important questions. Please answer every one.

1. Montenegro has an order called The Order of Danilo. Is there any possible way you could find out for me there what it would look like—whether a courtesy decoration given to an American would bear an English inscription—or anything to give versimilitude to the medal which sounds horribly amateurish.

2. Please have *no blurbs of any kind on the jacket*!!! No Mencken or Lewis or Sid Howard or anything. I don't believe in them *one bit* any more.

3. Don't forget to change name of book in list of works

---

1 In the summer of 1922 the New York brokerage firm E.M. Fuller & Co. declared bankruptcy. Edward M. Fuller, head of the company and a Great Neck resident, was soon indicted along with William McGee on charges of gambling with customers' funds. A series of trials that began soon after Fitzgerald moved to Great Neck led to their conviction, as well as the exposure of a complex web of financial impropriety—including plans to sell fraudulent securities over the telephone—involving a number of socially prominent people. It also emerged that Fuller had ties to gambler Arnold Rothstein, the model for Wolfshiem. Fitzgerald read up on the case in his effort to adumbrate Gatsby's criminal activities and account for his wealth. This background to the novel explains Gatsby offering bond salesman Nick the opportunity to partake in his "little business on the side" (Chapter V).
2 Close friend from Lake Forest of Ginevra King, Fitzgerald's first love; winner of the 1923 US Amateur women's golf championship.

4. Please shift exclamation point from end of 3d line to end of 4th line in title page poem. *Please*! Important!

5. I thought that the whole episode (2 paragraphs) about their playing the Jazz History of the world at Gatsby's first party was rotten. Did you? Tell me frank reaction—*personal*, don't *think*! We can all think!

F. Scott Fitzgerald to Maxwell Perkins, ca. 15 January 1925[1]

Proof hasn't arrived yet. Have been in bed for a week with grippe but I'm ready to attack it violently. Here are two important things.

1. In [Is] the scene in Myrt[l]es appartment—in the place where *Tom & Myrtle dissapear for awhile* noticeably raw. Does it stick out enough so that the censor might get it. Its the only place in the book I'm in doubt about on that score. Please let me know right away.

2. Please have *no quotations from any critics whatsoever on the jacket*—simply your own blurb on the back and don't give away too much of the idea—especially don't connect Daisy & Gatsby (I need the quality of surprise there.) Please be *very general*.

These points are both very important. Do drop me a line about them.

From Maxwell Perkins to F. Scott Fitzgerald, 20 January 1925[2]

You are beginning to get me worried about the scene in Myrtle's apartment for you have spoken of it several times. It never occurred to me to think there was any objection to it. I am sure there is none. No censor could make an issue on that,—nor I think on anything else in the book.

★★★

I certainly hope the proofs have got to you and that you have been at work on them for some time. If not you had better cable. They were sent first-class mail. The first lot on December 27th and the second lot on December 30th.

---

1 Source: *Dear Scott/Dear Max*, 91.
2 Source: *Dear Scott/Dear Max*, 92.

F. Scott Fitzgerald to Maxwell Perkins, 24 January 1925[1]

This is a most important letter so I'm having it typed. Guard it as your life.

1) Under a separate cover I'm sending the first part of the proof. While I agreed with the general suggestions in your first letters I differ with you in others. I *want* Myrtle Wilson's breast ripped off—its exactly the thing, I think, and I don't want to chop up the good scenes by too much tinkering. When Wolfsheim says "sid" for "said", it's deliberate. "Orgastic" is the adjective from "orgasm" and it expresses exactly the intended ecstasy. It's not a bit dirty. I'm much more worried about the disappearance of Tom and Myrtle on Galley 9—I think it's all right but I'm not sure. If it isn't please wire and I'll send correction.

2) Now about the page proof—under certain conditions never mind sending them (unless, of course, there's loads of time, which I suppose there isn't. I'm keen for late March or early April publication) .

The conditions are two.

> a.) That someone reads it *very carefully twice* to see that every one of my inserts are put in correctly. There are so many of them that I'm in terror of a mistake.

> b.) That no changes *whatsoever* are made in it except in the case of a misprint so glaring as to be certain, and that only by you.

If there's some time left but not enough for the double mail send them to me and I'll simply wire O.K. which will save two weeks. However don't postpone for that. In any case send me the page proof as usual just to see.

★★★

4) This is very important. Be sure not to give away *any* of my plot in the blurb. Don't give away that Gatsby *dies* or is a *parvenu* or a *crook* or anything. It's a part of the suspense of the book that all these things are in doubt until the end. You'll watch this won't

---

1   Source: *Dear Scott/Dear Max*, 92-94.

you? And remember about having no quotations from critics on the jacket—*not even about my other books!*

★★★

P.S. I'm returning the proof of the title page ect. It's O.K. but my heart tells me I should have named it *Trimalchio*. However against all the advice I suppose it would have been stupid and stubborn of me. *Trimalchio in West Egg* was only a compromise. *Gatsby* is too much like Babbit[1] and *The Great Gatsby* is weak because there's no emphasis even ironically on his greatness or lack of it. However let it pass.

From F. Scott Fitzgerald to Maxwell Perkins, ca. 18 February 1925[2]

After six weeks of uninterrupted work the proof is finished and the last of it goes to you this afternoon. On the whole its been very successful labor

(1.) I've brought Gatsby to life

(2.) I've accounted for his money

(3.) I've fixed up the two weak chap[t]ers (VI and VIII)

(4.) I've improved his first party

(5.) I've broken up his long narrative in Chap. VIII

This morning I wired you to *hold up the galley of Chap 40.* The correction—and God! its important because in my other revision I made Gatsby look too mean—is enclosed herewith. Also some corrections for the page proof.

★★★

Do tell me if all corrections have been recieved. I'm worried.

I hope you're setting publication date at first possible moment.

---

1 *Babbit[t]*, Sinclair Lewis's best-selling 1922 novel.
2 Source: *Dear Scott/Dear Max*, 94.

From Maxwell Perkins to F. Scott Fitzgerald, 20 April 1925[1]

I wired you today rather discouragingly in the matter of the sales and I could send no qualifications in a cable. A great many of the trade have been very skeptical. I cannot make out just why. But one point is the small number of pages in the book,—an old stock objection which I thought we had got beyond. To attempt to explain to them that the way of writing which you have chosen and which is bound to come more and more into practice is one where a vast amount is said by implication, and that therefore the book is as full as it would have been if written to much greater length by another method, is of course utterly futile. The small number of pages, however, did in the end lead a couple of big distributors to reduce their orders immensely at the very last minute. The sale is up to the public and that has not yet had time to reveal·itself fully. On the other hand, we have had a very good review, a very conspicuous one, in the Times and an excellent one also in the Tribune from Isabelle Patterson [*sic*]. William Rose Benet has announced preliminary to a review in the Saturday Review, that this is distinctly your best book. And the individuals whom I encounter like Gilbert Seldes (who will write also), Van Wyck Brooks, John Marquand, John Bishop, think this too.[2] Marquand and Seldes were both quite wild about it. These people understand it fully, which even the Times and Tribune reviewers did not.

I will send you anything that has much significance by cable. I know fully how this period must try you: it must be very hard to endure, because it is hard enough for me to endure. I like the book so much myself and see so much in it that its recognition and success mean more to me than anything else in sight at the present time,—I mean in any department of interest, not only that of literature. But it does seem to me from the comments of many who yet feel its enchantment, that it is over the heads of more people than you would probably suppose.

---

1 Source: *Dear Scott/Dear Max*, 100-01.

2 For the *New York Herald Tribune* review by novelist and critic Isabel Paterson (1886-1961), see *F. Scott Fitzgerald: The Critical Reception*, ed. Jackson R. Bryer (New York: Burt Franklin & Co., 1978), 200-02. The reviews by poet and critic William Rose Benét (1886-1950) and pioneering popular culture critic Gilbert Seldes (1893-1970) appear in Appendix B, items 2 and 5, respectively. Van Wyck Brooks (1886-1963), prominent American culture critic much admired by Fitzgerald; John P. Marquand (1893-1960), satiric novelist and contributor to the *Saturday Evening Post*.

From F. Scott Fitzgerald to Maxwell Perkins, ca. 24 April 1925[1]

Your telegram depressed me. I hope I'll find better news in Paris and am wiring you from Lyons. There's nothing to say until I hear more. If the book fails commercially it will be from one of two reasons or both.

1st The title is only fair, rather bad than good.

2nd *And most important*—the book contains no important woman character and women controll the fiction market at present. I don't think the unhappy end matters particularly.

It will have to sell 20,000 copies to wipe out my debt to you. I think it will do that all right—but my hope was it would do 75,000. This week will tell.

✷✷✷

In all events I have a book of good stories for the fall. Now I shall write some cheap ones until I've accumulated enough for my next novel. When that is finished and published I'll wait and see. If it will support me with no more intervals of trash I'll go on as a novelist. If not I'm going to quit, come home, go to Hollywood and learn the movie business. I can't reduce our scale of living and I can't stand this financial insecurity. Anyhow there's no point in trying to be an artist if you can't do your best. I had my chance back in 1920 to start my life on a sensible scale and I lost it and so I'll have to pay the penalty. Then perhaps at 40 I can start writing again without this constant worry and interruption.

From F. Scott Fitzgerald to Edmund Wilson, May 1925[2]

Thanks for your letter about the book. I was awfully happy that you liked it and that you approved of its design. The worst fault in it, I think is a Big Fault: I gave no account (and had no feeling about or knowledge of) the emotional relations between Gatsby and Daisy from the time of their reunion to the catastrophe.

---

1 Source: *Dear Scott/Dear Max*, 101-02.
2 Source: F. Scott Fitzgerald, *A Life in Letters*, 109.

However the lack is so astutely concealed by the retrospect of Gatsby's past and by blankets of excellent prose that no one has noticed it—tho everyone has felt the lack and called it by another name. Mencken said (in a most enthusiastic letter received today) that the only fault was that the central story was trivial and a sort of anecdote (that is because he has forgotten his admiration for Conrad[1] and adjusted himself to the sprawling novel.) and I felt that what he really missed was the lack of any emotional backbone at the very height of it.

Without makeing any invidious comparisons between Class A. and Class C., if my novel is an anectdote so is *The Brothers Karamazoff*.[2] From one angle the latter could be reduced into a detective story. However the letters from you and Mencken have compensated me for the fact that of all the reviews, even the most entheusiastic, not one had the slightest idea what the book was about and for the even more depressing fact that it was, in comparison with the others, a financial failure (after I'd turned down fifteen thousand for the serial rights!).[3]

F. Scott Fitzgerald to H.L. Mencken, 4 May 1925[4]

Your letter was the first outside word that reached me about my book. I was tremendously moved both by the fact that you liked it and by your kindness in writing me about it. By the next mail came a letter from Edmund Wilson and a clipping from Stallings,[5] both bulging with interest and approval, but as you know I'd rather have you like a book of mine than anyone in America.

---

1   Joseph Conrad (1857-1924), Polish-born English novelist whose works such as *Nostromo* (1904) and especially his "Preface" to *The Nigger of the "Narcissus"* (1897) significantly influenced Fitzgerald's understanding of novelistic form and aesthetic purpose; championed by Mencken in *A Book of Prefaces* (1917).

2   *The Brothers Karamazoff* (or *Karamazov*), 1880 masterpiece of Russian novelist Fyodor Dostoevsky (1821-81).

3   In fact Fitzgerald was unsuccessful at getting the $15-20,000 he wanted for serial rights to *The Great Gatsby*; two magazine editors turned him down. *College Humor* offered him $10,000, but he rejected the offer because he did not want to delay book publication and thought the venue would give a misleading impression of the novel.

4   Source: F. Scott Fitzgerald, *A Life in Letters*, 110-11.

5   Laurence Stallings (1894-1968), playwright and later screenwriter, author with Maxwell Anderson of the controversial 1924 play *What Price Glory?* He wrote a good review of the novel for the *New York World*.

There is a tremendous fault in the book—the lack of an emotional presentment of Daisy's attitude toward Gatsby after their reunion (and the consequent lack of logic or importance in her throwing him over). Everyone has felt this but no one has spotted it because its concealed beneath elaborate and overlapping blankets of prose. Wilson complained: "The characters are so uniformly unpleasant," Stallings: "a sheaf of gorgeous notes for a novel" and you say: "The story is fundamentally trivial." I think the smooth, almost unbroken pattern makes you feel that. Despite your admiration for Conrad you have lately—perhaps in reaction against the merely well-made novels of James' imitators—become used to the formless.[1] It is in protest against my own formless two novels, and Lewis' and Dos Passos' that this was written.[2] I admit that in comparison to *My Antonia* and *The Lost Lady* it is a failure in what it tries to do but I think in comparison to *Cytherea* or *Linda Condon* it is a success.[3] At any rate I have learned a lot from writing it and the influence on it has been the masculine one of *The Brothers Karamazov*, a thing of incomparable form, rather than the feminine one of *The Portrait of a Lady*.[4] If it seems trivial or "anecdotal" (sp) is because of an aesthetic fault, a failure in one very important episode and not a frailty in the theme—at least I don't think so. Did you ever know a writer to calmly take a just critisism and shut up?

---

1 Reference to followers of the austere preoccupation with novelistic form (especially economy of incident and point-of-view) evident in the novels and criticism of American writer Henry James (1843-1916).

2 John Dos Passos (1896-1970), American novelist noted for his use of multiple plots and social and psychological realism to engage modern historical experience. Fitzgerald championed *Three Soldiers* (1921) and admired *Manhattan Transfer* (1925), but said little about the sprawling three-volume epic *U.S.A.* (1930, 1932, 1936).

3 *My Ántonia* (1918) and *[A] Lost Lady* (1923), novels by Willa Cather (1873-1947); Fitzgerald wrote her out of concern that he might be misconstrued as having plagiarized some bits of characterization from the latter novel. *Cytherea* (1922) and *Linda Condon* (1919), novels by Joseph Hergesheimer (1880-1954).

4 *The Portrait of a Lady* (1880; 1908), novel by Henry James.

Appendix B: Contemporary Reviews

[Fitzgerald's early complaints about the incompetent or negligent reviews of his novel should not overshadow the fact that reviews of *The Great Gatsby* were generally positive. The novel received very strong reviews from some of the most distinguished critics of the day, most notably his recent friend Gilbert Seldes, an early champion of T.S. Eliot and James Joyce, and author of *The Seven Lively Arts* (a 1924 collection of appreciations of American popular culture). With the exception of his other friend H.L. Mencken's backhanded acknowledgment that the novel had style but little substance, the reviews reprinted below praised the novel and charted the author's career in terms that would have delighted Fitzgerald. These prescient judgments recognized *The Great Gatsby*'s formal virtue and stylistic brilliance, and anticipated Fitzgerald's posthumous canonization as an aesthetically rigorous novelist in the tradition of Gustave Flaubert, Joseph Conrad, and Henry James. The reviews by Mencken, Benét, and Curtis have been slightly abridged; the latter half only of Van Vechten's review has been reprinted; Seldes' review has been reprinted in its entirety.]

1. H.L. Mencken, "Fitzgerald, The Stylist, Challenges Fitzgerald, The Social Historian," *Baltimore Evening Sun* (2 May 1925): 9

Scott Fitzgerald's new novel, "The Great Gatsby," is in form no more than a glorified anecdote, and not too probable at that. The scene is the Long Island that hangs precariously on the edges of the New York city ash dumps—the Long Island of gaudy villas and bawdy house parties. The theme is the old one of a romantic and preposterous love—the ancient *fidelis ad urrum* motif[1] reduced to a *macabre* humor. The principal personage is a bounder typical of those parts—a fellow who seems to know everyone and yet remains unknown to all—a young man with a great deal of mysterious money, the tastes of a movie actor and, under it all, the simple sentimentality of a somewhat sclerotic fat woman.

---

1 Mencken seems to have in mind here the motif "faithful unto death," *fidelis ad uram* or *fidelis ad mortem.*

This clown Fitzgerald rushes to his death in nine short chapters. The other performers in the Totentanz[1] are of a like, or even worse quality. One of them is a rich man who carries on a grotesque intrigue with the wife of a garage keeper. Another is a woman golfer who wins championships by cheating. A third, a sort of chorus to the tragic farce, is a bond salesman—symbol of the New America! Fitzgerald clears them all off at last by a triple butchery. The garage keeper's wife, rushing out upon the road to escape her husband's third degree, is run down and killed by the wife of her lover. The garage keeper, misled by the lover, kills the lover of the lover's wife—the Great Gatsby himself. Another bullet, and the garage keeper is also reduced to offal. Choragus[2] fades away. The crooked lady golfer departs. The lover of the garage keeper's wife goes back to his own consort. The immense house of the Great Gatsby stands idle, its bedrooms given over to the bat and the owl, its cocktail shakers dry. The curtain lurches down.

This story is obviously unimportant, and though, as I shall show, it has its place in the Fitzgerald canon, it is certainly not to be put on the same shelf with, say, "This Side of Paradise." What ails it, fundamentally, is the plain fact that it is simply a story—that Fitzgerald seems to be far more interested in maintaining its suspense than in getting under the skins of its people. It is not that they are false; it is that they are taken too much for granted. Only Gatsby himself genuinely lives and breathes. The rest are mere marionettes—often astonishingly lifelike, but nevertheless not quite alive.

What gives the story distinction is something quite different from the management of the action or the handling of the characters; it is the charm and beauty of the writing. In Fitzgerald's first days it seemed almost unimaginable that he would ever show such qualities. His writing, then, was extraordinarily slipshod—at times almost illiterate. He seemed to be devoid of any feeling for the color and savor of words. He could see people clearly, and he could devise capital situations, but as writer qua writer he was apparently little more than a bright college boy. The critics of the Republic[3] were not slow to discern the fact. They praised "This

---

1 Dance of Death.
2 As used here, the term "choragus" refers to the leader of the chorus in classical Greek tragedy.
3 I.e., the United States.

Side of Paradise" as a story, as a social document, but they were almost unanimous in denouncing it as a piece of writing.

It is vastly to Fitzgerald's credit that he appears to have taken their caveats seriously and pondered them to good effect. In "The Great Gatsby" the highly agreeable fruits of that pondering are visible. The story, for all its basic triviality, has a fine texture, a careful and brilliant finish. The obvious phrase is simply not in it. The sentences roll along smoothly, spark[l]ingly, variously. There is evidence in every line of hard and intelligent effort. It is a quite new Fitzgerald who emerges from this little book and the qualities that he shows are dignified and solid. "This Side of Paradise," after all, might have been merely a lucky accident. But "The Great Gatsby," a far inferior story at bottom, is plainly the product of a sound and stable talent, conjured into being by hard work.

I make much of this improvement because it is of an order not often witnessed in American writers, and seldom indeed in those who start off with a popular success. The usual progression, indeed, is in the opposite direction. Every year first books of great promise are published—and every year a great deal of stale drivel is printed by the promising authors of year before last. The rewards of literary success in this country are so vast that, when they come early, they are not unnaturally somewhat demoralizing. The average author yields to them readily. Having struck the bull's-eye once, he is too proud to learn new tricks. [...] He begins to imitate himself. He peters out.

There is certainly no sign of petering out in Fitzgerald. After his first experimenting he plainly sat himself down calmly to consider his deficiencies. They were many and serious. He was, first of all, too facile. He could write entertainingly without giving thought to form and organization. He was, secondly, somewhat amateurish. The materials and methods of his craft, I venture, rather puzzled him. He used them ineptly. His books showed brilliancy in conception, but they were crude and even ignorant in detail. They suggested, only too often, the improvisations of a pianist playing furiously by ear but unable to read notes.

These are the defects that he has now got rid of [...]. ["The Great Gatsby"] shows on every page the results of that laborious effort. [...] There are pages so artfully contrived that one can no more imagine improvising them than one can imagine improvising a fugue. They are full of little delicacies, charming turns of phrase, penetrating second thoughts. In other words, they are easy and excellent reading—which is what always comes out of hard writing.

Thus Fitzgerald, the stylist, arises to challenge Fitzgerald, the social historian, but I doubt that the latter ever quite succumbs to the former. The thing that chiefly interests the basic Fitzgerald is still the florid show of modern American life—and especially the devil's dance that goes on at the top. He is unconcerned about the sweatings and sufferings of the nether herd: what engrosses him is the high carnival of those who have too much money to spend and too much time for the spending of it. Their idiotic pursuit of sensation, their almost incredible stupidity and triviality, their glittering swinishness—these are the things that go into his notebook.

In "The Great Gatsby," though he does not go below the surface, he depicts this rattle and hullabaloo with great gusto and, I believe, with sharp accuracy. The Long Island he sets before us is no fanciful Alsatia:[1] it actually exists. More, it is worth any social historian's study, for its influence upon the rest of the country is immense and profound. What is vogue among the profiteers of Manhattan and their harlots today is imitated by the flappers of the Bible Belt country clubs weeks after next. The whole tone of American society, once so highly formalized and so suspicious of change, is now taken largely from frail ladies who were slinging hash a year ago.

2. William Rose Benét, "An Admirable Novel," *Saturday Review of Literature* (9 May 1925): 739-40

"The Great Gatsby" is a disillusioned novel, and a mature novel. It is a novel with pace, from the first word to the last, and also a novel of admirable "control." Scott Fitzgerald started his literary career with enormous facility. His high spirits were infectious. The queer charm, color, wonder, and drama of a young and reckless world beat constantly upon his senses, stimulated a young and intensely romantic mind to a mixture of realism and extravaganza shaken up like a cocktail. [...] Scott Fitzgerald was born

---

1   Place of refuge for criminals, after the area in London around White-friars monastery throughout the sixteenth and seventeenth centuries.

with a knack for writing. What they call "a natural gift." And another gift of the fairies at his christening was a reckless confidence in himself. And he was quite intoxicated with the joy of life and rather engagingly savage toward an elder world. He was out "to get the world by the neck" and put words on paper in the patterns his exuberant fancy suggested. He didn't worry much about what had gone before Fitzgerald in literature. He dreamed gorgeously of what there was in Fitzgerald to "tell the world."

And all these elements contributed to the amazing performance of "This Side of Paradise," amazing in its excitement and gusto, amazing in phrase and epithet, amazing no less for all sorts of thoroughly bad writing pitched in with the good, for preposterous carelessness, and amazing as well for the sheer pace of the narrative and the fresh quality of its oddly pervasive poetry. Short stories of flappers and philosophers displayed the same vitality and flourished much the same faults. "Tales of the Jazz Age" inhabited the same glamour. "The Beautiful and Damned," while still in the mirage, furnished a more valuable document concerning the younger generation of the first quarter of the Twentieth Century. But brilliant, irrefutably brilliant as were certain passages of the novels and tales of which the "boy wonder" of our time was so lavish, arresting as were certain gleams of insight, intensely promising as were certain observed facilities, there remained in general, glamour, glamour everywhere, and, after the glamour faded, little for the mind to hold except an impression of this kinetic glamour.

There ensued a play, in which the present writer found the first act (as read) excellent and the rest as satire somehow stricken with palsy, granted the cleverness of the original idea. There ensued a magazine phase in which, as was perfectly natural, most of the stories were negligible, though a few showed flashes. But one could discern the demands of the "market" blunting and dulling the blade of that bright sword wildly whirled. One began to believe that Fitzgerald was coming into line with the purveyors of the staple product. And suddenly one wanted him back in the phase when he was writing so well and, at the same time, writing so very badly. Today he was writing, for the most part, on an even level of magazine acceptability, and on an even level of what seemed perilously like absolute staleness of mind toward anything really creative.

But "The Great Gatsby" comes suddenly to knock all that surmise into a cocked hat. "The Great Gatsby" reveals thoroughly matured craftsmanship. It has structure. It has high occasions of felicitous, almost magic, phrase. And most of all, it is out of the mirage. For the first time Fitzgerald surveys the Babylonian captivity of this era unblinded by the bright lights. He gives you the bright lights in full measure, the affluence, the waste, but also the nakedness of the scaffolding that scrawls skeletons upon the sky when the gold and blue and red and green have faded, the ugly passion, the spiritual meagreness, the empty shell of luxury, the old irony of "fair-weather friends."

Gatsby remains. The mystery of Gatsby is a mystery saliently characteristic of this age in America. And Gatsby is only another modern instance of the eternal "fortunate youth." His actual age does not matter, in either sense. For all the cleverness of his hinted nefarious proceedings, he is the coney caught. For he is a man with a dream at the mercy of the foul dust that sometimes seems only to exist in order to swarm against the dream, whose midge-dance blots it from the sky. It is a strange dream, Gatsby's—but he was a man who had hope. He was a child. He believed in a childish thing.

It is because Fitzgerald makes so acid on your tongue the taste of the defeat of Gatsby's childishness that his book, in our opinion, "acquires merit." And there are parts of the book, notably the second chapter, that, in our opinion, could not have been better written. There are astonishing feats that no one but Fitzgerald could have brought off, notably the catalogue of guests in Chapter IV. And Tom Buchanan, the "great hulking specimen," is an American university product of almost unbearable reality.

Yet one feels that, though irony has entered into Fitzgerald's soul, the sense of mere wonder is still stronger. And, of course, there is plenty of entertainment in the story. It arises in part from the almost photographic reproduction of the actions, gestures, speech of the types Fitzgerald has chosen in their moments of stress. Picayune[1] souls for the most part, and Gatsby heroic among them only because he is partly a crazy man with a dream. But what does all that matter with the actual narration so vivid and graphic? As for the drama of the accident and Gatsby's end, it is the kind of thing newspapers carry every day, except that here is a novelist who has gone behind the curt paragraphs and made the real people live and breathe in all their sordidness. They are actual, rich and poor, cultivated and uncultivated, seen for a moment or two only or followed throughout the story. They are memorable individuals of today—not types.

---

1 Small, of little worth.

Perhaps you have gathered that we like the book! We do. It has some miscues, but they seem to us negligible. It is written with concision and precision and mastery of material.

3. William Curtis, "Some Recent Books," *Town & Country* 81 (15 May 1925): 68

There has been a vast amount of fusfut over a stodgily inadequate play called "Processional,"[1] which claimed to interpret for an expectant public what some critic labeled the orgiastic danger of jazz. Beyond, however, some extraordinarily capable publicity work, this particular play failed to give local habitation to all those urges toward promiscuity, the loosening of the whole category of inhibitions, Freudian and economic, which this generation is pleased to associate with contemporary dance music. [...] The author of "Processional" is only one of a rather sizable group who have been trying to express the springtime restlessness of the human race, its half-believed disbelief in the moral conventions, which is as old as the Ohio mound dwellings and as new as Mr. Buckner's padlocks.[2] From where we sit, watching the swaying throng, it seems very much as if F. Scott Fitzgerald in "The Great Gatsby" [...] had succeeded rather startlingly in doing just this thing. This we state in spite of the fact that it seems rather an obvious thing to expect from Mr. Fitzgerald: his previous novels have all revolved around this motive, have been quite successful, and have failed only to be completely so because they were molded in too unsophisticated a form. [...]

It is one of the very special qualities of Mr. Fitzgerald's "The Great Gatsby" that, while proceeding in the calm manner of sophistication and taste, with no trace of the moral reformer or apologist, he has given us a picture which is, to us at least, as terrifying as any tragedy Aristotle[3] could have wished for. "The

---

1 1925 play by John Howard Lawson (1894-1977).
2 Probably a reference to the practice of padlocking the entrances to speakeasies—illegal saloons—authorized by Emory R. Buckner, US District Attorney of southern New York.
3 Aristotle (384-322 BCE), Greek philosopher, claimed that "pity and fear" were the emotions properly drawn out by tragedy, in his *Poetics* (ca. 330 BCE).

Great Gatsby" is an attempt to show the workings of an urge towards license upon the lower middle class and upon the very rich, taking those selected cross sections of each which have succumbed most completely. The unfortunate gentleman from whom the book takes its title is the descendant of starved farmers in the wheat-growing country of the Middle West, a man who, in the renascence, would have been a successful condottiere,[1] who, in the Long Island of today, however, was a meteor in the bootlegging world. He had lost all his inhibitions in his flight save his belief in the monogamous treatment of a "nice" woman. The other half of the tragedy, for a tragedy "The Great Gatsby" unmistakably is, is the nice young woman upon whom the adventurer's desires are focussed. She had married resplendently and, in the progress of her years, since she and the adventurer had touched orbits at a training camp, had lost all of her inhibitions save those dealing with the super-sacredness of Property and an Assured Income. When they finally met she is quite willing to become his mistress—and he wants a divorce and a scandal. This is to reduce "The Great Gatsby" to a few syllables, to the bare skeleton of the story, to the framework upon which is suspended a panorama of the wining and wenching and rhythmic movement, all of which today we call jazzing. The book succeeds most definitely in giving the sense of dissatisfaction with the majority code of conduct, the conventional method of ordering one's life; the continual excitation of all the senses, the ordinary interpretation of Pater's so often quoted and so dangerous gemlike flame theory,[2] that restlessness which we would so like to believe is our own discovery, is here, for the first time in our knowledge, satisfactorily crystallized inside the covers of one thoroughly praisable book. For in "The Great Gatsby" Mr. Fitzgerald passes from the able and conscientious school into the cool cloisters of the literary elect.

Professionally to us, it has always been a regret that we have not, in this generation, had writers of whom one could be really proud in intellectual groups which knew and admired the best contemporary British and Continental literary art—somebody

---

1 A mercenary or soldier of fortune.
2 Articulated by British philosopher and art historian Walter Pater (1839-94) in the Conclusion to *The Renaissance* (1873, 1893), a collection of essays on Renaissance art and poetry that influenced late-Victorian and high-modernist aestheticism: "To burn always with this hard, gem-like flame, to maintain this ecstasy, is success in life."

who did fine writing as distinguished from the "great," and dull, writing of the Victorian manner. We feel of "The Great Gatsby" that it can be put on the same book shelf with the best of London, Vienna, Paris, or Rome. And this is about as high a compliment as can be given any novel. When you get to a certain experience in reading, it is not so much what an author says as the way he says it that counts, the technic of his criticism upon his characters and, though them, upon life. Ever since Mr. Fitzgerald started in writing he has been saying practically what he has said in "The Great Gatsby." But meeting him again in this book is somewhat like realizing that a hopeful child has become adult. As an author Mr. Fitzgerald has ceased to chronicle events and has begun to marshal them in perspective and to give the comment upon them which, after all, are the only excuses for the existence of literature. Real life, raw, unassorted, kaleidoscopic, without meaning, is all about us. The justification of a novelist is to arrange these things into a pattern and to associate this pattern with the vast general background of conduct from the major stars of which we guide our existence. When somebody can do this in the manner not of a glorified newspaper reporter, nor of a pulpit orator, nor of a college professor, but of a thoroughly appreciative person of affairs, sympathetic in spite of sophistication, with the human touch in spite of technical writing ability far beyond average attainment, then the product has the claim to be called literature. There are two ways of achieving this: the patiently plodding, detail upon detail manner of Mr. Lewis [see p. 180, n. 2], the sort of thing one persists in reading through because of a shamed feeling that one should, or the flaming brilliancy of the specially gifted who, with almost flamboyant dexterity, sketch a situation in a series of singing sentences which one reads almost with a sense of elation, the elation with which one hears strongly emotional music or studies a perfectly poised painting. Whether or not "The Great Gatsby" has the popular sale of "The Beautiful and the Damned" [sic], it is a much abler, a much finer, a much more mature presentation of Mr. Fitzgerald's problem.

4. Carl Van Vechten, "Fitzgerald on the March," *The Nation* 120 (20 May 1925): 575-76

In "The Great Gatsby" there are several of Mr. Fitzgerald's typical flappers who behave in the manner he has conceived as typical of contemporary flapperdom. There is again a gargantuan drinking-party, conceived in a rowdy, hilarious, and highly titillating spirit. There is also, in this novel, as I have indicated above, something else. There is the character of Jay Gatsby.

This character, and the theme of the book in general, would have appealed to Henry James. In fact, it did appeal to Henry James. In one way or another this motif is woven into the tapestry of a score or more of his stories. In Daisy Miller you may find it complete.[1] It is the theme of a soiled or rather cheap personality transfigured and rendered pathetically appealing through the possession of a passionate idealism. Although the comparison may be still further stressed, owing to the fact that Mr. Fitzgerald has chosen, as James so frequently chose, to see his story through the eyes of a spectator, it will be readily apparent that what he has done he has done in his own way, and that seems to me, in this instance, to be a particularly good way. The figure of Jay Gatsby, who invented an entirely fictitious career for himself out of material derived from inferior romances, emerges life-sized and lifelike. His doglike fidelity not only to his ideal but to his fictions, his incredibly cheap and curiously imitative imagination, awakens for him not only our interest and suffrage, but also a certain liking, as they awaken it in the narrator, Nick Carraway.

When I read Absolution in the American Mercury I realized that there were many potential qualities inherent in Scott Fitzgerald which hitherto had not been too apparent. "The Great Gatsby" confirms this earlier impression. What Mr. Fitzgerald may do in the future, therefore, I am convinced, depends to an embarrassing extent on the nature of his own ambitions.

5. Gilbert Seldes, "Spring Flight," *The Dial* 79 (August 1925): 162-64

There has never been any question of the talents of F. Scott Fitzgerald; there has been, justifiably until the publication of The Great Gatsby, a grave question as to what he was going to do with his gifts. The question has been answered in one of the finest of contemporary novels. Fitzgerald has more than matured; he has mastered his talents and gone soaring in a beautiful flight, leaving behind him everything dubious and tricky in his earlier work, and

---

1   *Daisy Miller* (1878), Henry James' short novel about a young American woman traveling in Europe, all conveyed from the point-of-view of an admiring but cautious follower, Frederick Winterbourne.

leaving even farther behind all the men of his own generation and most of his elders.

In all justice, let it be said that the talents are still his. The book is even more interesting, superficially, than his others; it has an intense life, it must be read, the first time, breathlessly; it is vivid and glittering and entertaining. Scenes of incredible difficulty are rendered with what seems an effortless precision, crowds and conversation and action and retrospects—everything comes naturally and persuasively. The minor people and events are threads of colour and strength, holding the principal things together. The technical virtuosity is extraordinary.

All this was true of Fitzgerald's first two novels, and even of those deplorable short stories which one feared were going to ruin him. The Great Gatsby adds many things, and two above all: the novel is composed as an artistic structure, and it exposes, again for the first time, an interesting temperament. "The vast juvenile intrigue" of This Side of Paradise is just as good subject-matter as the intensely private intrigue of The Great Gatsby; but Fitzgerald racing over the country, jotting down whatever was current in college circles, is not nearly as significant as Fitzgerald regarding a tiny section of life and reporting it with irony and pity and a consuming passion. The Great Gatsby is passionate as Some Do Not[1] is passionate, with such an abundance of feeling for the characters (feeling their integral reality, not hating or loving them objectively) that the most trivial of the actors in the drama are endowed with vitality. The concentration of the book is so intense that the principal characters exist almost as essences, as biting acids that find themselves in the same golden cup and have no choice but to act upon each other. And the *milieux* which are brought into such violent contact with each other are as full of character, and as immitigably compelled to struggle and to debase one another.

The book is written as a series of scenes, the method which Fitzgerald derived from Henry James through Mrs. Wharton,[2] and these scenes are reported by a narrator who was obviously intended to be much more significant than he is. The author's

---

1   1924 novel by British novelist Ford Madox Ford (1873-1939), the first of his four-volume Tietjens series.
2   Edith Wharton (1862-1937), American novelist often regarded as a follower of her older friend Henry James because of her subject matter (the social world of the leisure class) and her careful management of scene, character development, and narrative point-of-view.

appetite for life is so violent that he found the personality of the narrator an obstacle, and simply ignored it once his actual people were in motion, but the narrator helps to give the feeling of an intense unit which the various characters around Gatsby form. Gatsby himself remains a mystery; you know him, but not by knowing about him, and even at the end you can guess, if you like, that he was a forger or a dealer in stolen bonds, or a rather mean type of bootlegger. He had dedicated himself to the accomplishment of a supreme object, to restore to himself an illusion he had lost; he set about it, in a pathetic American way, by becoming incredibly rich and spending his wealth in incredible ways, so that he might win back the girl he loved; and a "foul dust floated in the wake of his dreams." Adultery and drunkenness and thievery and murder make up this dust, but Gatsby's story remains poignant and beautiful.

This means that Fitzgerald has ceased to content himself with a satiric report on the outside of American life and has with considerable irony attacked the spirit underneath, and so has begun to report on life in its most general terms. His tactile apprehension remains so fine that his people and his settings are specifically of Long Island; but now he meditates upon their fate, and they become universal also. He has now something of extreme importance to say; and it is good fortune for us that he knows how to say it.

The scenes are austere in their composition. There is one, the tawdry afternoon of the satyr, Tom Buchanan, and his cheap and "vital" mistress, which is alive by the strength of the lapses of time; another, the meeting between Gatsby and his love, takes place literally behind closed doors, the narrator telling us only the beginning and the end. The variety of treatment, the intermingling of dialogue and narrative, the use of a snatch of significant detail instead of a big scene, make the whole a superb impressionistic painting, vivid in colour, and sparkling with meaning. And the major composition is as just as the treatment of detail. There is a brief curve before Gatsby himself enters; a longer one in which he begins his movement toward Daisy; then a succession of carefully spaced shorter and longer movements until the climax is reached. The plot works out not like a puzzle with odd bits falling into place, but like a tragedy, with every part functioning in the completed organism.

Even now, with The Great Gatsby before me, I cannot find in the earlier Fitzgerald the artistic integrity and the passionate feeling which this book possesses. And perhaps analysing the one and praising the other, both fail to convey the sense of elation which one has in reading his new novel. Would it be better to say that even The Great Gatsby is full of faults, and that that doesn't matter in the slightest degree? The cadences borrowed from Conrad, the occasional smartness, the frequently startling, but ineffective adjective—at last they do not signify. Because for the most part you know that Fitzgerald has consciously put these bad and half-bad things behind him, that he trusts them no more to make him the white-headed boy of The Saturday Evening Post, and that he has recognized both his capacities and his obligations as a novelist.

Appendix C: Consumption, Class, and Selfhood: Eight Contemporary Advertisements

["You resemble the advertisement of the man," Daisy tells Gatsby just before their fatal trip to the city in Chapter VII—an endearing observation that uncannily exposes something fundamental about his character. Gatsby is a walking advertisement for the full-blown consumer culture that became permanently established by the 1920s, for he is a model consumer, spending money to transform himself into an ideal shaped by the advertising industry. Like his counterpart Myrtle Wilson, he believes what the ads encourage him to believe: i.e., that class can be bought, that through careful imitation of models one can become (paradoxically) one's "real," classier self. Fitzgerald filled his novel with references to commodity culture and may even be deliberately echoing the language of advertising in some of the novel's memorable passages, as when Daisy goes through Gatsby's shirts (Chapter V), or when Nick describes Gatsby's enchanting impressions of Daisy's Louisville home (Chapter VIII). What follows are eight advertisements culled from 1922 issues of *Vanity Fair* and *Town & Country*, two magazines epitomizing urbane sophistication and moneyed leisure: an Arrow Collar ad featuring "the man" Daisy may have had in mind; a perfume ad graced with the image of the fashionable young American *femme du monde*; a Stutz car ad unabashedly promoting its product as a sign of wealth and success; a negligee ad flaunting the ever-widening array of colors consumers were becoming accustomed to; an ad for a cosmetic treatment designed to revive one's youth; an ad for instant "culture" in the form of Harvard president Charles Eliot's "Five-Foot Shelf of Books"; an ad for period furniture to fill American houses built in imitation of European period-architecture; and an ad for the fashionable sports car after which Fitzgerald may have named one of his characters.]

"Always favored above all other [sic] by French ladies of fashion and by most Americans who visit Paris—the choice, now, of the ultra discerning in this country."

MAKE THIS YOUR PERSONAL CAR

THE H.C.S. is owned and liked by men who have long since passed the Dollar Sign on the road to achievement.

$2400
AT INDIANAPOLIS

H.C.S. MOTOR CAR COMPANY

H. C. S.

DESIGNED BY HARRY C. STUTZ

Three Maytime Creations for Madame and Mademoiselle

DREAM-LIGHT NEGLIGEES

For The Morning Hours And Intimate Tea-Time

Model 2.—TEA GOWN OF CRÊPE CHIFFON, very artistic in color effect. Three layers of chiffon one over-laying the other and each a different color; light blue, French blue, orchid, coral, black, sherry or purple predominating. Flowing sleeves. . . 39.50

Model 4.—TEA GOWN OF CRÊPE SATIN, copy of French model. Long sleeves of crêpe chiffon bound in satin. Girdle of satin roses. In fuchsia, French blue, light blue, pink or black. 27.50

Model 6.—BOUDOIR COAT OF SILK CRÊPE DE CHINE in peach, light blue, orchid, rose or turquoise. Entirely trimmed with gracious ruffles of Margot lace 18.50

NEGLIGEE SHOP—*First Floor*

Franklin Simon & Co.

Fifth Avenue, 37th and 38th Streets, New York

Like a Wizard of the Ages—

MADAME LECLAIRE

Imparts the Secrets of the Mystical Fountain of Youth

The season is over but a summer season is about to begin.

You were beautiful when you made your first bow to society and now it frightens you to look back—it seems so many years ago.

If the beauty of yesterday could remain a beauty she would be without rival owing to a store of rich experiences. She would know how to direct her beauty. If you have been a beautiful woman and have watched your reflection in the mirror of the day gradually fade and wither, do not despair. I can make beauty blossom again. There are many so called Beauty doctors and Beauty parlours who play with cosmetics as children play with shadows. These are not for the thinking woman. There is

ARE YOU TIRED OF YOUR TIRED FACE?

a science of Beauty she must learn and I know some of its secrets. I can make any woman look as she would look in her cherished dreams. The charm of youth is the most desired thing in the universe when one has lost it. There is an early period when we do not think of it—and then there comes a period when we never cease to think of it. The streets are full of dead faces and half dead faces. No one looks at them a second time. When you gaze in your glass at the first crowfeet, the sagging throat, the hair with no lustre, the lips with no smile, do not make the hopeless mistake of endeavouring to cover age with cosmetics. Get back to a rebirth. Recreate the thing you sigh for. I can lead you to the Fountain of Youth.

MADAME LECLAIRE

14 East Fifty-Sixth Street   New York City

Note: Mrs. LeClaire begs you to realize that these are exceedingly serious invitations of her emotions. We can be deceived.

"I can make beauty blossom again.... The charm of youth is the most desired thing in the universe when one has lost it. There is an early period when we do not think of it—and then there comes a period when we never cease to think of it. The streets are full of dead faces and half dead faces.... Get back to a rebirth. Recreate the thing you sigh for. I can lead you to the Fountain of Youth."

"How can you gain, in just a few delightful minutes' reading each day, that knowledge of a few truly great books which will distinguish you always as a well-read man or woman?... The booklet tells about it— how Dr. Eliot has put into his Five-Foot Shelf 'the books essential to the Twentieth-Century idea of a cultivated person' [...]"

THE JORDAN BLUE BOY IN BLUE DEVIL BLUE

Built for those happy people who bought a Jordan Playboy
for their honeymoon, but now want a little more room for
the friends they take for an afternoon of golf.

The wheelbase has been lengthened for lowness. Cushions
hug the floor. The top fits like a swanky sport hat—and
all is slender—'cept the tires—they are fat.

JORDAN

"Built for those happy people who bought a Jordan Playboy for their honeymoon, but now want a little more room for the friends they take for an afternoon of golf."

Appendix D: The Irreverent Spirit of the Jazz Age

[Though published half-way through the decade we think of as "the Jazz Age," *The Great Gatsby* already views the period retrospectively. Indeed, it anticipates Fitzgerald's more justifiably retrospective description in his 1931 essay "Echoes of the Jazz Age," where 1922 is offered as the turning point of the decade, the year in which the Jazz Age "became less and less an affair of youth," and hence potentially tragic. The selections below strike a balance between conveying the rebellious spirit of the moment—as in Duncan Poole's *Vanity Fair* satire from the summer of 1922 or H.L. Mencken's typically contemptuous attack on Prohibition—and assessing it more objectively, if still sympathetically. (Even as Mencken derides Prohibition, he recognizes the widespread alcoholism it is causing.) The selections are headed by a substantial excerpt from Fitzgerald's impressionistic overview of the twenties, written after the stock market crash of 1929 and his wife's mental breakdown, and thus as pertinent to an appreciation of *Tender is the Night* as *The Great Gatsby*. They culminate in selections from Walter Lippmann's 1929 book *A Preface to Morals*, specifically its opening chapter on "The Problem of Unbelief." Not being identified with the post-war generation, Lippmann recognized the spiritual hazards of a rebelliousness that had no positive object to it, just as Fitzgerald arguably had in his novel. Zelda Fitzgerald's 1925 essay "What Became of the Flappers?" has been included here over her 1922 "Eulogy on the Flapper" (in the June issue of *Metropolitan*) because it tallies better with the novel's depiction of Daisy Buchanan as the flapper grown older and domesticated, and expresses in striking terms the conservative freedom claimed by the post-war emblem of sexual licentiousness.]

1. From F. Scott Fitzgerald, "Echoes of the Jazz Age," *Scribner's Magazine* 90 (November 1931): 460-62

It was an age of miracles, it was an age of art, it was an age of excess, and it was an age of satire. A Stuffed Shirt, squirming to blackmail in a lifelike way, sat upon the throne of the United

States;[1] a stylish young man hurried over to represent to us the throne of England.[2] A world of girls yearned for the young Englishman; the old American groaned in his sleep as he waited to be poisoned by his wife, upon the advice of the female Rasputin who then made the ultimate decision in our national affairs.[3] But such matters apart, we had things our way at last. With Americans ordering suits by the gross in London, the Bond Street tailors perforce agreed to moderate their cut to the American long-waisted figure and loose-fitting taste, something subtle passed to America, the style of man. During the Renaissance, Francis the First[4] looked to Florence to trim his leg. Seventeenth-century England aped the court of France, and fifty years ago the German Guards officer bought his civilian clothes in London. Gentleman's clothes—symbol of "the power that man must hold and that passes from race to race."

We were the most powerful nation. Who could tell us any longer what was fashionable and what was fun? Isolated during the European War, we had begun combing the unknown South and West for folkways and pastimes and there were more ready to hand.

The first social revelation created a sensation out of all proportion to its novelty. As far back as 1915 the unchaperoned young people of the smaller cities had discovered the mobile privacy of that automobile given to young Bill at sixteen to make him "self-reliant." At first petting was a desperate adventure even under such favorable conditions, but presently confidences were exchanged and the old commandment broke down. As early as 1917 there were references to such sweet and casual dalliance in any number of the *Yale Record* or the *Princeton Tiger*.

---

1 Warren Harding (1865-1923) became President in 1921, and died in office from what was widely assumed to be food poisoning.
2 Edward, Prince of Wales (1894-1972), who became Edward VIII in 1936 before abdicating so as to marry his mistress Wallis Simpson.
3 The "female Rasputin" probably refers to Nan Britton (1896-1991), who claimed to be Harding's mistress, confidante, and mother of his illegitimate child in a 1927 tell-all memoir, *The President's Daughter*; the lingering consequences of Harding's corrupt administration helped lend popular credence to her story. Fitzgerald's allusion links her to Grigori Rasputin (1871-1916), the notorious monk who had undue influence over Tsarina Alexandra before the Romanov dynasty fell during the Russian Revolution.
4 King of France from 1515 to 1547.

But petting in its more audacious manifestations was confined to the wealthier classes—among other young people the old standards prevailed until after the War, and a kiss meant that a proposal was expected, as young officers in strange cities sometimes discovered to their dismay. Only in 1920 did the veil finally fall— the Jazz Age was in flower.

Scarcely had the staider citizens of the republic caught their breaths when the wildest of all generations, the generation which had been adolescent during the confusion of the War, brusquely shouldered my contemporaries out of the way and danced into the limelight. This was the generation whose girls dramatized themselves as flappers, the generation that corrupted its elders and eventually overreached itself less through lack of morals than through lack of taste. May one offer in exhibit the year 1922! That was the peak of the younger generation, for though the Jazz Age continued, it became less and less an affair of youth.

The sequel was like a children's party taken over by the elders, leaving the children puzzled and rather neglected and rather taken aback. By 1923 their elders, tired of watching the carnival and with ill-concealed envy, had discovered that young liquor will take the place of young blood, and with a whoop the orgy began. The younger generation was starred no longer.

A whole race going hedonistic, deciding on pleasure. The precocious intimacies of the younger generation would have come about with or without prohibition—they were implicit in the attempt to adapt English customs to American conditions. (Our South, for example, is tropical and early maturing—it has never been part of the wisdom of France and Spain to let young girls go unchaperoned at sixteen and seventeen.) But the general decision to be amused that began with the cocktail parties of 1921 had more complicated origins.

The word jazz in its progress toward respectability has meant first sex, then dancing, then music. It is associated with a state of nervous stimulation, not unlike that of big cities behind the lines of a war. To many English the War still goes on because all the forces that menace them are still active—Wherefore eat, drink and be merry, for to-morrow we die. But different causes had now brought about a corresponding state in America—though there were entire classes (people over fifty, for example) who spent a whole decade denying its existence even when its puckish face peered into the family circle. Never did they dream that they had contributed to it. The honest citizens of every class, who believed in a strict public morality and were powerful enough to enforce the necessary legislation, did not know that they would necessarily be served by criminals and quacks, and do not really believe it to-day. Rich righteousness had always been able to buy honest and intelligent servants to free the slaves or the Cubans, so when this attempt collapsed our elders stood firm with all the stubbornness of people involved in a weak case, preserving their righteousness and losing their children. Silver-haired women and men with fine old faces, people who never did a consciously dishonest thing in their lives, still assure each other in the apartment hotels of New York and Boston and Washington that "there's a whole generation growing up that will never know the taste of liquor." Meanwhile their granddaughters pass the well-thumbed copy of "Lady Chatterley's Lover"[1] around the boarding-school and, if they get about at all, know the taste of gin and corn at sixteen. But the generation who reached maturity between 1875 and 1895 continue to believe what they want to believe.

Even the intervening generations were incredulous. In 1920 Heywood Broun[2] announced that all this hubbub was nonsense, that young men didn't kiss but told anyhow. But very shortly people over twenty-five came in for an intensive education. Let me trace some of the revelations vouchsafed them by reference to a dozen works written for various types of mentality during the decade. We begin with the suggestion that Don Juan leads an interesting life ("Jurgen," 1919); then we learn that there's a lot of sex around if we only knew it ("Winesburg, Ohio," 1920), that adolescents lead very amorous lives ("This Side of Paradise," 1920), that there are a lot of neglected Anglo-Saxon words ("Ulysses," 1922), that older people don't always resist sudden temptations ("Cytherea," 1922), that girls are sometimes seduced without being ruined ("Flaming Youth," 1922), that even rape often turns out well ("The Sheik," 1922), that glamorous English ladies are often promiscuous ("The Green Hat,"

---

1 Notorious 1928 novel about a wealthy Englishwoman's affair with a gamekeeper by British novelist D.H. Lawrence (1885-1930). Its explicit sexual subject-matter and language kept it an underground classic until obscenity trials between 1959 and 1962 cleared the way for its publication and sale in the United States, Great Britain, and Canada. Fitzgerald's mis-spelling "Chatterly's" is corrected here and elsewhere in the essay.

2 Heywood Broun (1888-1939), American critic and journalist.

1924), that in fact they devote most of their time to it ("The Vortex," 1926), that it's a damn good thing too ("Lady Chatterley's Lover," 1928), and finally that there are abnormal variations ("The Well of Loneliness," 1928, and "Sodome and Gomorrhe," 1929).[1]

In my opinion the erotic element in these works, even "The Sheik" written for children in the key of "Peter Rabbit,"[2] did not one particle of harm. Everything they described, and much more, was familiar in our contemporary life. The majority of the theses were honest and elucidating—their effect was to restore some dignity to the male as opposed to the he-man in American life. ("And what is a 'He-man'? demanded Gertrude Stein[3] one day. 'Isn't it a large enough order to fill out the dimensions of all that 'a man' has meant in the past? A 'He-man'!") The married woman can now discover whether she is being cheated, or whether sex is just something to be endured, and her compensation should be to establish a tyranny of the spirit, as her mother may have hinted. Perhaps many women found that love was meant to be fun. Anyhow the objectors lost their tawdry little case, which is one reason why our literature is now the most living in the world.

---

1   *Jurgen* (1919), by American novelist James Branch Cabell (1879-1958); *Winesburg, Ohio* (1919), interrelated short-story sequence by American writer Sherwood Anderson (1876-1941); *This Side of Paradise* (1920), Fitzgerald's own first novel; *Ulysses* (1922), by Irish novelist James Joyce (1882-1941); *Cytherea* (1922), see p. 193, n. 3, *Flaming Youth* (1923) by American writer Warner Fabian (pen name of Samuel Hopkins Adams [1871-1958]); *The Sheik* (1919 in Great Britain; 1921 in the United States), best-selling novel by British novelist E.M. Hull (pen name of Edith Maude Winstanley), the basis for the popular 1921 movie starring Rudolph Valentino; *The Green Hat* (1924), by British novelist Michael Arlen (1895-1956); *The Vortex* (1925; opened 1924), play by British playwright Noel Coward (1899-1973); *The Well of Loneliness* (1928), pioneering novel about lesbianism by British writer Radclyffe Hall (1880-1943); *Sodome [et] Gomorrhe* (1922), fourth volume of French writer Marcel Proust's masterpiece *A La Recherche du Temps Perdu* (which began appearing in C.K. Scott Moncrieff's English translation as *Remembrance of Things Past* in 1924).

2   1902 children's tale by English writer Beatrix Potter (1866-1943).

3   Gertrude Stein (1874-1946), American avant-garde writer whose home in Paris was frequented by an international array of artists, writers, and admirers.

Contrary to popular opinion the movies of the Jazz Age had no effect upon its morals. The social attitude of the producers was timid, behind the times and banal—for example no picture mirrored even faintly the younger generation until 1923, when magazines had already been started to celebrate it and it had long ceased to be news. There were a few feeble splutters and then Clara Bow in "Flaming Youth";[1] promptly the Hollywood hacks ran the theme into its cinematographic grave. Throughout the Jazz Age the movies got no farther than Mrs. Jiggs,[2] keeping up with its most blatant superficialities. This was no doubt due to the censorship as well as to innate conditions in the industry. In any case the Jazz Age now raced along under its own power, served by great filling stations full of money.

2. Duncan M. Poole, "The Great Jazz Trial: With a Few Illuminating Remarks on the Way of Reformers in General," *Vanity Fair* 18 (June 1922): 61, 108

Verily, the way of the Reformer is hard. Perhaps he likes it that way, but it has always seemed to me rather tough. It isn't as if he were always forging upstream, going contrary to the current so to speak, or always beating to windward. In both of these, some progress may be noted, some head-way made, and they are thrilling and exciting. But the Reformer's lot is much worse than that. His results appear so illusory, so evanescent. He no sooner gets some particular social evil all nice and reformed, than another breaks out to take its place. It is as though Public Morality were a large squashy hot-water bottle, partially filled. You know how the pesky things act. If you punch them in one place they bulge out in another. So it is with reforming.

Looking back over comparatively recent years, we can recall a sequence of popular vices which one by one have been attacked, suppressed and perhaps partially cured. Racing, gambling, prize-

---

1   Clara Bow (1906-65), one of the leading actresses of the silver screen in the twenties. Fitzgerald's memory is at fault here: Colleen Moore (1900-88), not Clara Bow, was the star of the 1923 movie version of Warner Fabian's sensational novel.

2   Socially aspiring Irish-American wife in the syndicated comic strip *Bringing Up Father*, created in 1913 by George McManus (1884-1954).

fighting, drugs, drinking and the most ancient and permanent forms of immorality have all come in for their share of attention. And the latest target for the Reformer's guns is Jazz.

Jazz is not defined in my Webster's Collegiate. It probably will be in the next edition. The nearest thing I find to it under the J's is "jig,"—a brisk dance movement in a rhythm of triplets. 2. A piece of sport, a prank. 3. A kind of trolling bait. 4. An apparatus for separating impurities by agitation.

It is quite remarkable how many of these definitions fit Jazz as we know it today. It is certainly a brisk dance movement and a piece of sport or prank. "A kind of trolling bait" is not so obvious, though it might apply. Whether "an apparatus for separating impurities by agitation" applies as a description depends entirely on how you look at it. The real dyed-in-the-wool Reformer holds that Jazz, far from separating impurities brings them together, and by this same method of agitation. Its defenders say that, on the contrary, it works just exactly as Mr. Webster says, that it is a perfectly grand thing, and by its festive agitation frees all sorts of repressed emotions that would otherwise find their outlet in horrid Sunday-School and church-choir scandals. Oh, you must not suppose for an instant that this great modern dance movement is without its champions!

Let us look for a moment at the forces arrayed against each other. Let us try to stage a trial scene, and let the prisoner, Jazz, be summoned to the Bar where the witnesses, pro and con, shall be heard. As usual in such cases, we will allow the plaintiff to prefer his charges first and introduce his testimony. Jazz, whom I visualize in my poetic way, as a very attractive young lady in a sketchy evening gown, is brought before Judge Morrill by Police-Matron Grundy, a veritable wizardess in arresting, on suspicion, all doubtful characters. The charge is formidable and impressive.

"This creature," says Officer Grundy, "is one of the most dangerous criminals at large. Her character is a compound of all the vices of the age. By her example the Youth of America is becoming degenerate and debauched. She has flagrantly paraded her vicious example before the innocent people who frequent our restaurants, cabarets and theatrical performances. The purity of our New York audiences is becoming seriously undermined. We demand that she be put away for an indefinite period. We recommend a year in a Dancing Reform-School where the regulation garb is a heavy wool waist and skirt extending to the ankles. It is evident that this——"

"Kindly do not plead the case," says Judge Morrill, "call your witnesses."

The Rev. John R. Straightjacket is called and duly sworn. Dr. Straightjacket is a vice-expert, and qualifies as such by relating in great detail his past experiences in a vast number of dens, dives, and—as he adds—worse. He is very much at home in the witness chair, which seems to fit his bulging form as if made for it.

"Let us start with a basic problem," he announces in a voice which swings the court-room chandeliers with its resonance. "All pleasure is dangerous. It has a corrupting influence. Whenever pleasure steals in, the moral censor sneaks out the back door. Enjoyment encourages iniquity. This is particularly true of dancing, which is the invention of the devil. In ancient times this was not so. Dancing was an individual exercise, a spiritual expression. David danced before Solomon."

"Oh, you Salome" (from the rear of the court-room).

Judge M.: "Order in the court. Proceed."

"But this Jazz, this wanton exhibition of lewdness which brings bodies of opposite sex into a juxtaposition which—"

Judge Morrill here requests Dr. Straightjacket to submit the rest of his testimony in the form of a brief, adding "and make it as brief as possible." The next witness is called.

This is the Rabbi Steven S. Stone of the Sho Maholem Synagogue, who repeats in substance the remarks of Dr. Straightjacket. He is, however, a much more snappy witness. His testimony is epigrammatic and pungent; he does not chin himself on his own rhetoric as does his Christian Brother. But he too is an expert. He refers to the age as "jassastrophic" and gets a good laugh from the jury. He speaks of the "mad hunger for a good time, a hunger which enables men and women to atrophy their senses through super-stimulation."

"Do you think Jazz is corrupting the stage?" he is asked.

"No. The stage is incorruptible. Most of my friends are theatrical managers and I can say——"

"You are a liar," shouts Dr. Straightjacket. "The stage is a hotbed of vice. I challenge you now to a debate on the platform of my church."

"Schlemiel!" screams the Rabbi, "Meet me at the synagogue!"

Both witnesses are forcibly removed and the sounds of a fierce conflict are borne in from the corridors.

Next we hear from a celebrated playwright who has written a play of which he reads the first act, showing clearly that Jazz not only destroys the home but that its horrid example is corrupting the honest labouring man of the country. It appears that the caddies at the country-club see these shocking performances going on and tell their fathers about it and thus the poison seeps into the veins of the industrial world until the first thing we know we have an enormous general strike on our hands! It is quite terrifying.

Homer Flitts, Jazz editor of the *Gotham Gazette,* says he was horrified when he saw nice people become wild and woolly under the influence of Jazz rendered by human gorillas who moaned and groaned over their musical instruments, and Professor Tasmalia, student of Infant Education paints a shocking picture of immorality in the nurseries and kindergartens introduced by Jazz records artfully included in the latest Bubble Books.[1]

Well, it looks very dark and gloomy for Jazz. She hangs her head and weeps a little. The jury is silent, impressed. But wait!

The young attorney for the defense is about to speak. He is a pleasant looking young chap and he carries a ukelele on a ribbon around his neck, upon which he occasionally plays a few chords in harmony with his musical voice.

"Your Honour," he chants, "ladies and gentlemen of the Jury, and (bowing to Jazz) Guest of Honour."

This graceful tribute brings a ripple of applause from the benches.

"Your Honour, we have listened patiently to a long line of testimony from a number of gentlemen who claim to be experts. It is customary, I believe, to be allowed to cast, if possible, some doubt on the reliability of such testimony and upon the character of such witnesses. As to its expertness, I can only point out that it is obviously true that none of these gentlemen has ever practised the vices which they so outrageously attack. They have not led the wanton and vicious life which they attribute to my client, the defendant, and they would be the first to agree with me in

---

1   Children's series of books with accompanying records published by
    Harper Columbia between 1917 and 1922.

this. But it is a curious fact that all Vice-Experts are invariably people who have made virtue their only pursuit. I, therefore, ask you, Your Honour, to dismiss the charges on the ground that they are supported by testimony [un?] worthy of belief, and I so move."

Judge Morrill hesitated but finally decided that it would hardly be proper not to hear a few witnesses.

"Very well then," continued the young barrister, "I will produce them and gladly. We have our experts, and real experts, too. Will Miss Zambino kindly take the stand."

An exquisite creature clad in a long cloak advanced to the rail: Standing composedly she faced the jury-box and said in a clear voice:

"Ladies and gentlemen, I have jazzed both in public and private ever since the craze started. It is now waning; other forms of dancing are taking its place, but I can assure you that I have never found in it anything but a helpful form of exercise, a physical and mental relaxation. I wish I could indicate more clearly how beneficial this may be, but without a partner ... Ah, how do you do! ... we met at Montmartre,[1] did we not?"

One of the younger jurors had leaped out of the pen. As he did so Miss Zambino dropped her long cloak disclosing the bare neck and shoulders of evening attire; an instant later, to the soft rhythm of the lawyer's ukelele they were jazzing daintily in the small inclosure before the bench.

"I object," shrieked Matron Grundy. "She is influencing the Juror."

"Objection sustained," said His Honour, with a sigh of disappointment.

The defense witnesses were called in in quick succession and an imposing array they were, a Health Commissioner, a noted Physician, a Psychologist, a Banker, one and all agreeing that Jazz was a delightful, harmless creature, and that they were united in their support of anything that made for human happiness. The jury was immensely bucked up. Even Judge Morrill looked happy when he charged them.

"Ladies and Gentlemen, you will now consider the evidence as presented to you. You have heard the charges and the evidence. It is for you to decide. You will now go out,—and don't come back."

The Jury are still out!

---

1 Section of Paris popular with artists, writers, and musicians, and known at the time for its bars and sexual promiscuity.

This is the great trial of Jazz. She is still at large, losing to be sure, a certain amount of her popularity, as is inevitable, but still found in certain localities. If she disappears entirely the Reformers will say they have killed her or driven her away.

But will they be down-hearted?

Never. For, as I said, when one reform is apparently accomplished another will surely spring up to take its place. Already we have those dreadful moving picture affairs!

But an even worse thing is going on. The young girls and children of our schools are going about with their goloshes all unbuttoned, actually flapping in the breeze! This is leading to all sorts of evils. The world is sure to go to hell as rapidly as progress—in goloshes—can be made.

3. From H.L. Mencken, ["Five Years of Prohibition"], Editorial, *American Mercury* 3 (December 1924): 420–22

Five years of Prohibition have had, at least, this one benign effect: they have completely disposed of all the favorite arguments of the Prohibitionists. None of the great boons and usufructs that were to follow the passage of the Eighteenth Amendment has come to pass. There is not less drunkenness in the Republic, but more. There is not less crime, but more. There is not less insanity, but more. The cost of government is not smaller, but vastly greater. Respect for law has not increased, but diminished. Even the benefits that were to come from the abolition of the open saloon, long damned as a constant temptation to the young, are not visible. On the contrary, the young are now tempted as the saloon, even in its most romantic and voluptuous forms, never tempted them. We were, in 1920, a nation of mild drinkers, moving steadily and certainly toward greater and greater temperance. Business and the professions had cast off strong drink; boozy lawyers and doctors were disappearing; the very drummers were practicing their science cold sober. Few American women drank at all; among the young the vine was almost as much a stranger as the poppy. Now all those gains are lost. The absolute number of users of alcohol has at least doubled, and few of the recruits show any sign of using it with discretion. [...] One or two cocktails, in the old days of freedom, made the average American dinner party, at least outside Manhattan Island, somewhat devilish. Today the dose is as much as the liver and lights will bear.

The Methodists who gave us Prohibition hate their fellow-men, but they are not altogether asses. The facts so brilliantly displayed on all sides are not lost upon them. Hence they quietly shelve their old arguments. One no longer hears from them—save perhaps when they address remote yokels, far from all reach of sense—that Prohibition has obliterated or will presently obliterate crime, or that it is abolishing poverty and disease, or even, indeed, that it actually prohibits. What one hears is simply the doctrine that it must be enforced because it is the law.

***

Meanwhile, the city man himself gets used to law-breaking, and all his old instinctive antipathy to it tends to disappear. [...] It is practically impossible, in any big town, to find a man above the level of a Methodist who does not violate the Volstead Act[1] deliberately and habitually. There may be pious minorities in back streets who obey it, but there is certainly no show of respect for it where collars are clean and there is regard for the tense of verbs.

So the matter stands after five years of relentless dragooning and blackjacking. The Bill of Rights has been suspended, the Federal courts have been reduced to impotence and absurdity, the enforcement of the ordinary laws has been impeded, the jails have been filled with men full of resentment and a bitter sense of injustice, millions and millions of the taxpayers' money has been wasted, the few remaining half-decent politicians have been converted into frauds and liars, a horde of professional thugs and blackmailers has been turned loose upon the country, and at least two-thirds of its adult citizens, not to mention millions of its younger ones, have been inoculated with the notion that breaking the law, and even violating the Constitution, is, after all, no serious thing, but simply a necessary incident of a civilized social life.

4. From Zelda Fitzgerald, "What Became of the Flappers?" *McCall's* 53 (October 1925): 12, 30, 66

Flapper wasn't a particularly fortunate cognomen. It is far too reminiscent of open galoshes and covered up ears and all other proverbial flapper paraphernalia, which might have passed unno-

---

1 Statute for enforcing Prohibition.

ticed save for the name. All these things are—or were—amusing externals of a large class of females who in no way deserve the distinction of being called flappers. The flappers that I am writing this article about are a very different and intriguing lot of young people who are perhaps unstable, but who are giving us the first evidence of youth asserting itself out of the cradle. They are not originating new ideas or new customs or new moral standards. They are simply endowing the old ones that we are used to with a vitality that we are not used to. We are not accustomed to having *our* daughters think our ideas for themselves, and it is distasteful to some of us that we are no longer able to fit the younger generation into our conceptions of what the younger generation was going to be like when we watched it in the nursery. I do not think that anything my daughter could possibly do eighteen years from now would surprise me. And yet I will probably be forbidding her in frigid tones to fly more than 3,000 feet high or more than five hundred miles an hour with little Willie Jones, and bidding her never to go near that horrible Mars. I can imagine these things now, but if they should happen twenty years from now, I would certainly wonder what particular dog my child was going to....

The flapper springs full-grown, like Minerva, from the head of her once déclassé father, Jazz, upon whom she lavishes affection and reverence, and deepest filial regard.[1] She is not a "condition arisen from war unrest," as I have so often read in the shower of recent praise and protest which she has evoked, and to which I am contributing. She is a direct result of the greater appreciation of beauty, youth, gaiety and grace which is sweeping along in a carmagnole (I saw one in a movie once, and I use this word advisedly)[2] with our young anti-puritans at the head. They have placed such a premium on the flapper creed—to give and get amusement—that even the dumb-bells become Dulcies[3] and convert stupidity into charm. Dulcy is infinitely preferable to the kind of girl who, ten years ago, quoted the Rubaiyat[4] at you and told you

---

1   Minerva (or Athene in Greek), the goddess of Wisdom, was born from the head of her father Jupiter (or Zeus).
2   As used here, a procession of dancers singing one of the favorite republican songs of the French Revolution.
3   Generic name for a dim-witted woman, after the heroine of Marc Connelly and George S. Kaufman's popular 1921 play *Dulcy*.
4   *The Rubáiyát of Omar Khayyám* (1859), twelfth-century Persian poem freely translated into English by Edward Fitzgerald (1809-83). The poem's religious scepticism and seize-the-day motif would have appealed to rebellious youth.

how misunderstood she was; or the kind who straightened your tie as evidence that in her lay the spirit of the eternal mother; or the kind who spent long summer evenings telling you that it wasn't the *number* of cigarettes you smoked that she minded but just the *principle*, to show off her nobility of character. These are some of the bores of yesterday. Now even bores must be original, so the more unfortunate members of the flapper sect have each culled an individual line from their daily rounds, which amuses or not according to whether you have seen the same plays, heard the same tunes or read reviews of the same books.

The best flapper is reticent emotionally and courageous morally. You always know what she thinks, but she does all her feeling alone. These are two characteristics which will bring social intercourse to a more charming and sophisticated level. I believe in the flapper as an artist in her particular field, the art of being—being young, being lovely, being an object.

For almost the first time we are developing a class of pretty yet respectable young women, whose sole functions are to amuse and to make growing old a more enjoyable process for some men and staying young an easier one for others.

Even parents have ceased to look upon their children as permanent institutions. The fashionable mother no longer keeps her children young so that she will preserve the appearance of a débutante. She helps them to mature so that she will be mistaken for a step-mother. Once her girls are old enough to be out of finishing-school a period of freedom and social activity sets in for her. The daughters are rushed home to make a chaotic début and embark upon a feverish chase for a husband. It is no longer permissible to be single at twenty-five. The flapper makes haste to marry lest she be a left-over and be forced to annex herself to the crowd just younger. She hasn't time to ascertain the degree of compatibility between herself and her fiancé before the wedding, so she ascertains that they will be separated if the compatibility should be mutually rated zero after it.

The flapper! She is growing old. She forgets her flapper creed and is conscious only of her flapper self. She is married 'mid loud acclamation on the part of relatives and friends. She has come to none of the predicted "bad ends," but has gone at last, where all good flappers go—into the young married set, into boredom and gathering conventions and the pleasure of having children, having lent a while a splendour and courageousness and brightness to life, as all good flappers should.

5. From Walter Lippmann, *A Preface to Morals* (New York: Macmillan, 1929), 6, 12, 14-18 ["The Problem of Unbelief"]

We are living in the midst of that vast dissolution of ancient habits which the emancipators believed would restore our birthright of happiness. We know now that they did not see very clearly beyond the evils against which they were rebelling. It is evident to us that their prophecies were pleasant fantasies which concealed the greater difficulties that confront men, when having won the freedom to do what they wish—that wish, as Byron said:

> which ages have not yet subdued
> In man—to have no master save his mood,[1]

they are full of contrary moods and do not know what they wish to do. We have come to see that Huxley[2] was right when he said that "a man's worst difficulties begin when he is able to do as he likes."

The evidences of these greater difficulties lie all about us: in the brave and brilliant atheists who have defied the Methodist God, and have become very nervous; in the women who have emancipated themselves from the tyranny of fathers, husbands, and homes, and with the intermittent but expensive help of a psychoanalyst, are now enduring liberty as interior decorators; in the young men and women who are world-weary at twenty-two; in the multitudes who drug themselves with pleasure; in the crowds enfranchised by the blood of heroes who cannot be persuaded to take an interest in their destiny; in the millions, at last free to think without fear of priest or policeman, who have made the moving pictures and the popular newspapers what they are.

These are the prisoners who have been released. They ought to be very happy. They ought to be serene and composed. They are free to make their own lives. There are no conventions, no tabus, no gods, priests, princes, fathers, or revelations which they must accept. Yet the result is not so good as they thought it would be. The prison door is wide open. They stagger out into trackless space under a blinding sun. They find it nerve-wracking.

---

1 From *The Island* (1823) by British Romantic poet George Gordon, Lord Byron (1788-1824).
2 Thomas Henry Huxley (1825-95), British biologist and essayist.

***

... [T]he position of modern men who have broken with the religion of their fathers is in certain profound ways different from that of other men in other ages. This is the first age, I think, in the history of mankind when the circumstances of life have conspired with the intellectual habits of the time to render any fixed and authoritative belief incredible to large masses of men. The dissolution of the old modes of thought has gone so far, and is so cumulative in its effect, that the modern man is not able to sink back after a period of prophesying into a new but stable orthodoxy. The irreligion of the modern world is radical to a degree for which there is, I think, no counterpart. For always in the past it has been possible for new conventions to crystallize, and for men to find rest and surcease of effort in accepting them.

***

But there is reason for thinking that a new crystallization of an enduring and popular religion is unlikely in the modern world. For analogy drawn from the experience of the past is misleading.

When Luther, for example, rebelled against the authority of the Church,[1] he did not suppose the way of life for the ordinary man would be radically altered. Luther supposed that men would continue to behave much as they had learned to behave under the Catholic discipline. The individual for whom he claimed the right of private judgment was one whose prejudgments had been well fixed in a Catholic society. [...] The reformers of the Eighteenth Century made a similar assumption. They really believed in democracy for men who had an aristocratic training. Jefferson,[2] for example, had an instinctive fear of the urban rabble, that most democratic part of the population. The society of free men which he dreamed about was composed of those who had the discipline, the standards of honor and the taste, without the privileges or the corruptions, that are to be found in a society of well-bred country gentlemen.

---

1 Martin Luther (1483-1546), leader of the Protestant Reformation in Europe after supposedly nailing his Ninety-Five Theses detailing abuses of ecclesiastical power to the church door in Wittenberg, Germany in 1517.

2 Thomas Jefferson (1743-1826), American founding father; main author of "The Declaration of Independence" (1776) and third President of the United States (1801-09).

The more recent rebels frequently betray a somewhat similar inability to imagine the consequences of their own victories. For the smashing of idols is in itself such a preoccupation that it is almost impossible for the iconoclast to look clearly into a future when there will not be many idols left to smash. Yet that future is beginning to be our present, and it might be said that men are conscious of what modernity means insofar as they realize that they are confronted not so much with the necessity of promoting rebellion as of dealing with the consequences of it. The Nineteenth Century, roughly speaking the time between Voltaire[1] and Mencken, was an age of terrific indictments and of feeble solutions. The Marxian indictment of capitalism[2] is a case in point. The Nietzschean transvaluation of values is another;[3] it is magnificent, but who can say, after he has shot his arrow of longing to the other shore, whether he will find Cæsar Borgia, Henry Ford, or Isadora Duncan?[4] Who knows, having read Mr. Mencken and Mr. Sinclair Lewis, what kind of world will be left when all the boobs and yokels have crawled back in their holes and have died of shame?

The rebel, while he is making his attack, is not likely to feel the need to answer such questions. For he moves in an unreal environment, one might almost say a parasitic environment. He goes forth to destroy Cæsar, Mammon, George F. Babbitt, and Mrs. Grundy.[5] As he wrestles with these demons, he leans upon them. By inver-

---

1 François Marie Arouet de Voltaire (1694-1778), French enlightenment philosopher renowned for his religious scepticism.

2 After German political philosopher Karl Marx (1818-83), in such works as *The Communist Manifesto* (1848) and *Capital* (1867, 1885, 1894).

3 After German philosopher Friedrich Nietzsche (1844-1900), in such works as *Beyond Good and Evil* (1886) and *On the Genealogy of Morals* (1887).

4 Caesar [Cesare] Borgia (1476-1507), powerful and ruthless cardinal and statesman in Northern and Central Italy, the model for Machiavelli's treatise, *The Prince* (1513); Henry Ford (1863-1947), pioneering American automobile manufacturer credited with creating modern assembly-line production and establishing higher wages for workers; also notorious as an anti-Semitic propagandist (see Appendix E2); Isadora Duncan (1878-1927), radically innovative American dancer who acquired a cult of admirers.

5 Caesar: as used here, the established political power; Mammon: the tyranny of money and the drive for material acquisition; George F. Babbitt: the small-city real estate salesman of Sinclair Lewis's popular 1922 novel *Babbitt*, whose name became synonymous with a small-minded, repressive, middle-Americanism; Mrs. Grundy: stock name for a conventional prude.

sion they offer him much the same kind of support which the conformer enjoys. They provide him with an objective which enables him to know exactly what he thinks he wants to do. His energies are focussed by his indignation. He does not suffer from emptiness, doubt, and division of soul. These are the maladies which come later when the struggle is over. While the rebel is in conflict with the established nuisances he has an aim in life which absorbs all his passions. He has his own sense of righteousness and his own feeling of communion with a grand purpose. For in attacking idols there is a kind of piety, in overthrowing tyrants a kind of loyalty, in ridiculing stupidities an imitation of wisdom. In the heat of battle the rebel is exalted by a whole-hearted tension which is easily mistaken for a taste of the freedom that is to come. He is under the spell of an illusion. For what comes after the struggle is not the exaltation of freedom but a letting down of the tension that belongs solely to the struggle itself. The happiness of the rebel is as transient as the iconoclasm which produced it. When he has slain the dragon and rescued the beautiful maiden, there is usually nothing left for him to do but write his memoirs and dream of a time when the world was young.

What most distinguishes the generation who have approached maturity since the debacle of idealism at the end of the War is not their rebellion against the religion and the moral code of their parents, but their disillusionment with their own rebellion. It is common for young men and women to rebel, but that they should rebel sadly and without faith in their own rebellion, that they should distrust the new freedom no less than the old certainties—that is something of a novelty. As Mr. Canby[1] once said, at the age of seven they saw through their parents and characterized them in a phrase. At fourteen they saw through education and dodged it. At eighteen they saw through morality and stepped over it. At twenty they lost respect for their home towns, and at twenty-one they discovered that our social system is ridiculous. At twenty-three the autobiography ends because the author has run through society to date and does not know what to do next. For, as Mr. Canby might have added, the idea of reforming that society makes no appeal to them. They have seen through all that. They cannot adopt any of the synthetic religions of the Nineteenth Century. They have seen through all of them.

---

1 Henry Seidel Canby (1878-1961), critic and professor, founding editor of the *Saturday Review of Literature*.

Appendix E: Race and the National Culture, 1920-25

[Recent scholarship has paid considerable attention to ways in which *The Great Gatsby* engages debates about American racial and cultural identity that were shaping a reactionary public policy while having a lively impact on popular and esoteric art and vernacular culture in general. The novel alludes to the issue early when Tom Buchanan spouts the thesis of a recent "scientific" book about the imminent doom of "the white race," and it makes the presence of darker immigrants or migrants felt throughout as constituents of the modern American scene. Below are two excerpts from Lothrop Stoddard's *The Rising Tide of Color Against White World-Supremacy* representing the "Nordicist" or Anglo-Saxonist narrative of American history as a potentially tragic process by which a pure founding stock is displaced by "alien hordes." Fitzgerald was certainly familiar with this idea and the racism it legitimized. (Indeed, both Stoddard's book and the Madison Grant book Stoddard cites enjoyed the respectable imprint of Fitzgerald's publisher, Charles Scribner's Sons.) Fitzgerald was probably equally familiar with counter-arguments to the effect that the immigrant experience virtually defines what it is to be an American, such as that re-printed here of former New York Commissioner of Immigration Frederick Howe in his contribution to a landmark 1921 collection of dissident essays, *Civilization in the United States*. Howe's essay on "The Alien" follows more disturbing selections from the popular anti-Semitic tracts of automobile magnate Henry Ford, which backhandedly acknowledge (even as they obsessively disavow) the extent to which the popular culture through which "modern" Americans were identifying themselves as such was being made by Jewish immigrants often drawing on the expressive practices of African-Americans. Finally included here is Miguel Covarrubias's 1924 caricature of the urbane, upstart "new Negro," a figure that leaves its mark on the novel only less emphatically than the figure of the sinister Jew.]

1. From Lothrop Stoddard, *The Rising Tide of Color Against White World-Supremacy* (New York: Charles Scribner's Sons, 1920): 261-62, 303-04

[The racial trajectory of modern America]

Probably few persons fully appreciate what magnificent racial treasures America possessed at the beginning of the nineteenth century. The colonial stock was perhaps the finest that nature had evolved since the classic Greeks. It was the pick of the Nordics of the British Isles at a time when those countries were more Nordic than now, since the industrial revolution had not yet begun and the consequent resurgence of the Mediterranean and Alpine elements had not taken place.[1]

The immigrants of colonial times were largely exiles for conscience's sake, while the very process of migration was so difficult and hazardous that only persons of courage, initiative, and strong will-power would voluntarily face the long voyage overseas to a life of struggle in an untamed wilderness haunted by ferocious savages.

Thus the entire process of colonial settlement was one continuous, drastic cycle of eugenic selection. Only the racially fit ordinarily came, while the few unfit who did come were mostly weeded out by the exacting requirements of early American life.

The eugenic results were magnificent. As Madison Grant[2] well says, "Nature had vouchsafed to the Americans of a century ago the greatest opportunity in recorded history to produce in the isolation of a continent a powerful and racially homogeneous people, and had provided for the experiment a pure race of one of the most gifted and vigorous stocks on earth, a stock free from the diseases, physical and moral, which have again and again sapped the vigor of the older lands. Our grandfathers threw away

---

1 Pseudo-scientific categories for different branches of the white "race" established in the late nineteenth century. Nordics (also commonly known as Teutons) were of predominantly Germanic and Anglo-Saxon descent; Mediterraneans were predominantly southern European and noteworthy for their dark complexion; Alpines, present predominantly in central and eastern Europe, derived from the peasantry that made up the vast core of the European peoples and were credited with establishing agriculture in Europe.

2 Madison Grant (1865-1937), leading eugenicist and advocate of restrictive immigration laws, author of *The Passing of the Great Race* (1916), from which the following excerpt is taken.

this opportunity in the blissful ignorance of national childhood and inexperience." The number of great names which America produced at the beginning of its national life shows the high level of ability possessed by this relatively small people (only about 3,000,000 whites in 1790). With our hundred-odd millions we have no such output of genius today.

The opening decades of the nineteenth century seemed to portend for America the most glorious of futures. For nearly seventy years after the Revolution, immigration was small, and during that long period of ethnic isolation the colonial stock, unperturbed by alien influences, adjusted its cultural differences and began to display the traits of a genuine new type, harmonious in basic homogeneity and incalculably rich in racial promise. The general level of ability continued high and the output of talent remained extraordinarily large. Perhaps the best feature of the nascent "native American" race was its strong idealism. Despite the materialistic blight which was then creeping over the white world, the native American displayed characteristics more reminiscent of his Elizabethan forebears than of the materialistic Hanoverian Englishman. It was a wonderful time—and it was only the dawn!

But the full day of that wondrous dawning never came. In the late forties of the nineteenth century the first waves of the modern immigrant tide began breaking on our shores, and the tide swelled to a veritable deluge which never slackened till temporarily restrained by the late war. This immigration, to be sure, first came mainly from northern Europe, was thus largely composed of kindred stocks, and contributed many valuable elements. Only during the last thirty years have we been deluged by the truly alien hordes of the European east and south. But, even at its best, the immigrant tide could not measure up to the colonial stock *which it displaced*, not reinforced, while latterly it became a menace to the very existence of our race, ideals, and institutions. All our slowly acquired balance—physical, mental, and spiritual—has been upset, and we today flounder in a veritable Serbonian bog,[1] painfully trying to regain the solid ground on which our grandsires confidently stood.

---

1 After English poet John Milton's name for Lake Serbonis in Egypt, a marshy tract covered with shifting sand (see *Paradise Lost* II, 592).

"Finally perish!" That is the exact alternative which confronts the white race. For white civilization is to-day coterminous with the white race. The civilizations of the past were local. They were confined to a particular people or group of peoples. If they failed, there were always some unspoiled, well-endowed barbarians to step forward and "carry on." But to-day *there are no more white barbarians*. The earth has grown small, and men are everywhere in close touch. If white civilization goes down, the white race is irretrievably ruined. It will be swamped by the triumphant colored races, who will obliterate the white man by elimination or absorption. What has taken place in Central Asia, once a white and now a brown or yellow land, will take place in Australasia, Europe, and America. Not to-day, nor yet tomorrow; perhaps not for generations; but surely in the end. If the present drift be not changed, we whites are all ultimately doomed. Unless we set our house in order, the doom will sooner or later overtake us all.

And that would mean that the race obviously endowed with the greatest creative ability, the race which had achieved most in the past and which gave the richer promise for the future, had passed away, carrying with it to the grave those potencies upon which the realization of man's highest hopes depends. A million years of human evolution might go uncrowned, and earth's supreme life-product, man, might never fulfil his potential destiny. This is why we to-day face "The Crisis of the Ages."

2. From Henry Ford, *Jewish Influences in American Life*, Volume 3 of *The International Jew: The World's Foremost Problem* (Dearborn, MI: Dearborn Publishing Co., 1921), 37, 39–43, 64–65, 67, 69–70, 72–74

"Jewish Gamblers Corrupt American Baseball"

There are men in the United States who say that baseball has received its death wound and is slowly dying out of the list of respectable sports. There are other men who say that American baseball can be saved if a clean sweep is made of the Jewish influence which has just dragged it through a period of bitter shame and demoralization.

Whether baseball as a first-class sport is killed and will survive only as a cheap-jacket entertainment; or whether baseball possesses sufficient intrinsic character to rise in righteous wrath and cast out the danger that menaces it, will remain a matter of various opinion. But there is one certainty, namely, that the last and most dangerous blow dealt baseball was curiously notable for its Jewish character.

★★★

The storm began to be heard as far back as 1919. The Cincinnati Nationals [Reds] had defeated the Chicago Americans [White Sox] in the World Series [*sic*] of that year, and immediately thereafter the country became a whispering gallery wherein were heard mysterious rumors of crooked dealing. The names of Jews were heard then, but it meant nothing to the average man. The rumors dealt with the shady financial gains for a number of Jew gamblers of decidedly shady reputation.

But "they got away with it," in the parlance of the field. There was not enough public indignation to force a show-down, and too many interests were involved to prevent baseball being given a black eye in full view of an adoring public.

★★★

Then came the big scandal. A Cook County grand jury was called into session at Chicago and asked to investigate. When this grand jury had completed its labors, eight members of the Chicago American League team were under indictment for throwing the World Series of 1919, the previous year, to the Cincinnati Reds. And all along the line of the investigation the names of Jews were plentifully sprinkled.

★★★

It becomes necessary at this point in the narrative to give a brief "Who's Who" of the baseball scandal, omitting from the list the names of the baseball players, who are sufficiently known to the public. The list will comprise only those who have been in the background of baseball and whom it is necessary to know in order to understand what has been happening behind the scenes in recent years.

★★★

[...] [T]here is Arnold Rothstein, a Jew, who describes himself as being in the real estate business but who is known to be a wealthy gambler, owner of a notorious gambling house in Saratoga,[1] a race track owner, and is reputed to be financially interested in the New York National League Club.

Rothstein was usually referred to during the baseball scandal as "the man higher up." It is stated that in some manner unknown he received the secret testimony given before the grand jury and offered it to a New York newspaper. However, the fact is this: the grand jury testimony disappeared from the prosecuting attorney's safe-keeping. It is stated that, when Rothstein found out it did not incriminate him, he then offered it for publicity purposes.

★★★

Rothstein is known on Broadway as "a slick Jew." That he is powerful with the authorities has been often demonstrated. His operations on the turf have led to suggestions that he be ruled off.

"Jewish Jazz Becomes Our National Music"

Many people have wondered whence come the waves upon waves of musical slush that invade decent parlors and set the young people of this generation imitating the drivel of morons. A clue to the answer is in the above clipping.[2] *Popular music is a Jewish monopoly.* Jazz is a Jewish creation. The mush, the slush, the sly suggestion, the abandoned sensuousness of sliding notes, are of Jewish origin.

Monkey talk, jungle squeals, grunts and squeaks and gasps suggestive of cave love are camouflaged by a few feverish notes and admitted to homes where the thing itself, unaided by the piano, would be stamped out in horror. Girls and boys a little while ago were inquiring who paid Mrs. Rip Van Winkle's rent while Mr. Rip Van Winkle was away.[3] In decent parlors the fluttering music sheets disclosed expressions taken directly from the

---

1 Also known as Saratoga Springs, city in upper-state New York.

2 Ford excerpted a *New York Times* article of 1920 recounting federal charges leveled against seven music publishing corporations (including Irving Berlin's) for violating anti-trust laws.

3 Allusion to the popular 1914 song, "I'm the Guy That Paid the Rent for Mrs. Rip Van Winkle," by George Fairman.

cesspools of modern capitals, to be made the daily slang, the thoughtlessly hummed remarks of high school boys and girls. [...]

★★★

It is the purpose of this [...] article to put Americans in full possession of the truth concerning the moron music which they habitually hum and sing and shout day by day, and if possible to help them to see the invisible Jewish baton which is waved above them for financial and propaganda purposes.

Just as the American stage and the American motion picture have fallen under the influence and control of the Jews and their art-destroying commercialism, so the business of handling "popular songs" has become a Yiddish industry.

Its leaders are for the most part Russian-born Jews, some of whom have personal pasts which are just as unsavory as *The Dearborn Independent* has shown the pasts of certain Jewish theatrical and movie leaders to be.

The country does not sing what it likes, but what the vaudeville "song pluggers" popularize by repeated renditions on the stage, until the flabby mind of the "ten-twent'-thirt'" audiences begin to repeat it on the streets. These "song pluggers" are the paid agents of the Yiddish song agencies. Money, and not merit, dominates the spread of the moron music which is styled "Jewish Jazz."

★★★

Tin Pan Alley is the name given to the region in Twenty-eight street, between Broadway and Sixth avenue, where the first Yiddish song manufacturers began business. Flocks of young girls who thought they could sing, and others who thought they could write song poems, came to the neighborhood allured by dishonest advertisements that promised more than the budding Yiddish exploiters were able to fulfill. Needless to say, scandal became rampant, as it always does where so-called "Gentile" girls are reduced to the necessity of seeking favors from the eastern type of Jew. It was the constant shouting of voices, the hilarity of "parties," the banging of pianos and the blattering of trombones that gave the district the name of Tin Pan Alley.

The first attempt to popularize and commercialize the so-called "popular" type of music was made by Julius Witmark, who had been a ballad singer on the minstrel stage.[1] He ceased performing to become a publisher, and was soon followed by East Side Jews, many of whom have become wealthy through their success in pandering to a public taste which they first debased.

Irving Berlin, whose real name is Ignatz or Isadore Baline, is one of the most successful of these Jewish song controllers.[2] He was born in Russia and early became a singer and entertainer. With the rise of "rag-time," which was the predecessor of "jazz," he found a new field for his nimble talents, and his first big success was "Alexander's Rag-Time Band"[3]—a popular piece which by comparison with what has followed it, is a blushing, modest thing.

It is worth noting, in view of the organized eagerness of the Jew to make an alliance with the Negro, that it was Jewish "jazz" that rode in upon the wave of Negro "rag-time" popularity, and eventually displaced the "rag-time."

Berlin has steadily gone the road from mere interestingness to unashamed erotic suggestion. He is the "headliner" in homes as well as in the not-too-particular music halls, but his stuff without its music sometimes savors of vile suggestion.

The motif of this business can be clearly seen in the "Berlin Big Hits." There are the so-called "vamp" songs, such as "Harem Life," and "You Cannot Make Your Shimmy Shake on Tea."[4]

Among the "successes" is the song entitled, "I Like It."[5] It is a "vamp" song which has been sung everywhere, even by myriads of children who could not appreciate the full suggestion of the words, but were hypnotized by the atmosphere which the words created when sung; and by older folks who would not under any circumstances *speak* the words of the song, but who are victims of the modern delusion that a little flashy music covers a multitude of sins.

---

1 Julius Witmark (1870-1929), songwriter, performer and, most successfully, partner with his two brothers in the music printing business M. Witmark & Sons (bought by Warner Brothers in 1929).

2 Irving Berlin (1888-1989), born Israel Isadore Baline, one of the United States' most popular and beloved song-writers; he wrote what is widely regarded as America's unofficial national anthem, "God Bless America," in 1918.

3 More precisely, "Alexander's Ragtime Band," popular Irving Berlin song published in 1911.

4 Berlin songs performed in the *Zeigfeld Follies of 1919*.

5 Mildly bawdy song of 1921 by Berlin.

Ministers, educators, reformers, parents, citizens who are amazed at the growth of looseness among the people, rail at the evil results. They see the evil product and they attack the product. They rail at the young people who go in for all this eroticism and suggestiveness.

But all this has a source! Why not attack the source? When a population is bathed in sights, sounds and ideas of a certain character, drenched in them and drowned in them, by systematic, deliberate, organized intent, the point of attack should be the cause, not the effect. Yet, that is precisely where the point of attack has not been made, presumably because of lack of knowledge.

It is of little use blaming the people. The people are what they are made. Give the liquor business full sway and you have a population that drinks and carouses. After preaching abstinence to the victims for a century, the country turned its attention to the victimizers and the abuse was greatly curtailed. The traffic is still illicitly carried on, but even so, the best way to abolish the illicit traffic is to identify the groups that carry it on.

The entire population of the United States could be turned into narcotic addicts if the same freedom was given the illicit narcotic ring as is now given the Yiddish popular song manufacturers. But in such a condition it would be stupid to attack the addicts; common sense would urge the exposure of the panderers.

A dreadful narcotizing or moral modesty and the application of powerful aphrodisiacs have been involved in the present craze for popular songs—a stimulated craze. The victims are everywhere. But ministers, educators, reformers, parents, and public-spirited citizens are beginning to see the futility of scolding the young people thus diseased. Common sense dictates a cleaning out of the source of disease. The source is in the Yiddish group of song manufacturers who control the whole output and who are responsible for the whole matter from poetry to profits.

Next to the moral indictment against the so-called "popular" song is the indictment that *it is not popular*. Everybody hears it, perhaps the majority sing it; it makes its way from coast to coast; it is flung into the people's minds at every movie and from every stage; it is advertised in flaring posters; phonograph records shriek it forth day and night, dance orchestras seem enamored of it, player pianos roll it out by the yard. And by sheer dint of repetition and suggestion the song catches on—as a burr thistle catches on; until it is displaced by another. There is no spontaneous popularity.

It is a mere mechanical drumming on the minds of the public. There is often not a single atom of sentiment or spiritual appeal in the whole loudly trumpeted "success"; men and women, boys and girls have simply taken to humming words and tunes which they cannot escape, night or day.

The deadly anxiety of "keeping up with the times" drives the army of piano-owners to the music stores to see what is "going" now, and of course it is the Yiddish moron music that is going, and so another home and eventually another neighborhood is inoculated.

But there is no *popularity*. Take any moron music addict you know and ask him what was the "popular" song three weeks ago, and he will not be able to tell. These songs are so lacking in all that the term "popular" means as regards their acceptableness, that they died overnight, unregretted. Directly the Yiddish manufacturers have another "hit" to make (it is always the public that is "hit") a new song is crammed down the public gullet, and because it is the "latest," and because the Yiddish advertisements say that it is a "hit," and because the hired "pluggers" say that everybody is singing it, that song too becomes "popular" for its brief period, and so on through the year. It is the old game of "changing the styles" to speed up business and make the people buy. Nothing lasts in the Yiddish game—styles of clothing, movies nor songs; it is always something new, to stimulate the flow of money from the popular pocket into the moron music makers' coffers.

There hasn't been a real "popular" song of Yiddish origin since the Jewish whistlers and back-alley songsters of New York's East Side undertook to handle musical America—not one, unless we except in genuine gratitude George Cohan's "Over There,"[1] a song which came out of a period of strain and went straight to the people's heart.

Two facts about the "popular song" are known to all: first, that for the most part it is indecent and the most active agent of moral miasma in the country, or if not the most active, then neck and neck with the "movies"; second, that the "popular song" industry is an exclusively Jewish industry.

---

1 George M. Cohan's popular patriotic song of 1917, the year of America's entry into the First World War.

3. **From Frederick C. Howe, "The Alien," in** *Civilization*
   in the United States: An Inquiry by Thirty Americans,
   ed. Harold E. Stearns (New York: Harcourt, Brace,
   1922): 337-42, 346, 350

The immigrant alien has been discussed by the Anglo-Saxon as
though he were an Anglo-Saxon "problem." He has been discussed by labour as though he were a labour "problem"; by inter-
preters of American institutions as though man existed for institutions and for institutions which the class interpreting them
found advantageous to its class. Occasionally the alien has been
discussed from the point of view of the alien and but rarely from
the point of view of democracy. The "problem" of the alien is
largely a problem of setting our own house in order. It is the
"problem" of Americanizing America. The outstanding fact of
three centuries of immigration is that the immigrant alien ceases
to be an alien when economic conditions are such as properly to
assimilate him.

There is something rather humorous about the way America
discusses "the alien." For we are all aliens. And what is less to our
liking we are almost all descended from the peasant classes of
Europe. We are here because our forebears were poor. They did
not rule over there. They were oppressed; they were often owned.
And with but few exceptions they came because of their poverty.
For the rich rarely emigrate. And in the 17th and 18th centuries
there was probably a smaller percentage of immigrants who
could pass the literacy test than there are to-day. Moreover, in the
early days only suffering could drive the poor of Europe from
their poverty. For the conditions of travel were hazardous. The
death toll from disease was very high. It required more fortitude
to cross the Atlantic and pass by the ring of settlers out onto the
unbroken frontier than it does to pass Ellis Island[1] and the
exploiters round about it to-day.

The immigration question has arisen because America, too,
has created a master class, a class which owns and employs and
rules. And the alien in America is faced by a class opinion, born
of the change which has come over America rather than any
change in the alien himself. America has changed. The alien

---

1 Federal immigration center and the point of entry for 70 per cent of
American immigrants between 1892-1924, located in Upper New York
Bay near the Statue of Liberty.

remains much the same. And the most significant phase of the immigration problem is the way we treat the alien and the hypocrisy of our discussion of the subject.

Sociologists have given us a classification of the immigrant alien. They speak of the "old immigration" and the "new immigration." The former is the immigration of the 17th and 18th and the first three-quarters of the 19th centuries. It was English, Scotch, Irish, German, Scandinavian with a sprinkling of French, Swiss, and other nationalities. From the beginning, the preponderance was British. During the 18th century there was a heavy Scotch inflow and during the first half of the 19th a heavy Irish and German immigration. The Irish came because of the famine of 1848, the Scotch in large part because of the enclosure acts and the driving of the people from the land to make way for deer preserves and grazing lands for the British aristocracy. Most of the British immigration was the result of oppressive land laws of one kind or another. The population of Ireland was reduced from eight million to slightly over four million in three-quarters of a century. The British immigrant of the 17th century, like the recent Russian immigration, was driven from home by economic oppression. Only a handful came to escape religious oppression or to secure political liberty. The cause of immigration has remained the same from the beginning until now.

The "old immigration" was from the North of Europe. It was of Germanic stock. It was predominantly Protestant. But the most important fact of all and the fact most usually ignored is an economic fact. The early immigrant found a broad continent awaiting him, peopled only by Indians. He became a free man. He took up a homestead. He ceased to belong to anyone else. He built for himself. He paid no rent, he took no orders, he kept what he produced, and was inspired by hope and ambition to develop his powers. It was economic, not political, freedom that distinguishes the "old immigration" from the "new."

The "new immigration" is from Southern and Central Europe. It is Latin and Slavic. It is largely Catholic. It, too, is poor. It, too, is driven out by oppression, mostly economic and for the most part landed. Almost every wave of immigration has been in some way related to changes for the worse in the landed systems of Europe. Wherever the poverty has been the most distressing, there the impulse to move has been the strongest. It has been the poverty of Europe that has determined our immigration from the 17th century until now.

The ethnic difference is secondary. So is the religious. The fundamental fact that distinguishes the "old immigration" from the "new" is economic. The "new immigration" works for the "old." It found the free land all taken up. The public domain had passed into the hand of the Pacific railroads, into great manorial estates. Land thieves had repeated the acts of the British Parliament of the 18th century. The Westward movement of peoples that had been going on from the beginning of time came to an end when the pioneer of the 80's and 90's found only the bad lands left for settlement. That ended an era. It closed the land to settlement and sent the immigrant to the city. The peasant of Europe has become the miner and the mill worker. He left one kind of serfdom to take up another. It is this that distinguishes the "old immigrant" from the "new." It is this that distinguishes the old America from the America of to-day. And the problem of immigration, like the problem of America, is the re-establishment of economic democracy. [...]

The "new immigration" from Southern and Central Europe began to increase in volume about 1890. It came from Southern rather than Northern Italy, from Poland, Hungary, Bohemia, Russia, the Balkans, and the Levant. There was a sprinkling of Spanish and Portuguese immigrants. In 1914 South and Central European immigration amounted to 683,000, while the North European immigration was but 220,000. Of the former 296,000 came from Italy, 123,000 from Poland, 45,000 from Russia, and 45,000 from Hungary. These figures do not include Jewish immigrants, who numbered 138,000. Of the North European immigrants 105,000 came from the British Isles, 80,000 came from Germany, and 36,000 from the Scandinavian countries.

Of the 14,000,000 persons of foreign birth now in the country, a very large percentage is of South and Central European stock.

We are accustomed to think of the old immigration and the new immigration in terms of races and religions. And much of the present-day hostility to immigration comes from the inexplicable prejudice which has recently sprung up against persons of differing races and religions. It is assumed that the new immigration is poor and ignorant because it is ethnically unfitted for anything different and that it prefers the tenement and the mining camp to American standards of living and culture. [...]

The "immigration problem," so called, has always been and always will be an economic problem. There are many people who feel that there is an inherent superiority in the Anglo-

Saxon race; that it has a better mind, greater virtue, and a better reason for existence and expansion than any other race. They insist there are eugenic reasons for excluding immigration from South and Central Europe; they would preserve America for people of Anglo-Saxon stock. As an immigration official I presided over Ellis Island for five years. During this time probably a million immigrants arrived at the port of New York. They were for the most part poor. They had that in common with the early immigrant. They had other qualities in common. They were ambitious and filled with hope. They were for the most part kindly and moved by the same human and domestic virtues as other peoples. And it is to me an open question whether the "new immigration," if given a virgin continent, and the hope and stimulus which springs from such opportunity, would not develop the same qualities of mind and of character that we assume to be the more or less exclusive characteristics of the Anglo-Saxon race. There is also reason for believing that the warmer temperament, the emotional qualities, and the love of the arts that characterize the South and Central European would produce a race blend, under proper economic conditions, that would result in a better race than one of pure Northern extraction. For it is to be remembered that it was not political liberty, religious liberty, or personal liberty that changed the early immigrant of Northern Europe into the American of today. His qualities were born of economic conditions, of a free continent, of land to be had for the asking, of equal opportunity with his fellows to make his life what he would have it to be. The old immigrant recognized no master but himself. He was the equal of his neighbours in every respect. He knew no inferiority complex born of a servile relationship. It was this rather than our constitutions and laws that made the American of the first three centuries what he was. It was this alchemy that changed the serf of Northern Europe into the self-reliant freeman of America.

The immigration problem was born when this early economic opportunity came to an end.

★★★

America is a marvellous demonstration of the economic foundations of all life. It is a demonstration of what happens to men when economic opportunities call forth their resourcefulness and latent ability on one hand and when the State, on the other, keeps its hands off them in their personal relationships. For the alien quickly adopts a higher standard of culture as he rises in the industrial scale, while his morals, whatever they may have been, quickly take on the colour of his new environment, whatever that may be. And if all of the elements which should enter into a consideration of the subject were included, I am of the opinion it would be found that the morals, the prevalence of vice and crime among the alien population is substantially that of the economic class in which he is found rather than the race from which he springs. In other words, the alleged prevalence of crime among the alien population is traceable to poverty and bad conditions of living rather than to ethnic causes, and in so far as it exists it tends [to] disappear as the conditions which breed it pass away.

★★★

The alien of to-day is not very different from the alien of yesterday. He has the same instincts and desires as did those who came in the *Mayflower*. Only those who came in the *Mayflower* made their own laws and their own fortunes. Those who come today have their laws made for them by the class that employs them and they make their own fortunes only as those aliens who came first permit them to do so.

4. Miguel Covarrubias, "The Sheik of Dahomey,"[1] 1924

"Nothin'—Ah don't care whut it is—can get mah boy recited. Nothin! And talk about havin' a way with wimmin, ain't nobody can tell him nuthin' ... He's a dressin' up fool, dat boy is, an' he sure's got luck with de high yalla ladies."

---

1 Source: Miguel Covarrubias and Eric D. Walrond, "Enter, the New Negro, a Distinctive Type Recently Created by the Coloured Cabaret Belt in New York," *Vanity Fair* (December 1924): 60.

Select Bibliography

Textual Resources

Atkinson, Jennifer E. "Fitzgerald's Marked Copy of *The Great Gatsby*." *Fitzgerald/Hemingway Annual* 2 (1970): 28-33.

Bruccoli, Matthew J. *Apparatus for F. Scott Fitzgerald's "The Great Gatsby*." Columbia: U of South Carolina P, 1974.

Fitzgerald, F. Scott. *The Great Gatsby: A Facsimile of the Manuscript*. Ed. Matthew J. Bruccoli. Washington, DC: Bruccoli Clark/NCR Microcard Books, 1973.

——. *The Great Gatsby: The Revised and Rewritten Galleys*. F. Scott Fitzgerald Manuscripts, Vol. 3. Ed. Matthew J. Bruccoli. New York: Garland, 1990-91.

——. *Trimalchio: An Early Version of "The Great Gatsby*." Ed. James L. W. West, III. New York: Cambridge UP, 2000. [Based on the unrevised galleys.]

Biography and Letters

Bruccoli, Matthew J. and Jennifer M. Atkinson, eds. *As Ever, Scott Fitz–: Letters Between F. Scott Fitzgerald and His Literary Agent, Harold Ober, 1919-1940*. Philadelphia: Lippincott, 1972.

Bruccoli, Matthew J. and Margaret M. Duggan, eds. *The Correspondence of F. Scott Fitzgerald*. New York: Random House, 1980.

Bruccoli, Matthew J. *Some Sort of Epic Grandeur: The Life of F. Scott Fitzgerald*. 2nd rev. ed. Columbia: U of South Carolina P, 2002.

Bryer, Jackson R. and Cathy W. Barks, eds. *Dear Scott, Dearest Zelda: The Love Letters of F. Scott and Zelda Fitzgerald*. New York: St. Martin's, 2002.

Donaldson, Scott. *Fool for Love: A Biography of F. Scott Fitzgerald*. New York: Dell, 1983.

Fitzgerald, F. Scott. *A Life in Letters*. Ed. Matthew J. Bruccoli. New York: Simon & Schuster, 1994.

Hook, Andrew. *F. Scott Fitzgerald: A Literary Life*. New York: Palgrave, 2002.

Kuehl, John and Jackson R. Bryer, eds. *Dear Scott/Dear Max: The Fitzgerald-Perkins Correspondence*. New York: Charles Scribner's Sons, 1971.

Mizener, Arthur. *The Far Side of Paradise: A Biography of F. Scott Fitzgerald*. Rev. ed. New York: Vintage, 1959.

Turnball, Andrew, ed. *The Letters of F. Scott Fitzgerald*, New York: Charles Scribner's Sons, 1963.

West, James L.W., III. *The Perfect Hour: The Romance of F. Scott Fitzgerald and Ginevra King, His First Love*. New York: Random House, 2005.

Bibliographies & Reference Guides

Bruccoli, Matthew J., ed. *F. Scott Fitzgerald's "The Great Gatsby": A Literary Reference*. New York: Carroll & Graf, 2000.

Bruccoli, Matthew J. *F. Scott Fitzgerald: A Descriptive Bibliography*. Rev. ed. Pittsburgh: U of Pittsburgh P, 1987.

Gross, Dalton and Maryjean Gross. *Understanding "The Great Gatsby": A Student Casebook to Issues, Sources, and Historical Documents*. Westport, CT: Greenwood Press, 1998.

Tate, Mary Jo. *F. Scott Fitzgerald A to Z: The Essential Guide to the Life and Work*. New York: Checkmark Books, 1998.

Critical Studies and Collections

Berman, Ronald. *"The Great Gatsby" and Fitzgerald's World of Ideas*. Tuscaloosa: U of Alabama P, 1997.

——. *"The Great Gatsby" and Modern Times*. Urbana and Chicago: U of Illinois P, 1994.

Bruccoli, Matthew J., ed. *New Essays on "The Great Gatsby."* New York: Cambridge UP, 1985.

Bryer, Jackson R., ed. *F. Scott Fitzgerald: The Critical Reception*. New York: Burt Franklin & Co., 1978.

Curnutt, Kirk, ed. *A Historical Guide to F. Scott Fitzgerald*. New York: Oxford UP, 2004.

Gleason, William. *The Leisure Ethic: Work and Play in American Literature, 1840-1940*. Stanford: Stanford UP, 1999.

Hoffman, Frederick J., ed. *"The Great Gatsby": A Study*. New York: Charles Scribner's Sons, 1962.

Kenner, Hugh. *A Homemade World: The American Modernist Writers*. Baltimore: Johns Hopkins UP, 1975.

Lehan, Richard. *"The Great Gatsby": The Limits of Wonder*. Boston: Twayne, 1990.

Mizener, Arthur, ed. *F. Scott Fitzgerald: A Collection of Critical Essays*. Englewood Cliffs, NJ: Prentice-Hall, 1963.

Nowlin, Michael. *F. Scott Fitzgerald's Racial Angles and the Business of Literary Greatness.* New York: Palgrave, 2007.

Piper, Henry Dan. *F. Scott Fitzgerald: A Critical Portrait.* Carbondale: Southern Illinois UP, 1965.

Prigozy, Ruth, ed. *The Cambridge Companion to F. Scott Fitzgerald.* New York: Cambridge UP, 2002.

Sklar, Robert. *F. Scott Fitzgerald: The Last Laocoön.* New York: Oxford UP, 1967.

Stern, Milton R. *The Golden Moment: The Novels of F. Scott Fitzgerald.* Urbana: U of Illinois P, 1970.

Tratner, Michael. *Deficits and Desires: Economics and Sexuality in Twentieth-Century Literature.* Stanford: Stanford UP, 2001.

Way, Brian. *F. Scott Fitzgerald and the Art of Social Fiction.* London: Arnold, 1980.

Articles in Journals and in Collections Cited Above

Breitwieser, Mitchell. "*The Great Gatsby*; Grief, Jazz, and the Eye-Witness." *Arizona Quarterly* 47.3 (1991): 17-70.

——. "Jazz Fractures: F. Scott Fitzgerald and Ephochal Representation." *American Literary History* 12.3 (2000): 359-81.

Berman, Ronald. "*The Great Gatsby* and the Twenties," in Prigozy, 79-94.

Clymer, Jeffory A. "'Mr. Nobody from Nowhere': Rudolph Valentino, Jay Gatsby, and the End of the American Race," *Genre* 29.1-2 (1996): 161-92.

Coleman, Dan. "'A World Complete in Itself': *Gatsby*'s Elegaic Narration." *Journal of Narrative Technique* 27.2 (1997): 207-33.

Curnutt, Kirk. "Fitzgerald's Consumer World," in Curnutt, 85-128.

Gidley, M. "Notes on F. Scott Fitzgerald and the Passing of the Great Race." *Journal of American Studies* 7.2 (1973): 171-81.

Goldsmith, Meredith. "White Skin, White Mask: Passing, Posing, and Performing in *The Great Gatsby.*" *Modern Fiction Studies* 49.3 (2003): 443-68.

Hitchens, Christopher. "The Road to West Egg." *Vanity Fair* (May 2000): 76, 80, 84, 86.

Irwin, John T. "Compensating Visions: *The Great Gatsby.*" *Southwest Review* 77.4 (Autumn 1992): 536-45.

Kerr, Frances. "Feeling 'Half Feminine': Modernism and the Politics of Emotion in *The Great Gatsby.*" *American Literature* 68.2 (1996): 405-31.

Margolies, Alan. "The Maturing of F. Scott Fitzgerald." *Twenti-eth-Century Literature* 43.1 (1997): 75-93.

Marsh, Joss Lutz. "Fitzgerald, *Gatsby* and *The Last Tycoon*: The American Dream and the Hollywood Dream Factory." *Litera-ture/Film Quarterly* 20.1-2 (1992): 3-13, 102-08.

Michaels, Walter Benn. "The Souls of White Folk." *Literature and the Body: Essays on Population and Persons*. Ed. Elaine Scarry. Selected Papers from the English Inst. 12. Baltimore: Johns Hopkins UP, 1988. 185-209.

Pauly, Thomas H. "Gatsby as Gangster." *Studies in American Fiction* 21.2 (1993): 225-36.

Prigozy, Ruth. "Gatsby's Guest List and Fitzgerald's Technique of Naming." *Fitzgerald/Hemingway Annual* 4 (1972): 99-112.

——. "Introduction: Scott, Zelda, and the Culture of Celebrity," in Prigozy, 3-27.

——. "'Poor Butterfly': F. Scott Fitzgerald and Popular Music." *Prospects* 2 (1976): 41-67.

Sanderson, Rena. "Women in Fitzgerald's Fiction," in Prigozy, 143-63.

Slater, Peter Gregg. "Ethnicity in *The Great Gatsby*." *Twentieth-Century Literature* 19.1 (1973): 53-62.

from the publisher

A name never says it all, but the word "broadview" expresses a good deal of the philosophy behind our company. We are open to a broad range of academic approaches and political viewpoints. We pay attention to the broad impact book publishing and book printing has in the wider world; we began using recycled stock more than a decade ago, and for some years now we have used 100% recycled paper for most titles. As a Canadian-based company we naturally publish a number of titles with a Canadian emphasis, but our publishing program overall is internationally oriented and broad-ranging. Our individual titles often appeal to a broad readership too; many are of interest as much to general readers as to academics and students.

Founded in 1985, Broadview remains a fully independent company owned by its shareholders—not an imprint or subsidiary of a larger multinational.

If you would like to find out more about Broadview and about the books we publish, please visit us at **www.broadviewpress.com**. And if you'd like to place an order through the site, we'd like to show our appreciation by extending a special discount to you: by entering the code below you will receive a 20% discount on purchases made through the Broadview website.

Discount code: **broadview20%**

Thank you for choosing Broadview.

Please note: this offer applies only to sales of
bound books within the United States or Canada.

The interior of this book is printed on 100% recycled paper.